THE
DEAN'S LIST

BY JON HASSLER

Staggerford
Simon's Night
The Love Hunter
A Green Journey
Grand Opening
North of Hope
Dear James
Rookery Blues
The Dean's List

FOR YOUNG READERS

Four Miles to Pinecone
Jemmy

THE
DEAN'S LIST

JON HASSLER

BALLANTINE BOOKS
NEW YORK

All rights reserved under International
and Pan-American Copyright Conventions. Published
in the United States by Ballantine Books, a division of Random
House, Inc., New York, and simultaneously in Canada
by Random House of Canada Limited, Toronto.

A portion of this novel first appeared in
Image: A Journal of Religion and the Arts, under the title
"Christmas Eve in Omaha," and subsequently in
Christmas, published by Augsburg
Fortress Press.

Another portion first appeared
as a short story entitled "A Classroom Skit"
in *Lake Country Journal.*

http://www.randomhouse.com

Library of Congress Cataloging-in-Publication Data

Hassler, Jon.
The dean's list / Jon Hassler.
p.   cm.
ISBN: 0-345-41637-6
I. Title
PS3558.A726D39   1997
813'.55—dc21   97-10177

Text design by Holly Johnson

Manufactured in the United States of America

First Edition: May 1997

10 9 8 7 6 5 4 3 2 1

In memory of my dean
Robert L. Spaeth
1935–1994

CONTENTS

FALL TERM

#233. The "O" stands for Oswald or Osbert as I recall, not "zero" as Angelo claims. Nobody knows what the "F" stands for. His grade in life, says Angelo.

I jot this in my pocket notebook as President O. F. Zastrow and his guest exchange their tedious thoughts on the subject of celebrities. The president's guest, a tiresome name-dropper named Bridges, is trying to impress the four of us with an account of a cocktail party he once attended on a Pacific beach with seven starlets and the assistant director of *Batman*. Fortunately, I'm compelled to excuse myself before he comes to the end of it.

"I'm already five minutes late for class," I explain, pocketing my notebook and getting to my feet. "I'm very sorry."

Smiling agreeably and shaking my hand, Bridges wishes me a merry Christmas. He's a handsome, youngish alumnus in a fawn-colored suit who's spent the last dozen years living in Hollywood. A pair of dark glasses, instead of a necktie, hangs down the front of his sky blue shirt, their bow hooked over its open collar. This meeting was called for the purpose of exploring how his acquaintance with certain famous people might be useful in raising money for our scholarship endowment.

The president, meanwhile, plants his elbows on the table and covers his nose with a tent of his stubby fingers, under which he emits a doglike noise, an unfriendly growl that causes Bridges to look a bit startled. It's an old story, President Zastrow's disapproval of me. My assistant, Angelo Corelli, maintains a serene appearance by raising his eyes to the ceiling and smiling vaguely, while the president's secretary, April Ackerman, an impatient woman of few words but extravagant gestures, lowers her forehead to the pad she's been writing on and sighs—an indication that she's heard altogether too many growls lately.

"It's Freshman English," I explain further, pushing my chair tight to the conference table and gathering up my folder of memos regarding celebrities. "It's our final class before exam week." I offer Bridges a look of amiable regret, and I exchange an understanding smile with Angelo and April. No use smiling at President Zastrow, of course. Any sign of goodwill is inevitably lost on the man. For too many years, he and I have been directing campus affairs from offices facing each other across Administration Row, exchanging countless memos, sharing the podium at faculty workshops, even sharing a room in the St. Paul Hotel whenever college business takes us to the capital, and yet nothing like warmth or sympathy has ever passed between us. I've never known anyone so robotlike, so empty of fellow feeling, so ossified, as our president. An absolute dud, Mother calls him.

"Do deans always teach, Dr. Edwards?" inquires Bridges, a hint of confusion coming into his eyes. I remember Bridges from his student days, twelve or fifteen years ago, but he doesn't remember me—or pretends not to because he flunked my course in History of the English Language. He's the middle of three sons belonging to the local furniture store family of Bridgeses. His first name is Portis, and he can scarcely read. I seem to recall his grandmother telling Mother it was some sort of health problem that forced him to drop out before earning his degree, but I've always doubted the truth of this, always suspected it was plain stupidity. We still had high academic standards in those days; near-illiterates had a hard time graduating.

"Yes, I teach one class each semester, and I'd better get there before they desert me." I chuckle then, indicating that this is a joke. Not that I haven't had students capable of walking out on me, but this semester's class wouldn't think of doing anything so disrespectful. This group has been a gem from Day One, twenty-seven men and women from various backgrounds, not all of them young, with whom I've achieved a remarkable level of rapport bordering on affection. Last time I was late, they sent a delegate, Mrs. St. George, to my office to see what was keeping me. "I promised them a quiz today," I add, backing away from the table. "We'll meet again, I'm sure. Happy New Year, in case I don't see you again."

"Beautiful," replies Bridges. Beautiful has been his favorite adjective this morning. Gorgeous came in second. In my boredom I counted nine beautifuls and seven gorgeouses.

Crossing the president's bookless office on my way out, I hear the president muttering, "Why he keeps teaching . . . a man in his position . . . always walking out of meetings early."

Remarks such as these no longer have the power to hurt me. O. F. Zastrow has been a fixture here for a quarter of a century, first as dean, then as president, so I've had ample time to grow accustomed to the smallness of his mind and the enormity of his inferiority complex—the latter founded upon a weak academic background and not at all well-concealed behind an abrasive and carping personality. He has two strengths as president: fund-raising (always the number-one priority in the eyes of the State College Board) and the spiffy maintenance of buildings and grounds (number two). As for the true mission of a college—teaching and learning—he leaves that whole side of things to his dean.

That's me: Leland J. Edwards, Ph.D., Dean of the College and senior member of the faculty; tenured in the English Department since 1963.

Happy anticipation is how I'd describe the faculty's overall feeling concerning the president's retirement this spring. Some believe I'll succeed him, but I don't want the job. I'm fifty-eight and sick of administration. Administration is meetings and memos and very little to do with students. If it weren't for my class of freshmen, the only students and alumni I'd get to know would be the lazy ones I suspend, the vandals I expel, and the stuffed shirts like Portis Bridges I patronize. No, after our new president is firmly in place, say a year from now, I want to step down as dean and finish out my career in the classroom. Mother, of course, won't hear of it. Mother prays to live long enough to see me installed as the sixth president of my *alma mater*. Mother has lung disease.

I half expect to find Mrs. St. George in my outer office, or some other emissary from Freshman English sent downstairs to conduct me to class. Instead, a phone call awaits me. My large and unrefined secretary, Viola Trisco, smiles as she hands me the receiver. Her smile, I notice, is composed of equal parts sympathy and derision, which means it's Mother on the line.

"Leland, your umbrella."

"That's all right, Mother. I can catch a ride home if it's still raining."

"It'll be sleet by that time."

"I shouldn't wonder, this late in the year."

"Did you hear my show?"

"I'm sorry, I was in a meeting."

"Everybody's wild about your apple crisp."

"Yes, we thought it would be a hit, didn't we?"

"Four people called in. What they like is the hint of lemon."

"Your idea, actually."

"It was not—don't try to humor your old mother. You know very well the lemon zest was your idea."

"Mother, I've got to run."

"Remember it's Friday."

"Yes, of course. I'll be home by three."

"Not a minute after. They never wait for us at the Hi-Rise."

"I'm late for class, Mother. I'm glad your breathing is better."

"It's not better. It's worse."

"It sounds better."

"It's worse."

"Three o'clock then."

"Not a minute later."

Viola Trisco takes back the receiver and loads me down with my oversized literature anthology, the student themes I spent last night correcting, and a stack of folded orange paper fresh from the copy machine.

"Schedule nothing more this afternoon," I instruct her. "I'm out of here at ten to three."

"Gotcha," she says, dragging a string of dyed red hair out of her eyes.

With my free hand I remove the coats—mine and Viola's—from the coat tree and lay them across one of my brocaded chairs for visitors.

"Hey, what's up?" she asks.

"A prop," I explain over my shoulder, carrying the coat tree out into the corridor.

"Lunch with Dr. Bloom at twelve," she happily calls after me. Viola Trisco, like most of the deanwatchers on this campus, interprets my friendship with Mary Sue Bloom as a budding romance—a fantasy I do nothing to squelch.

My class meets in a second-floor room known as the Little Theater because its creaky floor is canted toward a platform and its fifty desks are bolted down in a semicircular pattern. Many years ago, when my father chaired the History Department, this was the only auditorium on campus, the venue for plays, lectures, and chamber concerts. Larger gatherings—commencement exercises, choral concerts, political rallies—were accommodated in the gymnasium downstairs, which later became the library, and which is now partitioned into offices. In those early days, Rookery State College in its entirety was contained in this building, McCall Hall (named for an early and forgotten functionary in the state department of education), and my father was one of some thirty professors, supported by a janitor, three secretaries, and a bursar. Now there are nearly three hundred members of what I like to call our college family and President Zastrow refers to as his labor force. Very soon, with the completion of the new hockey arena rising on the riverbank, our buildings will number thirteen, including dormitories.

Entering the Little Theater, I measure out a bit of a smile and cast it here and there among my students, for it's late in the term and not much can go wrong as a result of cordiality. Three and a half decades in the classroom have taught me the danger of unrestrained chumminess. More than once, early in my career, I was affable too early and caused a class of freshmen to misbehave for the entire semester—late assignments, whispering, sloppy habits of attendance. It's true, of course, that some educators can get away with lightheartedness—my assistant, Angelo Corelli, a helplessly gregarious man, seems unhampered by his laughing and joking manner with students—but I can't risk it. My smile, I regret to say, is not the open, spontaneous expression Angelo's is. By studying it in snapshots, I've come to realize that there's a calculated, not to say sinister, aspect to my smile. It doesn't sit easily on my face.

It's my father's smile, actually. My father died when I was fourteen. In our family albums he never seems to be putting his whole heart into his happier expressions. Mother, on the other hand, before illness forced her to cut back on her social life and reduce her beloved radio work to three shows per week, was always a freewheeling laugher and smiler. These days, alas, Mother puts most of her energy into breathing.

After apologizing for my tardiness, I nod to the three classroom helpers I've appointed, and they rise from their desks and go quickly about their duties. The elderly Mr. Edgar Curtis, a retired Greyhound bus driver, comes forward and hands me a scrap of paper with the names of today's two absentees written on it. Mrs. St. George collects everyone's written work and ceremoniously lays the papers on my desk; she's a woman of forty-five or fifty years who began the semester wearing print dresses of a matronly design and carrying a purse, and who now favors sweatsuits and a canvas shoulder bag. Miss Kelly Evans, a young woman whose hobby is presumably her hair—its style and color keep changing—hands out half-sheets of paper for today's quiz.

On the chalkboard I write a short question requiring a long

answer bearing on "Bartleby the Scrivener," and the room falls silent. I move my chair and a stool to the far side of the platform and arrange them, together with the coat tree, for today's performance. Then I sit down and go over my lines. *Barbara, how good it is to see you,* I read silently, imagining myself crossing the platform to Miss Carol Thelen's outstretched arms and giving her the embrace the story calls for.

I have to say I'm rather proud of my idea of dramatizing scenes from fiction. It brings us to a clearer understanding of the characters and the nuances of language. It isn't my habit to take part in these skits, but the class insisted that I play this role, claiming that I'm the very picture of the aging financier described in the story—tall, lean, gray-haired, a scrupulous dresser, a good listener, a man of few and measured words. *Dean Leland Edwards as Martin Ferguson*—I'm listed on the stack of orange programs I've brought to class.

Carol Thelen as Charlene Trent.
Edgar Curtis as The Friend.
Kelly Evans as The Landlady.

I raise my eyes from the page of underlined dialogue and study the not-so-pretty Carol Thelen sitting in the front rank of desks. She's making intensely hard work of the quiz, her face down close to her exacting penmanship, her free hand gripping her dark, unruly hair. She's wearing an old-fashioned plaid wool skirt, long and tight, and a frilly white blouse under a blue cardigan that she must have found in a trunk of hand-me-downs. Seeing clothes this unstylish on anyone else, you'd assume she'd gotten herself up for her role as the older woman in Martin Ferguson's life, but on Miss Thelen you can't be sure. She comes to class in odd-looking outfits that somehow correspond to her odd-looking face. That her eyes are not symmetrical, one being smaller and a bit slanted, is obviously a birth defect, but I wonder if her chin was moved slightly to the right of center by a blow to the face. One hears such ugly stories of domestic violence these days. Miss Thelen, a first-semester freshman, is about to drop out of college. She confided to me last week, rather proudly I thought, that she'd landed a job as night checker at Petey's Price-Fighter Foods.

"Time's up," I announce at precisely twenty minutes after the hour, and Mrs. St. George collects the quizzes while I hand the orange programs down the rows.

Miss Carol Thelen comes reluctantly forward then, as do the other two cast members, old Mr. Edgar Curtis and Miss Kelly Evans, whose hair today is a straight fall of burgundy. I require each student to perform at least once during the semester, and I've seen some splendid acting, but it's typical of the final presentation of the term that these players should be self-conscious foot-draggers. They've obviously spent their academic lives trying to avoid the sort of embarrassing display I'm demanding of them. Stepping up onto the platform and forcing themselves to turn and face their classmates, all three of them wear expressions of extreme disappointment because the disaster they've been praying for—earthquake, flood, bubonic plague—has failed to intervene. I sympathize. I was the same way in my student days, and I'm still unnaturally shy for a professor of my years and experience. It's an incredibly long mile to the first class meeting. In this respect, each term is a kind of triumph for me. I remember how my voice trembled and my hands perspired in September as I introduced myself to these thirty strangers I've since learned to become so fond of.

Feeling the pain of their timidity, I make quick work of my introduction, concluding with the words, "Here, then, is the culminating scene between Martin Ferguson and his old flame, Charlene Trent."

We aren't half bad, we four uptight amateurs. It's only a staged reading after all—whispered blocking directions as you go, textbook in hand, no need to memorize. The reticent Kelly Evans fits perfectly the part of Martin Ferguson's landlady, welcoming Charlene Trent into her imagined parlor and serving her a cup of imagined tea while they await Martin's return from a stockholders' meeting of the Big Jake Tractor and Chainsaw Company. Miss Evans's is mostly a listening role, for Miss Thelen has a lot to say as Charlene Trent, speaking in her naturally plaintive voice about her long-term depression after the death of her husband and her decision, finally, to set off in search of her girlhood sweetheart.

I, as Martin Ferguson, enter then, bringing along with me my stodgy old companion, a part played haltingly yet convincingly by Mr. Curtis, a man whose imagination got pretty well atrophied during his forty years of driving the same tedious highway between Grand Forks and Grand Rapids. Discussing our investments, we hang up our coats and go into the parlor, which is to say we step up onto the platform, and when I see Charlene Trent sitting there, I have to be told who she is.

Here I'm afraid I overplay my part, standing stock-still in amazement far too long, drawing out the moment of drama to the point where it ceases to be breathtaking and evidently becomes comical, for I hear snickers. *Would you get a load of old Dean Edwards hamming it up!* Well, why not? I'm enjoying myself. I'm finding it curiously liberating to be Martin Ferguson for a few minutes instead of Leland J. Edwards, dean of the college. I adopt a gruff and blustery manner. I speak in a throaty voice that hurts a little, throwing in an "Urrr" here and there, the way President Zastrow does when he's confused or unhappy, which is most of the time. "Urrr, urrr," I growl, sending the class into stitches.

So enthralled am I by my newfound talent as a comedian that I can't stop showing off. Between "Urrr"s, I work my face into a wide-eyed overreaction to every line that's addressed to me. I fail to notice Carol Thelen throw her arms wide, as I instructed her to do in yesterday's fifteen-minute rehearsal, and we're over on the next page before I realize I've overlooked the single meaningful gesture in the entire scene, forgetting to give her the embrace the story calls for. I turn to my audience with a classic Jack Benny deadpan expression, and I say, "We forgot to hug." They all laugh like ninnies.

Except Miss Thelen. She doesn't laugh. She's drilling me with a look I take to be a well-deserved reprimand for stealing the scene and, worse, destroying the author's serious tone.

Later, the scene over, class dismissed, she remains sitting at her desk, and I apologize to her. "Forgive me," I say, "for being such a ham."

She shrugs. "No problem."

I'm vaguely aware of two or three students lingering in the doorway to hear this exchange, and I suppose it's partly for their instruction that I specify, "What we saw here this morning was a betrayal of the author's intention, and I am to blame. I violated the essence of the piece by playing it for laughs."

Do those lingering students stay for what happens next? I have the impression we are still being watched. Standing with my back to the door, textbook, papers and coat tree in hand, I'm ready to leave, but Miss Thelen is not. She's still sitting there—or languishing might better describe her—with her chin resting on her forearms and her forearms resting on her bulging bookbag and her asymmetrical eyes conveying a sobering kind of sadness as she says, "I don't want to go."

"Where?" I ask, not needing to be told that it isn't the skit that's made her so pensive; it's the prospect of spending a lifetime standing at one of the seven checkout counters of Petey's Price-Fighter Foods.

"Out in the world," she says.

"Ah, but you will always have the choice of returning to college someday." I consider the influx of nontraditional students one of the great advances in higher education in my lifetime. Every year I watch bridges built over the gaps between the mature and the young. "Look at Mrs. St. George," I tell her. "Look at Mr. Curtis."

She gets wearily to her feet, puts her arm through the strap of her bookbag, and adds, "Thanks for a good class, Dr. Edwards. I've loved it." She comes trudging toward me.

"Well then, in that case, let's have that hug we forgot." I gallantly set down the coat tree and we embrace briefly and awkwardly, she hindered by the heavy bag hanging off her shoulder, and I with the papers and book stacked in the crook of my arm. But it's okay. It seems fitting. She smiles a little, and I do too. I say something uninspired, like "Better late than never," and she says, "Thanks," once more, and out the door she goes.

The lingering students are gone as well. But standing there in the corridor and looking in at me with hate and accusation boiling in her deep-set eyes is L. P. Connor, the paranoid, unstable, highly explosive woman who has become my nemesis.

———

Over lunch I ask Mary Sue Bloom if she's ever been dogged by a student.

"Dogged? What do you mean, dogged?"

"Trailed," I tell her. "Continually inconvenienced. You know, dogged."

"Sure, who hasn't?" She smiles her brief little smile and stabs nervously at her lettuce. Mary Sue's expressions and gestures are all jerky and quick, for she's a woman in haste, a small, efficient dynamo—and pretty, too, if you like a pale face that colors easily with emotion, a quality I've always found irresistible in a woman. I'm also partial to dark russet hair and deep dark eyes like hers, and the rather sad tilt to her eyebrows. She's new on campus this year, our replacement for my old friend Kimberly Kraft in Education.

"There's this woman named Connor," I continue. "She's been hanging around campus for twenty years, off and on."

"L. P. Connor? She's back?"

"You know her? How do you know her?"

Mary Sue shrugs, her mouth full. She dips her head and swallows. "Her name comes up. Wasn't she an education major for a time?"

"That, as well as art and music and business management. She's never finished a course of study."

"I think she's the one Faith Crowninshield supervised in student teaching. Faith says she nearly drove her out of her mind."

"Yes, I remember that disaster. She slapped and spanked little kids, and Faith threw her out of the program."

"She says to this day L. P. Connor blames her for blocking her career path."

"She blames me to this day for not endorsing her as an English major. I was chair at the time, and had veto power. I knew her too well to recommend her."

We finish our salads and take up our hamburgers. We're lunching in the chilly student center, made to seem chillier today by the icy raindrops running down its north and east walls of windows. We're surrounded by youngsters squirting catsup on everything that passes into their mouths. I move my chair so I don't have to look at Dorcas Muldoon on her stool next to the cash register. Dorcas Muldoon used to manage this cafeteria, but now, dying of stomach cancer, all she can do is give you change while reminding you of your mortality. Her stool is high and her posture is bad—a buzzardlike hump to her shoulders. Her eyes, too, are buzzardlike, hooded and cold.

"Would you like catsup?"

"Actually I would," says Mary Sue, so I confer with the students at the next table and they let me borrow theirs. After fussing over our hamburgers—pickles, onions, catsup, pepper—we bite hungrily into them.

"How's yours?" she wants to know.

"So-so. A bit sinewy. How's yours?"

"So-so."

We share a birthday, Mary Sue Bloom and I. March eleventh. She'll be fifty-three—rather old these days for changing jobs. President Zastrow had his eye on a younger applicant, a man with a new Ed.D. degree whose undergraduate major had been geography (Zastrow makes a hobby of collecting road maps), but Mary Sue's credentials in teacher preparation were too impressive to pass up, and of course there was our gender balance to keep in mind. Fortunately, after granting contracts to a number of incompetents over the years, O. F. Zastrow now allows me the last word in hiring—as long as I allow him the last word in firing.

Zastrow loves firing people. He appoints a committee to find out who's expendable. He calls it his Search Committee, a gross perversion of the term. A Search Committee, when times were good, went searching for people to hire, but now, although certain departments (like English, like Philosophy) could do with new blood, new brains, our falling enrollment permits virtually no hiring. When a professor dies or retires or quits for any reason, he is usually not replaced, and by means of such attrition our teaching staff diminishes almost in proportion to the student population; but whenever, at our budget meetings, a deficit is discovered in the pot that salaries come out of, Zastrow will give me his imitation of a sad look, and say, "Guess we'll have to lop off a live one," and he'll gather his Searchers around him.

You can almost hear our president's heart speed up at the prospect of dismissal. Poor Kimberly Kraft was lopped off last spring. It made me sick to watch this old friend forcefully removed from her office, weeping and moaning. President Zastrow and his secretary April Ackerman made fast work of it. *Give us your keys, Dr. Kraft, and April will help you empty your desk. Your retirement package includes a year's free medical insurance, congratulations, good luck and good-bye.* Kimberly's been living in seclusion ever since. Mother and I are about the only people she'll let into her house, where she sits most of the day in her calico-covered rocking chair petting her stuffed owl.

"This Connor woman—will you point her out to me?" asks Mary Sue, chewing voraciously.

"You must have seen her. She wears a black cape, and a blacker expression. Her black hair is blond at the roots."

"How old?"

"Thirty-five, but older around the eyes."

"Only thirty-five? And she was here twenty years ago? What was she, a child prodigy?"

"No, no, she just hung around. Her father taught here. Connor the artist. Surely you've heard of him."

"He taught here? Connor, the famous drunk?"

I flinch at this. "Connor was my friend," I tell her.

Mary Sue is half a minute taking this in, her eyes trained on mine as she goes on chewing. I know what she's thinking. She's trying to imagine the tame likes of me as a companion to the wild likes of Connor, who during his time in Rookery had already become prominent enough as a painter to make his alcoholic episodes newsworthy. I recall the newspaper headline ARTIST COMATOSE, NEAR DEATH during one of his many bouts of pneumonia. Not his last, as it turned out. I explain this to Mary Sue. "His fatal binge occurred in 1980, in New Hampshire, where he'd lived with Peggy Benoit, another friend and fine teacher we lost."

She gives me an accusing look. "Rookery has trouble keeping faculty."

"No, our turnover is about average for a small state institution in the Midwest."

"I mean *good* faculty."

I can't deny this. In my ten years as dean, I've tried to raise standards around here, but a college faculty is a very heavy thing to lift. Every time I see a picture of the enormous hard-shell tortoises of Galápagos, I think of the sloe-eyed, snappish bunch of teachers who make up the bulk of our English and Philosophy departments, teachers whose minds have been crusted over by tenure and the esoteric journals they based their early lectures on and haven't changed a word of in thirty years. I have in place a network of scouts seeking out bright young instructors ready to change jobs as well as talented old professors looking for a light load during their last years, but Rookery has generally proved too remote for the ambitious on their way up and too cold in the winter for the popular on their way down.

It's a depressing subject, and one I'd rather not discuss with Mary Sue Bloom, for fear that she, too, will desert us at the end of the year, so I lead her back to ancient history. "We played in a musical combo together. Connor and I and three others, including this woman named Peggy Benoit. She was his sweetheart."

"She's not the mother . . . ?"

"No, no. The mother, Connor's wife, is a dreary little woman, sort of a mental case actually, who must have passed her faulty brain waves along to her daughter. The two of them live in a little house over on Mill Avenue with a stash of Connor's paintings. Whenever they run short of money, they sell one off."

"What's the 'L. P.' stand for?"

"Laura Patrice, according to her transcript. She's blessed with brains, but they're scrambled. She kept ending up in psych wards, both here and in the East. She'd go and visit her father in New England and have a breakdown. It was very hard for Peggy. She hated Peggy for taking her father away, you see."

"So why is she picking on you?"

"For refusing to welcome her into our house anymore. I mean that's my theory. There was a time, you see, during her teens, when Mother took her on as a reclamation project. She seemed so neglected and pitiful after her father moved away. Through good times and bad, food preparation was one of her abiding interests, so Mother had her in for cooking lessons. But of course we couldn't have her in the house when she turned dangerous, when every time she picked up a knife we wondered if she was going to slice bread or slash her wrists."

"Good God—suicidal?"

"For a while at least, as her mother had been from time to time."

Mary Sue looks thoughtful for a moment, then tosses off the chilling words, "Well, I know the feeling."

Why do I feel so deeply wounded by this remark? We fall silent, eating. Two men from Physical Education sit down nearby. The younger man, a musclebound athletic trainer, sheds his coat, revealing sweatpants, a Blue Heron T-shirt and biceps as big and hard as sewer tile. The older man is visibly upset. He's our athletic director, Ernie Burr. He says, "Not a Spect-O-Cheer for Chrissake, we don't have that kind of money!" This would be in reference to our hockey coach, an autocrat named Hokanson who thinks his program is the reason we exist as a college. Hokanson has been begging for a forty-thousand-dollar Spect-O-Cheer scoreboard as the crowning glory of our new hockey arena.

"The contractor says he needs to know right away, before he pulls his electricians off the job."

"Not a chance."

"Can't afford it," I put in, over the lunchtime din, in support of Ernie Burr.

"And new uniforms," replies the athletic trainer, whom Hokanson has trained as his mouthpiece so as not to let any of us rest, even when he's out of town. During the hockey season, Hokanson and his team spend alternate four-day weekends on distant sheets of ice.

"We got new uniforms three years ago," says Ernie Burr, loud enough for me to hear how loyal he's being. Actually, the moment Hokanson returns to campus he'll be talking out of the other side of his mouth.

"But the scoreboard's a must," insists the younger man. "Hokanson says it's a whole new ball game these days."

Ernie Burr turns to me. "Tell him, Edwards."

"Can't afford it," I repeat.

"But hockey carries the athletic department. It's bigger than football, bigger than basketball. Hokanson says without hockey income, the women's programs all go belly-up."

Ernie Burr looks to me to deny it.

"An old chauvinist threat," I tell him. "We've heard it before."

My attention is brought back to Mary Sue, who is looking far off while speaking in a monotone. "Actually I did have a student like that," she's saying. "His name was Lockhart. In Bismarck . . . He kept turning up in all my classes. . . . The thing was, you couldn't tell by looking at him how deranged he was."

She turns and focuses on me. "He had these strong features, you know? Dark hair, dark eyes, big wide nose. And he smiled all the time, which would have been my clue if it had been an idiotic smile, but it wasn't, it was sweet. He had the sort of presence that makes you call on him a lot, you know what I mean? The kid who looks like he's on your wavelength?"

Of course I know. I tell her about Mrs. St. George in her sweatsuit and Miss Kelly Evans of the everchanging hair color. "They're both like that. First to raise their hands at a question, last to doze off when I'm being dull."

"That's it exactly. The Bismarck mental case seemed very smart. He took every class I taught, then followed me to my office afterward and sat there looking at me. He was scary."

"So what did you do about it?"

"The wrong thing. I got stern with him and said he couldn't come to my office anymore." Mary Sue stops chewing and gives me a menacing scowl.

"It didn't work?"

"Oh, it worked all right. He went home and killed himself."

"Dear God!"

"At Christmastime, last year. That's why I had to get out of Bismarck."

I'm astounded. This didn't come out in her interview. "You mean you were somehow implicated?"

She dabs sadly at her lips with her paper napkin. "All last spring I kept seeing him sitting there in my office. Talk about being dogged. It got so I couldn't stand to go in in the morning. I carried my papers and books around with me all day and did most of my work in the library or the faculty lounge. It got so I couldn't sleep." With a plastic spoon, she carefully carves her bite marks out of her hamburger.

"You needed therapy."

"I talked to people about it—my chairman, my priest—and they said one solution would be to move away and start over. Here, take the rest of my hamburger—whenever I think about it, I can't eat. Steve was his name. Steve Lockhart. Dead at twenty because I kicked him out of my office."

"Nonsense, Mary Sue."

Her cheeks turn instantly red, her eyes hot with anger. "Don't say 'nonsense' to me, Dean Edwards!"

"Please. I'm just saying you can't feel responsible—"

She leans across the table and shakes a finger in my face. "And don't tell me how I should feel and how I shouldn't feel!" The noise in the student center is such that no one else seems to hear this; nor does the angry swing of her shoulders and hips attract attention as she stalks out of the cafeteria. I'm on my feet and ready to go after her when I realize what a spectacle this would make. *Hey, look at old Dean Edwards—would you believe it, on the make?*

The trainer and athletic director ask me to join them, so I move over. Finishing Mary Sue's hamburger, I listen to their tug-of-war regarding the athletic budget. Ernie Burr stands firm. Out the streaky window I watch Mary Sue hurry along the walk toward McCall Hall, a lovely, compact, fast-stepping figure pushing her red umbrella against the wind.

I pull up at the front door and go around the car with the umbrella to help Mother to her feet. Due to her increased weight and loss of muscle tone, she has trouble getting up out of low seats. In the entryway, we sit on a bench until she catches her breath. She'll be eighty-two in June. Cold rain is hell on emphysema.

"There's Sally," she wheezes, peering through the glass door into the lobby.

"Yes, there she is," I agree flatly, watching Sally McNaughton, manager of the Sylvan Senior Hi-Rise, cross the lobby and disappear into the dining room. For most of my life I couldn't have said even these four words about Sally without the inflection of love in my voice. As recently as last year we were still capable of turning on the old electric current that ran all the way back to our days as students at Paul Bunyan Elementary. It took Mary Sue Bloom to turn it off. I sense, however, that Sally would still like to ignite the spark. She still dresses to please me. This afternoon she's wearing one of my favorite outfits, a silky pantsuit of gold medallions printed on a dark rust background. After three divorces, Sally's gone back to her maiden name, McNaughton. Her last husband, Pug Patnode, was my predecessor in the dean's office. A used-car dealer named Roy Spang was her first husband. I was her second.

I stand up and pull open the inner door, but Mother clamps a restraining hand on my arm. "Wait," she says because her breath is still rattling and whistling. So I turn to scan the bulletin board and find only one new notice since last week. It's lettered in the shaky hand of Johnny Hancock.

BAT HOUSES. BAiTED WITH GUANO.
BUiLT with GALViNiZED
NAiLS. 75 bat capacity $49.
100 bat capacity $79.
see Johnny.

Pointing this out to Mother, I tell her, "God knows what anyone would want a bat house for."

"God and Johnny Hancock," she says.

I move along the wall to the bronze plaque and scan the names of the city officials who spearheaded the erecting of this five-story stack of widows and widowers, the tallest building in town. Also acknowledged in bronze is the Department of Housing and Urban Development, whence came a dignitary for the dedication ceremony, a poorly attended affair I remember very clearly. It was conducted on the lawn, under a tent, four summers ago. Mother was here for the speeches, taking notes for her radio show, while I was helping our old friend Hildegard Lubovich move in. I had already made several trips with Hildegard's belongings, and when I arrived with the old lady herself, she refused to get out of the car because she thought the gathering on the lawn was gypsies.

"I won't sleep any place that lets gypsies anywhere near," she declared, giving me a fearsome scowl, and hugging her big black purse to her chest. "Listen to them rave."

I told her the echoing, amplified voice was that of the Reverend Worthington Pyle reciting a prayer of consecration, and standing behind him, waiting his turn at the microphone, was the mayor of Rookery, but nothing I said convinced her to follow her twenty-five boxes of belongings up to her new apartment on the third floor. I pointed to Mother and Sally McNaughton and other people she knew under the big top, but she refused to look. Therefore, since I was content to listen to the speeches and Hildegard was content to sulk, we sat there with the windows rolled down to the pleasantly warm breezes of June. There were maybe forty people in the shade of the enormous tent to hear the mayor introduce a city councilman, who introduced the man from HUD, who said our federal government had come to Rookery like an angel of mercy and paid for 82 percent of this wonderful facility. After the concluding prayer and before the lemonade was served, I crossed the newly sodded lawn and asked Mother and Sally to come to my aid, which they did, but Hildegard refused to be cajoled. "Why are you consorting with gypsies?" she asked Mother.

So we ended up taking Hildegard to our house and feeding her supper. We went back in the evening, after the tent had been taken down, and she allowed herself to be taken peaceably up in the elevator to her new home.

I hear "Lolly and Leland," "Leland and Lolly" spoken aloud as we make our entrance into the dining room, an expansive, windowless area with a blue tile floor and mustard walls. About two-thirds of the residents sit facing each other across the long trestle table; I count twenty-four elderly women and two men. Sally McNaughton, moving along the far side of the table, pouring coffee, gives us a warm, welcoming smile. "Lolly and Leland" is repeated and passed along. We show up every Friday afternoon for this somber little coffee party—this is home to Mother's few close friends left alive—but a number of the residents are either sight-impaired or memory-impaired or both.

"Who?" ask the hard-of-hearing.

"Lolly and her boy."

I help Mother off with her heavy red coat, a capelike garment with fur at the collar and black braid running over the shoulders and down the front. She's wearing about five pounds of jewelry today, some of it valuable, pinned to her dress and hanging in chains from her neck. The dress is a shapeless wool smock of blue twill. She has rings on eight of her fingers.

We settle onto folding chairs in the vicinity of her three closest friends, and without a moment's hesitation the conversation begins. No greetings, no groping for a topic, no warm-up required—the chatter comes pouring forth. "What you got against cauliflower?" asks Hildegard Lubovich, presumably referring to something I missed on Mother's radio show. Flatulence is the answer, and while Mother is explaining this discreetly to Hildegard, Dot Kropp carries on about the outrageous price of lettuce at Petey's Price-Fighter Foods, and Nettie Firehammer reports the latest news disseminated by Twyla Todd up in 507. Twyla Todd, immobilized by arthritis, seldom shows up at this gathering, and yet she will quite often dominate the conversation because of what she learns from her police-band radio.

Mother confides to Hildegard, "I was terribly gassy as a girl."

"The ambulance went out twice last night," Nettie Firehammer reports, "once to your neighborhood, Lolly, somebody on Sawyer Street, they didn't say who. Twyla asked me to ask you." Nettie Firehammer is a wisp of a woman caved in by osteoporosis and cigarettes. She and her husband, in their heyday, were the proprietors of Firehammer's Five and Dime, where I bought leaden toy soldiers and candy and Halloween masks as a child.

"Nothing serious," Mother assures her, adding that had anyone died in Rookery last night she'd have heard about it at the radio station from Benny Smith, who is responsible for "Cliff's Obituaries."

"Petey says it's because of the storms and flooding in California," Dot Kropp explains to me, "so I said to Petey, I said, 'No way will I pay over a dollar and a quarter for one of these mushy little heads of lettuce, I'll go without.' "

"Very wise of you, Dot," I tell her. She's one of the many people I've known over seventy who were traumatized in their youth by the Great Depression, and although she's a former high school librarian she seems to have swept her once-lively mind clean of every concept but the cost of living. Hildegard has informed Mother that Dot hangs up her used paper towels to dry.

"How come it's still called 'Cliff's Obituaries' if it's always Benny Smith reading them?" asks Hildegard. Unlike Nettie and Dot, both of them shrinking and bending with age, and unlike Mother, who becomes heavier and more shapeless by the year, Hildegard has the tall, angular look of a woman much younger than her seventy-eight years. Her appearance is flawed, however, by her atrocious taste in clothing, which runs to polyester slacks and short-sleeved, flowered tops from bargain counters with buttonholes not quite matching their buttons and threads hanging loose under the arms.

"Cliff Mason started the show," Mother tells her, "and then when Cliff deserted us and went on to fame and fortune as a newscaster on the Statewide Network, we just hung onto the name. Wouldn't 'Benny's Obituaries' sound kind of, I don't know, less serious?"

Sally McNaughton summons Nettie and Hildegard to their turn in the kitchen, slicing and serving the treat of the week, and they come out bearing trays of something runny called peach delight, a kind of cobbler pastry under which apples have been replaced by canned peaches that slip around like fish on your plate. It's been the dessert of choice here for about the last three years. I sense, however, that we're coming to the end of the peach delight phase of Hi-Rise history, for today, when Johnny Hancock calls out "Where's dem cherries?" a number of the women pause in their nimble mastication to remark in favor of the cherry parfait that's been served more and more often of late. The golden age of Hi-Rise desserts, in my opinion, occurred in the late 'eighties when you could count on chocolate cake and vanilla ice cream every week.

Dot Kropp needs to know, confidentially and urgently, if KRKU, in which Mother has the majority financial interest and Dot has a few of her own closely watched dollars invested, is going to be bought out, as threatened, by the Statewide Network. Mother emits a long, wheezy laugh, assuring her that KRKU will only pass from her control over her dead body, but Dot doesn't seem pacified. She's worried, she says, that the network's horribly wild talk shows will come to Rookery, which retains, according to various friends and relatives living elsewhere, the last unbesmirched airwaves in Minnesota.

"My niece wrote from Minneapolis that she heard a whore arguing with a Franciscan sister on WCCO."

We fall silent at this, eating our cobbler. I gaze around this most dismal of dining rooms, imagining how it might be improved with wallpaper and a few windows cut into its walls. I think what I dislike most are the framed jigsaw puzzles hanging on all sides at eye-level—laughing children and exotic landscapes and card-playing dogs dressed up in funny clothes. Sally has explained her motive in permitting such a travesty of interior decoration, and I understand it, but I can't help being repelled by it. Granted, these old folks, after a lifetime of industry, don't have any meaningful work to do, and so these five-hundred-piece puzzles represent the fruits of their labors—but a drunken Native American looking cross-eyed at his horse? Why, at a certain age, must we relinquish all taste and good sense?

When I finish eating, I go, by popular demand, to the piano in the corner and play "Cruising Down the River." A few cracked voices sing along. A few more join in on "Daisy, Daisy, Give Me Your Answer True." Except for "... the living is easy," nobody knows the words to "Summertime," so I end up playing it solo, improvising and getting into an insistent sort of Brubeck beat until I can tell by the growing sound of their gabble that I've lost my audience; so I stand and take my customary bow and go and sit at the men's end of the long table. None of the residents remarks about the trick I've played, slipping summer songs over on them instead of Christmas carols. Without a window to see out of, maybe they've momentarily forgotten what month it is, forgotten the sleety rain that's been spitting down all day.

Johnny Hancock and the Reverend Worthington Pyle are currently the only two men living here. Father Pyle, on my right, is telling a woman sitting across from him that it's all over. She stares blankly at the collar of his loose, gray turtleneck, and he repeats at a higher pitch, "It's all over, I tell you!"

This woman, a new resident, a stranger to me, is apparently unacquainted with the residents' habit of segregation at table. Or maybe, having been told, she still prefers sitting here, in which case the other women will condemn her as man-crazy. She wears a great deal of makeup on her gaunt face, and her fresh hair coloring—oxblood, carelessly applied—has colored the rims of her ears as well. She shifts her gaze from Worthington Pyle to me, as if to ask, What's the matter with this old coot? Nestled in her left ear is a big hearing aid.

"It's all over," Father Pyle repeats to Johnny Hancock, and he proposes a toast to ignorance, but this companion of his, dressed in a soiled flannel shirt and bib overalls, this builder of bat houses, grunts and turns away.

"It's all over," says Father Pyle to me.

"What's all over?" I ask, though I have a pretty good idea.

"Goodness is over. Ethical behavior. The higher attainments of the human race. Civilization at its best is down the tubes, at least in America. I don't speak for the third world, the developing nations. I speak only for America."

"You're wrong," I tell him, as I've insisted countless times in the past. The moment Worthington Pyle retired from the active priesthood, he gave himself up to this bitterly sardonic train of thought. He used to be rector of our church, St. Blaise Episcopal, the site of my baptism and my wedding, my father's funeral and my son's. He's a narrow-shouldered old man with a sour mouth, sleepy eyes and quite a lot of uncontrollable white hair. His half-glasses ride low on his short nose. I recall how he would occasionally let drop a shockingly pessimistic statement from the pulpit, but in those days you had the feeling that he was at least struggling to hold his darker impulses in check. No more. Now he preaches a single message—the efficacy of ignorance—which I find particularly offensive.

"It's God's plan, Edwards, that each generation of Americans will become stupider than the last. Dummies will graduate from college and give us the laws of the land. Morons will carry the day. God in his wisdom will see to it, because an intelligent population would be too restless in the kind of culture we're developing—the TV culture."

"Now, now, Father," scolds Sally McNaughton good-naturedly, coming around with the coffeepot and standing close to my shoulder. "We aren't corrupting poor innocent Leland with our bad thoughts, are we?" She's teasing me, of course, standing with her hip an inch from my elbow, her scent in my nostrils. She remembers how I used to heat up in her presence.

Worthington Pyle is unstoppable. "We've become an over-populated, leisure-time culture that's getting stupider by the minute. Two hundred and fifty million smart people would get in each other's way, don't you see? Brains need elbowroom. Ignorance doesn't care." He raises his cup, trembling and dribbling his coffee. "Here's to ignorance."

"I can't drink to that," I tell him. "That's a despicable thing to drink to."

"No more coffee for me," Johnny Hancock tells Sally. "One cup's my bladder's limit." It's a limit dictated also by Johnny's need for chewing tobacco, the shredded kind, a packet of which he now fishes out of a hind pocket of his overalls.

"Johnny, why would anybody want a bat house?" I ask him.

He directs a brown-toothed smile at the red-eared woman while shaking his head and pointing at me as though he's never known anyone so incredibly stupid. "For bats."

"Well, obviously. But why?"

Turning politely away from the New Woman (as she will be known here until the next new resident moves in), he drags an enormous pinch of stringy tobacco from his pouch to his mouth and stuffs it into his cheek.

"Keefe um owf yuh howf," he replies around his wad.

Sally translates for me. "Keeps them out of your house."

"But our house doesn't have any bats."

"Some houses do," she says. Then she leans over to whisper a number in my ear, "Five-oh-six," and moves quickly away.

The Reverend Worthington Pyle is chuckling. "You aren't going to believe this, Leland. I once had bats in my belfry."

"No!" I've heard this before, but "no" is the line he wants fed to him.

"My church in Owl Brook had a belfry. Tried everything. Couldn't keep the bats out." His narrow shoulders shake with false laughter.

"Shud had a baf howf," Johnny Hancock advises.

The Reverend Pyle then turns to the New Woman, willing to share with her his rare good humor. "I once had bats in my belfry."

"Doesn't surprise me," she shoots back.

"Leland!" calls a voice from down the table. It's Hildegard pointing with alarm at Mother, who's having a coughing fit. It's one of her silent fits, on a scale of one to ten only a five or six, but I stand up anyhow to show Mother and Hildegard and her other friends that I'm ready to come to her aid if necessary. I'm the faithful son who always does what's expected of him. If I didn't, they'd natter about it for days.

Hildegard alerts Sally as well, and she goes and leans over Mother and holds her by the shoulders as the coughing dies away.

"Who's that spitting up?" the New Woman wants to know.

"My mother."

"Looks like she's about had it."

It's true. Mother emerges from these episodes with the most helplessly bleary look in her eye—an imploring eye that fastens itself on me and says it's time to go home.

Helping her from the dining room, I hear Worthington Pyle call to us, "Remember, Edwards, brains need elbowroom!" I turn to wave good-bye, and see Hildegard appropriate Mother's unfinished plate of peach delight. I see Johnny Hancock dribbling brown spit into the middle chest pocket of his bib overalls, and the New Woman looking extremely offended and pointing a tattling finger at him. I can understand the New Woman's disgust, for she doesn't see the small cylindrical orange-juice container Johnny carries in that pocket as a spit depository.

Sally accompanies us through the lobby, supporting Mother and saying how sorry Twyla Todd will be not to see her. Twyla Todd, imprisoned upstairs not only by her arthritis but also by the unvarnished drama that now and then comes over her short-wave radio, usually receives Mother for a lengthy visit in her room. Sally and I don't always spend this time making love in an empty apartment. We do it maybe two or three times a year, at Sally's discretion. Bidding her good-bye in the vestibule, I read sexual frustration in her flashing eyes.

The New Woman comes up and stands beside her. "Who are them two?" she asks.

"Lolly and her little boy," Sally answers.

The woman fiddles with the dial in her ear and asks again: "Who?"

Not "who," but "why" might be more apt.

How does a man my age become trapped in this life of service to his mother? Why is he driving her home through the sleety rain of late afternoon when he could be lying in the single bed of 506 with his former wife?

It's a story.

When I was fourteen my father died, as I've said, and immediately thereafter Mother and I fell into a tight, almost suffocating, dependence on each other, a kind of brittle, extrasensory hookup that had us anticipating each other's thoughts, spoken and unspoken. I could sense, for example, the depth of her sorrow. Known to all her chatty friends as a jolly extrovert, Mother concealed her lingering grief from everyone but me. This troubled me greatly. I'd learned how to read the weather in her eyes and always tried my best to either conform to it or bring her out of it. When she was pensive, I was pensive. When she was silly, so was I. Capriciousness I could handle. Even petulance. But her sadness was impossible for me to deal with. I was helpless to console her when she grieved, because the proven method of doing so—endless chatter—was something I was incapable of. I set myself the task of learning loquaciousness—I'd seen how motor-mouths worked whenever she had her bridge club in—but I just couldn't master it. Perhaps because my own grief was as deep as hers.

"Speak!" she would demand of me after her bridge club had broken up and gone home or she'd hung up the phone or turned off the radio and the hush in the house was more than she could tolerate. "Speak to me, Leland!" So what I'd do then, I'd present her—for the umpteenth time—with some fond but worn-out memory from the days when my father was alive, say a summer picnic on the riverbank or a Christmas visit to Omaha, and she'd get a soft, nostalgic look in her eye and we'd try to have a conversation about it. But I invariably lacked the words to hold up my end of it, so we'd fall silent and she'd brood and complain about what she called my secret nature. If there's one abiding thorn in Mother's side, it's my reticence.

Eventually, growing older, I turned this reticence to my advantage. While Mother called it my vice, it actually became my salvation, for it was only behind this screen of silence that I was able to develop a life of my own. It was either that, or choke on her well-meaning but relentless attention. I did this in my thirties—opened myself up to the sort of complexity most boys experience in their adolescence. Pretty late by normal standards, but so what?—I've always been a late starter. I didn't shave until I was eighteen. I didn't attain my full height, six-one, until I was out of college. I was thirty-five years old the night I first went to bed with Sally.

We had kissed, once, in the 1940s. I was nine, Sally was ten.

Mother, Father, and I had returned the previous September from our twenty months in Bloomington, Indiana, where my father had earned his doctorate in history. We moved into the house Mother and I occupy to this day, our large and lovely half-timbered Tudor on Sawyer Street, near campus.

I discovered that my time away had cooled the few uncertain

friendships I'd had at Paul Bunyan Elementary, and none of my fourth-grade classmates, except girls, lived in my new neighborhood. No matter. Never much of a friend-seeker, I was content to while away the afternoons and evenings of that first fall and winter in solitary pleasures such as reading comic books or expanding my father's stamp collection or prowling around the house and yard pretending I was a fighter pilot shot down behind enemy lines and sneaking back to safety. Autumn Saturdays I spent a lot of time with my father, either fishing or following the Blue Heron football team through its inglorious autumn schedule. Winter Saturdays, even back then, the hockey team was a winner, but my father preferred fishing through the ice, as he used to say, to watching people skate around on it beating each other up. It was on one of those Saturdays, with no one at home to talk to, that Mother started her radio show and spoke to all of Rookery.

After school one very cold day in January, tunneling through a hardpacked snowdrift in our backyard and progressing inch by inch across Norway and back to my outfit, I broke through into daylight to find myself being spied upon by a twelve-year-old boy who lived two streets over from ours. I'd seen him in school but never spoken to him. His name was Otto McNaughton. To my great disappointment, he said we should become friends. I agreed to this proposal, because to have declined would have been impolite, but I sensed from the start how overbearing he'd turn out to be. I was nine and meek, the very sort of flunky he needed, by his nature, to order around.

We spent hours in Otto's basement, building things out of his father's scrap lumber—hours I found intensely disagreeable because I had no skill with tools, because the basement was dank, and because Otto's mother kept shouting for us to keep the noise down so she could hear the radio. I might have stopped going to Otto's house altogether if it hadn't been for its one great attraction—his sister Sally, who seemed rather fond of me.

I'll never understand how a girl growing up with a complaining mother, a bossy brother, and a father seldom home, acquired her sweetness, but that's what Sally was—sweet. Repeatedly, therefore, I went to Otto's in the hope that his sister, a fifth-grader, would be home and smile at me and say hello. At that age, of course, a boy can't admit to liking a girl without suffering ridicule and humiliation, so I told no one about her but Mother. And I told her obliquely, describing Sally's agility in gym class, which the fourth, fifth, and sixth grades took together. Sally was better than boys, I said, at climbing ropes and swinging along the parallel bars. Nobody could outrun her.

Mother was amused. "Don't tell me romance is raising its pretty little face," she said.

One day after school, Otto and I were in his basement building bazookas for the final push across France and into Berlin. It was my job to hold the boards and broomsticks as Otto sawed and hammered and sanded and glued. His crosscut saw slipped on a knotty piece of oak and cut my thumb to the bone. I shot up out of the basement, bleeding and screaming, and ran home, to be fussed over and bandaged by Mother and (what a relief!) forbidden to play in Otto's basement anymore.

Next morning I was excused from the rigors of gym class because of my bandaged thumb. Sally, waiting her turn on the ropes, came and sat beside me on the bleachers. She was all smiles and solicitude, wanting to know how serious my wound was.

"Pretty bad," I told her. "You want to see the bone?"

I made as if to unwrap the gauze, expecting her to do something girlish like scream or faint or at least say, "No, please, I can't stand the sight of blood," but she shocked me by saying, "Yes."

Luckily my homeroom teacher, Miss Tucker, came over to us at this point, saving me the embarrassment of exposing my wound and fainting myself, for if anyone couldn't stand the sight of blood, it was I at that age. Having inquired about the circumstances of the accident, Miss Tucker asked, "And what were you building, Leland?"

I didn't answer. This teacher of mine was a frail, mellow-hearted, elderly woman, a friend of Mother's, who'd been treating me as something of a teacher's pet, a position of favor I didn't want to jeopardize by admitting I'd been manufacturing weapons of violence.

"A birdhouse?" she prompted.

"Yes, a birdhouse," I lied, shielding her from the awful truth. And then I cringed, realizing that Sally must have known about the bazookas.

When Miss Tucker left us, going off to supervise some fourth-graders falling off the parallel bars, I turned to Sally expecting a reprimand. Instead, she looked delighted. She shocked me by taking my face in both her hands and planting a firm kiss on my forehead. "Oh, you're so cute!" she exclaimed.

Somehow I managed not to tell Mother about the kiss. Mother would only be amused. The kiss was too precious to be laughed at.

Then my father died, and I sensed that a girl's kisses would no longer be amusing to Mother. Not that I attracted any, but I got the message: Mother needed a full-time man in her life, and I was that man. The message became explicit when I was sixteen and accompanied a girl named Constance Overgard to a musical program in the college auditorium. The artists, known as Whitmore and Lowe, were touring the Midwest playing duets on two pianos. Constance and I, who had been taking piano for several years, had performed a duet the previous May at our annual recital, and I admired her proficiency with difficult chords. She was a farmer's daughter, one of those muscular, sunburned, strong-fingered girls who come from dairy farms with not enough brothers to take care of all the milking and fieldwork.

Looking back, I see that we were unusually serious for our age, Constance and I, and this seriousness we respected in each other without ever getting serious *about* one another. Our backgrounds were too dissimilar for any sort of kinship except that of the keyboard. What did Constance know about the books and magazines I spent hours reading in the college library? What did I know about tractors and milking machines and the price of alfalfa?

Coming away from the performance that night, we were reluctant to part, both of us enchanted by Whitmore and Lowe's artistry, and so, for half an hour, we drove the streets of Rookery in the Overgard Buick, discussing keyboard technique, and when she dropped me in front of my house, we parted with an awkward touching of shoulders and arms and squeezing of hands—our fingers, I suppose, trying to express the harmony we normally conveyed in our music.

Mother, as usual, was waiting to hear about my evening. She liked to keep radioland apprised of every cultural event in town, whether or not she'd been there. Having praised the performers' rendition of Mozart and Schubert, I should have known better than to go on to say how the recital had enchanted us, how eager Constance and I had become to work up new duets. I guess I praised her fingers.

Mother's face instantly darkened. I'll never forget the look of reprimand that came into her eyes as she pronounced, "Sex raises its ugly head." You wouldn't think disapproval could be all that harmful, but to this day, when Mother's eyes turn icy, I'm devastated. I can't stand it.

Our piano teacher, almost certainly at Mother's urging, removed duets from her spring program.

Skip about twenty years, to an autumn weekend in 1970. When I think back to that certain Saturday in October, I have a hard time believing it was actually my life Sally entered. Anything as miraculous as love, it seems, must have happened to someone else—someone, if not more worthy than I, at least more ready.

I was raking leaves at our cabin on Owl Lake, near the town of Owl Brook, where Sally lived with her husband the used-car dealer. I had been unwell, but I was happy. This annual chore of cleaning up the yard I found restorative. It was a lovely warm day of haze and migrating geese and long-shadowed sunlight lying along the lakeshore. The long grass, after weeks of drying wind, was covered knee-deep with brittle, drifted leaves.

We'd owned the cabin since before my father died in 1949. He was fishing in a canoe not two hundred yards from the dock when lightning struck. Because of this tragedy just out the front door, and since she was, and still is, too social for cabin living, Mother had no fondness for the place. She made the hour-long trip to Owl Lake only twice each summer—once to entertain her bridge club for an afternoon, and once to host the staff from KRKU radio and their families for a weekend of tenting, fishing, and grilling hamburgers.

Which suited me just fine. I liked being at the cabin alone, painting it, planting flowers around it, repairing the dock, napping, reading, fishing for northern pike and panfish. I'd have preferred catching walleyes, the way my father used to, but the walleyes of Owl Lake were night feeders, and, except on the KRKU weekend, I never stayed overnight at the cabin. I drove home to Rookery in the evening, because Mother didn't like to be alone in the house after dark.

On this Saturday morning, however, leaving the house, I'd withstood Mother's disapproval and insisted that I'd have to be away overnight. I'd been reading about William James, and seen how similar to mine was the nagging, mysterious illness that dogged him as a youngish man. His biographer, with the aid of a hundred years of hindsight, speculated that his malady was not physical in origin, but caused by the strain of playing a role in life that went against his nature. Once he broke out of the confining lifestyle dictated by his strong-willed father and followed his instincts into the refreshing and far-reaching field of psychology, his illness disappeared.

Dizziness, nausea, headaches, and fatigue. Dr. Mittleholtz, our family physician, after numerous blood tests, X rays, and probings into all my orifices, was stumped. He was unable to do for me what James's biographer did for him—say the word that made sense of all my symptoms: depression.

Like William James, I'd been living a life not my own—in my case a life mapped out by Mother. By breaking out of her control, might I not become healthy again? Dr. Mittleholtz agreed, though vaguely, his agreement expressed slantwise out of respect for the woman whose voice came booming over the air every morning and dominated the thinking of Rookery. Dr. Mittleholtz was a meaty-faced little man with an inward smile and a cryptic way of speaking. When, with a guilty sense of betrayal, I set forth my theory and asked him if, furthermore, a relationship with a woman unrecommended by Mother (I didn't identify Sally by name) might help unblock my path through life, he nodded and smiled inwardly and mumbled astonishingly, "Something I was taught in medical school, my boy—the world revolves on a stiff prick."

Carrying this truth home with me, I broke free that Saturday morning, offering Mother the soundest of reasons for my staying overnight at the cabin. This being a dangerously dry autumn, the forest service forbade lighting fires before dark, when the wind ordinarily subsided, which meant I wouldn't have all the leaves and brush burned before ten or eleven or midnight; plus, I needed to be back at the cabin the next day to shut off the water system, a complicated job taking half a day to complete. We knew from experience that if I didn't drain the pipes before the hard freeze predicted for Sunday night, the plumbing would burst.

Mother responded with all the injury and resentment she could integrate into her scolding expression, and when she saw that it wasn't getting her anywhere, she changed her tack. "Suit yourself," she said breezily, indicating it didn't matter, yet coldly, indicating it did.

And so there I was, happily raking leaves in the sunshine and feeling supremely gratified to have won this initial skirmish in my struggle for independence. I was thirty-five years old. Next summer, I decided, I would make a habit of staying at the lake overnight. Let Mother grow up, I told myself. Hadn't her widowed friends long ago learned to live alone around the clock, daylight and dark?

I was sweeping the flood of leaves downhill toward the beach when I heard a car door slam. I squinted into the low sun and saw a woman come around the corner of the cabin. Could this be Sally? What a coincidence! Though I hadn't seen her for four or five years, I'd had Sally on my mind all morning. I'd imagined driving into Owl Brook and looking her up and visiting with her over coffee at the Owl's Nest. I pictured her as the girl she'd been in high school and college—smoky teal green eyes expressing empathy and amusement by turns, a turned-out lower lip I'd always longed to kiss, tight angora sweaters she wore to class and took off in my dreams. "Oh, you're so cute," she'd said, kissing me in gym class when I was nine—and that was about the last spontaneous thing any woman or girl ever said to me.

The approaching woman raised her hand in greeting, and I shouted across the lawn, "Sally! I can't believe it!" I dropped my rake and tried to summon the courage to kiss her. "How did you find me?"

It wasn't Sally. I saw, as she drew closer, that although she was Sally's height and Sally's shape and her hair was the color I remembered Sally's to be, this was a stranger. She was older. She wore a long skirt and a plaid shawl. She ignored my embarrassed apology, my attempt to explain about the difficult slant of sunlight. She shook my hand and said she was a realtor. She said it was a seller's market in lakeshore these days and wanted to know if I was interested in making a lot of money on this property. She had a waiting list of buyers from Rookery, from Minneapolis, from as far away as Chicago.

No, I told her, it wasn't for sale.

"How long have you had it?" she asked. "It looks charming."

"My father bought it in 'forty-eight."

"Hmmm, twenty-two years. I can probably get you six or eight times what he paid for it."

Again I told her no, it wasn't for sale.

"Well, I just wondered. I come by here pretty often and there's hardly ever any sign of life."

"That's going to change," I said, picking up my rake.

Within half an hour I was driving slowly along a dirt street in Owl Brook, trying to determine if a certain house with no number was Sally's. It wasn't the neat rambler or colonial I'd imagined her to be living in. There was an enormous Winnebago camper parked in the side yard and a pickup out front with a flat tire. In the driveway was an old red Cadillac. A Weber cooker stood in the weeds on one side of the front door. On the other side was a motorcycle covered by a ragged tarpaulin.

At the corner, in the middle of a U-turn, I lost my resolve. After talking to the realtor, I'd hopped in the car, driven to town, and found Sally McN. Spang in the phone book, but this house, if indeed it was hers, seemed unapproachable, the window shades drab, the grass long and wiry, the pickup truck eaten by rust.

From the end of the block, I saw a bald man with a stomach come out the side door and get into the red car. He wore a white shirt with rolled-up sleeves and a dark necktie. He didn't look like the Roy Spang I'd known in Rookery. He was too young. He started the engine, picked his teeth for a few seconds, then flicked the toothpick out the window and backed into the street. I followed his cloud of dust to his destination two blocks away, a car lot called Spang Auto, which convinced me that this was either Roy or his brother, who went by the name of Cub, and the house he'd come out of was Sally's. But I didn't return there. I went instead to the Owl's Nest and drank coffee, wondering if I should dial her number. Could anyone married to Roy Spang for fifteen years be the same charming woman I remembered?

For although I hadn't seen either of them in a long time, I'd been keeping track of Roy and Sally from a distance. Whenever students from Owl Brook turned up in my class, I'd ask if they knew the Spangs. Most of them did. Sally worked in the Owl County Courthouse, directing a federal program whose goal was to rehabilitate the lame, the halt, and the blind-drunk to the point of becoming employable. What a perfect job, I thought, for Sally the caretaker. Even as a girl, she'd habitually befriended the friendless, taken in stray dogs, paid calls on invalids.

Her husband's reputation, it seems, was that of a lazy drudge. One of my students had been employed by Spang Auto to keep the vehicles washed in fair weather and to scrape off the snow and ice in winter. He said nobody could figure out what Sally saw in Roy. He was old enough to be her father. He and his brother now operated three sales lots, this one in Owl Brook, the original Spang Auto in Rookery, out past the industrial park on Highway 2, and the other one in Staggerford, some sixty miles to the southwest. Had I noticed, this student inquired, Roy's special affinity for recreational vehicles? All three lots carried an inventory top-heavy with RVs, particularly the more luxurious models. One such RV, a monstrosity called the Overland Rover, nearly the size of a semi-truck trailer, with bay windows and a retractable porch, served as Roy's office in Owl Brook. My student described it as having a hot tub, two bedrooms, three TV's, and velveteen upholstery throughout, even up the walls, in tones of peach and green.

He said when the weather was inclement Roy never stepped out of the Overland Rover from morning to night. He phoned from it, sold cars from it, made his lunch in it, napped in it, drove it home in the evening and parked it as close as possible to the side door of the house, thus necessitating a mere five- or six-step walk through the elements.

Another curious thing I heard about Roy Spang was confirmed by several students. It was evidently well-known in Owl Brook that whenever Roy and Sally were invited out to dinner, which was seldom, they arrived in the Overland Rover because Roy liked to lie down after a meal. "Thanks a lot, I feel a nap coming on," he'd say, having licked up the last of the dessert, and he'd go to bed in the driveway. This left Sally alone with the hosts, who seemed to prefer it that way, for they were invariably Sally's friends from the courthouse and it was Sally's company they sought.

Calling all this to mind, I finished my coffee, went to the pay phone at the back of the Owl's Nest and, probably out of curiosity as much as old affection, dialed her number.

A man answered.

"I'm calling for Sally."

"Not here."

"Will she be back?" A dumb thing to ask, surely, but I had trouble picturing her living in that house with the yard uncared for and the flat-tired pickup eaten by rust.

"Who is it?"

"An old friend."

"Edwards?"

How did he know?

"Lee Edwards—I be damned!"

"Who am I talking to?" I needn't have asked. The only person who ever called me Lee was Sally's brother, Otto McNaughton.

"Hey, Lee, it's your old buddy Otto. Jesus, Lee, you sound just like you used to, you know that?"

"Otto. How you doing, Otto?"

"Hey, fine. Hell of a long time since we talked."

"A long time," I agreed, thinking not long enough. I pictured the dank basement of the McNaughton house where we built weapons of war out of scrap lumber. I saw once again the dull crosscut saw jumping its groove and leaping to my thumb, watched myself running home spurting blood.

"Where are you, out at the lake? Hey, come on into town, we'll have ourselves a beer."

"No, I was just calling . . ." I couldn't think how to explain myself. I couldn't very well say I wanted to see how his sister had weathered fifteen years married to a slob.

"Tell you what, come on into the Legion later on. I'm tending bar. Buy you a brew."

"No, thanks a lot, Otto. I was just—"

"Hey, what's your number out there at the lake? I'll tell Sally."

I made up a number, rather than admit that the cabin had no phone and I was calling from down the street.

"Swell, Lee, I'll tell her."

"Otto, nice talking to you."

"Like to buy you a brew, Lee. Anytime."

I couldn't help asking, "How did you know I had a place on the lake?"

"Shit, man—town this size, you get to know things."

I drove back to the lake.

The wind died around five-thirty, and I touched a match to one of several mountains of leaves on the beach. I would spend about three hours tending fires until the last spark was out. I loved to feel unhurried as night came on instead of driving the twisty road home to Rookery. I loved standing at the water's edge listening to the wingbeat and splash of mallards and the crack of acorns falling onto the dock. My supper would be a beer and two hot dogs roasted on a stick. The copper sun hung in the evening haze over the far shore. There wasn't the hint of a breeze. Smoke rose fifty feet straight up, and then slanted south.

Again the slam of a car door. Again a woman approaching across the grass. This time—incredibly—it *was* Sally. She was wearing jeans, a sweatshirt, a windbreaker, long beaded earrings that swayed as she walked. She carried a bottle wrapped in a paper sack.

"Sally," I said, dropping my rake and my matchbook and

taking a step toward her, then stopping to wonder if I had the courage to give her the meaningful kiss I'd imagined.

You don't wonder about meaningful kisses beforehand—that's the first of many things I learned from Sally McNaughton Spang. I learned it when she strode up to me with a grin and a giggle, tossed the bottle into a cushion of leaves, and planted a kiss on my mouth. Love is spontaneous—for love it was. I knew for certain by the time the kiss had ended that I was in love.

"You called?" she said, bending over and feeling around in the leaves for the bottle.

"I talked to Otto. Does he live with you?"

"Off and on. Otto never grew up." Although her voice was lower than I remembered it, there was a lighthearted current running through it, a kind of sultry jocularity.

"I drove by your house. Saw a man coming out."

She came up with the bottle, removed it from the sack. "Man with a belly?"

"Yes, a short man, heavyset."

"Roy's brother Cub. They're partners. Roy's away, buying cars in the Cities."

"Cub lives with you too?"

"No, but he comes for lunch quite a bit. He lives down the street, alone since his wife left him. Cub never grew up either. Have you got a corkscrew?"

"No, sorry."

"I knew it." She pulled one out of her windbreaker pocket and went to her knees on the sand to remove the cork.

I dropped into the leaves beside her.

"So, Leland, why did you call?"

"I thought it would be fun to see you again."

"Well, is it?" She laughed.

"Yes, of course."

"It's fun seeing you too."

"I mean . . . I always liked you so much."

She smiled at me. "Then why didn't you ever say so?"

There seemed to be no answer to this. I said nothing.

"I liked you too," she said.

"You did?"

"Sure." She laughed again. "Don't we sound like a couple of teenagers?"

"You should have told me."

The cork went "pop."

"I never told you because you didn't seem to need me," she said.

What a curious remark. I studied her in the gathering dusk. The eyes were as intriguing as ever, the smile as quick and cheery, but added to her expression now was what appeared to be a trace of guile, as though life had taught her to be wiser than she'd been as a girl, a little less sweet perhaps, a little ironic, more interesting.

"I mean, if you'd needed me, I might have had to marry you," she said. "I'm the kind of person who needs to help the needy. You knew that surely." She added, with a laugh, "That's why I married Roy—he never grew up either."

"'Are you off your rocker?' my mother used to ask me whenever I did somebody a strange kind of favor, like the time I brought home Leonard Habstreet's monkey because it had scabies or lice and Leonard couldn't stand to watch it scratch itself practically to death. Remember Leonard Habstreet?"

I shook my head no, the bottle to my lips. We were sitting in one leafpile and watching another burning down to a blanket of sparks. We'd eaten the hot dogs and a few marshmallows, and now we were finishing off the wine. The name Habstreet I didn't recognize.

"Leonard was a divorced bartender who lived across the alley from us for a year or two when I was a girl and he was real proud of this scrawny little monkey he'd bought in Florida or some-where. It used to ride on his shoulder when he walked to work."

"Oh, him." The bartender with the pet monkey came back in memory.

"It sat at the table with him to eat its meals. He'd bring it over to our yard because it liked to swing from clotheslines and Leonard didn't have clotheslines. After a while it got this itch."

She took the bottle and sipped, careful to leave me a swal-low. Leafsmoke rose into the night. There was a splash and a gull-squawk nearby in the reeds. It was a blue and silver evening, the water flat as a plate.

"My mother had a fit. Leonard showed us the pet-store papers declaring it was inoculated against all normal monkey diseases, and it was neutered or spayed or whatever it is with monkeys, but this itch came on all of a sudden and it clawed its poor little belly and crotch all raw, which caused Leonard to practically have a nervous breakdown until I took the creature off his hands and bathed it in oatmeal and applied tar to the raw places. Don't ask me how I knew about oatmeal and tar, I was only fifteen, I must have heard about it somewhere. It did the trick. The monkey got better and none of us caught the itch, though my mother had a fit anyway, and made me promise never again to bring home a plant, animal, or person with a disease." She laughed again. "She about died when I brought home Roy."

"What was his disease, if I may ask?"

She hooted and lay back in the leaves. "Inertia's all that's ever been wrong with Roy, though he likes to call it a muscular disability. He had the whole world believing it back then. Had *me* believing it, otherwise I might not have married him. I mean, I could no more turn down a cripple than fly. That's *my* disability."

"You married in college."

She nodded. "Left class one day and went straight to the altar."

I thought it over. "Amazing. I didn't know you were that much of a caretaker."

"Enabler's the word. How *could* you know? We never talked."

"But we did, Sally. We were in those courses together, remember? We talked a lot."

"Not seriously, Leland."

I thought back. "Really?" I seemed to remember important conversations.

"I don't think so, Leland. We never *really* talked."

Hearing this made me incredibly sad. I sat with my back to her for a minute or two, listening to a fisherman motoring, slowly, far out on the water, dragging his bait through the darkness. Then I got up and lit another leafpile.

When only two mountains of leaves remained, we burrowed into one of them to keep warm, for a chill had descended with the dark, and we lay there watching the other burn and pop and send sparks high in the air. We kissed a long kiss, then Sally rolled over on top of me, her weight on her elbows, and asked me, nose to nose, "Do you have a bed, or do you always sleep in the leaves?"

"Actually I have two."

"We could probably make do with one."

My heart leaped. I was mute with joy, anticipation, uncertainty, fear. When I recovered my voice it was to ask, "Won't Otto tell Roy you're out late?"

"Otto works late. I'll be home before he will." She giggled. "Are you always this much of a worrywart?"

"Don't rest your weight on your elbows," I told her. "I want to feel all of you on top of me."

She nestled down then, her head on my chest.

I had another question, which I tried to stifle, but it wouldn't leave me alone. With my eye on a bright star, I asked, "Have you done this before?"

She tried to make light of my concern. "Not in a leafpile I haven't."

I had no business inquiring further, of course, but I couldn't seem to help it. "You know what I mean—with other men?"

I felt her fingers on my face. She gently covered my mouth.

We lay still and silent, growing warmer as the night grew colder. She might have dozed off—her breathing was soft and slow. She stirred finally, and said, "Let's go in." We crawled out of our nest and set it afire.

Introducing her to the one-bedroom cabin, I had a heightened awareness of its musty smell, the smallness of its sitting room, the quaintness of the ruffled curtains Mother had put up fifteen or twenty years earlier.

"Oh, good, a fireplace," said Sally.

"Sorry," I told her. "The chimney's plugged."

"So don't you ever have a fire on chilly nights?"

"I'm never here nights."

"How come?"

I didn't explain. I showed her the bathroom. I found a bedsheet on a shelf and spread it on the daybed in the sitting room.

"That's your bed?" she asked.

I nodded.

She crossed to the bedroom and switched on the light. "Did you know there's a nice double bed in here?"

"That's Mother's."

"She's not in it, is she?"

Two minutes later, lying with her in Mother's sheets, I had to ask: "Are you protected from having a baby?"

"Yes, don't worry."

I was silent for a time, holding her, then obtusely asked, "What method of protection?"

She laughed until the bed shook. "You kill me, Leland, you're so romantic."

I didn't see the humor. "I don't want to father a child."

"You won't, not with me. At least not tonight."

I suppose no one is ever quite prepared, the first time, for the shuddering act itself. My involuntary, throaty moaning. Her choked-off cry. The long moment of stasis before collapse. "Oh, Sally." I groaned, "I've always loved you."

Again her fingers covered my mouth.

I awoke to find her sitting on the edge of the bed in the dark. She was feeling among the clothing at her feet, separating hers from mine. I threw off the blanket and sat beside her, shivering. She allowed me to hold her for a last lingering minute before she began to dress.

"I'm going to be so sad without you," I told her.

Pausing, resting her chin on my shoulder, she whispered, "Why be sad?"

"Because now I know what's missing from my life."

"But it's not missing anymore," she said, kissing me.

EXAM WEEK

In my outer office, Viola Trisco and her student assistant are addressing my three hundred Christmas cards to our college family, and I listen to their discussion of professional wrestling as they work. Viola will take her grandson Billie to next Saturday's match at the armory, she says, because the Compactor's on the card. "Billie's nuts about the Compactor."

"What's the Compactor?" asks her assistant, a genteel young woman named Nancy Andrews.

"His real name's Howard Pribble, but they call him the Compactor because he's so huge he crushes people when he falls on them. He's real cute too. Strong as an ox and cute as a bug. Don't tell me you never heard of the Compactor."

"I never did," Nancy admits. "I've never been to a wrestling match."

"God, what have you been doing with your life?"

Out of the dozen student applicants for this job, Nancy Andrews was my choice to work with Viola because I was hoping for precisely this kind of exchange. Viola, a burly, domineering fifty-year-old, is at her best when instructing innocents like Nancy in the ways of the world outside these ivied halls.

"When I was single and working in Minneapolis, my girlfriend and I used to go to wrestling all the time, because wrestling was about the only thing you could go to if you didn't have a date. I mean it looked funny to see two girls go to a movie or a bar or anywhere else together, but wrestling was different. You could go to wrestling and nobody'd think you were too homely or retarded to get a boyfriend."

"What are you talking about?—I go to movies with my girl-friends all the time," says Nancy Andrews.

"Thirty years ago things were different. If you didn't hook up with a guy by the time you were twenty-one, you figured you'd had it."

During a typical day of deanly tedium, there's nothing like straight talk from Viola to freshen the air along Administration Row.

The phone rings and Viola buzzes me, transferring the call. "The president," she warns me.

"Leland here."

"Edwards?" says the president.

"Speaking."

"We're meeting."

"Who's meeting?"

"My advisory staff and Portis Bridges. We're ready to start."

"Go ahead," I tell him. I used to jump when he summoned me, but I got over that. "I'll be a few minutes late."

"No you won't, we're meeting in your office." He hangs up.

Meeting with larger groups, O. F. Zastrow will usurp my office because it's nearly twice as large as his. The first time he did this, years ago, came marching into my office without warning and brought with him half a dozen architects and contractors who spread their blueprints all over my desk and conference table, I offered to exchange offices with him. He declined. "Bad idea, Edwards." What made it a bad idea, I thought at first, was that it was I who'd thought of it, but I later came to realize that from his vantage point at the front of the building he can keep a watchful eye on the campus foot-traffic, particularly that of his faculty. He likes to send out memos reprimanding people for late arrival and early departure. My office, at the back, overlooks the river valley, a view I much prefer.

I buzz Viola and ask her to send Nancy Andrews to the student center for seven doughnuts and one bagel.

"Last time he asked for two," says Viola, referring to the president's fondness for bagels.

"One's plenty, Viola. We mustn't indulge him." It would be indiscreet of me to spell out for her that the bagel, like his glittery gold watchband and his glittery gold wife, has become one of President Zastrow's status symbols, that whenever lower forms of life are eating doughnuts, the bagel sets him apart. It would also be unnecessary, for Viola has his number.

First to arrive is Angelo Corelli, my eager young assistant. "O. F. is on his way," he says, rubbing his hands in eager anticipation. Angelo is thirty years old, two years out of graduate school, and looks, despite his name, more Irish than Mediterranean. He's a pale redhead with a bridge of freckles across his nose and a sparse new mustache under it. "This should be interesting. I hear Bridges went out and got us a big name."

How does Angelo maintain such a passionate love of meetings? After a committee has adjourned, he loves reviewing who said what to whom and analyzing everyone's motives. Although I find his enthusiasm a bit wearing, I rely quite heavily on his zest for details and his gladsome perseverance. I don't believe I could be dean without him.

"How's your mom's breathing, Leland?"

"Not so good. The cold and dampness."

"What do the medicos tell her?"

"Same as always—don't overdo."

Next into my office come the Advisory Committee, the makeup of which is so laboriously arrived at each autumn you'd think we were choosing the Joint Chiefs of Staff. It's always a tug-of-war between Zastrow and the faculty. Appointees need to be jointly agreed upon, and until recently there were five members, but nowadays the faculty, grown more militant, and Zastrow, more headstrong, can no longer find five mutually trustworthy people on this entire campus, so the Committee's been reduced to three.

They're an odd mix this year—Emeric Kahlstrom from Philosophy, Francine Phillips from Chemistry, and Reggie VanderHagen from Speech and Theater. They enter my office in that order, as though mindful of seniority, Philosopher Kahlstrom being very old and perhaps our most eminent burnout; Chemist Phillips middle-aged and tough-minded, a vociferous advocate of funding for the various sciences; and finally Stage Director VanderHagen, the sort of flashy young fellow I have a hard time taking seriously because he's such a complete narcissist. Every word out of his mouth strikes me as false or self-serving, usually both.

"Edwards, we've got to put in an elevator," sighs Emeric Kahlstrom wearily, down from his aerie on the third floor. As usual, he goes immediately to a chair facing the window, and I hurry to sit beside him before anyone else does. It doesn't take a philosopher to know that if you're gazing at something as beautiful as the Badbattle River, you stand a better chance of enduring a presidential meeting to its end.

"Leland, my friend, we're running out of lab supplies in Physics," says Francine Phillips. She's a petite woman wearing jeans under her lab apron. Tucked into the button-down collar of her shirt is an attractive silk scarf of a floral design.

"Leland, my friend, hi," says young VanderHagen, mimicking her and giving me a funny handshake.

"Christ, the stupidity of students nowadays," mutters Kahlstrom, rubbing his face like a man waking from sleep. He, like most of the faculty, has been spending this last day of Exam Week poring over papers for evidence of something a student may have learned. Here and there a professor will be pleased to come across a comprehensive grasp of his subject, or at least the professor's *view* of his subject, and occasionally even an insight or two beyond that, but generally it's discouraging work. If it weren't discouraging, professors of Kahlstrom's ilk wouldn't enjoy it so much. They take pleasure in passing around the ridiculous miscalculations and stupid conclusions their dimwitted students hand in. If all his students had brains, who would Kahlstrom feel superior to?

"I never write out an exam, I always dictate it to them," he says. "That way I find out who's been reading the text and who hasn't by the way they spell Camus and Sartre."

"How many haven't?"

"Yesterday five wrote S.a.r.t. Three wrote C.a.m.o.o."

"Students brought up on phonics, no doubt."

"Students brought up in a goddamn educational wasteland."

There is laughter in my outer office, and we all turn in amazement, for we recognize the rare sound of mirth from President Zastrow. It's a sucking, choking noise that you earnestly hope won't last long, and it never does. What stops it this morning is the absence of a pastry box on my conference table. Portis Bridges accompanies him into the room, untying a creamy silk scarf and looking jovial, but whatever was funny is no longer funny to Zastrow.

"Nothing from the cafeteria?" he asks me accusingly.

"On its way, O. F."

His attention is then drawn to Reggie VanderHagen, who has gripped his hand and is shaking it while praising a memo the president lately sent out concerning parking regulations. Francine Phillips interrupts, stridently insisting that the science hall be given a larger budget for office and lab supplies. It seems each year there's one adviser who vexes the president more than the others, and this year it's Chemist Phillips. Philosopher Kahlstrom, who has philosophized himself into peaceful despair, is too melancholy and foggy-minded to defy Zastrow, while young VanderHagen is too much the sycophant. While Phillips grows shrill in her appeal, VanderHagen grows syrupy. "Perfectly sensible to move visitor parking closer to McCall," says VanderHagen and the president looks pleased. "A bigger budget or we might as well shut down the physics lab," says the chemist. The president looks pained.

Believe it or not, it is possible to feel sorry for President Zastrow. Never having mastered any but the most basic form of human communication—in other words, being a dope—he can't understand why he enjoys so little cooperation from his faculty and staff. He treats people like dogs and, as a result, our college family has become obstructionist, closing ranks against his ideas, both the bad and the not-so-bad. For instance, you can't say that spreading our nine-month salaries over twelve months in order to gain a bit of interest for scholarships is a bad idea, but the faculty voted it down. And what's wrong with bringing visitor parking closer to the center of campus? The faculty, forced to walk fifty feet farther to their offices, is spoiling for a fight on that.

And being the world's worst communicator isn't Zastrow's only failing. He's pitifully unaware of the world around him. Take Paul Bunyan, for example. Years ago, when "Paul Bunyan's *Alma Mater*" became our official and ill-advised motto, Zastrow, then dean, didn't know Paul Bunyan was a mythical character. We had a brassy speech professor here at the time—her name was Georgina Gold—who spoke up one day at a faculty meeting and suggested that Paul Bunyan be asked back to his *alma mater* as our commencement speaker. There were a few chuckles at first, but then we all held our breath when we saw the unmistakable signs that Dean Zastrow was thinking it over—his brow furrowed, his right eye narrowed, his lips tightened—and sure enough, he told us—confirming our awful suspicions—that he'd have his secretary inquire about Mr. Bunyan's fee. He said we shouldn't get our hopes up because celebrities charged a lot of money.

I actually went home sick from that meeting. Mother and I had enough connections here and in St. Paul to know that Dean Zastrow was the fair-haired boy of the State College Board, and they were grooming him for president. He was the type of heartless autocrat the Board hoped would whip our flabby old campus into shape.

His first task, back then, was to weed out the older members of the faculty, and to reseed with rookies on the low end of the salary schedule. He was also charged with such things as tightening up office procedures and cutting down on the cost of heating fuel. He wasted no time. He replaced 27 percent of the faculty and staff, sold our reliable old mimeograph machines and bought used ditto machines that bled purple ink, blew fresh insulation into the walls of McCall Hall, and locked all campus thermostats at sixty degrees. In his first two years on the job, while professors wore overcoats to class and secretaries worked in snowmobile suits, he saved the State of Minnesota something like a hundred thousand dollars.

Thus, while endearing himself to taxpayers, he quickly came to be despised by most of the faculty and support staff. I withheld judgment. Often a new administrator, having made loud noises and done dramatic things to get your attention, will then settle back and let your campus proceed at its natural pace. Those that don't, my father used to say, seldom last very long. Hunker down and give the man time, I said—O. F. Zastrow will either be good for us, or gone. And sure enough, during his third year, the Middle East fuel crunch eased up and he unlocked the thermostats. But then came the day he decided to inquire about Paul Bunyan's speaking fee. Walking home in the late afternoon of that day, I had a vision of his career in Rookery stretching out endlessly before us, and I stepped behind a tree in a neighbor's yard and vomited.

And now, twenty-five years later, this same man, bound up in his tight blue suit and carrying his several chins on his chest and his small appointment book in his left hand, comes striding straight to his accustomed place opposite me at the conference table, where he can keep his eye on the doorway. It's a square table with ample room for two on a side, and I'm glad that he asks Portis Bridges to sit beside him today instead of the toadyish Reggie VanderHagen, whose face I cannot look at without an intense feeling of repugnance—an unjust reaction, surely, but I do wish that once in a while the boy would wipe that fawning smile off his face. I've spoken to Mother about VanderHagen. She agrees it's an unhealthy bias of mine, a kind of generational hangup. She says it's a matter of conscience and I should talk to our new rector, Father Tisdale, about it.

Not that Portis Bridges is much easier to look at, a fact I confirm for myself as I watch him remove his very dark sunglasses from the top of his head and apply the palms of his hands to his greasy blond hair, brushing it back over his ears, then wiping the goo on his handkerchief. He then draws the sunglasses down over his eyes, and looks at me (I think) and smiles. It isn't the ignorant, uncertain smile he gave me at last week's meeting, nor does it contain anything of VanderHagen's obsequiousness. It's more a smile of triumph. Over what, God alone knows.

Reggie VanderHagen and Angelo Corelli take the chairs to my left. Opposite them sit Francine Phillips and the president's secretary April Ackerman, who has hurried in with her notepad. Emeric Kahlstrom, sitting at my right hand, sighs and says he's hungry. I assure him pastry is on its way.

President Zastrow is about to open the meeting when I hear my name called. It's Faith Crowninshield, Chair of Education and our newly elected human rights officer. She's standing in the doorway.

"Yes, Faith?"

"One moment, Leland?"

"Urrr," growls the president as I leave my place and step over to take a large manila envelope from her.

"Sorry," she says.

"What's this?" I ask.

"It's self-explanatory." She hurries away, looking grim. The envelope, I see, is triply sealed—licked, clasped, and taped. It's from the Human Rights Office.

"Urrr," says the president, summoning me back to the table.

After April Ackerman reads the minutes, we learn why Bridges is looking so victorious. It has to do, alas, with Addison Steele.

"She's agreed to be our celebrity," President Zastrow announces, not entirely in triumph but rather defensively, his head bent forward, looking up at me through his shaggy eyebrows, uncertain how I'll receive this incredible news.

Reggie VanderHagen receives it with a little squeal of delight.

"The British rock star," Bridges explains with his eyes on me and Philosopher Kahlstrom—I suppose to save us old fogies the trouble of asking. Actually I don't have to ask—I scan the tabloids at the checkout counters like everyone else. Kahlstrom doesn't appear to be listening. He's squinting out the window, watching the traffic crossing the Eleventh Avenue Bridge.

"Addison Steele the sex deviant?" inquires Francine Phillips. "What do you mean, our celebrity?"

"She'll promote our endowment campaign," replies the president.

"Who asked her?" Francine wants to know.

"Bridges here."

"Through my agent," says Portis Bridges proudly.

"Why, for God's sake?"

"Name recognition," replies the president.

"But she's a tramp."

"Bridges says that's only her image."

Francine's grilling of the president is interrupted by the arrival of Viola Trisco with pastry from the cafeteria, followed by Nancy Andrews, who carries the coffeepot and paper cups. As the doughnut box goes round the table, beginning with the president, who removes the bagel, I ask Nancy Andrews how she likes Addison Steele, considering it useful to have the opinion of someone reared on heavy metal.

"Oh, she *used* to be cool," Miss Andrews tells me.

"And now?"

"I don't know, sort of uncool, you know? Like an exaggerated version of herself."

My suspicion that eavesdropping through my office doorway works both ways is confirmed when Viola offers, "If you guys need a celebrity, I know the Compactor's unpublished phone number."

Only Angelo responds to this. "Hey, that's cool, Viola," he says happily.

Pouring coffee into Zastrow's cup, she adds, "I came by it illegally, but he doesn't need to know that."

"Who's the Compactor?" asks Francine Phillips.

"Big stud of a wrestler," Viola tells her. "Wrestlemania champ three years running."

"I don't like paper cups," says Zastrow. "Where's your Styrofoam?"

"Ask the dean," Viola tells him.

"Ask the chemist," I tell him.

Francine Phillips says, "Styrofoam's less environmentally friendly than paper."

Zastrow gingerly brings his coffee to his lips. "Paper's too hot."

"Use a double cup," Viola advises.

After Nancy and Viola return to the outer office, the advisory committee takes up the issue of two paper cups as opposed to one Styrofoam cup—which is more wasteful?—and I turn my attention out the window where a ray of sun breaks through the overcast we've been under for days, casting a patch of spectacular amber light along the far bank of the river. The water is moving slowly, dotted with saucers of ice. I see two figures upstream, diehards fishing from the pier below the abandoned railroad yards— Mr. and Mrs. Roman almost certainly, Rookery's hardiest outdoorspersons. I watch the smaller figure lean back, jerking up her rod; the other figure crouches with a net. A tense half minute passes before there's a glittery splash in the icy water and a fish is brought up.

I bring out my pocket notebook and turn to my list. It's headed, *CTIWBIDU,* which stands for *Committee Thoughts It Would Be Indiscreet of a Dean to Utter.* What I mean is, they're ideas that cry to be expressed, but at the moment they cross my mind I have no one to express them to. I make it a point to jot something down at every meeting for two reasons. The number indicates precisely how many meetings I attend each year—a useless and depressing record if ever there was one—and it encourages my mind to wander and thus saves me from sleep or death by boredom.

> *#234. Curses, it's Friday—Hi-Rise coffee at three. Dear Lord, how I long to be over there on the pier with the Romans, angling for the last time until spring. Tomorrow the river will be ice.*

"A tramp and a whore!" Apparently Francine Phillips has been keeping up with Addison Steele's career, for she reviews for us the rock star's alleged felonies. On her last American concert tour alone, she was charged with public nudity, statutory rape, possessing cocaine, and inciting a riot.

Bridges insists, and Francine admits, that not all these acts were committed onstage. Ms. Steele, they agree, partakes of cocaine and sexual intercourse in private.

I speak up then, saying to Bridges, "I thought we were looking to Hollywood for our celebrity."

"Ah, Dean Edwards." My ignorance elicits his most benevolent smile. "We work with Hollywood agents, but their clients come from all over. With Addison Steele, you get worldwide name recognition. I mean this is over-the-top promotion. Even on a bad night, this baby's concert will draw at least a hundred thousand fans. Her agent—"

"Wait a minute," I interrupt. "There aren't a hundred thousand people in all of Rookery County."

"Just let me finish." Bridges exchanges an insider glance with Reggie VanderHagen, and they both snicker, possibly at my stupidity, possibly at the thought of this world-famous vamp performing up here in the sticks. "Her agent's a friend of my agent, Dean Edwards. He's agreed to bring her to the State Fairgrounds in St. Paul next July, where she can draw upwards of a quarter of a million people, with Rookery State College getting two dollars on every ticket we sell."

"*We* sell?"

"Well, we don't really have to *sell* them. Once the concert's publicized in the Twin Cities, tickets will sell themselves."

"And the publicity is paid for by . . . ?"

"The college budget," Zastrow puts in.

"A couple ads in the Sunday papers will do it," says Bridges. "Your money will be returned a hundred-thousandfold."

"Who handles the tickets?"

"Ticketmaster, I've already spoken to them."

"They don't do that for nothing."

"Their service charge is added to the price."

"And who polices this mob?"

My obvious distaste causes Bridges's smile to turn a bit sinister. "Off-duty cops," he says abruptly.

"Paid for by . . . ?"

"Listen, it's all included in the price of tickets, Dean Edwards. The permits, the opening band, the sound technicians, the cleanup crew, the advertising, the insurance—the audience pays for the whole nine yards."

"Tickets must cost a fortune."

Bridges turns to VanderHagen for counsel. "What are we paying these days, Reggie? You saw the Stones in Chicago last summer."

"I don't know, thirty, forty bucks."

Bridges tips his head from side to side, a gesture meaning give or take ten or twenty. "And it was a fantastic experience, right?"

"I'd have paid twice that for the Stones."

"Beautiful," concludes Bridges, resting his case.

I decide to rest mine as well. I turn to Francine Phillips, trusting her to prevent our getting into bed with this vulgar sex kitten.

"All right now," she says, taking my cue, "let's consider the perverted ethics of our sponsoring a sociopath like Addison Steele. To say nothing of the bad taste."

She is prevented from saying more by President Zastrow, who utters his attention-getting "Urrr." Ethics and taste are concepts the president is not comfortable with. He prefers the logic of numbers. "We'll get back to you on that, Dr. Phillips. April, give us that rundown of financial estimates."

There are a few moments of silent tension while Francine fumes and April Ackerman searches for the estimate. Zastrow detests inefficiency, and we're all a little afraid for April as she shuffles through her file folder. I am distracted, fortunately, by Viola Trisco in the outer office:

"The Compactor doesn't talk with a gravelly voice in real life—only on TV. In real life he's got a normal voice, almost sweet, you might say."

"No kidding," says Nancy Andrews.

"I know because when I was a telephone operator in Minneapolis, I sometimes placed calls for him, that's how I got his private number. He used to call Oshkosh a lot."

"Who's in Oshkosh?"

"Who knows? It was against the rules to listen. Ma Bell's real strict about that kind of thing. Guys used to call up and flirt—they wanted to know my name and address—but I never told them because if I did, I'd lose my job."

"No kidding?"

"Some of those guys had real cute voices, too, but I never once gave out my name and address."

"Statutory rape?" blurts Philosopher Kahlstrom, rising suddenly out of his reverie or coma or whatever it is that a lot of people mistake for a mind deep in thought. "Public nudity? What does that say about the state of our national soul?"

"It wasn't rape really," says VanderHagen condescendingly. "It was consensual sex with a boy of fifteen. And wouldn't you know, it had to happen in one of those backwater places where fifteen-year-olds aren't supposed to do it with adults." Vander-Hagen looks to Bridges for agreement.

Bridges, no doubt grateful to have found this harebrained ally in our midst, nods happily and says, "Kansas or someplace."

Emeric Kahlstrom declares, "I tell you what it says—we've succumbed to the forces of evil. Our national soul has gone in the toilet."

"Here it is," says April, waving a sheet of Zastrow's illegible scratching over her head in mock victory.

"Give it here," the president demands, and he applies his pen to the paper, circling things and drawing arrows between them, all the while uttering the sort of mathematical mumbo-jumbo I trust Angelo Corelli to follow and brief me about later. This lasts about three minutes, during which time a happy thought crosses my mind and I open my notebook again.

Alleluia, no coffee party today, no peach delight, because of the Hi-Rise Christmas dinner at six. That gives me at least an hour on the pier this afternoon.

Breathing noisily through his nose and snapping his gold watchband, our president looks up from his arrows and circles and glances across the table for my reaction—a glance only, and yet it reveals so much, because it's a glance of inquiry, expectancy. O. F. Zastrow is trying to read me. Needless to say, reading people is not one of his skills, and he doesn't often bother, but lately, when something stumps him, he'll now and then pay heed to my opinion. In my ten years as dean, perhaps my convictions have proven worthy enough to be listened to. I hope so. I don't like to sound excessively proud, but I see the dean's office, under the current regime, as the heart and soul of Rookery State. I wish this weren't true. I wish it were a delusion of grandeur, for I am neither wise nor consistently decisive, but I can't escape the notion that until a new and better administration is installed, this dear old campus—beloved of my father and to which I have devoted my entire adult life—will live or die by the wisdom of my decisions.

Looking around the table, I calculate that we can put this matter to rest with a four-two vote (Bridges and April Ackerman, not being faculty, have no voice in the matter), and so I am about to call the question when Angelo Corelli, to my astonishment, allies himself with the forces of evil:

"Half a million dollars," he exclaims. "We're talking mega-bucks here, guys. I mean, that's one-fourth of our endowment goal in one evening."

Unfazed by the look of displeasure I direct at him, this right-hand man of mine is brimming over with the cheer that money instills in him. His hobby being investments, Angelo has made some fair-sized profits in his day, for others (including Mother) as well as himself. Mornings when I accompany him to the Student Center for our coffee break, he picks up a copy of the *Morning Call* on the way and turns immediately to the financial pages, so that along with the greetings of students on the walkways and the birdsong overhead, I hear at my side the satisfied chuckling and humming of the successful investor.

While Angelo quotes the figures to prove that our past endowment campaigns took years and years to bring in what Addison Steele might raise overnight, I calculate my defense. With Kahlstrom and Phillips arming themselves with the sophisticated weapons of ethics and taste, I decide to take up the cudgel of state regulations.

"Let me remind everyone that all our past campaigns were scholarship fund-raisers. A scholarship fund is the only money each campus is free to raise on its own. We've never been permitted to establish endowments for buildings." Though aiming my words at Zastrow, I keep my eyes on Angelo because lecturing my president would be uncivil. "All but scholarship funding—capital outlay, supplies, salaries—has to come down to us through the State College Board. It's the law. It's been the law since the beginning, as my father learned when he was reprimanded for soliciting money for baseball uniforms in 1946."

Zastrow responds, decimating my argument. "I called St. Paul about that. The chancellor says we can do it."

Angelo lets me down gently. "That's right, Leland. The system was changed by the new chancellor, last summer when money was tight. Moorhead planted trees this fall with contributors' names engraved on brass and pressed into the bark. Winona raised its own money for library books and basketball hoops."

"Let's vote," squeals Opportunist VanderHagen, sensing at least a three-three tie, making another meeting on this question mandatory.

"Not yet!" I snap.

VanderHagen looks momentarily wilted by my tone. Bridges smiles confidently. The old philosopher sighs. Chemist Phillips says, "Addison Steele's name will be linked to Rookery State over my dead body."

"Urrr," says our president. His confounded expression tells me that his vote is still in doubt. I cast about desperately for another defense, and find myself putting fairly sensible things into words without premeditation.

"Does anybody but me wonder why this world-famous celebrity whose idea of public service is to demonstrate sexual acts in front of mobs of teenagers should be willing to do a benefit concert for higher education? I'll tell you why. She's past her peak. She's on her way down, according to the young woman in my outer office. At the rate rock stars come and go, by next summer Addison Steele could be so dated we'd have an audience consisting entirely of Bridges and Vanderhagen here, along with seven or eight other teenyboppers." Picturing what I've just said—I can't help it—a giggle escapes me.

"By next summer the woman could be in prison," Francine Phillips adds.

"She's passé," I declare, and I'm about to add "uncool" and "old hat" when Portis Bridges erupts with babble so intense that we all draw back in astonishment. Surely he has more than Rookery State's interest at heart. Only a financial kickback would inspire a man to explode with such a desperate-sounding sales pitch. "Never again such a deal . . . chance of a lifetime . . . window of opportunity . . . twentysomethings and thirtysomethings turn-ing out in droves." He raves like a man being led to the scaffold. Sweat breaks out on his upper lip. Moisture forms on his dark glasses. He shuts up only when he runs out of spit, a good bit of which has landed on my unfinished doughnut and sleeve.

"I move we vote," blurts VanderHagen, caught up in the thrill of the moment.

"I second," pants Bridges, who has no right to do so.

"Sorry," says Zastrow, "*I'll* second."

"What's the question?" inquires April Ackerman.

The president dictates, "That we pursue the possibility of inviting Addison Steele to be our celebrity." He watches her write, and adds, "Capitalize 'celebrity.'"

April looks to Francine for her vote.

"No."

She looks across the table at Angelo and VanderHagen, both of whom say, "In favor."

The old philosopher joins me in saying no. Reason leads bar-barism by one.

All eyes are on the president. At least a tie is assured, which gives Francine and Emeric and me until after Christmas to work on Zastrow and Angelo. VanderHagen, of course, is beyond hope.

But I'm floored—there'll be no need. "Urrr, abstain," says the president, and it's all over. The rock concert's wiped out, three to two.

Francine hurries off to her next ethical challenge. Angelo and April remain, chatting across the table. The philosopher remains too, scratching around in the waxed paper of the doughnut box, looking for more nourishment. Finding none, he suggests we adjourn to the cafeteria.

Disguising his disappointment, VanderHagen resumes his subservient role. "Sensible approach, Dr. Zastrow," he says, walking out with him. "Caution can sometimes be the best policy."

Portis Bridges is slow to rise from his chair. He removes his sunglasses so I can see his anger. He glowers at me for a dramatic moment, then says, "Edwards, you turd," and strides out of my office, tying his creamy silk scarf tightly at his throat.

———

Once we get past Dorcas Muldoon transforming herself into a cadaver on the high stool at the cash register, we're cheered by the sight of Mary Sue Bloom inviting us to sit at her table. The cafeteria is nearly empty, most of the students having left for what used to be called Christmas vacation before the term was declared offensively parochial by the State College Board. I notice L. P. Connor, my nemesis, moving along the far wall. She's wearing black and shades of purple today. She turns and scowls at me out of a powder-white face before she leaves by another door.

Mary Sue Bloom, by contrast, is looking particularly sharp in a red blouse and a sweater of deeper red. Red, too, are the rims of her weepy eyes, we discover as we approach—eyes that dart from one to another of us as we settle in with our paper cups. "Two deans and a philosopher," she says without smiling. "Just what a girl needs on a day this miserable."

A cold and cloudy day, I suppose she means. Because my mood has never been brought low by weather of any sort, I feel sorry for anyone sensitive to overcast skies and subzero temperatures. I always thought it was only those reared in fairer climates who suffered, but Mary Sue comes from Bismarck.

"At your service," Angelo tells her, scanning a front-page photo in the *Morning Call*—Toni Morrison delivering her Nobel lecture.

"The soul of the nation has gone in the toilet," announces Kahlstrom, about to bite into a heavily-glazed sweet roll.

With her dark hair swept severely back and tied in a tight knot, Mary Sue's face looks sharp and birdlike this morning. Stirring her coffee nervously, her eyes darting alertly among us, she says, "I need a sabbatical, you guys. I need a year of fresh air. It hit me this morning in Tests and Measurements. I was writing a word on the blackboard and I realized I'd written too many words on too many blackboards over the years. Like, what difference did any of them make?"

Oh my. Not another burnout, and this one so lovely, so freshly hired. The bromide I offer is stale, but she obviously needs to hear it: "We make a lot of difference without ever knowing it, Mary Sue. In college teaching, we don't get much feedback."

"Who needs feedback?" asks Kahlstrom. "The only feedback I ever get is grousing and griping."

I turn to Angelo for help in holding off the dark philosopher, but Angelo's caught up in the tiny print of finance.

"I feel like I can't pick up another piece of chalk without turning into chalk myself."

"Now, now, Mary Sue."

"Don't 'Now-now' me, Leland Edwards. I need time away."

"Just let me say your problem is not unique in the profession. A bad day in the classroom—it blows over."

"Oh, sure, easy for *you* to say it blows over."

Kahlstrom speaks slowly, shards of sugar glaze falling out of his ragged mustache. "They come to me, they say Plato's too hard, Heidegger's too hard, Bertrand Russell's too hard. I tell them, 'Look, is it my fault you can't read philosophy? It's either your fault or the philosophers' fault, it sure as hell isn't *my* fault.' "

"I'll tell you what I feel like, Leland. I feel like with every word on the blackboard something of my spirit, my vitals, is drawn down my arm and fingers and out through the stick of chalk. Have you got anybody who can take over for me? Because if I'm not feeling better after Christmas break, I'm applying for medical leave."

"Oh, don't!" I plead. How colorless the campus will seem without her, how boring my noon hours without our lunches on these catsup-stained tabletops.

"One kid says to me, 'Dr. Kahlstrom, reading metaphysics drives me nuts.' I tell him, 'Go see a psychiatrist.' Another kid says to me, 'Dr. Kahlstrom, after three pages of Wittgenstein, it all blurs together.' I tell him, 'Go see your eye doctor.' "

Mary Sue persists. "What I mean is, I feel like my soul has turned to chalk. Like everything I ever believed and felt is dusty and erasable."

Angelo folds his paper shut and says, "What say we start a support group for disillusioned professors, Leland? I mean, gee whiz, the year's not half over and we've got all these burnouts on our hands."

"All?" I ask. "Who else?" *Besides our wasted old philosopher here,* I could add, but don't.

"Oh, I know half a dozen. I'll ask around, see if they'd like to meet. How does that sound to you, Mary Sue—a support group?"

She shrugs.

Angelo jots down names on his newspaper. "How about you come to the first meeting, Leland? Give them a pep talk."

"No, sorry."

"Oh come on, tell them how you've done it day in, day out, for thirty-five years."

"I don't *know* how I've done it, Angelo. When you teach as long as I have, it defies analysis. It's all instinct."

Angelo presses Mary Sue's hand. "Will you come?"

She shrugs. "Why not?"

"Late afternoon? Say four?"

She nods.

"What day's best?"

"Today. I'm leaving for Bismarck tomorrow."

Mary Sue, I gathered from her résumé last spring, is even more of a homebody than I, having spent all her life in Bismarck, North Dakota. I at least ventured as far as St. Paul (M.A., Macalester, '57) and Minneapolis (Ph.D., University of Minnesota, '63) for my education, whereas Mary Sue got her B.S. from someplace called Mary College in her hometown and went on to teach there—indeed, after her parents' death, to actually live there, on campus, as the guest of the sponsoring order of nuns. Coming out of a convent like that, she surprised me with her wit and polish—I expected to meet some demure and saintly little waif. And she's tough: for her graduate degrees, she commuted across the frozen wastes of North Dakota to its university in Grand Forks.

"Just drop in and leave again," Angelo insists. "Tell them how you persevere."

"I persevere by casting my jigs and spoons off the railroad pier, Angelo."

"Just ten minutes. A short keynote address."

"By watching daylight die, all purple and silver in the water, Angelo."

"But it's freezing out."

"All the more reason. Tomorrow the river will be ice."

Mary Sue implores me. "Leland, I'd feel a lot better if you came. I mean can't you just picture half a dozen of us losers in one room? How dismal."

"No room is dismal with you in it, Mary Sue."

"Please."

"Look, I will instruct you by my absence. I can't function on this campus without leaving it when the fish bite. There was a time I would have met with you and tried to say bright things, but I'm beyond that now." All this is true. Plus the fact that I grow agitated whenever I have to share Mary Sue's conversation with others. As now. I love talking with her alone.

She and Angelo give up on me then, and turn—I regret to say—to Emeric Kahlstrom. I can just imagine the philosopher's malignant influence on such a group, for he's gone beyond burnout and hit the wall of absolute cynicism. Which prevents him from accepting, thank God. He says, "What'll you call it, the Futility Committee? Don't waste my time. I'm not what everybody thinks I am. I'm not the wise old man of the Philosophy Department." Who thought he was? Very few. He takes another enormous bite of his sweet roll, and continues. "I'll tell you a secret. Over the years my students have forced a vacuum cleaner up my nostrils and sucked out all my brain cells."

Disgusted by his dark blather, I turn my attention to Faith Crowninshield's manila envelope, which I've brought with me. I slit it open with my pocket knife and spill out a booklet with a blue cover, three pamphlets, and a number of newspaper clippings. It's all about sexual harassment—regulations, warnings, policies, accounts of egregious cases in the workplace. Nothing new. I'm amazed it still happens. People accused of harassing must be incorrigibly stupid.

"Oh oh, what's this?" says Angelo, drawing away as though the pamphlets were contaminated.

"Not our dean!" says Mary Sue, looking genuinely horrified.

I assure them it's a packet meant for my files. I was on the committee that drew up the policy. I open the booklet to the title page and point out my name among others.

"Are you sure you're not in the soup?" says Angelo, uncovering a typewritten letter I'd overlooked.

"See you later," says Mary Sue, and she's gone. Angelo follows her out. Kahlstrom eats, slouching in his chair and gazing at nothing.

I take up the letter. It's written in the comma-stuttering style that Faith Crowninshield mistakes for the language of lawyers.

Attention: Dr. Leland Edwards, Dean of the College.

It is my duty, as Human Rights Officer, of Rookery State College, to inform you, that you were observed, and stand accused of, violating the Human Rights, on Friday, December 18, 1993 at 10:55 a.m., in McCall Hall 212, of a student named Carol Thelen; specifically, to wit, behaving in a Sexually Harassing manner, that is, hugging and kissing said victim, and generally taking advantage of the power differential between yourself, as dean and professor, and said victim, as student.

The complainant, who is not Carol Thelen, states further, that this incident is only one in a long series of gender-related offenses, perpetrated by yourself, in Freshman English, Midwestern Literature, and History of the English Language; specifically, to wit, your persistent exclusion of, and/or verbal dismissal of, female poets, novelists, short story writers, essayists, and scholars, as well as your stubborn and demeaning use of "Miss" instead of "Ms." as a word of address.

Upon receipt of this complaint, you have *five working days* to respond, in writing, to this Human Rights Officer, who shall provide a copy of your response to the complainant. If the matter is not resolved through this exchange of correspondence, the complainant may proceed to Step Two.

The complainant's identity shall remain protected in order to prevent reprisal or retaliation. Any reprisal or retaliation against said complainant, shall, in itself, be considered a Human Rights violation.

Have a good day.

By the time I arrive at the abandoned Soo Line yards across the river, it's after four o'clock, the dying end of a dark, shadowless day. I park the Lincoln in a stand of young birch and bundle myself into my ankle-length overcoat. A grainy snow shower has begun to fall, sugary flakes almost too fine to be seen by the naked eye. Sitting above me on a frosty branch is a bluejay contemplating the cold, its beak buried in its puffed-out breastfeathers.

With my rod and minnow bucket in hand, I follow the winding trail down to the riverbank. It's steep in places, and greasy with snow. At a treacherous turn, I steady myself by gripping a signpost. Reuben Gresser's name is painted on the sign below its message: *NO DUMPING*. Reuben Gresser, a high school classmate of mine, has been sheriff of Rookery County for over twenty years. Since the advent of managed, pay-as-you-dump landfills, this slope is where a certain number of our citizens leave their trash in secrecy, at no charge. Besides the normal stuff, such as tires and garden bags leaking old leaves and a pickup load of old shingles, there are today a couple of eye-catching deposits: a fuchsia sofa with gold metallic threads, and the fresh, steaming bowels of a poached deer. The sofa has arrived as recently as the intestines, I assume, otherwise why haven't the diehards who fish here eased it downhill to the pier and sat there in comfort? I once found Mr. and Mrs. Roman and a third fisherman sharing a ragged overstuffed chair, the woman sunk deep in the springs and flanked by the two men on the arms.

It's dusk. Nobody's fishing. This is a spot for northern pike, and lore has it that this species won't bite in the dark, which isn't precisely true. I've known northerns to stay active into the night, particularly as freeze-up approaches—their last chance to eat the exotic stuff floating on the surface. Acorns, for instance, or seed pods, or even ducks. If a northern pike is large enough it will eat a small duck.

I walk out on the concrete pier and lean on the rusted railing, my eyes on the campus downriver. I take deep, cold breaths, expelling from my lungs—from my thoughts—the staleness of

Administration Row. Good-bye and good riddance forever, Portis Bridges and Addison Steele. Merry Christmas, Reggie VanderHagen—I won't have to lay eyes on you again until after the holidays. Please, Mary Sue Bloom, please, please come back after winter break and make a fresh start—I will make your way as smooth as it's possible for a dean to do. And bend all your efforts, Faith Crowninshield, I beg you, to keeping L. P. Connor at bay; for if we proceed to Step Two, a meeting between the complainant and the accused, I'll be mightily tempted to take her to court for defamation of character. She's been tormenting Mother and me for decades. Talk about harassment.

The dark water below me, within half a degree of ice, is moving like syrup. First I try a spoon with multiple hooks in order to spare myself the finger-freezing process of attaching a minnow. On my eighth or tenth cast I feel the tug of a fish, but I lose it. I keep casting over the same spot to no avail, so I decide to try still-fishing—fish move slower as their body temperature drops. I remove the spoon from the leader and shake a size-five out of my pocket-sized Velvet-tobacco can, the hook-container I inherited from my father. I attach the hook to the leader, and to the hook I attach a wriggly minnow from the icy water of the bucket. I clip on a sinker and bobber and heave the line upstream.

Watching the current carry the bobber slowly past me, I slip my wet hand inside my coat to warm it under my arm. In doing so, I feel folded sheets of fax paper in the pocket of my shirt. It's a letter from Peggy Benoit in New Hampshire, which came in as I was leaving the office. As soon as my fingers are warm enough to bend, I stand the rod against the railing, take out the letter, and read its two pages in the dimming daylight.

Dear Leland,

Wondering why you didn't respond to my news about Richard Falcon's desire to visit. Expected you to jump for joy and send him a plane ticket by return mail. (Well, knowing you, maybe not actually *jump* for joy.) Sooner the better, he says.

Here's a new poem he asked me to send you.

Late fall's been lovely here. Darkening colors overlaid with misty sun.

Love to Lolly.

And of course to you,

During the school year 1968–69, the Icejam Quintet—clarinet, sax, piano, string bass, drums—had a lot of fun practicing for engagements that never materialized. Peggy doubled as our sax player and vocalist. She was not only the best choral director Rookery ever had, she was, for a time, a candidate in a series of women who struck Mother as ideal daughter-in-law material.

It was both amusing and pathetic the way Mother kept bringing home women as though for auditions. I actually came to like most of them. Kimberly Kraft, for example. Kimberly was the one Mother had the hardest time giving up on. We became good friends, Kimberly and I, but she was considerably older than I was, and the last thing I needed was a second mother. As for the others, their only impediment, in my opinion, was that they weren't Sally McNaughton, the girl who kissed me when I was nine. In my early twenties, I was still secretly in love with Sally, who'd grown into a sandy-haired beauty with intelligent green eyes, a strong chin, and a caring manner undiminished since she was fifteen and cured Leonard Habstreet's monkey of the creeping crud. As freshmen at Rookery State, we had spent the occasional lunch hour studying together. Sally was better at college algebra than I was. I helped her with literature and history. I found her as congenial and desirable as she'd been in grade five, but of course she didn't qualify as a bridal candidate because she was engaged to marry Roy Spang, a disabled young man who just then was starting up Spang Auto, a dealership in old cars and pickups with patched tires, cracked windshields, and engines that sounded like jackhammers. Roy Spang promised to take Sally's brother Otto into the business, but never did.

Peggy Benoit, on the other hand, would have been the prize of Mother's candidates, but Peggy was never really in the running. What I understood, and Mother didn't, was that Peggy, from the day she set foot on campus, was nuts about Connor, our string bassist. Connor the painter of portraits. Connor the alcoholic husband of a chronically depressed wife. Connor the troubled father of a troubled teenage daughter named Laura, who now goes by the initials L. P. and who seems to have been put on this earth to trouble me. Though perhaps not the genius Peggy made him out to be, Connor did—does—have a strong reputation in our part of the country. At last count, I believe, there are eighteen of his landscapes and portraits hanging in museums around the Midwest.

Peggy was good for Connor—you'd hear it said over and over in those days. When, after two years in Rookery, Peggy was offered a job in her beloved New England, Connor packed up his paints and canvases and went with her, leaving his wife and adolescent daughter behind. Not that Peggy was a homewrecker—Connor and his wife had been estranged for some time. Word filtered back to us that Connor had stopped drinking.

Peggy wasn't good for his daughter, however. Laura Connor, feeling forsaken, turned her frightening attention on Mother, who'd been so kind to her—and on me. I'll never understand why we became the targets of her pent-up resentment. Instead of attacking us straight on, she was sly and calculating, working her damage in ways so elusive that she'd be long gone by the time we realized what she'd done—usually gone to Minneapolis, I guess, where she'd lived as a young girl.

For instance, the dozen letters of complaint about my teaching that dribbled into the Chancellor's office in St. Paul weren't traced to L. P. Connor until several months after the last letter was mailed. Some were typed; most were written with a variety of pens in a variety of hands, from nearly illegible cursive to large block printing. To this day they might have been thought the work of ten or twelve different people—what seemed to me, and to the Chancellor, an almost universal condemnation of my work—if L. P. Connor hadn't mislaid her notebook in the student center and Dorcas Muldoon hadn't found it, opened it, and seen therein all the early drafts in the several forms of handwriting. I sought to confront Miss Connor then, but couldn't locate her. She disappears for months at a time.

She also tried to discredit Mother's radio show. She spread false rumors about the unreliability of the recipes that went out over the air. The worst rumor, concerning food poisoning, we actually traced directly back to her. It was a vicious piece of slander not only against Mother but also against the grocer who sold her the ingredients, and the poor man had to throw out and restock whole shelves of goods. That time she fled for a year or more.

But it's been a long time now since she gave Mother trouble. I'd like to believe she's not completely heartless, that Mother's illness has caused her to let up. That's my generous interpretation. What's likelier, however, is that since L. P. Connor has taken up radical feminism as her choice of weapons, she attacks only men.

The second page of Peggy's fax is a poem called "Postal." Peggy has done this before, honored me with a Richard Falcon poem which his readers around the world haven't yet seen. This one's in longhand. It's six lines long. Surely not an autograph; it must be a photocopy, but it's hard to tell in the poor light. The handwriting is tiny. Trying to make it out in the near darkness, I see it's about letters between lovers; highly romantic at first, their tone changes with time. I can't study it further without hurting my eyes. I fold the pages and tuck them into my overcoat.

Poetry is a recent interest of Peggy's, presumably prompted by her friendship with Richard Falcon—yes, the same Richard Falcon who won a Pulitzer nearly fifty years ago for his first collection, *Under the Weather,* and whose book of children's verse you either listened to as a child or read to your own children, depending how old you are. Richard Falcon, now in his late seventies, is surely our nation's most famous living poet. Although twenty years have passed since he published his last book, *Fording the Bee,* he still occupies a place in our consciousness as the quintessential spokesman of rural America in a simpler time. Throughout our schooldays his poems were strewn around us like apples or plums in the orchard grass, many of them too perfectly unbruised—it seems to critics nowadays—but each one tangy and juicy and (in my opinion) perfectly delectable right down to its seedy moral center. My entire generation of Americans has lines by Richard Falcon stuck in our memory.

The fish that takes the fatal bite
Is victimized by appetite,
Both his and mine.

This simple little thing my father and I would bat back and forth across creeks, fishing for trout.

Because I'm better at deceit,
I satisfy his urge to eat
So I can dine.

I gather from what Peggy's said in recent letters that some of her neighbors and colleagues are astounded by their friendship, for it's well-known that the great man has spent most of his old age holding the world at bay. Yet it's not hard for me to imagine Peggy breaking through his reclusive tendencies without even trying very hard. Besides being wonderfully bright and attractive, Peggy is helplessly drawn to creative geniuses—particularly if they're male, and a bit off center. I have no idea what Richard Falcon's idiosyncrasies might be, but it appears—if her letter is to be believed—that I'm on the verge of finding out.

I try to picture the poet on our campus, a prospect I didn't allow myself to imagine when Peggy first mentioned it. I didn't respond because I didn't want to embarrass her for suggesting the impossible. It seemed a fantasy, a passing whim. Now, however, reeling in my bait and casting it out again, I permit myself a vision. I picture the roads into Rookery clogged by people driving hundreds of miles to hear Richard Falcon read from his work, people from all over the Midwest who, until now, have known Rookery only as the nation's icebox, or the source of the Unbreakable Blue Heron Hockey Stick, or the last stop this side of Winnipeg. The last time I went to a Modern Language convention, in Chicago, a woman from Maine looked at my nametag and said, "Mmm, Rookery—isn't that where hockey was invented?"

It's been known to happen—a poet drawing droves of listeners. Many years ago, T. S. Eliot appeared at the University of

Minnesota, where, to everyone's astonishment, so many thousands of his readers turned out that his presentation had to be moved into Williams Arena—capacity: eighteen thousand. I saw pictures in newspapers of people crammed in under the ceiling, sitting on I-beams. Our new hockey arena will have nearly five thousand seats. Imagine filling it to the walls with devoted readers of Richard Falcon. Imagine Rookery State College a new star in the cultural firmament. Never again would I have our stupid motto—"Paul Bunyan's *Alma Mater*"—thrown in my face. Never again, at conventions, would I have to stand there discussing, with smirking academics from Penn State and Duke, the Unbreakable Blue Heron Hockey Stick factory.

My bobber has gone under. I pick up my rod and feel the unmistakable pull of a big one. I release the drag, count to six, and set the hook. I have him. He heads out toward the middle of the river, then turns abruptly downstream. He's counting on the current to help him break the line, but the line won't break. It's thirty-pound test. Like my father before me, I fish for food. There are certain dilettantes with spinning tackle and monofilament line who laugh at my heavy old reel, my sturdy fibrous string, but I'm less interested in the drama of playing the fish than I am in eating it. I love fish on the plate, fresh out of water this cold. Lemon and tartar sauce and a baked potato—I taste it as I reel the fish in.

But my reel jams. The line comes freezing out of the water, thick as a pencil with ice, and the spool can't take it up. I drop the rod and draw the fish upstream hand over hand. It's like hauling in an anchor. Stepping back onto the bank so I can ease him onto the sloping shore rather than lift him over the rail, I tense myself, ready for his last desperate run. When it comes, when he foresees his death by open air, he puts all his muscle and nerve into a splash and a turn—and I am left holding the broken line. Damn it to hell. That's why we fish with rods. Rods bend and bounce and absorb the line-snapping surges of energy. He must have been a monster.

I climb back to the car and start the engine. Removing the iced-up reel from the rod, I place it on the floor by the heater vent, along with my iced-up gloves. I go to the trunk, open my tackle box, and start over again—hook, leader, sinker, bobber.

"Hi," says a man's voice in the dark that startles me. I turn and see a shadow emerging from the trees. He's carrying a rod and reel.

"Roman?" I ask.

"Any bites?" Roman's high-pitched voice.

"One. I lost him."

I catch his scent a moment before his white beard and black coat materialize in the light cast up from the trunk. He smells of kerosene. This reclusive man lives with his even more reclusive wife in a shanty in the woods, a short way down the abandoned railroad track. He smiles at me from under his long-billed cap. "Any size?" he asks.

"Big."

"I lost a big one too," he says. "This noon."

"Catch any?"

"Eight—me and the wife." His smile turns sheepish. The daily limit is three apiece.

"Any size?"

"A couple fair-sized. The rest hammerhandles."

Roman is the shortened form of an unspellable Slavic name nobody around here has learned to pronounce. He and his wife must be very old; they've been fixtures in Rookery all my adult life. Besides fishing and hunting—in and out of season—they subsist on their income from a seven-acre garden, specializing in cucumbers, berries, potatoes, pumpkins, and squash. They seem to have cornered Rookery's jack-o'-lantern market; in October there's a three-acre slope beside Highway 2 that turns orange with their pumpkins for sale.

He follows me down the dark hillside to the pier. When I warn him to step around the deer's innards, he chuckles.

"Not your deer, is it, Roman?"

More chuckling. "You think I'd be dumb enough to dump deer leavings this close to my house?"

We stand on the pier fishing together, discussing the latest controversy on Mother's radio show—the extension of a sewer and water system to this area that has not been annexed to the city. Roman fears he'll have to start paying taxes.

"You mean you're not paying taxes now?"

"Naw," he says. "Not property taxes."

"How do you get away with that?"

"Easy. Don't own property."

"But your house, Roman. You own your house—you built it yourself, you told me."

"Built it, but don't own the land it's on. All this woods here is tax-forfeit land. Belongs to the state."

"You can't build on state land, Roman. It's against the law."

"Wasn't state land when I built. Was railroad land."

"But you can't build on railroad land either."

"Oh yeah, the trainmaster okayed it. I was crossing guard in those days. Full-time job back then, guard at Eleventh Avenue crossing. Before the days of the automatic gates, remember?"

"Sure, back in the 'forties."

"Thirty, thirty-five trains through here a day, and Eleventh Avenue every bit the main drag it is now. Busier, maybe, before they built the bypass. Trainmaster back then was Sammy St. Pierre, remember?"

"No, I don't."

"We made a deal. Sammy St. Pierre let me build on the property as long as I took the night shift seven nights a week. Nobody wanted night shift, sit there in that cubicle all night waiting for trains. I didn't mind. More time to talk to people, nights, back then. Hobos mostly. At first, I lived in a spare room in the depot, remember the depot?"

"Sure."

"No place for a woman—spare room in a depot."

Though I don't remember the trainmaster from those years, nor Roman himself, I do recall crossing guards halting traffic with their little handheld stop signs, and I remember the hobos. I was a small boy during the Depression, the golden age of those curious strangers we called tramps. Our house must have been well-known to the hobo nation, because they made a beeline from the railyard to our back door for the sandwich and coffee Mother always handed out.

"You were married at the time, Roman?"

"Wasn't married to the missus quite yet then. But I wanted to live with her, see, and so we had to build us a house. Couldn't ask a woman to live in a depot."

I've shared this fishing pier with Roman many times without ever hearing this. It must be the darkness. It seems safer to reveal things when you can't see your listener.

I try nudging Roman ahead. "Mrs. Roman was a local girl, was she?"

"Nope, a hobo."

"A hobo!"

"Freight trains full of people riding the rails in them days. Mostly men, of course, but now and then a hobo's wife, or a couple of women together. One night we had the Hobo Queen through here."

"The Hobo Queen? Who was that?"

"The hobo nation would elect a queen, or appoint a queen, or the queen appointed herself—I don't know."

"You married the Hobo Queen?"

Roman's laugh is husky and moist. "No, God no. The Queen was kind of a dumpy dame, about fifty, I guess. Wore a crown made out of agates. Sat by the campfire not forty feet from where my house now stands, and told stories."

Roman is interrupted by a fish, a small sucker, which he releases back to the cold river. Then he brings in a larger fish, which he keeps, dangling him into the water on a stringer he ties to the railing. In the beam of my flashlight, I see it's a bullhead.

"You must be fishing deep."

"Yep, dragging the bottom," he says. "No use fishing shallow in the dark."

"The big one I had was shallow."

"A fluke." He baits his hook, and the moment I switch off the light, he continues his tale of romance.

"The wife and her sister came through from Montana one day, heading out East. Running away from home, more or less. Sort of spunky types, both of them." I hear him chuckle fondly at the memory. "I like that in a woman. That's why me and the wife always make it a point to catch Lolly on the radio. Lots of spunk in your mother."

He pauses for a time, and both of us watch the continuous

flow of rush-hour headlights crossing the bridges downstream. He laughs softly. "I said to the two of them, I said, 'How about hanging around here a few days?' Said it to the good-looking sister, mostly, but the other one—the one I married—was the one that answered. She said, 'Why should I?' 'There's good fishing right here in the Badbattle,' I told her. 'Okay,' she said. 'I will.' Just like that. Her sister, the good-looking one, told her she was stark-mad demented, but she stayed."

"What became of her sister?"

"Probably died."

"Probably? You never saw her again?"

"Oh sure, saw her every year on her way home for Christmas. Her and her husband. She'd write and say what train they were coming through on, and we'd be at the station to see her."

"Freight train?"

"God, no." More laughter. "She married a tiler in New Jersey—not sewer tile, a guy who laid floor tile. No more riding in boxcars for Helen."

"But you're not sure if she died?"

"Well, last time we saw her—ten years ago maybe—things wasn't so good between her and the tiler. He was a hard man, she said. She told the wife she'd like to strike out on her own again, like they did as girls. So maybe she did, but we never heard a thing about her after that."

"Didn't you ask the husband?"

"My wife wrote once to ask, but never heard back."

"And you let it go at that?"

"Yup." There's a long silence before he explains. "My wife didn't really care, one way or the other. Down through the years, every time Helen stopped through, she'd say my wife was stark-mad demented for staying with me. That gets pretty old after a while."

"So she could be still living."

"I suppose."

"What makes you think she's dead?"

"Her age. She'd be old as the hills by now—six, eight years older than my wife."

Though it's indiscreet of me, I can't help asking, "How old is your wife?"

"Six, eight years younger than me." He laughs.

No more bites for either of us. I reel in and release my minnow into the cold river. "I've got to go, Roman."

"Me too. Want my fish?"

"No, thanks. Want my minnows?"

"Sure." He releases the bullhead, and stuffs the stringer into his pocket. "Isn't worth cleaning just one. Anyhow, our freezer's full."

He picks up my bucket and we trudge uphill in the dark.

"Roman, do you know the poetry of Richard Falcon?"

"Name rings a bell."

"Very famous. He might be coming to Rookery."

"The wife probably knows him. She reads."

He lingers at my car while I stash my gear and shed my overcoat. He wants a ride but is too proud to ask.

"Want a ride to Petey's, Roman?"

"Don't mind if I do."

I drive him downtown against the traffic and out along Skidder Street to Petey's Price-Fighter Foods, as I've done before, and I wait in the car while he shops. He's left his scent with me, an aroma, besides kerosene, of some kind of peppery spice I can't identify.

Roman's a quick shopper. Here he comes wheeling out a cartful of the staples he and Mrs. Roman can't hunt or gather themselves—sugar, flour, coffee, cartons of cheap beer.

"How about having supper with me and the wife?" he asks on the way home. "See if she knows your poet."

"Thanks. Another time. It's holiday night at the Hi-Rise. Mother and I go every year."

"Too bad. We're having venison."

In the woods bordering the railroad yards, I drive as close as possible to his house, which is inaccessible by road. Following the aroma of woodsmoke through the birch grove, I help him carry his supplies.

"Roman," I ask, "if you don't have a car or truck, how do you transport your crops?"

"Wheelbarrow."

"But all those pumpkins beside the highway. They cover the entire hillside."

"Two wheelbarrows. Wife on one, me on the other."

We pass between walls of neatly stacked firewood and come to his front stoop. He pushes open the door and says, "Dee."

His wife appears in the small, low-ceilinged front room, smiling out of her small, wrinkled face, asking about the fishing and taking the sacks I carry. While her husband disappears inside with the beer and the flour, she thanks me profusely for transporting her husband and says I must stay for their venison dinner. She's so tiny and bony you wonder if she's become skeletal through privation. She wears a down vest over a sweatshirt, a tiny glass bead in each earlobe, her gray hair pulled neatly back in a knot tied with an orange ribbon.

"Another time, thanks. Mother and I are due at the Hi-Rise in half an hour."

"Oh, the fund-raising dinner—Lolly told about it this morning. It sounds so posh."

"It's anything but posh. A slice of ham and lots of gravy—catered by the VFW."

"So Lolly said. It sounds delicious." Does she mean this, or do I detect a hint of guile in her tone?

"It's been the same meal the last four years, and seldom warm."

In another room, I glimpse a dim lamp, a great length of stovepipe, and throw rugs nailed to the wall, perhaps as insulation.

Her husband reappears. "Leland's got a poet he wants to ask you about, Dee."

"Richard Falcon. Do you know his work, by any chance?"

"Sure. 'The fish that takes the fatal bite.'"

" 'Is victimized by appetite.'"

Roman looks amused as she and I exchange more lines. "He's coming to Rookery," I tell her.

"No."

A clock in the second room sets off a pretty chime. "Gotta run," I say, backing out the door.

"You'll come another time," says Dee.

I assure them that I will.

"Another time the venison won't be this fresh," calls Roman. His laughter follows me through the corridor of firewood.

Mingling with the residents and guests during the premeal punch and pickles, I find that everyone except Johnny Hancock and the New Woman has heard of Richard Falcon. Many claim to remember one or two of his poems. Some, in fact, can quote him. " 'There isn't much left in the house I desire,' " recites the Reverend Worthington Pyle, sitting down at his assigned place at the table next to ours.

I respond with the second line of the sonnet. " 'The screen door and wreath are the same shade of rust.' "

"Show off!" he spouts, with heat. He wanted to say it himself. I clam up, but he continues to glower at me. Nobody does the hurt and angry act so convincingly as our old rector.

The trestle table has been pushed aside tonight; we're eating in groups of four, sitting at cardtables covered with runners of Christmassy wrapping paper. On all the tables, in vases of crystal and china belonging to Mother, stand sprigs of imitation holly. This is an annual fund-raising affair, to which each resident is encouraged to invite a guest willing to pay twenty-five dollars a plate. Tonight's plate, as I predicted, is the VFW specialty—ham, slaw, baked potato.

Hildegard Lubovich sits on my left, wearing three or four of her best necklaces and her sourest expression, along with an ill-fitting oxford-cloth blouse tight at the breast and a bit longer in one sleeve than the other. To Mother's assertion that Sally McNaughton looks lovely tonight, Hildegard replies, "She gets my goat." By which she means that Sally plays no favorites among the elderly, that Hildegard isn't deferred to as the banker's widow the way she used to be as the banker's wife.

On my right sits Hildegard's perpetual sidekick, Nettie Firehammer, whose holiday attire consists of a blaze-orange hunting vest over her black pantsuit and a dried rose in her sparse gray hair. "Looks yummy," she says, surveying the contents of her Melmac plate and trying to decide where to begin. Following Hildegard's lead, she stabs open her potato.

"Richard Falcon—didn't he write the one about the snow-plow on the highway?" asks Mother, sitting opposite me. "It was buried in snow and along came ..." She frowns, trying to remember.

"Along came a spider!" Johnny Hancock gleefully shouts, silencing nearly everyone in the room. Johnny, in bib overalls, and the Reverend Pyle, in turtleneck and sport coat, are sharing their table with a middle-aged niece of Johnny's, and a well-dressed elderly man with shifty eyes. The elderly man, whose name is McAllister, is a former certified public accountant who was decertified a number of years ago for being careless with other people's money. Some of it belonged to St. Blaise, for he used to be a trustee of our church.

"There's one about a cat," says Johnny's niece, who wears a spiny green Christmas corsage high on the shoulder of her green suit.

" 'Little cat feet,' " agrees Worthington Pyle erroneously. " 'Over city and harbor.' "

"No, that's Carl Sandburg," says Mother, accurately and surprisingly—I've never known her to read poetry. "Butchering hogs in the world, or some such atrocious thing. Why can't they write poems like we learned in school?"

"Because beauty is dead in the modern day," proclaims Worthington Pyle darkly. "When our generation is gone, all the good poems will go with us."

To this, there is hearty agreement from the tables nearby. Verses are called up and exchanged, quotations going back as far as the seventeenth century and spreading out across the dining room. Most of the lines are pleasing and provocative enough to bring tender smiles to this collection of wrinkled old faces, the exceptions being Johnny Hancock's mischievous contributions.

" 'What is so rare as a day in June.' "

" 'This is the forest primeval.' "

" 'I hear those gentle voices calling Old Black Joe.' "

" 'Chink, chink Chinaman sitting on a fence, trying to make a dollar out of fifteen cents.' "

"Shame on you, Johnny!" calls out Sally, who has seated her-self with Marigold Mack and a pair of friendless old ladies in a far corner of the room. Marigold Mack, Hi-Rise caretaker, is second in command to Sally. She doles out everyone's meds. When residents need rides, she calls the Medi-van; when they need a lecture, she calls a relative. When a faucet leaks or a fuse blows, she fixes it. Should death come along and empty an apartment, it's Marigold who goes in with her mops and pails and Lysol and Windex and makes the place shine for the newcomer. A silent, muscular woman with a secret past, a blurry tattoo on her forearm, and seams in her face that make her appear older than her forty-five years, Marigold was recruited from the CREW program Sally used to manage before she became manager of the Hi-Rise. Unlike Sally, who lives in a house of her own—a 'fifties style rambler with no basement and scarcely any yard and open to strays and misfits of the sort she used to deal with at CREW—Marigold resides here on the premises.

After a few more quotations from the ladies, Johnny Hancock slips in, " 'Grass grew tall, tickled his ball, he shit all over his overall.' Hee, hee." His niece cries, "For shame!" and covers his mouth.

After a pause for muttering and sighing, to signify how tiresome we all find Johnny Hancock, Father Pyle gets the verses rolling again. " 'Stone walls do not a prison make,' " he declaims. " 'Nor iron bars a cage.' "

Comes a response from Nettie Firehammer: " 'I think that I shall never see, a nest of robins in her hair.' "

" 'The lowing herd homeward plods its weary way.' "

" 'Beautiful dreamer, waken to me.' "

" 'Tiger, tiger, burning bright, something, something of the night.' "

" 'Be it ever so humble, there's no place like home.' "

" 'Grass grew tall, tickled his—' "

"Johnny, *please!*"

Sally and Marigold eventually come round with trays of dessert—butterscotch pudding and a sugar cookie. Then Sally, standing in front of the serving table, delivers her annual address of welcome and gratitude. She's wearing a black skirt and a red jacket tonight. Her white blouse was a gift from Mother years ago, its collar embroidered by Mother in a holly design. Her

chestnut-dyed hair is piled in a topknot, exposing the small earrings of red enamel and silver I gave her last Christmas. Despite
her smile and her spirited voice, she looks worn out. It's a hard
season at the Sylvan Senior Hi-Rise. Outbreaks of loneliness and
discontent—even dementia—spread through the place as Christmas approaches; she has to do a lot of soothing and reassuring.
Sometimes she even has to go out searching for wanderers.

The money collected tonight, she announces, will go toward
the rest-room facilities being installed on this main floor, which
were foolishly left out of the architect's plan. When the plumber
and tiler finish their work next week, it won't be necessary for
those needing relief to take the elevator up to their apartments,
or—if caught short—to use the bathroom in Marigold Mack's
tiny apartment off the lobby. Good news indeed for this roomful
of deteriorating bladders. A round of applause.

Next, she asks the residents with guests to introduce them. At
the next table, Johnny Hancock keeps it simple, standing up with
his niece and saying, "Jennie," and sitting down again. There is
scattered clapping. Mother writes Jennie's name on a notepad—
news for her radio show.

Worthington Pyle launches into a tedious panegyric concerning his guest, the man with the shifty eyes; a paragon of
virtue, he says, a financial wizard, a saint.

Mother, writing down the man's name, laughs wheezily and
nudges Hildegard Lubovich and says, "Donald McAllister's a
saint—did you catch that?"

"A shyster, you mean," says Hildegard.

More laughter from Mother, and a seething noise from Hildegard, none of it loud enough, it seems, to cause the former trustee
of St. Blaise to lift his eyes from his plate, nor Worthington Pyle
to desist. He grinds on, speaking of his days in the active min-
istry, his lifelong friendship with Mr. McAllister, and then concludes with a prayer for the well-being of faithful Episcopalians
everywhere. This is followed by a general "Amen," with all eyes
averted because Johnny Hancock, seated on his right, begins to
dribble spit into the upper middle pocket of his overalls.

"Donald McAllister feathered his own nest for years with
church funds," Hildegard mutters like the insider she's not, and

drawing a black look from Reverend Pyle. Her friendship with Mother led Hildegard into Episcopalianism, but only after the death of her husband Anton, a devoted Catholic.

"Emptied the coffers," Mother agrees pleasantly. A true insider, Mother knows the amount to have been terrifically exaggerated by rumor.

"Who?" asks Nettie Firehammer. Nettie is losing, with age, her ability to follow conversations, except at a distance.

Hildegard points to the man.

"That old thing?" says Nettie in disbelief.

Next, Sally designates our table. Hildegard stands up and says, "You all know Lolly Edwards, and her boy Leland."

We draw, or I should say Mother draws, louder and longer applause than even the main-floor toilet did. Mother is loved. There's scarcely a hearing aid in this building that isn't turned to the radio when "Lolly Speaking" comes on the air. Not that she does all that much speaking anymore. With the onset of lung disease, she's reluctantly allowed her studio guests to share more and more of her fifteen minutes of airtime. But these faithful listeners still trust her to ask the same incisive questions they themselves would ask of the public servants who, week after week, appear on her Monday show. Dog droppings on downtown sidewalks and the extension of city water to the northeast bank of the river are the two hottest topics this season. Her Wednesday show she devotes entirely to cooking, because the dictating of recipes, repeating and pausing, repeating and pausing, is so well suited to her rate of breathing. If she's short of breath on Friday, call-in day, she'll let her callers rant and ramble to their heart's content; if her pipes happen to be clear, however, the angries, the bores, the lonelyhearts, and the loonies quickly find themselves cut off and replaced by Mother herself and the backlog of opinions that's been building up during her latest siege of lung trouble. What a cruel irony that this particular malady should strike someone whose primary talent is talk.

Tonight she's in good voice. Christmas is a powerful tonic for Mother. Social festivities always speed up her heart rate, her adrenaline flow, her brain waves. Next we'll host our annual open house, and then, after two days of cleanup and recuperation we'll get in the car and make our annual trip to the farm where she was born in 1912. I'll drive seven hours, and she'll chatter all the way at my side, energized by the prospect of spending Christmas with her people, the O'Kelly clan of Grimsby, Nebraska. We'll come home exhausted, both of us, and she'll be at low ebb for most of January. You'll be able to notice it on the radio, in fact, her voice diminished, her delivery a drone.

Myself, I won't own up to being exhausted. Mother doesn't like it when I'm tired, so I've trained myself to be resilient. I'll go to the office the very next morning and examine grade-point averages with Angelo Corelli. We'll plan who to put on probation, who to suspend, who to include on the Dean's List. Angelo calls it Bureaucracy Day.

Sally's mention of money puts Mother in mind of her certificates of deposit. "I'm locked in for another eight months," Mother laments, comparing her financial holdings to Nettie's and Hildegard's.

"Get out of CDs," orders Hildegard, digging into her butterscotch pudding. "The rates are dreadful."

"But I'm locked in. Nobody told me the economy was going to collapse."

Nettie Firehammer speaks up, offering posthumous advice from her husband. "Municipal bonds let you keep what you earn, Horace always said." Following Hildegard's lead, she tastes her pudding. Mother and I save ours for later, upstairs, with Twyla Todd.

Mother scoffs at municipal bonds. "Lower rate than CDs, and they tie you up for years."

"But they aren't taxed. Horace always hated paying taxes."

"Who doesn't," says Mother, "but that's no reason to settle for three percent. Leland, what is Angelo saying these days about Procter and Gamble?"

"I'll ask him."

"Stay away from Procter and Gamble," orders Hildegard. "You can't trust corporations anymore, what with takeovers and insider trading. I'd give my money to gypsies before I'd give it to Procter and Gamble."

"Horace always liked a bar of Ivory in the tub, the way it floats."

"Ask Angelo about treasury notes too, would you, Leland?"

"No good," declares Hildegard. "Treasury notes are worthless. I'd keep my cash in a sock before I'd put it in treasury notes."

"The worst thing is commodities," says Nettie. "Horace said, to his dying day, never get into commodities."

Mother laughs. "We learned our lesson about commodities, remember, Leland?"

I nod, regretting the bundle we lost on pork bellies. It cured me of dabbling in the market. The more ignorant I've remained since, the better off we've become.

"It was so sad and touching, how he died," says Nettie of her beloved Horace. "He'd been unconscious since midnight, and about noon he opened his eyes. The doctor was there in the room, and all my sisters. So was our brother-in-law, Les. So was our dog. Horace was lying there, looking me straight in the eye—I'll never forget it. He said, 'Nettie, never get into commodities,' and then he died."

We fall silent for a moment, out of respect for Horace in his wisdom.

"Commodities will make you some money," Hildegard says, her eyes fastened on mine, "if you have the brains for it."

The VFW delivered Twyla Todd's meal in a small Styrofoam box. She hasn't bothered to transfer it to a plate. Imprisoned by stiffening joints, she sits eating beside her window on the fifth and highest floor, facing an overloud news program on the television screen. When the newscaster pauses for breath, I can hear her police-band radio crackling away on her lamp table. Mother and I greet her by carefully lifting her left hand, and she looks up at us with the half-smile of a puzzled child. Twyla Todd is declining at about the same gradual rate as Nettie Firehammer. Through her eyes, you can watch her brain at work. She recognizes me first—I suppose because I'm the only man she sees from one week to the next—and then her smile opens into joy when her eyes meet Mother's.

"How are you, Twyla?"

"Not so bad." She chews slowly and tentatively because her jaw, like every other hinge in her body, is painful to move. She swallows and says, "They say it's cold out."

"Very cold," says Mother, sitting down on the couch. "Though it didn't stop Leland from going fishing."

"How . . . ?" Mishandling the remote, Twyla raises the volume on the TV but doesn't appear to notice. I take it from her and silence the newscaster. We then hear the staticky voice of the police dispatcher directing an ambulance to a rural address. Reaching across Twyla, I turn the radio down, but not quite off, and then, before taking my place next to Mother on the couch, I look down on the steaming paper mill, the brightly lit car dealerships on Court Street, the dense traffic funneling into the shopping mall beyond the rendering plant.

Mother repeats, "Leland went fishing this afternoon."

"Oooh, my," says Twyla, giving me the big, encouraging smile little boys get for accomplishments beyond their years. "Is it cold out?"

"Very cold," I tell her, as I sink into the couch.

Twyla puts down her fork, takes a shaky sip of water, and asks, "Who lives at Thirty-three Vendome Avenue South, Lolly?"

Mother frowns, thinking.

"Vendome," I offer, "that's the street with the skating rink next to the fire station."

"But Thirty-three. I can't picture Thirty-three." Twyla looks distraught.

"Police or ambulance?" Mother asks.

"Ambulance. Somebody lying in a backyard. It wasn't half an hour ago. Dead or alive they didn't say."

"Man or woman?"

"Man, I think."

"We'll drive past and let you know," Mother assures her.

With her ear to shortwave day and night, Twyla stays ahead of the news passed by word of mouth in the dining room and lobby downstairs—car accidents, crimes, heart attacks—but sometimes the victim's name is not broadcast with the address, and that's where Mother and I come in, since we're virtually her only visitors with a car. The radio was a gift from her husband their last anniversary together. He couldn't have known what an asset it would be in the Hi-Rise, where nothing is held in higher regard than gossip when it's fresh and local.

Mother asks, "It wouldn't be Charlie Peabody, would it?"

"Well ..." Twyla peers down Vendome Avenue with her mind's eye. "But the Peabodys don't have a backyard. It's all pigs."

"It's not pigs anymore."

"It isn't?"

"Not for years. It's zoning, Twyla. You can't keep pigs in the city. Neighbors can't stand the smell."

Twyla's eyes brighten and pierce us with a sudden alertness. "Wasn't it a tragedy, losing to St. Albert?"

"Certainly a surprise," I tell her, "if not a tragedy."

"But they scored with Jeffy in goal. I worry he'll get benched again." Twyla became a hockey fan when her grandson began playing. St. Albert College, last weekend, was supposed to be a pushover.

"Jeffy got in the game?" Surely Twyla's confused. Last year, her grandson began the season as our star goaltender, but falling grades disqualified him and he hasn't played since.

"He started the second period, till St. Albert scored twice, then Coach Hokanson took him out. His father's just sick about it."

Jeffy's father and mother, like hockey parents everywhere, are possessed. They had the boy on skates at the age of two. At five, he was speeding around the public rinks flailing a hockey stick and tripping up kids twice his size.

Twyla laments, "I worry scouts will come to see him, and he'll be sitting on the bench."

The door opens and the weightless Nettie Firehammer comes fluttering in. Her wraithlike shape, together with her orange and black attire, is remindful of the wrong holiday—Halloween.

"How are you, Twyla?"

"Not so bad. I hear it's cold out."

"Freezing." Nettie Firehammer perches on the edge of a straight chair facing Twyla, and politely waits for her daily briefing. She understands—as Mother and I do—that Twyla doesn't like to be asked for the news, but prefers to portion it out slowly in conversation because visitors stay longer that way. Nettie will go back to the half-dozen widows on the third floor, including Hildegard Lubovich, and report whatever knowledge she doesn't lose in the elevator. It used to be Hildegard who represented the third floor, but she proved too pushy for Twyla Todd, who began withholding things from her. The day she didn't tell Hildegard about the mayor's wife's car accident, the third floor began sending up Nettie. Hildegard's reports hadn't proved all that reliable in the first place, for she liked to shade the facts with her own colorful suppositions. They might have designated someone of sounder mind to take her place, but what Nettie lacks in memory, she makes up for in honesty. She would never think of withholding gossip because of a grudge or even a temporary snit, as Hildegard was known to do.

After a lengthy discourse on today's arthritic pain as compared to yesterday's, Twyla gets down to business. "There was spray paint on the Eleventh Avenue bridge again this morning."

"Oh, dear," says Nettie. "Bad pictures again?"

"Just bad words this time."

"What were they?"

"The dispatcher said some of them, but I couldn't make them out, it was scratchy and she was laughing."

"The dispatcher was laughing?" Mother is amused. "That would be Bess Kurilla—Bess is such a live wire."

"But the dispatcher shouldn't be laughing," says Twyla.

"Oh, why not?" says Mother. "We aren't hearing enough laughter these days."

"On shortwave, Lolly? It's not becoming."

Mother throws her hands dramatically high over her head. "Oh, well, into each life a little levity must fall."

This is met with a reproving silence from both women. Twyla resents levity on her premises; it implies a lack of respect for her pain. Nettie resents it, for the moment at least, adapting herself to

Twyla's mood. Nettie is a chameleon. Another day, she might just as easily be laughing with Mother.

Twyla starts over. "Is it cold out?"

Mother prompts me with a nudge—I'm to take over the weather.

"Pretty cold," I say, "but there's no wind."

"Well, that's good, anyway."

Nettie says, "There was a bad wind earlier, I think."

"No, Nettie." I foolishly try to straighten her out. "Yesterday was the wind. Today was calm all day."

Again, Twyla's eyes brighten. "Wasn't it a tragedy, losing to St. Albert?" she asks. "Jeffy's father's just sick about it. We lose to little schools like that, he says, scouts will stop coming to Rookery."

It's a widely believed myth that representatives from the National Hockey League come pouring into Rookery whenever the Blue Herons take the ice. The fact is that we average one scout every fourth or fifth game. I know; their passes are issued through my office.

"It couldn't have been Jeffy in goal, Twyla. He can't play this year because of his grades."

She scowls at me. "You were there?"

"No, I wasn't there." I'm never there. Hockey I can't watch. The fighting disgusts me, and I can't see the puck.

"You listened on the radio?"

"No, I didn't, but—"

"Jeffy was in the game."

Mother speaks up, mischievously changing the subject. "It must be twenty years since pigs were allowed in the city."

We watch the thinking of both women shift from hockey to pigs. It takes a few moments.

"Pigs in the city?" asks Nettie.

During the confusion that follows, I feel Mother chuckling silently at my side.

"They found a man lying in his backyard on Vendome Avenue," says Twyla.

"A man?" We watch Nettie switch from imagining pigs to imagining men. "What man?"

"They didn't say who it was."

"Who didn't?"

"Lolly said it sounded like Charlie Peabody's house, but Charlie hasn't any real yard."

"Charlie always had pigs," says Nettie.

They fall silent. So does the police dispatcher. If I were Mother I'd leave it there, but she can't resist toying. I sometimes wonder where her pity is.

"It was probably the f-word," she says, putting both women completely at sea. I stand up to leave.

This time it's Nettie who finally catches on. "The bridge, you mean."

Twyla still gropes for a mooring, her eyes darting among us.

"The graffiti," Nettie prompts her. "On the bridge."

"What about it?"

"Lolly says it probably said the f-word."

Twyla continues to look mystified, pretending not to know what the f-word is. She's always been slightly more proper than her contemporaries. "Is it cold out?" she asks.

OPEN HOUSE

It's so cold that some of our guests, the older ones, phone to ask if the party is canceled. It never is. We've held this open house in blizzards, in ice storms, and at thirty below. Once we even held it while the garage next door was burning to the ground and firemen were hosing down our house to wash away the sparks. "No, my dear," Mother replies happily on the phone to one and all, "ours is the oldest continuous Christmas party in Rookery."

Nowadays it's a pretty tame affair, so many of our guests being elderly. It used to be livelier. You could never predict, in the old days, if it would be a wholesome party, full of song and good cheer, or a reckless bash where the drinking got out of hand. One time we disturbed the peace until 2:00 A.M., and the neighbors called the police—a scandal kept alive for days afterward by people bringing it up on Mother's call-in show. Another time somebody—we think it was Kimberly Kraft—charged seventy-five dollars' worth of long-distance calls to Fargo on our upstairs phone. One of Mother's proudest moments, despite the shock and anguish involved, was the time Anton Lubovich, Hildegard's husband, keeled over and died in our kitchen and we didn't have to call the doctor, the rector, or the undertaker, because all three were in the next room singing carols. In the days when the *Morning Call* had a society page, they sometimes sent a photographer.

I have, in the past, fetched as many as three carloads from the Hi-Rise, but today, because of the extreme cold, I gather up only three willing residents—Hildegard Lubovich, Nettie Firehammer, and the New Woman with the oxblood ears. The Reverend Worthington Pyle insists on driving his own car, claiming that it needs starting once a day in weather this cold. Johnny Hancock rides with him. Sally says she'll be along later.

The old rector is not a good driver. Bearing heavily down on the horn and the gas pedal, he trails me across town, swerving and skidding on the icy streets. We find Mother stationed in the entryway, dressed in red and white, with silver slippers on her feet and a silver bow in her hair. She greets everyone except Johnny Hancock with repeated hugs and kisses. Johnny's the sort of rascal women dare not touch for fear of the touching he'll do in return. We're glad, at least, that Sally's talked him into putting on a clean flannel shirt and a clean pair of overalls. Crossing our threshold, he asks Mother, "Would you make some orange juice?"

"You'll find orange juice on the buffet, Johnny, with the liquor." She points.

"No, no," he says, looking suddenly irritated. "Make some fresh."

"Later," she tells him, and turns her attention to the next group coming up the walk. This is the vanguard of the college crowd, approaching in the order of their importance—President Zastrow first, with his zombielike wife on his arm, followed by Angelo Corelli and his handsome wife Gloria, both of them looking jaunty and even younger than their tender years. Trailing behind them is Emeric Kahlstrom, our pessimist-in-residence, and trailing behind Emeric, with an expression no happier than you'd expect of a woman who must wake every morning to mutterings of gloom and doom, is his wife Edna.

"Greetings, merry Christmas, welcome, welcome." Kiss, kiss, kiss—Mother greets them one by one, braving the frigid air sucked into the entryway.

The stiff, unsmiling Mrs. Zastrow, wearing a brown suit with a stylish and very short skirt, keeps her eyes trained on Mother's feet as she allows me to take her coat and allows her husband to steer her through the living room to the fireplace. In her twenty-five years among us, we have learned next to nothing about the soul of this eccentric woman whose expensive clothes are always of an inappropriate cut for a woman her age, and whose tanning-booth-blackened face is so thickly overlaid with cosmetics that you can't help imagining the hours of toil at her dressing table. Does she have a mind? The Corellis say yes, and I believe them because Angelo and Gloria are now and then invited to play Scrabble at the president's house. Does she have a voice? Yes, I have heard her utter words, though not sentences. Does she have a thirst for hard liquor? You bet.

O. F. Zastrow goes straight to the bottles and splashes together a Manhattan for her. I join him there, mixing a grasshopper for Hildegard. His crooked bow tie is patterned with tiny x's and o's.

"I have to say, O. F., how relieved I am to have staved off Addison Steele. We'll never be sorry we avoided that disaster."

"Well, we need somebody. Bridges promises he'll come up with another high-profile name."

"Actually, Bridges isn't the right person for that job, O. F."

"Nonsense. Totally trustworthy, Bridges. Where's your bitters?"

I hand him the bottle, while insisting, "Bridges goes against everything we stand for, O. F. He'll contaminate us. He'll keep presenting us with these intellectual deadbeats like a cat dragging in mice, and we'll have to keep voting them down."

Ignoring me, he measures out the bitters by the drop.

"Look, O. F., I can go along with the concept. I mean, in this day and age of slick advertising, I can see drawing attention to ourselves by hitching our wagon to a big name. But if we're really the center of learning we claim to be, then the name had better be in keeping with our goals."

Had I not already, while setting out the liquor, knocked back a couple of stiff brandies, I wouldn't allow myself to become so heated and carried away. Ordinarily I limit myself to one drink, because nothing is quite so disheartening to a college community as the sight of a dean in his cups. Seeing my predecessor, Pug Patnode, so frequently looped convinced me of this. But today I'm not feeling up to the occasion. Christmas, never a totally fulfilling season for me, has caused my spirit to go into a bit of a dip. Brandy, at least for the moment, buoys me up.

"Urrr," says my president—not ordinarily his expression of assent, but I'm gratified to see him nod as though I have actually caught his attention.

"I mean, a name standing for the life of the mind, O. F."

"Einstein," he replies astutely.

"That sort, yes."

"We'll ask Bridges to get ahold of him."

Oh, the breathtaking ignorance of the man. I break the news to him softly, "Einstein's dead."

"No."

"It's true."

While I mix an old-fashioned for Nettie Firehammer, Zastrow carries the Manhattan to his wife, who stands at the fireplace slightly bent forward at the waist, warming the backs of her exposed knees and thighs. Her eyes are still fastened on the silver slippers, following them across the room as Mother flutters between the Hi-Rise ladies, settling them into chairs. Zastrow says, "Loretta," and his wife, without turning to him, extends her jeweled hand automatically for the glass.

The ebullient Angelo Corelli appears at my side to examine the two wine decanters, red and white. His ugly new sweater— nubby threads of yellow and gray—gives off the dye-smell of the Discount Sweater Mart on Fox Avenue.

"Great party, Leland."

"I have to say your vote for Addison Steele disappointed me, Angelo."

"Yes, I know. It was the prospect of making all that money in one fell swoop."

"Think of her trashy image."

"The money swept me away, sorry. Incidentally, did you hear that Jeffy Todd played hockey the other night?"

"Heard it without believing it."

"St. Albert scored twice with Jeffy Todd in goal."

"Impossible. Hokanson knows the penalty for using ineligible players."

"It was in the paper, the box score."

I'm stunned. "He'll have to forfeit."

"He'll have a seizure."

"I'll have to confront him."

Angelo pours himself a glass of red and looks around. "Great party, Leland. Good wine, good cheer, strange people." He pours a glass of white for his wife.

"Strange people, Angelo? You've known them all for years."

"Known how strange they are," he says happily. "What's Mrs. Zastrow done to her face, do you suppose? I haven't seen skin like that since the last time I grilled Cajun chicken."

"Angelo, I sent you a memo—I think we can bring America's premier poet to campus. We should do some planning."

President Zastrow returns to the bottles, asking, "When did he die?"

"Sorry?" says Angelo.

"Einstein. When did he die?"

"Years ago," I tell him.

"You're sure of that? Nobody told me."

Angelo departs, smothering a chuckle.

"Yes, O. F., it's true. There are other good minds left alive, however. Have you heard of . . . ?" Here I falter, fearing he hasn't. I start over. "There's a very famous man in New Hampshire I think we could get, probably the foremost name in American literature currently—"

"Famous in New Hampshire doesn't mean diddly in Minnesota."

"No, I didn't say that right. What I mean is, he's universally famous, but he just happens to live in New Hampshire. He's truly a citizen of the world."

"What's his name?" asks Zastrow.

Assuming everyone, even my president, remembers this passage from childhood, I recite, " 'The fish that takes the fatal bite . . .' "

"What is he, Indian?"

"No."

"Name like that, sounds Indian."

"No, that's not his name, O. F. It's a popular line he wrote." I go on to recite the entire poem.

A thoughtful look comes into his eye. "It rhymes."

"Yes! It rhymes!" How astonishing that my president should notice. "Many of his pieces rhyme, O. F., though some of his longer works are written in blank verse. There's the one about strawberries, maybe you remember—Ned Rorem set it to music."

"Port tree."

"Pardon me?"

"He writes port tree."

"Yes, he's a *poet*, O. F.!" I shout this victoriously, I'm so excited at having led this philistine from point A to point B of my presentation. "I think he's our man, O. F. His name is Richard Falcon."

Zastrow looks stunned. "I didn't know he wrote port tree."

"All his life. What did you think?"

"Seems odd for a running back, is all."

"No, no, he doesn't play football, O. F. He's—"

"Richard Falcon? Of course he does. He plays for the Bears."

Mother calls across the room, reminding me that Hildegard and Nettie are without drinks. I find them perched side by side on the edge of our matching needlepoint chairs. They're conveying to Mother the latest report from Twyla Todd's police band radio.

Hildegard takes a large swallow from the glass I give her, smacks her lips and says, "A chimney fire on Tenth Street." She's covered tonight by a short-sleeved floral dress, and wears bracelets of tin up to her elbows.

"No, Eighth Street," says the emaciated Nettie, whose stockings, skirt, jacket, and hair are all of a uniform gray and imbued with the stench of cigarette smoke.

"No, Tenth, Nettie—don't you listen?"

"Twyla said Eighth."

"No, you said she said Tenth. The eight hundred block. Lolly, could you ask Leland to check it out? They didn't give the homeowner's name."

"Of course, Leland, you'll be glad to, won't you?"

"When I have time."

I move down the room and confide to Angelo, "Zastrow's trying to tell me Richard Falcon is a running back for the Bears."

Angelo laughs. "Wrong again. He's thinking of Richard Baer, running back for the Falcons."

At the end of the room, I spy the New Woman sitting on the love seat, apart from the others. I go and ask her what she'd like to drink.

"Schnapps," she snaps. She wears a sweater even uglier than Angelo's—swirls and zigzags of orange, purple, and pink. Her scent is lilac.

"I'm sorry," I tell her. "I'm afraid—"

"I knew it—rich people never keep schnapps in the house. Well, what the hell, anything with a kick will do."

I go and fill a snifter half full of brandy, and down a couple of quick swallows myself. When I present it to her, she sips, nods with satisfaction, and says, "Your wife's coughing is better."

"Not my wife's, my mother's. Yes, she's been much better the last few days."

"My bowels are better. Couldn't hardly move 'em since I went in the Hi-Rise."

I shake my head in sympathy.

"I tried all the laxatives."

"Well, I suppose dislocation will do that."

"Had some luck with Metamucil this morning."

"Good news indeed."

Johnny Hancock sidles up to me to ask if I'll make some fresh orange juice. Understanding his need, I lead him into the kitchen, where Helen Walker is preparing plates of sweetbreads, cold cuts, fruit, and nuts. Helen Walker is a neighbor who cooks and caters for us; Mother keeps her on a retainer. I present Johnny with a cylinder empty of its frozen orange concentrate. I've been saving it for him. It's the six-ounce size that fits in the pocket of his bib, its metal top still attached, the way he likes it. Now he's free to gnaw on his stringy tobacco all afternoon without having to open the door and spit into the icy wind.

We're joined in the kitchen by Worthington Pyle and Emeric Kahlstrom, discussing television. I recall finding them here last year, discussing astrophysics. They evidently prefer the relative privacy of our kitchen for comparing their matched set of melancholy philosophies.

"It's a horrible world lies ahead for youngsters these days, Kahlstrom."

"The pits, yes, but don't blame me, there's nothing I can do about it." There's always been this rather paranoid element in the old philosopher's manner of speaking.

"There's no future for a youngster with brains," says the retired rector, holding a bottle of beer to his lower lip and smiling bitterly at me, at Helen Walker, at Johnny. His tired turtleneck hangs loose at his sinewy throat. "Look at MTV, look at soap operas, look at All-Star Wrestling."

"Don't be simplistic." Kahlstrom snatches up a handful of nuts and goes to the window. Staring out at our snowy backyard, he says, "It's not TV alone that put civilization in the toilet."

"Look at the inane sitcoms, the nudes on HBO, the endless, mindless, meaningless football games."

"No, it goes back in history," mutters Kahlstrom, his mouth full of nuts. "It goes back to Greta Garbo."

I interject, louder than I intended: "Greta Garbo!!!"

Kahlstrom turns to me ruefully. "Figuratively speaking, of course." He goes on to lay out a premise too convoluted to follow—something about women's faces enlarged on grainy film—and so I pretend to be called away to the dining room. Johnny follows me, dribbling brown juice into his pocket.

"Hey, Leland, how goes it? I hear you've been charged with sexual harassment." This is Benny Smith, manager of Mother's radio station. He's a large, agreeable young man with shaggy blond hair and only one sport coat to his name—the baggy old camelhair he wears each week to brunch with Mother at the Van Buren Hotel and each December to this party.

"Charged? Hardly!"

"Got it right here in a news release from the college." Smiling benevolently, he draws an envelope from his pocket. "Dean charged in sex case, it says."

Speechless, I shake my head.

"Some crank, you think? Here, take a look."

The letter is typed on college stationery all right. I imagine the sinister and resourceful L. P. Connor mailing similar letters to all the media in Rookery.

"Do you mind?" I ask, tearing it up.

"Not at all." He takes the pieces from me, says "Pardon me" to Mrs. Zastrow, and casts them into the fire. The president's wife turns her vacant eyes on him for a moment, then directs them back at Mother's feet. Mother is absorbed in discussing Nebraska with Gloria Corelli, who looks radiant in black tights and a jacket of a black and red design. Like Mother, Gloria grew up in Nebraska.

I look around to check everyone's drink. The brandy is gone, I see, from the New Woman's snifter. Johnny Hancock has joined her on the love seat and is pointing out who's who. "That's Kahlstrom's old lady there, the one with the blue thingamajig on a strap."

"It's a purse."

"And that dame over there at the fire, that's the president of the college's old lady, she's a funny duck."

"Which one is the president?"

"Leland here's the president, ain't you, Leland?"

"Far from it, Johnny. Would you like more brandy, Mrs. . . . ?"

"You bet. Nice kick to it."

"You ain't president? I thought you was president."

"Dean, Johnny. I'm the dean."

"Dean? Dean's above president, ain't it?"

"Nobody's above the president, Johnny."

"Then that ain't your old lady?"

"You're pulling my leg, Johnny. I'm not married."

"Not married? Pyle said you was married."

"I was, once. To Sally."

"Sally at the Hi-Rise?" inquires the New Woman, looking amazed.

"Yes, years ago."

She narrows her eyes shrewdly, obviously trying to imagine us as a couple, and says, "Well, I'll be dipped."

When I return with her brandy, I find her alone again on the love seat, still wearing her shrewd expression. She says, "Sally, huh?"

"Can you picture it?"

She looks me up and down. "I guess I can at that," she says, and I am suddenly very sad. It's Christmas, and I sense her next question before she asks it:

"You got kids?"

"Had a son." To this day, saying his name will bring tears to my eyes, but I risk it. "Joey. He died."

"How old?"

"Two."

She deliberates further, then casts all doubt aside. "Yep, I can see where you'd be an all right couple."

My sorrow intensifies. I lower myself to the seat beside her and hang my head. "We were happy." My voice is shaky.

"How come you split?"

I shrug. I'm weeping.

"Who divorced who?"

"I divorced Sally."

"How come?"

Again I shrug. I'm not up to looking the New Woman in the face and telling her I divorced Sally because I couldn't stand to think of her in bed with Pug Patnode, our drunken dean. She'd done it, she said, because she wanted me to understand what it felt like to be married to a bigamist—by which she meant, of course, a man excessively attached to his mother.

"Do you mind?" I ask, taking the snifter from the New Woman and holding it to my lips.

"It's your booze."

I wipe away my tears and stand up as Mother approaches, ushering Edna Kahlstrom down the room, the melancholy philosopher's melancholy wife. "Edna, I want you to meet the new woman at the Hi-Rise. Her name is the same as yours." Saying this, Mother deftly removes the snifter from my grip, aware, of course, that I've gone over my one-drink limit. "Edna, this is Edna Kahlstrom, her husband's in Philosophy."

"Sorry to hear it," says the New Woman, then adds proudly, "mine was in plumbing."

Edna Kahlstrom, taking her hand, smiles a rare little smile. "Where did you live before the Hi-Rise?"

"Had a house in North Siding, but my husband died." The New Woman reaches up and takes the brandy from Mother. "I don't recollect ever seeing a philosopher before. Which one is he?"

"He's not in the room at the moment," says Mother. "I'll point him out when he comes back."

"I hope you like Rookery," says Edna Kahlstrom, sitting down beside the New Woman. "What do you think of the Hi-Rise?"

"Constipated at first."

The doorbell rings, and Mother goes to the entryway. I head back to the brandy bottle, but not before hearing the New Woman ask, "What do philosophers eat anyway?"

People stream into the house. Neighbors. Professors. Advertisers on "Lolly Speaking." The Triscos arrive, Viola wearing a bright blue pantsuit, her scrawny husband Bud looking wiry and tough in boots, jeans, and cowboy shirt. The current rector of St. Blaise Church, Reverend Tisdale, arrives along with Mrs. Tisdale, whose knee-length cardigan features eight reindeer coursing up the back from her right hip to her left shoulder. By this time Tisdale's predecessor, Worthington Pyle, has come skulking out of the kitchen with a look so bitterly Scroogelike that we all step nimbly out of his line of vision. He prowls through the rooms looking for our television set, muttering, "Kahlstrom's never seen MTV, it'll make a believer out of him." Philosopher Kahlstrom has evidently been delayed in the kitchen, doubtless snacking on the next tray of finger food.

I watch Rector Tisdale bravely take Father Pyle out of circulation by drawing him over to the window seat in the dining room and engaging him in conversation. I watch Mrs. Kahlstrom carry out this same sort of mission when her husband the philosopher finally appears. She steers him directly through the crowd to the coat closet and helps him on with his tight pullover and rubbers.

Crossing the room to say good-bye to them, I bounce off Benny Smith and realize I'm dizzy from drink.

"Steady, Leland."

"Sorry, Benny."

"You don't look so hot."

"Little bit looped is all."

"What's the matter with your eyes? They're runny."

"Little bit sad."

I speak unctuously to Mrs. Kahlstrom. "Thank you, *thank* you, Edna, for *leaving*. Time and again I've seen you sacrifice yourself for the rest of us by taking this doomsayer home before the party's over. Indeed, before he *destroys* the party with the deadly blight he spews wherever he goes." More surprising than the words I blurt is the fact that I'm not horrified to hear myself blurting them. It's the brandy. Whether the Kahlstroms are horrified, I don't pause to notice as I shut them outside.

I float through the living room feeling sad. God, I feel sad. If Bismarck weren't hundreds of miles away, I'd hop in the car and go and find Mary Sue Bloom. Have I fallen in love with her? What fascinates me about Mary Sue is her candor, her guileless honesty, her willingness to confide in me as no one else has ever done. Not even Sally. With Sally I always felt there was territory I'd never be allowed to explore, particularly after I learned of her infidelity. Coming as it did on the heels of Joey's death, her fling with Pug Patnode doubled my grief, shook my foundations, made me crazy.

Benny Smith steadies me, sets me on course toward the dining room. Approaching the two clergymen on the window seat, I feel strangely powerful. And taller than usual. Does booze do this, I wonder—make you seem taller? I look down at the pair of them sitting there with their hands on their knees like two little boys on a schoolroom bench. I preach to them, employing much the same stirring tone I use at Commencement when I introduce the valedictorian. "Father Tisdale," I say, "you are the most noble person in these rooms. You spare the rest of us the *ghastly* business of listening to the everlasting whining of Father Pyle, and may God *bless* you for that." Father Tisdale raises his hand to caution me, but I can't shut myself up. Brandy allows me to conclude this deliciously gratifying tirade with these words: "I know you're an affable sort of man, Father Tisdale, so I understand what a sacrifice it is for you to be sitting here in the corner taking in the morbid hallucinations of this decaying soul, instead of circulating among your friends. I don't say it's *quite* the same thing, at least not in degree, but your sacrifice puts me in mind of soldiers who throw themselves on grenades to spare their comrades in war."

Ungracefully, I turn on my heel and bump into Sally, who has come in through the kitchen. She's all in green tonight—an ankle-length, deep green skirt I haven't seen before, a pale green blouse, a jade necklace. Our greeting is cut short by Father Pyle, who rages, "Oh, ye of little faith, Edwards! MTV will make you believe in the perdition awaiting us in the days ahead."

I follow Sally into the other room, where Mother greets her in the overfervent manner she reserves for those few people who perplex her. Mother is always effusive with guests, but she seldom buries her face in their necks unless she's unsure of herself. Materialism and snobbishness, I dare say, are not qualities that first come to mind when you think of the host of "Lolly Speaking," and yet in 1972 when I introduced Sally to her as my bride-to-be, I know Mother was shocked to think of her beautiful oak-shaded house and furniture and linens and silver someday falling into the hands of the daughter of a second-rate barber with a weakness for high-ante poker. Sally's unfailingly kind and happy disposition weighed nothing in the Edwards scale of marriageability when compared to her several impediments. Besides her inferior background, Sally manifested no particular love or allegiance to Rookery State; indeed she'd never finished her degree. Furthermore, she'd been appointed to her position in the Owl Brook courthouse by the Owl County Commissioners, all seven of them being, at the time, registered Republicans. And worst of all, of course, she was divorcing her husband.

Not that any of this mattered to Sally and me. We were married on March 19, the Feast of St. Joseph, 1973. Winters we lived in Rookery's premier apartment house, the Badbattle Arms, whence Sally commuted to Owl Brook, and we spent the first of two idyllic summers together in the cabin on Owl Lake. We were married a little over a year when Joey was born.

Joey was the light of our lives. I swear no baby was ever doted upon so relentlessly by three adults as that boy of ours. So swiftly did Mother slip into the role of the jolly grandmother that you'd think she'd been rehearsing it all along. Everything about Joey amused her. He'd frown, belch, and inadvertently produce a bubble on his lips, and she'd laugh and laugh. He walked at ten months, which proved him to be, according to Mother, coordinated beyond his years. He said his first word, "radio," soon after, which made him the most remarkable prodigy ever born to mankind, she said. On his first birthday he said "Nanam," interpreted as "grandma," and of course this clinched it; the kid was a genius.

For me, in addition to the wonderment of this very miracle of new life that Sally and I had created, there was the excitement of seeing Joey effortlessly and instantly draw my wife and my mother together in friendship. We became a tight little unit, we three adults and the wee one, and not a day passes that I don't picture us proceeding down through the years like that, a tightly knit family of four, picnicking, gardening, traveling, Joey enriching every hour of every day for us, and no doubt transforming us, making us into people we might not even recognize as ourselves. Joey, who never reached his second birthday, would be twenty this year. I picture him as a college sophomore, majoring in (given his early utterance of "radio") modern languages and engaged in (given his coodination) athletics. Had Joey lived, I might even be a hockey fan.

Sally, in the crowded living room, disengages herself from Mother and tells me she'd love a stinger. I head back to the bottles where I find myself shoulder to shoulder once again with President Zastrow. I ask him if his wife wouldn't like to sit down; she's been standing like a bent scarecrow in front of the fire for what seems like hours. He says, "No, she's better off upright, it's her spine." Then he says something amazing—something to the effect that he'd like to prepare for his retirement by beginning to read books.

I laugh. It's a concept so sensible, I can't picture his doing it. "Ho, ho, O. F., what's come over you?"

Undaunted by my levity, he presses me for a recommendation, and so, after mixing Sally's drink, I lead him upstairs to my book-lined bedroom and draw down a James Thurber collection.

"Here, O. F., is exactly what you need, a lesson in lightening up."

Handling the book gingerly, holding it at arm's length and off to one side as though it might blow up in his face, he opens it at a random page and frowns at what he sees. He then turns to me and says, "I didn't know there weren't any pianos in Japan."

Oh dear, I should have known this book is beyond him. I offer him something less whimsical—*A River Runs Through It*— but no, he's intrigued by Thurber's misinformation. Descending the stairs, he conceals it under his crossed arms for fear (I'm sure) he'll be thought unprincipled for reading things other than memos.

The Hi-Rise delegation is crowded into the entryway, getting into their coats and mufflers, overshoes and mittens. With his long-billed cap pulled low, all that's visible of Johnny Hancock's face is his mouth and brown-stained chin. His mouth is asking Mother, around its wad of tobacco, if we have bats in our attic, while Hildegard reminds me that I must drive them home past the site of the chimney fire. Nettie Firehammer is helping the New Woman, who is looped, wind her endless pink scarf around her head and neck like a turban.

Worthington Pyle is mad at me. Gripping my arm as I try to get into my coat, he tells his fellow residents, seethingly, "Don't ride home with this intoxicated fish. He's stewed to the gills." There is a terrible power in the old rector's steely blue eyes, in the shaky hand he's clamped on my sleeve, and yet I don't regret calling him, to his face, a decaying soul, for his power to do psychic harm is equally terrible. He sucks all the hope out of any room he occupies, and it's high time somebody challenged him.

I'm sorry to see how seriously his fellow Hi-Risers take him. Do I actually *look* drunk? Their suspicious eyes go from me to Mother, to see her reaction to his warning—all eyes, that is, but Johnny's; he's checking the spit level in his pocket. Mother's reaction, after giving me a scrutinizing look, is a hearty laugh of dismissal as she retreats, wheezing, from the entryway. Sharing any small enclosed space with Nettie Firehammer's smoky stench always impairs her breathing.

Though unsteady when I bend over, I manage to get my over-shoes on, then my hat and gloves. Buttoning my overcoat, I follow the five of them out into the moonlight. The shortest day of the year has turned to night. Fearing icy patches and a broken hip, Hildegard clings to my left arm, Nettie to my right, and despite the fact that I have salted and chipped away every last slippery spot in preparation for this party, we proceed along the sidewalk like a cluster of invalids, prodding Johnny ahead of us and leading the New Woman by the hand. "I'm night-blind," the New Woman keeps saying, apparently unaware that her silky scarf has fallen over her eyes.

Worthington Pyle stands at his car, parked behind mine in the driveway, and calls, "Last warning, my friends, ride safely home with me or risk going through the windshield with that drunken lout."

"With you," declares Hildegard, deciding for the group as a whole, and tugging our ten-footed cluster in his direction.

It's a minute or more before Johnny will agree to give up the front seat to Hildegard, who suffers motion sickness riding in back; then it's a slow chore, this being a two-door compact, bending three stiff spines into the tiny backseat, and then low-ering Hildegard into the front seat and strapping her in.

The jaded old rector gets in behind the wheel and fumbles with his keys. Standing at his window, waiting for the engine to start, I am caught in the headlights of a dark, low sports car roaring around the corner and speeding down the street. From its open window a strong, young female voice calls out, "Hey, Dean Edwards, merry Christmas."

"Same to you!" I shout in return.

How gratifying to be wished well by an anonymous voice in the dark. A small but astonishing surge of joy comes into my heart, and fits itself between my grieving for Joey and my longing for a heart-to-heart talk with Mary Sue Bloom. It's a buoyancy caused not entirely by brandy, but also by the realization that this is, after all, a holy season, and I sense a cleansing purity in the frosty darkness. Am I not, all things considered, a fortunate man? Am I not, given my history of nagging illnesses, quite healthy for my age? Is my house not full of trusted friends? Has this not been, given the impediments I work against, the end of another successful semester in the dean's office? Will not President Zastrow's long and futile career come to an end at the close of next semester? Am I not the luckiest man in Minnesota to meet Richard Falcon in person, perhaps even have him as a houseguest? Am I not taller than usual?

The Reverend Worthington Pyle—far below me, it seems—opens his window an inch and asks, "What did you say?"

"Nothing."

"Yes you did. You shouted something."

"Oh, I did. I said merry Christmas to somebody going by."

"Bah! Shut your mouth."

I'm stunned for a moment, and then I laugh. My laughter hangs briefly in front of my face, a little moonlit cloud of dissolving steam. I'm immune to Father Pyle. I'm euphoric. It isn't entirely the brandy, as I've said; it's due in large part to the loveliness of the sub-zero night, so clear and bracing and still. Bells sound from some distant direction. Snow-covered houses stand about me like a calendar picture entitled *December*. Look at the Christmas trees in the windows. Look at the moonlit smoke standing straight up from the chimneys. Look at Mr. and Mrs. Cooper in their glassed-in, four-season porch across the street, sitting there in their accustomed chairs with their Franklin stove between them—an illustration by Norman Rockwell entitled "Serenity."

Worthington Pyle's starter moans, protesting the cold. The engine fires, then dies. It dies a second time, but sounds encouraging. Waiting there to make sure they get going, shivering a little, flapping my arms against my torso, I gaze at the Coopers sitting snugly behind their wall of glass, perfectly framed between the sturdy trunks of two ancient Norway pines standing like pillars in their snowy yard. Mr. Cooper, a muscular, ruddy-faced man of perhaps seventy years, a retired railroad engineer, sits to the left of the woodstove reading his newspaper. Mrs. Cooper, a grandmotherly teacher's aide at Paul Bunyan Elementary, sits in the rocking chair on the right, bending over her counted cross-stitch. The Coopers seldom close their drapes. They seldom socialize. Year after year, gently and apologetically, they decline our party invitation, preferring, it seems, to put themselves on display in this contented manner, as though to show the rest of humankind the way to a rewarding old age.

The engine starts. Mr. Cooper lowers his newspaper, his eyes caught by the rector's taillights. Mrs. Cooper looks out as well. The Reverend Pyle, for some reason, floors the accelerator as he shifts gears, and the car shoots backward across the street and bounces up onto the bank of plowed snow at the edge of the Coopers' yard. The Coopers sit forward, alarmed. The engine, still getting too much gas, whines at a higher pitch as the wheels spin in the snowbank. The Coopers step forward to their wall of floor-length windows, shading their view from the interior light. Spinning down through the snow, the wheels find traction and propel the car backward across the yard, but a bit slower now, the four or five inches of level snow retarding its progress. I run after it, crossing the street, waving my arms and shouting, "Take your foot off the gas!" I see violent movement in the car—arms flying, heads bumping—and I hear the muffled screaming and shouting of all five of its occupants. The Coopers have backed away from their wall of glass; Mr. Cooper has dropped his newspaper and picked up a stick of firewood, holding it high, like a weapon, helpless to stop the car from picking up speed as it passes over the bare ground between the pine trees, and Mrs. Cooper covers her face with her cross-stitch and I cover mine with my hands as the car crashes into their parlor.

Not far in. Their brick foundation, which prevents all but the back bumper from extending into the room, saves the Coopers from being pinned against the wall, but they are sprayed by glass falling like a sheet of water at their feet and engulfed by exhaust fumes spewing from the tailpipe at floor level. I fling open the passenger door to see why the engine is still racing and discover that the accelerator can't be raised because Hildegard Lubovich, rigid with panic, has planted her left foot firmly down on Pyle's right foot. "Turn off the ignition," I shout, but Pyle is too busy defending himself against Hildegard's clawing attack to his face to hear what I'm saying. The engine slows as I roughly release Hildegard's seat belt and pull her out of the car. Before liberating those in the backseat, I reach across to the steering column and switch off the ignition. I am cursed by the Reverend Pyle, and I hear cursing as well from Mr. Cooper, who stands with his wife, above us, shivering, and up to his ankles in glass.

All four passengers are able to stand up. Nettie Firehammer complains of pain in her chest, shoulders, neck and head. Hildegard is sobbing convulsively. I remove Johnny Hancock's hands from the front and back of the New Woman, who leans drunkenly against a tree. The old rector remains cursing behind the wheel. Our party guests come streaming across the street in the moonlight. Gloria and Angelo Corelli step through the open wall of the parlor, offering solace to the Coopers. Someone puts Hildegard in a car and drives off with her. Someone else takes the New Woman off my hands. "I've called the authorities, Dean," calls Viola Trisco from our front stoop.

Having helped Benny Smith lead the whiplashed and whimpering Nettie Firehammer to his car and seen them off in the direction of the hospital, I go back and stand beside Father Pyle's open window for a minute, waiting for the police, intending to explain to them that this wasn't a case of the driver's recklessness but the involuntary panic of one of his passengers. However, his damn-this and damn-that and his "Damn you to perdition, Leland Edwards" contain more hatred than I can bear, and I leave him to defend himself.

Growing agitated, I cross the street and see that Sally's van is gone. My heart grows heavy again. I change directions, proceeding along Sawyer Street in the moonlight and realizing that Sally is the only party guest I can talk to in my shuddering, trembling condition. In my mind's eye, the accident I've just witnessed keeps being replaced by my collision with the Black and White Taxi in November of 1975.

Mother and I were on our way to KRKU, with Joey standing between us on the front seat. The streets were slick with freezing rain. Sally, having left for work at 7:00 A.M., had phoned from Owl Brook to say the roads were treacherous and I mustn't drive anywhere until the ice thawed. I promised I wouldn't. I had no class until afternoon, no reason to venture out. With Joey playing at my feet, I was sitting in our kitchenette sipping coffee and correcting a stack of student papers when Mother called to say she didn't trust herself in her big car on ice and would I please give her a ride downtown. Joey and I were in the car and creeping along Sawyer before I realized I was breaking a promise to my wife—even though I hadn't for a moment forgotten her warning. Who can understand this? Soldiers in the trenches? Vassals to the king? For no one else, probably not even for Sally herself, would I have gone out and risked our lives in the car that morning, and yet because I'd been doing my mother's bidding for nearly forty years, her summons was somehow of a higher order than my promise to Sally. Would I have obliged her had I been fully aware of what I was doing? I don't know.

Mother almost fell on the steps coming out the door, and I, hurrying to her aid, went down on the sidewalk front first, and it seemed a full minute before I could get air into my lungs again.

Delayed thus by my fall and the need to keep our speed under ten miles an hour, Mother was certain to be late for her show; yet she didn't urge me to step on it. She sat there chattering away, her white-knuckled right hand gripping the door handle while, with her left, she patted the red cover of a fondue cookbook in her lap.

Carefully braking and hugging the right curb, I was following the Phoenix Avenue curve downhill to the First Street Bridge when one of the old Black and White Taxis spun out of control on its way up. Although it was traveling slightly faster than we were, and sideways at that, the impact when I hit it broadside didn't seem all that jolting—neither Mother nor I was hurt—but this was before mandatory car seats for little children, and Joey was dashed against the windshield and died instantly.

Nearly twenty years, O Lord, haven't assuaged the misery. I sink so low whenever I remember. Grant me at least a portion of the cheer I felt only minutes ago. Better yet, grant me Sally. I need to convey my crummy state to Sally, the only person I've ever allowed to know my weaker self.

Passing under a streetlight, I hear Angelo call after me, "Hey, Leland, where you going?" I veer left, drifting out of the light and down a side street, pretending not to hear him. Angelo's a dear friend, but not for all seasons. His defect is his chronic happiness. When you're overcome by the pall of Christmas as well as the shock of a car accident, the last thing you want is cheery prattle and jingle bells. It's Sally I need, my former wife, former love, former one true friend.

By the time I've circled the block, I find a squad car standing in front of the Coopers' house. Two men, a patrolman and I think Rector Tisdale, appear to be trying to coax Father Pyle out from behind the wheel of his Colt. The lights are out in the Coopers' parlor; the door is closed to the rest of their house. A dim flame flickers in the little window of their Franklin stove.

I return to our party. Although a number of guests have left, there's still enough going on in the living room to keep Mother occupied. She's on the couch visiting with Mrs. Tisdale and Mrs. Cooper, the latter throwing her hands in the air as she describes the shock of seeing the car backing into her parlor. Her husband the former railroader is standing with Bud Trisco at the liquor table, listening respectfully to President Zastrow expounding, perhaps, on the woeful lack of pianos in Japan. Angelo follows me into the kitchen to say that Sally tried to reach me by phone.

Ah.

Sitting down in the breakfast nook, I write a check for Helen Walker, who interrupts her work at the dishwasher to listen to my account of the accident. I instruct her to tell Mother I'm going to the hospital to follow up on Nettie Firehammer's whiplash injury. Then I leave by the back door and head for the Hi-Rise.

"Sally, I've said this before . . ."

"I know. Dozens of times." She chuckles quietly in the dark. "I told you a single is the only size that will fit these rooms." She's referring to this narrow bed in which we've made fast work of dispelling my loneliness.

"But you've had married couples living here."

"The bedrooms are bigger on the second floor."

"What about the Seversons? We used to visit them up here on the top floor."

"The Seversons got divorced shortly after moving in, remember? They took separate units."

"I can see why. I'd hate to spend my declining years restricted to sixteen inches of mattress."

"No, it had to do with finances." She lays her head on my shoulder and nuzzles into my neck—our falling asleep position from twenty years ago. "Each of them was better off drawing their retirement as single people. See, it happens sometimes, if you and your spouse both worked for most of your married life, then you . . . then you . . ."

I've always envied the instantaneous quality of Sally's sleep. And its depth. Of course I can't allow myself to fall asleep here, but at least I can dream for a few minutes. Before rising and putting on my clothes, I lie here remembering, as usual, a few happy scenes from our marriage. This always requires an act of will on my part, for in order to replay my life from twenty years ago, I have to get past the hulking figure of Pug Patnode who stands like a sentry at the end of our happy life together. I call to mind those two Christmas trips to Nebraska with Mother when Sally hit it off so well with all my cousins. Those two idyllic summers we spent on Owl Lake. Tonight, however, something is missing from these mental pictures. They've lost something of their nostalgic punch. I sense another figure looking at them with me and telling me, "Get over it, Leland."

Mary Sue Bloom.

Theodore ("Pug") Patnode, my predecessor in the dean's office, was a directionless blowhard in possession of the qualities Zastrow most admired in an administrator. He was loud, large, overconfident, and he came from industry. He'd arrived on campus when businesses were trimming their nonessential labor force, and "coming from industry" was a phrase applied to a good many people seeking refuge in higher education in those days, competing for the secure if underpaid positions on even the most remote and undistinguished campuses. Surely a dean drawn from business, reasoned our illogical president, would set the college on a businesslike course.

Dean Patnode's industry had been the manufacture of textbooks. His specialty was glue. Having developed a miracle compound that improved the adhesives used in bookbinding, he came to us with a reputation as a creative genius in the field of chemistry. While not understanding the first thing about teaching or learning or any other aspect of campus life, but based simply on his renown as a gluemaster, he was granted instant tenure along with an honorary Elks' membership and unlimited use of the college car. He was young for a dean, in his middle thirties. At first, I have to admit, he seemed like the quintessential administrator. He was articulate, handsome, and sociable, and he seemed actually to enjoy his work. People said he looked like a dressed-up Paul Bunyan; he had a reddish beard, smoked a smelly pipe, and wore double-breasted blazers with gold buttons. His voice was a resounding baritone; when he spoke to the student body, it rang like a deep bell, and when he sang in the Methodist church, I was told, those around him turned timid and shut up. His wife, Maisie, was a nurse. Their little daughter, Molly, had braided blond hair and mild mental retardation.

I don't say Pug Patnode left no improvements behind. He did streamline Administration Row by firing a couple of useless functionaries, and he began the series of monthly convocations that survives to this day. He went on the radio with Mother every few weeks to talk in large, idealistic terms about higher education, and in no time at all he had as much campus-wide respect as anyone in history—except my father of course, who'd been canonized by a previous generation. I recall Mother saying, during his first couple of years on campus, that she wished my father had lived to see the magic worked by Pug Patnode.

Unless you believed untraceable rumors, you wondered what had made him expendable in the book trade. One of the rumors implied that Pug was a philanderer and he drank too much. Another said that his bookbinding glue hadn't stood the test of time, and that a whole generation of textbooks had gone on the market with spines susceptible to fracture. A third claimed that he and his wife were first cousins. The speculations about his glue were unprovable in Rookery, and I suspect the rumor about their consanguinity was based on the mild retardation of their little daughter, but the things we heard about his dissolute behavior turned out to be accurate. Pug was a rake.

Mrs. Patnode was a large, strong woman with tightly curled hair, dark eyes, and a small, reedy voice she didn't use very often because Pug did most of the talking. At our Christmas parties in those years you'd find Maisie in a corner softly discussing diabetes or pinkeye with one or two other guests, while at the center of the room her husband's commanding voice was drawing attention to his reckless opinions, his memorized passages from the Founding Fathers, his scatological jokes.

"Leland, my good fellow, what's the white stuff in chicken shit?"

"Beats me, Pug."

"Why, it's chicken shit!" He'd laugh uproariously at his punch lines while casting laugh-soliciting expressions at everyone else in the room.

"Leland, answer me this. Who was known as 'the Master Builder of the Constitution'? I suppose you think it was George Washington."

"That would be James Madison, Pug."

"Madison, Jesus! It was Thomas Jefferson!"

Time after time, Pug would challenge me like this, taking my ignorance for granted and forgetting that American history had been my father's discipline and therefore my lifelong hobby. He was wrong at least half the time. Embarrassed for him, I refrained from correcting him. I didn't bother, on this occasion for example, to point out that James Madison had earned the title of Master Builder because he (along with Alexander Hamilton, and more clearly than Thomas Jefferson) had seen the need for a complete overhaul of our system of government. Pug's pretentions in the field of history, so weak as to be laughable among our historians, was motivated by his fear of being thought of as a narrow-minded scientist. Of that I'm certain. But I have no idea why I should have become his favorite target for these darts of historical trivia. I was reminded of junior high school, when certain bullies used to single me out for ridicule because of my superior grades.

Later, after I married Sally, I saw Pug's attitude change. He softened toward me, as though Sally somehow verified my worthiness as an interesting human being. He stopped trying to catch me out in historical mistakes. He deferred to me at faculty meetings. We went fishing together. I have to admit I was flattered by his friendship. With our wives, who were fond of each other, we went to basketball games. I learned too late that it was Sally, not I, he found interesting.

Mother claims to have been suspicious from the start, but I didn't have a clue. It seemed only natural that a caretaker like Sally should volunteer to teach Molly how to read, and that when Maisie took a two-month leave from Mercy Hospital to nurse her widowed father after his heart attack in Arizona, Sally should press on with her tutorial, sometimes spending most of a Saturday afternoon at the Patnodes' cabin in the tamarack swamp in the northwest corner of the county, and coming home tired and a bit disheveled. I assumed merely that she was battling a particularly stubborn case of retardation. I guess I've always been too innocent for my own good.

Like Sally's brother Otto, that bossy companion of my boyhood, Pug Patnode was forever embarking on some leisure-time project too strenuous, in my opinion, to enjoy. Out for a day in my canoe, he'd insist that we portage impossible distances in order to fish secluded lakes and streams I knew were all but fishless. And, like Otto, he was careless. While I crept stealthily along riverbanks with my flyrod, he'd go slogging downstream in hipboots and frighten off any trout that might have taken an interest in our bait.

Let Pug's cabin in the woods stand for exactly this kind of unthinking, overreaching effort. From the day he came to town, he dreamed of building a cabin in the wilderness, and he was forever studying survey maps at the courthouse, searching for the most remote acre of tax-forfeit land in Rookery County. When he finally found it and bought it—a hump of dry ground in the middle of a tamarack swamp twenty-five miles northwest of town—there was no way to get his pickup into the site, and we had to load his tools in a wheelbarrow and push it along a soggy path through the trees. Some of the lumber we sawed on-site from the tamaracks, but the specialized pieces, the braces, the doorframes, the rafters—we carried in on our shoulders.

"Get somebody with a dozer, Pug, and have him build you a road," I said one day, lying exhausted under a tree. We'd just carried in the last of the pressure-treated plywood for an enormous deck.

"Are you nuts?" he asked, strapping on his carpenter's apron. "A road, for God's sake—what do I want with a road?"

"You mean, what do *I* want with a road." I was thinking of the shingles yet to be carted in. Also the chimney blocks and the window frames. "I'm exhausted, Pug."

"Where's my level? You seen my level?"

"I'm not going to be your beast of burden anymore, Pug." Ignoring my declaration, he switched on his power saw and zipped through a board. With the sound of the saw dying in the forest, I added, "Anyhow, I can't see a sociable guy like you sitting out here beyond all human contact. Who's going to want to come slogging through these woods to see you?"

"Maybe I don't plan to be seen, Leland. A dean needs a hideaway."

"Why?"

I don't recall his answer. Now, of course, in my tenth year as dean, I see the need for a sanctuary, a place to clear one's mind of campus clutter. But Pug's methods of clearing his mind turned out to be shocking. Pug brought women, one after another, to this cabin I'd helped him build, and they spent the night. Two of the women were faculty wives. Three or four were professors. In what order, and why, they fell under the spell of this abominable lecher has been the subject of gossip ever since he left town. Some say Josie Travers was first. Josie was the wife of our government professor. Others say it was Phyllis Cameron, head of the Art Department and niece-by-marriage of Hildegard Lubovich. Everyone knows who was last. Sally, my wife, was last.

WINTER BREAK

Nebraska, though snowless, wears its wizened, wintry look—the unvarying miles of frosty russet fields and hillocks broken here and there by the sudden neon of fast-food shops along the freeway. Mother wakes from a short doze as we pass a treeless housing development, a sprawling strip mall, an exit sign into Omaha.

"It still seems strange not stopping here, doesn't it, Leland?"

"It does."

"Next year we really should. After all, he *is* your first cousin."

"You said that last year."

She laughs. "But next year we'll do it. Aren't you a tiny bit curious to see him?"

"Not in the least."

"And have a look at that skinny little wife of his? And see what's become of those fat little babies?"

"We know what's become of them. They're fat little husbands and fathers."

This, too, amuses her. "Now, Leland, don't be contrary."

"Sorry, I have a headache."

"Your glasses."

"Glasses! I don't wear glasses."

"You're overdue for a checkup."

"No, it's driving into the sun all day."

We've been making this annual trip since I was a boy. Until eight or ten years ago, we always spent Christmas Eve in Omaha with my father's family, and then early on Christmas morning set out for the O'Kelly farm near Grimsby where Mother grew up. However, now that Aunt Cora and Uncle Herbert are dead, there's nobody left in Omaha but my cousin Wesley and his wife and twin sons. Cousin Wesley doesn't—nor did he ever—have any interest in seeing us.

Mother examines her face in her sun-visor mirror. "Wrath of God," she sighs, disapproving of it, "but I'm too tired to fix it." She lowers her seat to a reclining position. In a minute she's sleeping again.

Christmas Eve with my father's people in Omaha, during my boyhood, was invariably stiff and unfestive, whereas we always spent a jolly Christmas Day at the O'Kelly farm. Not that the Edwardses were unkind or inhospitable. It's only that the O'Kellys, by nature, were more spontaneous and high-spirited. The minute we entered the farmhouse, we heard stories so uproarious they must have been invented, though they usually began or ended with the phrase, "Swear to God." The laughter and tall tales continued through dinner and into the evening as more aunts and uncles and cousins came pouring through the house to greet us. Any given Christmas, we probably saw thirty-five O'Kellys.

A Christmas *Eve* conversation, on the other hand, followed a serious, predictable line, beginning with the unreliability of the weather and leading on through the deteriorating condition of their ailing friends and neighbors and automobiles. As a boy, I considered this talk painfully dull, but over the years I learned to take a certain pleasure in the constancy of it—the way you will sometimes come to appreciate a cheerless old hymn in church simply because it's so familiar. I suppose, as we age, any sign of permanence consoles us, no matter if it bores us besides.

Isn't it curious, therefore, that despite the high colors of the O'Kelly Christmases, the Edwards family is more clearly etched in my boyhood memories? Grandfather Edwards, a small fragile man with a mustache and a mottled face, was made to seem even smaller by the engulfing overstuffed chair he always sat in. "Come, Leland, we'll read," he used to declare before dinner, and I would climb onto his lap and be read to from a book of moralizing tales about a virtuous boy named Henry. Grandmother Edwards, humbly deflecting all credit or praise, would serve the dinner for eight, and then take her place at the foot of the table where she silently nibbled and smiled at me whenever our eyes met.

Aunt Cora was my father's younger sister. She lived on the other side of Omaha with her husband Herbert and their son Wesley. Aunt Cora operated a beauty salon in her living room and smelled of permanent goo. Uncle Herbert was a butcher, a silent man with nine fingers and a full head of red hair. Cousin Wesley, two years older than I, was never any fun. Throughout his teens, he fancied himself a superb baseball pitcher and found me useful as a receiver of his fastball, which numbed my hand up to the elbow. His father called him "Hotshot." Wesley is retired now, after forty years of driving a delivery truck for a lumberyard.

I remember how Grandmother Edwards's smile, never quite joyous, turned very sad on the Christmas when my father was stationed in California and waiting to be shipped out to the war in the South Pacific. I recall the phonograph record he sent home to his parents that winter. *Don't open without Lolly and Leland present,* he'd printed on the envelope, but Cousin Wesley was discovered opening it before we got there. He was reprimanded by his parents and prevented from putting it on the Victrola, and when Mother and I arrived, he was still pleading his innocence—which I found easier to accept than his parents did, for neither Uncle Herbert nor Aunt Cora would admit even to themselves what I knew: their eleven-year-old hotshot hadn't yet learned to read.

It was unlike any phonograph record I'd ever seen—small, thin, bendable, nearly transparent, with grooves on only one side. It had a white and blue label on which

U.S.O.

SAN FRANCISCO

was smudgily printed. Grandfather set it on the spindle, lowered the needle, and we were astonished to hear my father's voice. He was singing, *a cappella*, "I'll Be Home for Christmas."

Mother laughed and wept. Grandmother only wept. I felt supremely gratified and far superior to Wesley, for not only did his father have no singing voice, he'd also been rejected as physically unfit for the armed forces, having lost his trigger finger in a meat slicer. We played the record over and over, far into the night.

The next year a glimmer of joy appeared in Grandmother Edwards's smile; the war was over and my father was safely home. But four years after that the smile turned severely sad again, and it remained that way for the rest of her life, for by that time my father had been struck dead by lightning.

My own sorrow, though secret, was devastating. Had I allowed my feelings to be touched by the open air, perhaps they would have evaporated, but Mother made it clear from the start that while a widow might indulge herself in an ongoing sort of lament, her fourteen-year-old son must quickly cast his grief aside and console her with a happy face. Thus my sadness, mostly unexpressed, lingered like a low-grade fever. Fortunately, my father had left me a legacy of absorbing hobbies—fishing, coin-collecting, reading history, playing the piano—and these I pursued with a kind of mad intensity; yet I could never quite throw off the gloom I felt whenever it struck me that I must go on living in a world bereft of this dear man.

It's too bad that a tragedy of that magnitude was required to bring me into closer union with my paternal grandparents, but that's what happened. I acquired an affinity for—indeed I found myself imitating—the Edwards reticence, their measured, mournful ways. True, I still enjoyed Christmas Day on the O'Kelly ranch, but every December I found myself looking forward with the same degree, if not the same type, of eagerness to Christmas Eve in Omaha, where my father's memory was held in sacred trust.

When, with time, my memories of him began to fade, my melancholy did not. It was compounded, in fact, by guilt. Why hadn't I written down examples of my father's wisdom? Why, without the help of photos, could I not bring his face clearly to mind? I wanted to be able to dwell on his life the way they did in Omaha. No Edwards ever seemed to tire of my inquiries. Were there snapshots of my father I hadn't seen? How big were the fish he'd caught in the Missouri River when he was my age? What were his favorite piano pieces? Told and repeated every Christmas, the facts of my father's days on earth became as familiar to me as the Gospels, and as holy.

And as intimidating. So intensely reverent was the Edwards form of devotion that I began to feel extremely unworthy. In retrospect, of course, I see that my common sense was telling me to quit probing my wound and get on with my life, but to do so then would have seemed a kind of betrayal.

It took the upheaval of a moving day to shake me out of this state of unhealthy nostalgia. I was nineteen or twenty when my grandparents decided to leave their house in Omaha and take a new suburban apartment. In planning to be packed and moved by Christmas Eve, they'd overestimated their endurance, with no idea of how much time it takes to dig the accumulation of a lifetime out of the corners of the attic and closets and little storerooms under the stairs. When Mother and I arrived around noon, we found Grandfather exhausted and deeply asleep in his overstuffed chair and Grandmother full of tearful apologies. The house was in disarray—curtains down, cupboards half empty, dozens of half-packed boxes scattered through the rooms. Aunt Cora was upstairs emptying the linen closet. Soon, Wesley and Uncle Herbert returned for another pickup load and we all pitched in.

Working into the night, we moved about half their belongings, including beds, to the apartment before we all wore out. Christmas Eve dinner was take-out Chinese, eaten around midnight in a new dining nook that smelled of fresh drywall. We were sipping tea, dunking Aunt Cora's holiday cookies, and feeling dislocated when I brought out the celluloid record of my father's voice. Earlier, while helping Grandmother clear out the attic, I'd come across it in a hatbox of mementos. I put it on the turntable. The sound was amazingly clear. So fresh and melodious was my father's voice that he seemed to be present in the room. "I'll be home for Christmas," he sang, and we sat there enchanted. I played it a second time, and we exchanged a few reverent remarks. I played it a third time, and each of us gazed off in a private direction, calling up private memories. Even Cousin Wesley seemed moved.

I switched it off then, and a curious conversation ensued. It began with Grandfather, who declared, "Typical of that boy not to say right out that he was coming home."

"Yes, that was his sweet way," Aunt Cora said of her brother. "Tell us in a song like that. And the next thing there he was."

"Typical," Grandfather repeated with a growl, as though the memory irked him. "Surprise you like that. Never say it straight out."

Uncle Herbert quietly agreed. "Just give us that one clue."

"But he didn't—" began Grandmother, her memory evidently clearer than theirs, but she wasn't given a chance to finish. Aunt Cora was recalling the gifts he'd brought from Hawaii:

"To this day I keep the Pearl Harbor pillow on the daybed. And, Wesley, don't you still carry that jackknife?"

Cousin Wesley said he did.

Aunt Cora turned to Mother. "Lolly, you must've been the most surprised of all when he showed up. You and Leland."

Mother and I exchanged a look, and before either of us could point out that they had their Christmas memories mixed up, Aunt Cora was going on:

"Or did you and Leland know ahead of time and not tell us?"

"Seems like yesterday," mused Uncle Herbert.

"I thought he'd be in uniform," said Wesley accusingly, "but he wasn't."

Grandmother timidly made another attempt. "I don't think he came home that Christmas. . . ."

And Mother came to her aid. "It was the following year he brought the things from Hawaii."

Grandfather declared both of them mistaken. First the record appeared, then my father himself, the next day. Wesley and his parents all nodded their support.

"Oh, so that's how it was," said Grandmother, and I watched a little smile spread across her face as she allowed herself to believe this erroneous version. It made such a pleasing story after all.

I spoke up then, pointing out that the song wasn't about actually coming home for Christmas, only dreaming about it. Mother, too, persisted, repeating the facts—the recording one Christmas, his homecoming the next.

None of this made the least impression. With Grandmother forsaking the truth and going over to the other side, we were outnumbered five to two. There were a few moments of strain, a kind of silent standoff, before Mother laughed and said, "Well, what's the difference?—at least we have his voice. Would you play it again, Leland?"

And so we listened once more, all of us sitting there in a kind of stupor of satisfaction: Grandfather, Uncle Herbert, Aunt Cora, and Wesley happily picturing the day they'd invented; Grandmother putting their invention together, piece by piece, in her imagination; Mother not caring what they thought, only relishing the sound of the voice preserved so fortuitously by the U.S.O., San Francisco.

And I, of course, was relieved beyond measure to watch a pleasing myth replace the truth, for I saw how trivial were the memories I'd been trying so hard to preserve. Memories, fading and flawed, were all they had in Omaha, while I had my father's fishing tackle, his coin collection, his library, his sheet music. I lived in his house. I had his knack for catching fish. I didn't have his singing voice, but I had his talent at the piano. I had his smile, I was told by those who knew him. I had his way of walking, said Mother, with my left foot turned out a little. I knew from photographs that I had his hairline and eyes. And I had this family of his, who, I sensed, would go on worshiping his memory over the years, preserving it, in their way, from oblivion, while I went ahead and lived the life he lost.

We drive the last seventy miles in darkness. It was primarily for the purpose of making this trip more comfortable that we bought the most luxurious road car on the market, yet by the time we pull into the farmyard, Mother is worn out and wheezing. My rump is numb, my neck aches. We roll to a stop between a Jeep and a pickup, and we just sit there, both of us momentarily stunned to be at a standstill, neither of us feeling quite equal to the high spirits we're sure to encounter in the house. The glare of the yard light falls through the windshield and across our laps.

"We should've got rooms in Grimsby for the night," says Mother.

"We still can."

"No, it's too late now." For the kitchen door is thrown open and a head peers out. It looks like my cousin Ron O'Kelly.

"Is Ron's new wife named Jerry or Judy?" I ask. Ordinarily we rehearse the names of the new in-laws as we travel, as well as the recent offspring, but today Mother kept dropping off to sleep.

"Lucy," she wheezes. "She's a nurse."

"Are you sure? I thought it started with 'J.'"

"Lucy," she insists.

O'Kellys come streaming across the frozen grass to welcome us, Cousin Ron in the lead. He carries a bundled infant in the crook of his arm.

"And what did they name their baby?"

She utters a phlegmy laugh. "Lord, I forgot they had one. Was it a boy or girl?"

"Boy, I think. A really odd name."

"Maybe not odd in her culture." By which she means Lucy is African-American.

O'Kellys surround the car, everyone talking, nobody listening. Cousin Ron, shifting the infant to his other arm, opens Mother's door, leans in, kisses her, and helps her to her feet. Cousin Maylene roughly nudges Ron aside, embraces Mother, then stands back to allow Uncle Bill, the patriarch, to receive her. Uncle Bill, a brawny, bossy man, is the last survivor of Mother's siblings. Like his daughter Maylene, he wasn't blessed with the full quota of O'Kelly affability, and he's become even more ungiving in his old age, as though surviving his several brothers and coming into sole possession of 880 acres of rich Nebraska bottomland compels him to act the part of the exalted squire. But at least he's solicitous of Mother. Turning abruptly away from me after a brief handshake, he helps Mother across the grass.

I follow, accompanied by Cousin Ron and his baby; by Cousin Maylene and her silent husband Detlef and their twin teenage sons; and by Cousin George with his wife Claudette and their grown-up son and daughter, Scott and Georgia, and their eight-year-old girl named Bridget.

I ask, "What's the baby's name, Ron?"

"How could you forget?" his sister Maylene asks me. "Think where Lucy came from." Maylene's my loudmouth cousin, habitually butting in.

"Michigan O'Kelly?" I propose, knowing I'm wrong.

"No, silly. The city."

"St. Clare Shores? It isn't Clare, I know that."

"Oh, come on, one more guess."

Then it comes to me. "Detroit."

"Detroit William O'Kelly," says Ron proudly.

Aunt Mary, the patriarch's warmhearted and imperturbable wife, is setting out snacks on the kitchen table. Her kiss tastes of buttery cookie dough and she smells like cinnamon. Uncle Bill went three hundred miles to find this wife of his, for Mary was a Callahan from Scotts Bluff. Her bachelor brother, Jack Callahan, a reticent, agreeable man who works the fields under Uncle Bill's supervision, gives me an arm-squeeze, a punch to the shoulder, and a handshake. "Howdy, Leland," he drawls. "What do you know about Savonarola?"

"Savonarola? Burned at the stake in Florence, if I'm not mistaken."

"Unfairly, wouldn't you say?"

"I've no idea, Uncle Jack." Though technically no relation of ours, we've been calling him Uncle Jack ever since 1950 when he moved into the hired-man's mobile home hidden in the oak and willow of the windbreak. He haunts the Grimsby Public Library. "Well, from what I've been reading," he says, and goes on to defend the martyred reformer while eight-year-old Bridget tugs at my pant leg, telling me, "I'm in gifted, I'm in gifted."

George and Claudette's daughter Georgia, my prettiest cousin-once-removed, tells me she's enrolled in a genealogy class at Kansas State and wants to know if Mother and I will help her with the names missing from her family tree. I assure her we will. Meanwhile her brother Scott, a high-school teacher in Lincoln, wants to know if college teaching might be a worthwhile aspiration—are there openings in sociology? No, it's a hopeless job market, I frankly tell him. Their little sister keeps at me, shouting, "I'm in gifted."

Ron's wife Lucy enters the kitchen from another room, her dusky African face a startling sight among all these pale Irish complexions. We didn't meet her last Christmas, because she and Ron were on their honeymoon. She's evidently one of those rare women unconcerned about not being quite so svelte as those around her; on the contrary, she gives the impression of wearing the few extra pounds under her burgundy sweatsuit with pride. As Ron introduces us, she gives me a radiant smile, then darts over to Mother, sensing her fatigue, and leads her to a chair in the parlor.

"I'm in gifted," repeats the little girl, speaking of her accelerated progress through the third grade. Scott says if it isn't college teaching, then it will be politics—do I know anyone in Washington? Uncle Jack, meanwhile, keeps insisting that Savonarola was on the right track in arousing the faithful against corruption among the clergy.

This, then, is a typical gathering at the farm; cousins and cousins-in-law vying for everyone's attention, voices raised in argument, lowered in gossip; Uncle Jack spouting esoteric knowledge gained from his avid but directionless reading; Uncle Bill loudly bemoaning the price of corn; Maylene, less agreeable and more like her father as she ages, loudly ordering her husband Detlef around, telling him where to sit and when to speak—all of this against the background buzz of talk in other rooms. To think that Mother grew up in this welter of hit-and-miss communication. No wonder she craves more talk than I provide.

But she doesn't crave it tonight. When I finally manage to move through the kitchen and into the parlor, she's not there. I find her upstairs in the guest room, where Lucy has unpacked her bag, hung up her clothes, laid out her various nighttime medicines, and put her to bed. Descending the stairs with me, Lucy says she's alarmed by Mother's general weakness, her labored breathing, her swollen ankles. If she's no better tomorrow, she ought to see a doctor. Lucy's alarm I find alarming, of course, because she's a nurse.

But a bit later, returning to the guest room and looking in on her, we find her deep in a placid sleep. Bending down to judge her breathing—as I've done how many hundreds of times in the past several years?—I hear only a bronchial scrape and whistle brief as a robin's good-night chirp.

A hush momentarily falls over the gathering when we return downstairs. She's better, Lucy tells them, and their voices rise to a noisier level than before.

My room, as in years past, is in Grimsby, in Cousin George's house. Pleading exhaustion, I ask George and Claudette if I might drive myself there and let myself in, but Claudette insists on taking me home in the Jeep; she must get her gifted third-grader home to bed. Lucy, who also lives in town, says she'll go with us; Baby Detroit is wailing with hunger. Ron will drive George home later in the pickup. Scott has his own car. Georgia will stay with her grandparents on the farm tonight.

Bridget tucks herself between her mother and me in the front seat and immediately falls asleep. Lucy gets in back with the baby. Claudette confesses, over the rumble of the gravel road, that the older she gets the sooner she tires of her in-laws' chatter. Claudette isn't Irish, but of some stoical northern-European stock. Finnish, I think. "With all their talk," she tells me, "you'd think they'd get to the bottom of things."

"What do you mean, the bottom of things?"

"Jack's cancer, for example."

"Uncle Jack has cancer?" I'm shocked; he looks so vigorous.

"Prostate. And Aunt Mary has heart trouble."

"Really? But she's the picture of health."

Lucy speaks up from the dark backseat, where sucking noises tell me she's breastfeeding Detroit. "Mary's supposed to lose twenty pounds. She was in the hospital with circulation trouble in October. I wanted to write and tell Lolly, but Mary said not to." She laughs. "I'm not about to go against my brand-new mother-in-law."

"Oh, but you should've. You've no idea how you people are on Mother's mind from one Christmas to the next."

"Well, I might have, if it would've been just Mary. But if she told Bill that I'd gone behind her back, there'd a been hell to pay. Bill can be so *cross* sometimes."

"Yes," I agree. "He's always been my one antagonistic uncle."

"Just be glad he's not your father-in-law."

It's a cold night. Clouds have dimmed the moon. We ride along in silence for a time, until I can't help asking Lucy, "Is Uncle Bill a racist?"

"No," Claudette answers for her. "He's equally hard on all of us."

Lucy concurs. "Oh, I'm sure he was shocked when Ron brought me into the family, but shock is a far cry from hostility. Actually I don't think it's been easy for him, what with some of his farmer friends being so Afro-phobic."

"Did you know Maylene and Detlef are in counseling?" asks Claudette, getting back down to the bottom of things.

"What for?" I ask.

"Rocky marriage."

"They're a bad match," says Lucy. "Mrs. Aggressive married to Mr. Passive-aggressive."

"And those spooky twins of theirs?" I ask. "Where did they disappear to?"

"God knows," says Lucy. "You can tell what those twins are up to by looking in their eyes."

"Why? What are they up to?"

"Drugs."

A mile or two of silence again, during which I wonder if I'm witnessing the disintegration of a family—or if the O'Kelly clan has weathered problems of this magnitude in the past without my being aware of them. I suppose it's likely they have. Apparently only now, pushing sixty, do I qualify as a confidant—at least in the eyes of these in-laws. The O'Kellys themselves have always been too busy talking to tell me anything important.

At the outskirts of town Claudette asks, "How's the college these days? You're still dean?"

"Going on ten years."

"It must suit you."

"It doesn't, actually. I'd rather be teaching."

"So why don't you?"

"I would, if we had a competent president."

Lucy speaks up. "You mean you're covering for a dolt?"

"It feels like that, most of the time."

"That's the pits. I was assistant to a supervising nurse like that in Detroit. Bad decisions. Bad morale. It's no fun having to come along behind somebody, righting her wrongs, but if I didn't keep at it, it seemed like the whole unit would collapse."

"Precisely." I want to turn and look at this woman with such a clear understanding of my predicament, but the baby's still sucking. "Obviously you did leave though."

"Left to get married."

"And the unit collapsed?"

"Almost. Until she screwed up so bad they fired her, and then everything was okay again."

"Well, we can't risk a near-collapse at Rookery State—our campus isn't all that vigorous to start with."

"Enrollment down?" asks Claudette.

"A little. We've got a recruiting staff the size of a small army, but still if you took a poll of Minnesotans, asking them to identify all the four-year colleges in the state, I'm sure Rookery would have the least name-recognition."

"What do you specialize in?" Claudette wants to know.

"Nothing, unless being all things to all people up north is a specialty."

"Specialize, Leland. Even high schools are doing it these days. Scott's high school in Lincoln is turning into a magnet school for science and math, that's why he's looking for a way out."

"Even grade schools," says Lucy. "The one in our neighborhood's got a Spanish-immersion program."

"What you ought to do, Leland, is take your field, American history—"

"Literature," I remind her. "History was my father's field."

"Okay, literature. What you do is, you build up American lit as your speciality. Do some high-profile things, that way instead of thinking of snowbanks and jackpines when they hear the name Rookery State—which is what I do—people will think of a literary center. You're dean, you can swing it."

I feel my heart speed up, as it always does when anyone speaks hopefully of my dear campus in the forest. I'd forgotten that Claudette, as a younger woman, had been in public relations and advertising. "What do you mean by high-profile?" I ask, leading her on, excited to have Richard Falcon up my sleeve.

"Oh, you know, distinguished lecturers, a writers' workshop, stuff like that."

"How about Richard Falcon? Would he be distinguished enough?"

"Richard Falcon," gasps Lucy in the backseat. "My all-time favorite poet."

"You don't need to go *that* far—bringing people back from the dead."

"Richard Falcon isn't dead. He's alive and well and living in New Hampshire, and for some reason he wants to come to Rookery."

"Just today, driving out to the farm," gushes Lucy, "I saw this tree of birds against the sky and I thought, 'houndstooth.' Remember how it goes, Leland?"

I do indeed. I recite the haiku:

"Heavy with blackbirds
Before a houndstooth sunset
The leafless trees pose."

"God," sighs Lucy. "Isn't that perfect!"

"I thought he was dead," says Claudette.

"And the one about geese landing, remember?"

I try reciting that one as well—"Beaks and wingtips down,"— but can't get past the first line.

Claudette wants to know, "So why haven't I heard of Richard Falcon, except as a mythical figure, for the past twenty years?"

Lucy has one opinion: "It's been a long time since his last collection came out."

And I have another: "That, and critical taste turned against him for a time. He was thought to be too simple for the mature reader. We were told to dig into Pound and Eliot instead. Wallace Stevens. More recently, John Ashbery. But now that poetry is becoming a performance art—you know, readings all over the place—poets are writing accessible poems once again, and that bodes well for what somebody once described as 'Falcon's clean and dancing line.' Just wait, his next book will bring him back from being a myth and restore him as a vital part of our culture."

Claudette is skeptical. "I wonder," she says, pulling up in front of Ron and Lucy's house. "I mean, isn't there such a thing as being *too* accessible? Birds and trees and all those pretty images—don't you want something deeper now and then, something just a little dark?"

"It's there," says Lucy.

"It's there all right," I agree. "Remember the one about the two pheasants? Light as a child's poem on the outside, but dark on the inside."

Lucy and I recite half of it together:

"Two golden pheasants
In a climate too cold
For corn to grow
Couldn't die old.

One I shot.
It ran though stricken. . . ."

"Our teacher read us that one," says the little girl, awake now that the car has stopped.

"And what does it mean?" asks her mother. "Can you tell us?"

"It means I'm in gifted."

Christmas Day seems less chaotic than in past years. Conversation, after the din and nervous drivel that greeted our arrival, becomes less a competitive sport than a sharing of family warmth, and Aunt Mary's dinner, of course, is superb. Mother, though a bit more subdued than usual, and requiring a lengthy nap after the meal, wears a constant expression of bliss, for the entire clan dotes on her throughout the day. Even Uncle Bill allows himself a few hearty laughs over the tales she tells about radio work. The time she cut off what she thought was a crank caller who turned out to be the governor. The time she mistook "sugar" for "salsa" in a handwritten recipe for green apple pie that she read over the air, and all those angry calls coming in from people who feared their taste buds had been destroyed. When she begins to reminisce about her girlhood on the farm, it's amazing the way everyone listens. Do they sense, as I do, that she may not be back again?

The day ends as yesterday did, with Lucy's helping Mother up to bed, and then my enjoying another late-night conversation with Lucy and Claudette in Grimsby because their husbands can't tear themselves away from a poker game with Scott and Detlef and Uncle Bill. The three of us settle into the warm, over-furnished living room of Lucy and Ron's house just off Main Street, a house I remember as very austere during Ron's first marriage to a tax auditor for the State of Nebraska. Lucy owns two volumes of poems by Richard Falcon, the early *Plants and Animals* and his most recent, a small attempt at autobiography entitled *Fording the Bee*. We pass them back and forth, reading our favorites, and before long we're talking about heartbreak, of all things. Major heartbreak. The breakup of Lucy's first marriage in Detroit. The death of Claudette's parents in a house fire in Lincoln. I feel free, as never before, to speak about losing both my father and my son. I jabber on about both of them: Joseph J. Edwards, the great-spirited man who gave me life and led me only partway into my teens before he was wiped off the face of the earth in a millisecond on the afternoon of August 15, 1948. Joey Tobias Edwards, the baby I created with Sally, the person who was supposed to follow us down the street of our days after we'd disappeared around the corner, the soul of our souls, instantly dead at seventeen months when I crashed into the black taxi, November 27, 1975.

Lucy has never been told about Joey. Small wonder I've always felt vaguely uneasy surrounded by O'Kellys. Afraid to get serious, they cover up tragedy. How gratified I was to see a number of them come north for Joey's funeral, but never since, in our many Christmas visits to Grimsby, have I heard Joey's name uttered even once. Now finally, sitting under Lucy's tassel-shaded lamp, with Richard Falcon's poems in my lap and tears pressing behind my eyes, I listen to Claudette tell Lucy what Joey looked like: his fat cheeks, his slow smile, his grave eyes. It dawns on me then how much I love both of these women. Claudette I've known for a quarter century without ever being truly acquainted with her mind. Lucy brings a wonderfully fresh strain of energy and goodwill into the aging O'Kelly clan. I can't possibly wait a year to see them again.

The next morning, both of these two dear cousins-in-law are at the farm to see us off with hugs and kisses and tins of home-made pastries. I haven't felt this sorry to leave Nebraska since I was thirteen and Ron and George and Uncle Jack took me fishing in the Missouri.

Driving between Grimsby and Omaha, I tell Mother the family secrets I learned from Claudette and Lucy, beginning with May-lene and Detlef's marriage counseling, then moving on to Uncle Jack's cancer. She's strangely reticent. Ordinarily, Mother is able to take bad news in stride. Indeed, thirty-five years of radio interviews have taught her to face the worst with aplomb, taught her the perfectly diplomatic platitude to match every lament. But today she keeps turning away from me, gazing out her side window at the chilly drizzle, the foggy fields dropping away toward the river. Aunt Mary's heart failure, Uncle Bill's stern-ness, the twins on drugs—each item I bring up seems to make her shrink a little, seems to close off another passage to her lungs. By the time Omaha comes into view, she's gasping for breath.

"You need a doctor."

She closes her eyes.

"A hospital," I say more emphatically, though I mean it as a question. You can't hospitalize Mother without her permission.

She tries clearing her throat, but her problem lies deeper than that. She coughs a tight, strangling cough, then sinks back in her seat and nods, gasping, "Doctor."

Signs direct me off the freeway to a new suburban hospital, a confusing, one-story sprawl of hubs and spokes. Red neon points to Emergency. I press a button on a post, and a woman's voice makes inquiries from a grill in the wall. "A case of acute lung disease," I shout at the brick. "She can't breathe!" A door folds open and a young woman wearing a sweatshirt and jeans emerges pushing a wheelchair. Before taking Mother inside, she instructs me where to park. Her sweatshirt says CORNHUSKERS.

Inside, I'm held at the registration counter answering countless questions before I'm permitted to follow Mother deeper into the maze. I need to tell whoever's treating her, in case they don't notice her swollen ankles, that her heart isn't strong enough to withstand the shot of adrenaline or any other of the speed-up drugs typically given to wheezers and chokers. A vaporizer is usually a great help, along with a very small dose of a certain antihistamine.

I find her in an examination room, alone, waiting in the wheelchair. Her breathing is terribly labored—eight or nine on our ten-point scale. Struggling for oxygen, she has torn her scarf away from her throat and torn the two top buttons off her dress. She throws her chest out with each inhalation, tipping her head back to straighten her windpipe. After waiting for what seems eternity, I go back out in the corridor, looking for help. In another examination room, I find the CORNHUSKER woman bending over an old man on a gurney. "We need a doctor!" I tell her.

"Dr. Yance will be along. He's somewhere in the building."

"Somewhere in the building! Isn't this Emergency? Why isn't he here?"

"It's Sunday."

I raise my voice. "Find the doctor! Find a nurse! Find somebody! My mother is . . ." I almost say "dying," but of course she isn't.

"I'm the nurse," she says, turning her attention back to the old man.

I return down the long hallway to the registration desk and plead for a call on the intercom. The receptionist complies: "Doctor Yance wanted in Emergency, Doctor Yance wanted in Emergency," and then she holds me there with yet more questions for her files.

When I return to Mother, the doctor is already there, sitting face to face with her, bending forward, exploring her chest with his stethoscope. Nurse Cornhusker stands nearby holding a chart on a clipboard and clicking a ballpoint pen. I explain about Mother's heart. The doctor nods, listening to it very intently. Then he stands and faces me, folding his stethoscope into a pocket of his blue smock. He's a squat young man. His mouth is extremely wide, with thick lips that seem to reveal about four dozen very large and perfect teeth when he smiles—which he does when I recommend a vaporizer and an antihistamine capsule.

"Is that so funny?" I want to know. "It's relieved her in the past."

"I'd be careful with antihistamine, the way her blood pressure is." His smile, I realize, isn't one of amusement or derision. It's an expression of empathy, friendliness, condolence. "I want to admit her for bed rest, with oxygen. She's very weak."

"Can't we arrange that at home? We're just passing through."

"Where is home?"

"Rookery, Minnesota."

"Ah," he says. "Hockey sticks." Then, pursing his fat lips over his magnificent teeth and shaking his head, he turns to Mother. "Five hundred miles at this point would be life-threatening."

Life-threatening! Obviously this stranger mistakes her chronic rattles and wheezes for something fatal, perhaps because she looks so forlorn under these harsh, unflattering lights. I protest. I explain to him and to the woman in the sweatshirt, who stands ready to jot his next observation on her clipboard, that Mother has always resisted hospitalization, preferring instead to rent an oxygen tank, hire a nurse, and prevail upon Dr. Mittelholtz to come to the house. "We'll take a portable oxygen tank with us. She's quite comfortable in the car."

Dr. Yance's response is to stand beside Mother and gently lay a hand on her shoulder. Adding pity to his empathetic smile, he looks down at her and says, "We'll let the lady decide whether to go or stay."

Mother throws out her chest and forces the word "Stay!" out with a gust of breath. Her eyes roll with fury or fear—I can't tell which. I've never before seen such a wild expression on her face.

She's given a private room looking out over an acre of mud. Her breathing grows steadily worse, noisier, more desperate. I've never seen her like this. On our ten-point scale, this is twelve. By midafternoon, a hideous moan has been added to each inhalation, as if her last available air passage must lead through her voice box, and this is soon matched by a high-pitched *"Eeeeee"* uttered as each breath is expelled. The oxygen tube to her nose seems to have no effect. Nor has the medicated IV solution flowing into her arm brought relief. The wild look is gone from her eyes; she's so intent on making her lungs work that she can't seem to spare the energy required by a facial expression.

The nurses on duty in this wing take turns trying to alleviate her suffering—a rearrangement of pillows, a stronger dose of oxygen, soothing words and pats on the arm, a cool damp cloth to the forehead. Nothing helps. *"Eeeeeeeee."* Pacing the hallways, I can hear this as far away as the nurses' station and beyond. I notice patients sitting up alertly in their beds, expressions of horror on their faces, waiting to hear if her next breath will be her last. One by one, the staff coming on evening duty are drawn to the room by the appalling noise emanating from her throat and distended mouth. All of them, from the custodian to the head nurse, give me what I'm sure they think is a reassuring smile, but I can tell from the nervous, confounded look in their eyes how uncommon is death by suffocation.

For isn't that what we're witnessing? This awful suspicion, which I have allowed to dawn on me only gradually through the afternoon, is confirmed by Dr. Yance, whose last act before going off duty is to take me aside and ask if I've called the family.

"Family? Mother and I *are* the family."

"No other relatives?"

"Several, in Grimsby, but they've just seen her." My clipped manner of saying this apparently strikes the doctor as interesting, for he purses his heavy lips and tilts his head while looking me deep in the eye. When I raise my hand to wipe away a tear, he flinches as though fearing I'll strike him. His tone is cautious:

"For your own sake then, Mr. Edwards? Someone to be with you? I'm afraid your mother—"

"I have a cousin here in Omaha I can call, thank you."

He understands he's dismissed—he's no dummy. I regret being so abrupt. I'm flustered by grief.

His replacement is Dr. Kim, a youngish woman of vaguely Asian appearance. At first sight of her at Mother's bedside, I experience a renewal of hope. She's a woman, after all. The first thing she does is order me out of the room. If Dr. Yance had used her peremptory tone on me, I would have burned with anger. "Out," says Dr. Kim as though to a dog, and I retreat willingly, nay gladly. She closes the door.

Cooling my heels in the corridor, I ponder my faith in womanhood. I guess the reason is obvious. I've been conditioned to think of women as the tougher and more resourceful half of the human race. From seeing my father dead early in what everyone agreed was to be a distinguished career, I went on to watch Mother endure for another half a century as Rookery's steady opinionmaker. In classrooms, over time, haven't I come to expect young women to excel at reading and writing, while any gifted young man always turns up as a pleasant surprise? And, as dean, haven't I had much better cooperation and good advice from women than men? When I see Mother's door swing open and Dr. Kim call down the hallway to the nurses' station, "Get this woman over to ICU," I know she'll save her life.

Mother comes out of her room on wheels—a gurney equipped with an IV sack and an oxygen tank. She's propped up with a mound of pillows at her back. Our eyes meet for a moment, but she gives me no sign of recognition, for the look of wild fright has returned to her face. Striding with me along the corridor, Dr. Kim repeats Dr. Yance's advice about rounding up relatives. She points to an alcove with upholstered chairs and a telephone. Obediently, though not quite willingly, I stop and place a call to Grimsby. Claudette answers. As much as I'd like to forestall an influx of O'Kellys, I don't gloss over the facts. Claudette's not surprised. She says Lucy had predicted as much. She calls George to the phone. Waiting for George, I hear two voices behind me, the moaning voice of a man and a woman's hysterical laughter. I turn and see a door labeled *Press bell and wait*. This alcove, I realize, leads to the psychiatric wing.

George reprimands me, albeit gently, for not calling earlier. He promises to round up the clan and bring them to Omaha.

I hang up and sit back in the deep leather chair. I'm

exhausted. A fidgety young man comes into the alcove and sits in the chair facing me. He smiles. I say hello. He looks suddenly troubled. I comment, as soothingly as possible, on the weather. He laughs, crosses his eyes, and puts two fingers up his nose. I hurry off to ICU.

By 9:00 P.M. enough O'Kellys have arrived to overflow the visitors' lounge, overtax the patience of the nursing staff, and cast me into a state of desperation. I'm not used to having people around when I'm upset. My method of dealing with stress—when Sally's out of reach—has always been to go to my room, go for a walk, go fishing. I need space and time to chew over disasters, digest them. Afterward, of course, when emotion leaks away and language takes over, I'll seek out someone to talk to, say Angelo Corelli, but in order to reach that point, I need the steadying state of solitude.

No self-respecting O'Kelly has ever been acquainted with solitude. They surround me in the lounge like a yapping wolf-pack, vying for my attention. I'm shocked to hear them speak of Mother in the past tense. Having stolen into her room and seen the terrible respirator hose down her throat and all the other wires and tubes she's attached to, they've clearly convinced each other she's a goner.

"Lolly was the salt of the earth, Leland," says Uncle Bill. "When the time comes, will you bury her Catholic or Episcopal?"

Uncle Jack says, "I remember when your dad died, Leland. It was snowing like hell."

Uncle Bill corrects him: "Not when his dad died, Jacko. His dad died in August. He was struck by lightning, for God's sake."

When Cousin Ron tells me, "It's good she's going quick, very little suffering," I respond snappishly:

"Excuse me, but I'm not ready to believe Mother is dying." Their morbid talk weakens my faith in Dr. Kim. I keep looking for my two soulmates, Lucy and Claudette, to show up and help me fend off their in-laws, but they've both apparently stayed home with their children.

Cousin George: "I hope the funeral's not Wednesday. I've got to be at a meeting on Wednesday."

Cousin Maylene: "That's the way I want to go when my time

comes. Up and doing in the morning, and off to the great beyond by nightfall."

Uncle Bill: "We'll all go up to Rookery together, we'll hire us a bus."

Uncle Jack looks bewildered. "August was it, Leland? Your dad died in August?"

Aunt Mary reminisces, "The Christmas she brought you to the farm, Leland, with that bloody rash all over your face, I felt so sorry for both of you."

Cousin George, laughing: "Remember the time we all went to Midnight Mass together? We didn't like the hymn the choir was singing and so we started in on 'Come All Ye Faithful' and swayed the whole congregation over to our side. Wasn't that rich, Leland? It takes a good-sized family to do that."

Maylene puts in darkly, "Takes a few drinks beforehand, is what it takes." Then she turns to me. "Leland, we can't let you drive back to Rookery alone. Time like this, you need companionship."

"It may surprise you to know Mother's riding home with me."

"Don't kid yourself, Lolly can't last the night." Maylene's my stubborn cousin, the hardest to defy. She turns to her younger brother. "Ron, you ride to Rookery with Leland. We'll bring you home on the bus when we come to the funeral."

Ron regrets to say he can't; he has appointments to meet.

Somebody says, "George will go, George has vacation time coming." But because of George's meeting, other suggestions are put forth:

"Jack will go. It'll do Jack good to get away."

"Mary should go. Leland's always been fond of his Aunt Mary."

"Tell you what, Mary and Jack should both go. Do them both good to get away."

Maylene dictates, "You'll come back to Grimsby tonight, Leland, stay with us and get a fresh start in the morning."

I'm telling her politely, "No, please, Maylene, I'll be perfectly fine," while thinking, Get off my back, you tiresome crab.

"Nonsense, I'll take you home with me. Detlef and the twins can follow in your car."

I have caught sight of her Teutonic husband at the edge of this gathering, wearing a hangdog expression, as though engaged in sour meditation. I imagine the twins out in the parking lot, sharing a joint.

"And then tomorrow morning," she continues, "you and Mary and Jack can set off for Minnesota. We'll see to the transport of the body—we're friends of the undertaker in Grimsby. Do you a world of good to be with family overnight."

"No! I'm staying here."

Unaccustomed to being defied, she scowls and stretches her mouth in a teeth-gritting expression before asking, "Where will you find a room at this hour?"

"My cousin Wesley's." This is out before I quite realize what a perfect ploy it is. "Excuse me, I haven't yet notified him that we're in town. I'm sure he has a bed I can use."

I escape to the relative peace and quiet of the telephone alcove and the voices of the mad behind the locked door.

"Sally, I'm calling from Omaha."

"How come? I thought you were coming home today."

"Mother's in the hospital."

"Her breathing?"

"And heart."

"How bad?"

"Intensive care."

"Oh, my."

There's a five-second pause, during which Sally is probably searching for a diplomatic way of asking if she's going to die. A lot of people are going to take a great interest, someday, in watching me adjust to Mother's death, and foremost among them will be Sally.

"What's the doctor saying?"

"Notify the family."

"Will you?"

"I've done it. Most of them are here, driving me batty."

"Wesley too? Are Wesley and Bernadine there?"

"No."

"You haven't called them?"

"I wonder if I should."

"Of course—Lolly's his godmother, for goodness' sake."

Sally remembers Cousin Wesley from the first of our two Christmases as a married couple. We stopped in Omaha that year, Aunt Cora being still among the living, and Sally rather enjoyed meeting Wesley's tiny wife Bernadine. I don't recall any conversation of my own with Bernadine advancing beyond hello, how are you, how nice to see you again. Nor has Mother, for some odd reason, ever put any effort into befriending her. Mother has always seemed satisfied simply to laugh at how little she is. To this day Sally gets a handwritten Christmas note from Bernadine, while Mother and I get only a card with no signature, only *Wesley and Bernie* printed in red.

"You want me to call Bernadine for you, Leland?"

"You have her number?"

"I'll get it. Where are you, what hospital?"

I have to ask a passing nurse.

"Can you believe it's called the United District Hospital, Sally? It sounds like the Soviet Union."

"Okay, Leland, keep me posted."

"Sally, come to Omaha."

She laughs.

"I need you, Sally. Motels are so lonesome."

She says, mockingly, "You poor thing."

"You cured that monkey's itch, and now you won't cure mine?"

She laughs and hangs up.

I'm summoned to Mother's room, where Dr. Kim explains to me, her Asian-black eyes fixed on the monitor, that the heart signs have stabilized, thanks to the right mix of pharmaceuticals. Now it's her bronchial infection that needs to be remedied. By morning, if her heart continues at its present workmanlike efficiency, we ought to see much of her congestion relieved. Perhaps in two or three days she can be taken home.

I hold Mother's hand, thanking God for sparing her and feeling how painful it must be to have a machine doing your breathing for you. She half opens her eyes. She's sedated, Dr. Kim explains.

"Can I stay in here?" I ask.

"Pull up a chair." She leaves the room.

And that's how I escape the O'Kellys—the same method I used as a little boy eluding nightmares, my parents' bed my refuge.

In a few minutes Dr. Kim is back to say, "I'm sending home your horde of relatives, Mr. Edwards. They'd like to say good-bye to you."

It's now 10:30. The clan is beginning to look a little weary, though they have no less to say. They're buzzing with Dr. Kim's optimistic prognosis.

"Never expected otherwise," says Uncle Bill, and they all concur, adding their own versions of how hopeful they'd been.

"Lolly's always been a tough old girl, Leland."

"Just wait, she'll be hundred percent in no time."

Maylene says, "Shame on you, Leland, losing hope like you did. I said to Detlef all along we'd see Lolly back in Grimsby next Christmas, didn't I, Detlef?"

Detlef, skulking in the doorway, sneers, then turns to lead his twin haggard-looking sons outdoors.

"Now take good care of your mother," says Aunt Mary as I help her on with her coat. "She's the only mother you've got."

Her brother Jack needs help too, getting his second arm into the sleeve of his windbreaker. "Call us in the morning, Leland. Your Aunt Mary worries, you know."

Maylene gives me a frightfully accusing look. "Listen to Leland long enough and we'd all be in the dumps."

Uncle Bill laughs one of his rare laughs, saying, "Just saved ourselves the cost of a bus to Rookery."

"Oh, look at the snow," exclaims Aunt Mary on the doorstep. The O'Kelly shoulders and caps turn white as they stroll out into the snow falling in thick, silent curtains, snow blanketing the cars in the amber-lit parking lot and glittering like a million chips of amber as they brush off their windshields, snow veiling their headlights as the three cars move slowly and silently out of the lot and form a procession toward Grimsby. Standing at the entrance, I wave good-bye. I allow the cooling snow to wet my face for a minute or more, before I return to Mother's room and fall instantly asleep in the chair.

Next thing I know, Dr. Kim is encouraging me to find myself a motel and go to bed. She says I mustn't fret about Mother. Let her know where I'm staying, and she'll do the fretting.

I find my coat in Emergency. Stepping out into the windless, beautiful night scarcely twenty minutes after the O'Kellys have left, and I find their footprints already obliterated by snow.

Waking in the morning, I need a few moments to remember where I am. I reach for the bedside phone and call the hospital. Mother's off the respirator, breathing on her own. She'll be moved out of intensive care in an hour or so.

"Hold on, not so fast," I tell the nurse. "She was out of intensive care yesterday and just about died."

"I'm sure Dr. Yance knows best, Mr. Edwards."

"Please can I talk to the doctor?"

"Dr. Yance is with another patient, but your mother has a guest who's been asking for you."

Waiting for the guest to come on the line, I imagine it's going to be Bernadine, presumably alerted by Sally. I'm delighted to hear instead, "Howya doin', Leland?"

"Lucy! Bless your heart. When did you get there?"

"Been here an hour. Didn't come with the others, I was working the night shift. Just as well—the last thing a nursing staff wants in an emergency is an outsider sticking her nose in their business."

"Is Mother really okay?"

"She's coming along just fine. Here, let her say."

A whisper: "Leland . . . pretty bed jacket."

"What?"

"A present . . . from Lucy."

"Why are you whispering?"

"Lace over pink . . . satin."

"It's hard for her to talk, Leland. Her throat's pretty raw from the respirator. I've been feeding her ice chips."

"Did Ron come with you?"

"Ron's home with the baby this morning. The whole clan was going to come again today but I told them, Cool it."

"Thank God."

"I gotta run now, Leland."

"Wait till I get there."

"Can't. Gotta relieve Ron, he's going to the dentist. Lolly'll be just fine. Color's back in her face."

"But you'll come again?"

"Tomorrow's Claudette's turn. Say, have you got a cousin named Bernadine?"

"I do, a cousin's wife."

"Well, she's been calling. See you day after tomorrow, if you're still here. If you leave tomorrow, Claudette will want to go with you. I'll baby-sit her sixth-grader, and I will drive up to Rookery to bring her back this weekend."

"Lucy, it's wonderful you came. You're probably the reason Mother's better."

"Not me—it's the ice chips."

My room faces a field, and when I draw back the drapes, I see nothing but whiteness. I scratch the windowpane, assuming it's frost, but no, it's the thick, disorienting snowfall that fell through the night, lying like a painter's white dropcloth over all of Nebraska. The beginning of a Richard Falcon poem springs to mind.

> I wade and explore
> In hazy noon light
> The countryside smothered
> In snow overnight
> And find I'm unable
> To comprehend white
> With everything dark
> Having vanished from sight.

I follow a snowplow along a thawing thoroughfare, sipping a cup of McDonald's coffee on the way. The sun is high and blinding, the hospital corridors mercifully dark by comparison.

Approaching Mother's room, I see two figures in black jackets, a heavyset man and a small woman, standing next to her empty bed, their eyes out the window, their backs to the doorway. My initial impulse—to flee—is unreasonable; I'm reacting to the surly teenage Wesley of forty years ago and the pain of his punishing fastball in my catcher's mitt. He must have matured since then, I tell myself, and to prove that I too have come of age, I sweep into the room and shake their hands and tell them how perfectly wonderful it is to see them again.

Tiny Bernadine squeals with delight. She's always been one to smile with every muscle of her face—a brow-raising, eye-squeezing, cheek-tightening expression so dissimilar to the impassiveness of her husband that you might mistake them for different species. Wesley, averting his eyes, mumbles a greeting and shakes my hand. Wesley's hand doesn't feel like a pensioner's hand; it's too calloused. I wonder if word of his retirement from the lumber delivery truck was a false rumor. *Lennox Lumber* is printed on the visored cap he fits onto his balding head as he says, looking at his wife, "We was just leaving."

"But now we're staying," she informs him. "We've got to hear all about you, Leland, like how's your college these days, and how's your health been, and why haven't you stopped to see us these last eleven years?"

I feign astonishment. "Eleven years! Maybe four or five, not eleven." I hear voices in the bathroom, Mother's husky whisper and the coo of a nurse.

"At least ten," Wesley confirms, risking a glance directly into my eyes. "We was still on Dill Street last time you stopped."

"Eleven," his wife repeats. "Nineteen eighty-two. The Christmas before Jimmy married Nancy. Did you know both our boys are still married to their original wives, Leland?"

"I expected no less."

Displayed on their matching jackets of black satin is a *Bassbusters International* insignia on the right breast and their names stitched on the left. *Bernie* is the name she wears. The insignia portrays a fiercely scowling fish rising to take a treble-hooked spoon into its jagged-toothed maw. Wesley's stitching says *Hotshot*.

"You simply have to come and stay with us, Leland. You

never thought, did you, how you might have hurt our feelings last night by going to a motel." Bernadine's undiminished smile indicates the wound wasn't serious, but I apologize anyhow:

"Sorry, but you know how it is late at night, you'd rather drop into a rented bed than bother people."

"Oh, I love it, you're such a gentleman, Leland. Get your things together tonight, and move into our guest room."

Wesley says, "We're clear the other side of Omaha. Been there it'll be nine years come April."

"I heard you retired."

"Did. Took early pension it'll be two years come June. Got in a accident." He holds out his left hand, displaying half a thumb. "Nothing serious—a band saw—but it seemed like a good enough excuse to retire, workman's comp and all. I been fixing up the place on Dill to sell."

"Your grandparents' place," Bernadine explains. "We rented it out for a while, but then decided to fix it up and sell it so we can start traveling more and forget it. It needed quite a lot of work."

"Needed new soffits and rain gutters. Needed new windows. Been working on it it'll be nine months come this Friday."

"We'd never go anywhere with the house on our hands— Wesley's such a worrywart. He's the kind of landlord that has to be by the phone all the time, in case his property burns down or a tornado hits it."

"Well, Jesus, it's the house my ma was born in," says my cousin with more sentiment than I thought him capable of.

"And my father," I add.

"Sally says you're still Dean of the College, Leland. She called us, you know. Sounded perky as always, that old Sally. What a sweetheart."

"Needed new steps down the basement."

"I said to Wesley, just you wait, someday we're going to hear Sally and Leland are hitched again."

"Needed the chimney tuck-pointed, needed a new electric line running out to the garage."

"That's a divorce that never made sense to me, Leland—you and Sally."

"Built a deck out back."

The bathroom door opens and Mother emerges on the arm of a smiling young nurse. She wears a shapeless hospital garment and her step is a shuffle. She looks depleted but not entirely drained. "I'm planning my wake," she says in a forceful whisper. "Last night, lying here dying . . ."

"Just listen to this, Leland," Bernadine gushes. "Your mom's got this loopy idea."

Standing shakily at the foot of the bed, Mother turns her cheek for my kiss, and then she sets forth her outlandish proposal, pausing every few syllables to catch her breath. "I lay here imagining . . . my own wake. It was fun . . . all those old friends together in one room . . . Bernadine and Wesley have promised to come. We have to . . . notify the folks in Grimsby."

"Mother, that's preposterous. You're not dying, you're getting better."

"I know it, don't look so upset . . . We'll have it at St. Blaise and serve snacks . . . as soon as I'm feeling up to it. We're going home tomorrow."

"You're up to going home?"

"Medicare says I'd better be."

The three of us stand aside as the nurse helps her into bed, reattaches the IV to the shunt in her arm, the oxygen supply to her nose. Her dyed oily hair is pulled back in a bun and her eyes are surrounded by scores of tiny new wrinkles, but the deathlike pallor, as Lucy said, is gone from her cheeks and a smile continues to play about her lips as she goes on: "When I first told Bernadine . . . she about flipped." She begins to quiver with laughter, and soon the bed is shaking and the IV sack is swinging on its hanger.

"I told her it's going too far, Leland, having your memorial service while you're still alive." Bernadine utters a worried laugh. " 'What you plan to do,' I said to her, 'lie in a rented coffin pretending to be dead?' "

"Won't sell the place till summer," Wesley interrupts, perhaps finding Mother's idea as morbidly repellent as I do. "We got to paint it and patch the foundation yet. You can't paint till spring in these parts. March if you're lucky, usually April."

"You have renters in it now?" I ask, hoping to steer us further away from the living wake.

"No, no, it's too torn up for renters right now. Water shut off, gas shut off, no furnace."

While pretending to listen to Wesley's tedious account of his remodeling plans, I watch Mother's smile go lax and her eyes go sleepily shut. "The phone company likes to play hardball," Wesley is saying as I nudge both of them toward the door. "Cheaper to keep the phone in service, because they charge you eighty bucks to reconnect."

"Wesley's serving as his own contractor," says his wife proudly.

"Let's give Mother a chance to rest," I whisper.

In the corridor, I can't shake them loose. When I stop at the nurses' station, they stop with me, Wesley describing the eventual blistering of paint applied in cold weather. I walk farther, as far as the entrance. Again they stop, enumerating the advantages of being your own contractor rather than hiring one. We cross the slushy parking lot. Standing beside their red pickup, they give me directions to their house. I notice *Bernie* painted in small black letters under the passenger window.

They get in, finally, and Wesley starts the engine, but Bernadine won't let him shift gears until I promise to come to dinner and bring my suitcase. They make a U-turn then, and honk at me on their way out of the lot. Under the driver's window is printed *Hotshot*.

Dinner, thanks to Bernadine, is not unpleasant. She's more curious about Wesley's family than Wesley is, and seems genuinely interested in what I have to say about my father. I talk mostly of baseball teams he coached and fishing trips he took me on, and of course I give her what I suppose is a rather florid account of the U.S.O. record of 1944 and his sweet rendition of "I'll Be Home for Christmas." Tears well in her eyes.

"By the way," I say to Wesley, who's left the table by this time and is lying in his Stratolounger, "do you know what became of the record? I never saw it after that Christmas Eve at our grandparents' apartment."

Wesley, without opening his eyes, emits a negative mumble, and his wife adds, "Oh, Wesley wouldn't know. There's scads of boxes in the garage he hasn't looked at since his mother died. I'll find it and mail it to you."

Helping her clear the table, I answer her inquiries about Sally—her health (superb), her job at the Hi-Rise (demanding work for a middling salary), the prospects of our remarriage (nil).

"And your son?" asks Bernadine.

"Joey."

"Does she still miss him terribly?"

"Terribly," is my guess. Sally never mentions his name.

"And you, Leland, Joey must have meant the world to you."

I nod, turning away, suddenly choked up with love for Bernadine. *Joey* is obviously the password to my heart.

Next morning on the way to the hospital they lead me to the house at the corner of Barker and Dill which, except for six months in 1963–64, has been in the family for eighty-one years. The year I found the record in the hatbox in the attic, the house was sold on a contract for deed, but the buyer defaulted after six payments, and Grandfather and Grandmother Edwards got it back. They sold it then to their grandson Wesley, newly married, for a fraction of its worth, and he and Bernadine raised their sons in it.

Say what you will about Wesley's lack of family feeling, he certainly lacks no skill when it comes to remodeling. Though everything is covered with sawdust, the place has a bright, fresh feel about it. He has single-handedly sanded the oak floors, painted four rooms and papered three, installed new kitchen appliances, and built a new stairway leading into the new family room in the basement. With the help of subcontractors, two of whom are on the job today, he has fed new insulation into the walls, upgraded the plumbing and wiring, replaced chilly old windows with triple glazing, and topped it all off with a new roof.

"Wesley, I'm really impressed," I tell him, standing in the upstairs bedroom my father occupied as a boy.

He frowns at the floor, scratching his forehead, trying not to look proud. His wife straightens the collar of his Bassbusters jacket and gushes, "Isn't my Hotshot the handiest thing?" She grips his chin and gives his head a playful wiggle, which causes him to look almost happy. I probably haven't seen this man smile four times in my life, and here he is actually raising his eyes and looking pleased with himself, pleased with this house, pleased with this wife who pleases him. What a remarkable woman.

An electrician comes into the room, goes to his knees, and cuts a small hole in the newly painted wall. Wesley goes over and watches him fish around for a wire.

"My father would love what you've done to his room," I tell them. "Blue was his favorite color."

"Runs in the family then," says Bernadine. "Blue's Hotshot's favorite too, isn't it, Honey?"

Wesley nods, embarrassed, it seems, by her revelation. I'm amazed to think of this cousin of mine holding an aesthetic opinion. I can't resist the urge to press him further:

"You didn't always like blue best."

Ignoring me, he tells the electrician to come up an inch with the outlet.

"I mean, when we were boys you told me you liked red."

That I should recall this from fifty years ago confirms his view of me as a nutcase—I see it in the glance he gives his wife as he and the workman leave the room.

Stepping over to the dormer window, I look down on the roof of the bungalow next door. "After my father died, I used to come up and stand right here, looking out."

"Oh, that's so sweet," says Bernadine.

"I suppose I was trying to see the world as he had."

"Oh, Leland." She puts her arm around my middle.

"That house wasn't here then. It was a vacant lot where we played catch."

"Oh, Hotshot and I just *love* playing catch. Summers, we're on a salt-and-pepper softball team."

"He still fancies himself a pitcher?" I ask.

"Show him the strike zone and he'll burn it right in there."

"And you're able to catch it?"

"Usually." She laughs. "When it doesn't knock me over." She hugs me briefly and leaves the room.

I linger there, feeling closer to my father than at any time since I last heard his voice on the phonograph.

BUREAUCRACY DAY

There was an old rector named Pyle
Who abandoned his affable style;
    He bitched and he spat
    Like a (---) cat
Till he choked on his poisonous bile.

If I'm ever to become as lighthearted as I've always secretly wished to be, it will no doubt transpire through my association with Angelo Corelli, a man of irrepressible good humor. Even on occasions such as today when his silliness is inappropriate and irksome, you can't help envying him his bubbly chemistry and wishing you'd been born under a star like his.

This limerick, for instance. He composes it during the two minutes I'm on the phone with Coach Hokanson's secretary. I no sooner put the receiver down—fuming because I'm unable to arrange a meeting with Hokanson before his hockey team leaves for Colorado—and Angelo reads it to me, seeking my help with the missing adjective.

"What brought this on?" I inquire, puzzled because we haven't touched on Father Pyle this morning, or any other aspect of our Christmas party. This being bureaucracy day, our business has been the fall-term Dean's List and the spring semester calendar, particularly Richard Falcon's appearance, which we've scheduled for the first of February. It's the only foreseeable Sunday not in conflict with some civic activity, such as the annual ice-fishing contest on Lake Lamond, or some athletic event on campus. True, February first will be St. Blaise Sunday this year, a momentous day in our parish, but the faithful can get along without my reading from the pulpit for once.

"I thought a dose of poetry might uplift you," says Angelo. "You've been a little down in the mouth all morning."

"It's his mother." This from Viola Trisco in the outer office.

"Never mind, Viola," I bark.

"Whenever Lolly's under the weather, Dean goes into a tailspin," she explains to Angelo.

He replies brightly, "He's so crazy about Richard Falcon's poetry, I thought he might like mine as well."

"That's not poetry," I pointed out.

"Really?"

"It's doggerel."

"No kidding?" He looks pleased.

"It's also the truth," says Viola from her desk. "Every time I lay eyes on that broken-down, so-called clergyman I want to smack him in the mouth." She rises from behind her word processor and lumbers over to the doorway, filling it with a roundness that seems much larger than a week ago—the greater girth of Christmas feasting, I suppose. "He did a wedding for the niece of a friend of mine and he acted real shabby—hurried through the ceremony like the church was on fire, and then never showed up at the reception."

Angelo seeks her aid. "What's the adjective I'm looking for, Viola? He bitched and he spat like what kind of cat?"

"A pole cat."

"No, a longer word."

"A rabid cat."

"No, three syllables. A *dum*diddy cat."

She turns back to her desk, repeating thoughtfully, "A *dum*diddy cat—I'll think about it."

But instead of thinking about it, she jabbers on about Mother and lung disease and KRKU and our Nebraska relatives. She says she wants to meet the cousin who returned with us from Grimsby. Usually, on occasions such as this when Viola can't shut up, there's a student worker to absorb her chatter, but students haven't returned to campus yet. So, in order that Angelo and I can concentrate on grade-point averages, I send her around to the various departmental mailboxes to distribute our second Richard Falcon memo. Then I sign eighty-two letters of merit, of warning, of suspension. Looking over my notepad from last semester, I'm momentarily puzzled to see what looks like *Faith-sex* scribbled under unfinished business. I show it to Angelo.

"Sexual harassment—don't you remember?"

"Oh, God, yes. What a bother."

I get Faith Crowninshield on her cellular phone. She's in her car, on her way to the Court Street Mall. It's a scratchy connection and we have to raise our voices:

"Faith, tell me, is this another of L. P. Connor's tactics to bring me down?"

"Sorry Leland, I can't divulge that information."

"Faith, for pity's sake, she's a maniac."

"You know the rules, Leland. You helped draw them up."

"But how can I respond unless I know who I'm responding to?"

"Your first response is to me. If that doesn't satisfy the complainant, we go to Step Two."

"My response to you is this: Not guilty."

"Oh, it's too late for that. Anyhow, it should have been in writing."

"Too late!"

"Five working days, remember? We're going to Step Two."

"So who's been working? It's winter break."

"Winter break's for our student body, Leland—and I guess our dean. Meantime your faculty toils away preparing for next term."

"Well, of all the outrageous, legalistic—"

"Look, did I choose to be human rights officer?" Her voice rises to a painfully shrill level. "Didn't my dean ask me to submit my name for nomination, and didn't my colleagues vote me in? You think this is a fun job?"

"Just a minute, Faith: if the faculty is so busy working while their dean is on break, why am I sitting here in my office while you're out shopping?"

"Now let's not get personal, Leland." There's a raspy silence before she adds, "How's this afternoon for Step Two, before the semester gets under way? I'm really eager to get this over with."

"You and me both."

"Super. Pick a time."

"Three-thirty."

"I'll inform the complainant. Happy New Year, Leland."

Angelo, surprisingly, advises caution. He furrows his freckled brow, licks his young mustache, and claims that I'm on thin ice, involved in an area of law largely untried in the courts. He says the accused have no safety nets. He says anyone at all can bring charges, whether they have any stake in the case or not, and the accused are guilty until proven innocent.

"Nonsense. That's unconstitutional."

"So it is, in the real world," he replies with a grin, "but this is college."

Although he's heard it before, I patiently review my unassailable position for him. "At semester's end we performed a classroom skit, three students and I, in which the script called for me to give Carol Thelen a hug. I flubbed my part and forgot to hug her. Ten minutes later, leaving the room, she came up to me with tears in her eyes. She was sad that the course was coming to an end—"

"Why?" asks Angelo suspiciously.

"Why! Because she liked it! Is that so hard to believe, that a student might like a course I teach?"

He gives me a weak, noncommittal smile.

"She said something sentimental, something nice about my teaching, I guess, so I said to her, 'Let's have the hug we forgot,' and I gave her an innocent, unromantic, absolutely asexual farewell embrace that lasted maybe two seconds, and out the door she went. And that's when I saw L. P. Connor in the corridor, glaring in at me."

Angelo casts his eyes at the ceiling, as though pondering my chances for acquittal.

"Sounds open-and-shut to me." This from the outer office. Viola is back.

"Thank you, Viola."

"I say *sounds* open-and-shut. Gotta remember, L. P. Connor's a ballbreaker."

"Viola, don't you have work to do?"

"Get yourself a legal eagle, Dean, or she'll skin you alive."

As if the interference of L. P. Connor weren't enough to impede a dean's progress through this day of bureaucratic details, my way is further blocked by O. F. Zastrow, back in town a day early from his vacation in Fargo. Summoned to his office, Angelo and I cross the hall and find the starstruck young idiot, Portis Bridges, making himself at home behind the president's desk. Tipped as far back as the president's leather chair will allow, his head lolling, his mouth full of the president's jelly beans, Bridges is laughing and speaking into the president's phone. Zastrow, meantime, is nowhere to be seen.

Portis Bridges covers the mouthpiece to assure us, "O. F.'s in the john"; then he's back on the line, saying, "Okay, George, see what you can do. Johnny and Elizabeth both. Get *those* two up here and we'll put this little campus of ours on the goddamn *map*!" He winks at me and giggles.

We sit down at the small presidential table. "Johnny?" Angelo inquires of me.

"Carson?" I suggest.

"My guess would be Cash," says Angelo.

"Yes," I agree, "that seems more likely. And Elizabeth? Taylor, or the Queen of England, do you suppose?"

O. F. Zastrow emerges from the toilet that was installed at incredible expense in his closet during a recent siege of his chronic bladder infection. Buttoning the tight buttons of his double-breasted suitcoat, he stands over us, announcing that the rest of his advisory committee are on their way to join us for an impromptu meeting with Portis Bridges, who has new celebrities for us to consider. As usual after a vacation, our president is looking particularly beady-eyed and fretful—the way I feel myself. Absent from campus, he doubtless loses sleep as I do, imagining how Rookery State might go adrift without our respective hands on the tiller.

Angelo asks cheerily, "How was your vacation, sir?"

"You mean on a scale of one to one hundred?"

"Whatever."

"One." He gives us a pouty look.

"Not so hot, then," says Angelo.

"Too crowded for swimming. Dust in the room. Food not up to par."

"Swimming? In Fargo?"

"Holiday Inn. Other years it's been fine, but this time not. New management, I guess."

"Bummer."

"The wife's allergic to dust, you see."

"Double bummer."

Zastrow shoots me an accusing look. "Tried reading your book by that Thurber fellow."

I acknowledge this with a wordless nod of my head. His expression tells me what he thought of it.

Reggie VanderHagen sweeps into the room, shocking us with his transformed appearance. He's shaved his bullet-shaped head and somehow bronzed it. He's wearing gold rings in his ears. He looks like a Samoan beachcomber. Leaning across the desk, he exchanges an exuberant high-five with Bridges, who's still giggling into the telephone, and then he shakes the president's hand. I have the clear impression that Zastrow doesn't recognize him. "Ciao," he says to the president.

Angelo and I get to our feet to welcome Francine Phillips, who's well-dressed for a change. Slipping out of her slim black coat, she looks splendid in a white turtleneck under a belted white cardigan and a burgundy skirt revealing knees none of us have ever seen before. We're used to seeing her in a lab smock.

"You caught me on my way to Bismarck," she tells the president. "This better not take long."

"Bismarck, good Lord," I exclaim, estimating the distance. "Surely you're not driving."

"Three hundred miles—are you nuts? God, no, I'm taking the plane. It leaves in an hour." Pulling up a sleeve, she displays her watch to the president, and I half expect her to tell him, *When the big hand's on two and the little hand's on twelve.*

"Is it Mary Sue?" I inquire, suppressing my anxiety.

"Mary Sue's on the edge," she replies darkly. "She needs coaxing back to Rookery."

"Depression's the pits," Angelo says.

"You can say that again," I tell him, recalling my emotional nosedive after divorcing Sally.

"Depression's the pits, get it?"

Bridges brings the president's chair upright and comes around the desk to shake our hands, joyously bragging, "There's a good chance we can get Johnny Cash to come to St. Paul in July for a benefit concert, and Elizabeth Plimpton has openings in May."

"Funky!" says Reggie VanderHagen—approvingly, I think.

The president's eyes have not left VanderHagen. "What happened to your head?" he asks, causing the newly bronzed face to grin impishly, and Bridges to break into peals of laughter.

VanderHagen, who goes a little crazy every Christmas, delegates my assistant to answer for him. "Tell him, Angelo."

"It's called a makeover, sir."

"A makeover? Like women have?"

"Yes, sir, for men."

VanderHagen puts in, "A new year, a new look."

The president turns to me for confirmation. "Did you know men were having makeovers, Edwards?"

"I've heard of it."

"Why?"

"That I haven't heard."

Francine wants to know if Bridges is talking about the real I'll-Walk-the-Line Johnny Cash. She thought he was dead.

"There's only one Johnny Cash, and he's not dead because I have access to him through my agent, George Ephistopholi. George can bring this superstar to the state fairgrounds August eighth for a mere sixty thousand dollars because he'll be traveling through on his way home from the We-Fest in Detroit Lakes.

Have any of you thought of the great possibilities for a slogan? I mean the tie-in between Johnny Cash and cash money?"

None of us have, apparently. I know I haven't. Thinking of it now, I can't help but snicker for some reason, perhaps to cover my impatience with this entire business of celebrities. And then, to cover my snicker, I ask, "Who's Elizabeth Plimpton?"

"The first woman to do a heart transplant," Bridges replies in stirring tones. He turns his attention to Francine. "You said you wanted a different type of woman than Addison Steele."

" 'Nobler' is what I said. 'A nobler example of womanhood.' "

"Well, here you are. I can arrange with George Ephistopholi to bring Dr. Plimpton up from Houston to deliver your commencement address."

"No good," says Angelo sadly. "We've already voted on this year's speaker."

"So we did," says the president brightly.

"Who did?" asks Francine.

"You were absent," says the president, smiling benignly.

I break the news to her. "This year's speaker is our president."

Francine looks to me in disbelief. I verify it with a nod—one final honor for Zastrow, on his way out the door.

There's a grunting, sighing sound from the doorway—Emeric Kahlstrom struggling to get out of his woolly pullover. With Angelo tugging on the sleeves and me peeling the waistband up his back, we inadvertently pull the old philosopher off balance and he goes to his knees with a muffled shout. He's flailing his arms and moaning by the time Francine steps in and discovers he hasn't unzipped the collar. We guide him to a sitting position on the edge of the president's desk, where he's eventually freed of his treacherous garment.

We all seem energized by this little crisis and ready to move forward with our advisory meeting. I propose going across to my office and getting started, but Bridges says that's unnecessary. All he wants this morning is our authorization to go ahead with his negotiations, and we can take care of that with a voice vote here and now. "All in favor say aye."

Angelo and VanderHagen express their approval.

I speak up and remind everyone that nonvoting visitors do not call questions. It's in our bylaws.

"God, Edwards," whines VanderHagen, "how did you get to be such a fussbudget?"

Our obstructionist-in-residence, Emeric Kahlstrom, says helpfully, "What's the issue?—I'll vote no." He's still sitting on the desk, still panting, his wispy white hair standing on end.

"I have another proposal for you," I tell them. I choose my words carefully, this project being crucial to the future of Rookery State College. "You're right," I concede, "we *do* need to attract attention beyond the Rookery city limits, and the best way to do this is to bring exciting new life to our campus. We *used* to do it. Do you realize that in my father's day, Rookery State was recognized far and wide for its music program? The Minneapolis Symphony came up here on two buses every August and gave a preseason concert that was reviewed, without fail, in all the Twin Cities newspapers. And every spring we hosted the biggest choral festival in the state. I'm talking about fifty years ago. We had a summer music camp for high school musicians. Our glee club toured the Midwest. One year they went as far as Toledo."

VanderHagen is amused by Toledo. "How droll," he says, giving me the same pitying smile one might use on the senile and the out-of-touch.

Bridges points out that music is exactly what we're getting, with Johnny Cash.

Chemist Phillips wants to know what possible objection I could have to Dr. Plimpton.

"None whatsoever," is my reply. "A famous surgeon is the very sort of speaker I would love to introduce at commencement, but we already have a speaker. Indeed, Dr. Plimpton is the sort of person our campus needs to attract, a person of intellectual achievement." I pace the small office, gathering momentum and conviction as I go. "And I'll concede further that if it takes a gravel-voiced cowboy from Nashville to get a foundation laid under our new science wing, then go ahead, bring Johnny Cash to the state fairgrounds and soak his fans thirty bucks a ticket. But in the meantime, let's get serious about Richard Falcon."

I stop and face my listeners. I can tell by their expressions who has read my pre-Christmas memo concerning the poet, and who hasn't. Chemist Phillips and Philosopher Kahlstrom, who haven't, look puzzled. VanderHagen yawns to indicate he has.

"We have within our grasp the most famous writer in the nation, my friends, winner of the most prestigious literary awards, and he's ready and willing to come and present a reading on our campus."

Francine Phillips says, "You don't need our approval to bring in a speaker, Leland. Tell the English department and let them handle it."

"Listen, for the event I have in mind, I'll need the cooperation of the entire faculty. First, I want to overspend our advertising budget and cover a five-state area with posters and radio spots. I want people driving up here from Des Moines and Madison and Sioux Falls, and I want two thousand visitors, at least, from Minneapolis and St. Paul."

"But, Leland," says VanderHagen, coming out of his long yawn, "our auditorium only seats fifteen hundred."

"The new hockey arena seats three times that many."

Bridges says, "I don't think George Ephistopholi deals in poets, Dean Edwards. He's strictly into showbiz and surgeons."

"The hockey arena?" asks Chemist Phillips, her eyes lighting up in a way that I find endearing. As a man of very few original ideas, I'm excited to see one appreciated.

"That's what I said, Francine. We inaugurate the arena with every American's favorite poet."

Zastrow puts on his squinty, shrewd expression. "We'll never get thirty dollars a ticket for a poet."

"We don't charge thirty dollars—we don't charge anything! Don't you see?—we throw open our doors and invite people in from all over the Midwest for the experience of a lifetime. Look what it does for us, my friends. By filling the arena with civilized readers of poetry, it counteracts our reputation as a hockey factory. It reminds people that our main work is *not* the training of gladiators on ice skates, but the shaping of hearts and minds."

My listeners look stupefied. Even Angelo, privy to the plan, looks skeptical.

"Jesus Christ," sighs VanderHagen, hanging his head of polished bronze and shaking it—a gesture of despair.

"What is it, Reggie?" I shout at him, enraged.

Silence. Evasive looks. My audience further stunned by my angry tone.

"I may be a fussbudget, Reggie, but what makes you such a stumbling block? Exactly what is it that makes you sigh like that?"

When Bridges answers for him—"Your idealism, Dean Edwards"—it's my turn to be stunned. I didn't know he knew the word.

Then everyone is suddenly speaking at once. Angelo takes on VanderHagen, promoting poetry over hockey and country western music—though hopelessly—while Bridges argues against poetry, imploring the president not to jeopardize Rookery's reputation for blood sports. "What did I miss?" Kahlstrom inquires, and Angelo gives up on VanderHagen and goes to the old philosopher's side to tell him about Johnny Cash.

"Is this a meeting or isn't it?" Francine Phillips wants to know, "because if it isn't, I'm outta here."

"Me too." I help her on with her coat while listening to President Zastrow's exchange with Bridges. The latter's tone is incredulous: "No pianos in Japan?"

"I could hardly believe it myself."

"Of *course* there are pianos in Japan."

"No, I read it in a book."

"What about Yamahas? Yamahas are made in Japan."

"I said pianos, not motorcycles."

I bid Francine good-bye, urging her to phone me with the news from Bismarck, and I cross the corridor, scanning my memory for substitute professors in the event Mary Sue Bloom doesn't return. I wonder if her predecessor, Kimberly Kraft, might be lured out of seclusion. In my outer office I try phoning Kimberly. Standing at Viola's desk, listening to Kimberly's answering machine explain at tedious length why she can't come to the phone just now, I look across to Zastrow's office, where Bridges is again seated in the president's chair and VanderHagen is helping himself to fistfuls of jelly beans. Zastrow himself is getting into his tight black overcoat for his trip downtown, where he lunches five days a week at the Elks'. Angelo, having helped Kahlstrom into his pullover, follows him out into the corridor, bringing the old philosopher up to speed on Elizabeth Plimpton.

"She transplants hearts in Dallas," I hear him say.

The old man isn't impressed: "Too many people alive these days. Gotta let more people die when their time comes."

"Viola," I ask, replacing the receiver, "why is Portis Bridges working so hard on the president these days? What's it to him, getting us off to a strong start on our building campaign?"

Viola looks thoughtfully up from her keyboard, patting a lock of frosted orange hair into place.

"I mean, a man like that, I can't believe it's entirely for the good of the college, can you? As a student he was a zero, he never joined the alumni club, and until last month he hardly ever set foot on campus. Now look at him, he's spending the morning on O. F.'s phone."

Viola swivels around to squint across the corridor. "Guy like that, it's got to be money, right?"

"A kickback, do you think, from the agent he's always talking to?"

Viola takes a hit of caffeine from her can of Mountain Dew. I can tell from her expression that she's no more convinced of the money motive than I am. The Bridges family has money to burn. "Know what it might be?" she says, peering shrewdly up at me. "Could be that boy's practicing up for president."

"Good Lord, Viola."

"Leave it to me, I'll find out."

"Don't ask him directly, don't put ideas in his head."

"Don't worry." Viola picks up her phone and punches a number from memory. "Who do we call in this town when we want to know what's up?"

I'm curious to know.

"Hello, is Lolly there?" she inquires.

Preparing lunch, we laugh a good deal over Mother's role as gossip-on-call. Claudette O'Kelly, dribbling dressing onto a bowl of chicken salad, says it's unprecedented that somebody should have an entire city in her grasp the way Mother does, her finger on every pulse. She says the only other being she knows of with this kind of omniscience is God Herself.

Mother's laughter becomes a cough. She turns from the lettuce she's been shredding and faces her bulletin board until she recovers. This wall of cork, Mother's center of operations as long as I can remember, is covered with news clippings, appointments, hand-scrawled notes, photos, grocery coupons, and phone numbers. It's her game board, her wailing wall, her book of life. I see her in memory standing there by the hour after my father's death, arranging and rearranging, weeping and not weeping, her mouth abristle with straight pins.

"Better cut the comedy," I tell Cousin Claudette. "She'll have a relapse."

"Nonsense. There's no disease on earth two aspirins and a good laugh won't fix."

When Mother resumes work on the salad, she asks, "What have I been missing on campus that Viola Trisco should be delving into the Bridges family?"

I describe Portis Bridges's behavior in the president's office, his urgent attempts to foist celebrities on us.

"Very ambitious, that whole Bridges dynasty," says Mother.

"He was an aimless washout in college," I explain to Claudette. "He was gone from Rookery for about fifteen years, and now he's suddenly back, and feigning great interest in helping us put up a new wing on the science hall."

"How do you know he's feigning?" says Claudette. "Maybe he's found himself."

"In Hollywood? Out of the question."

"What was he doing out there?"

"Meeting the stars," says Mother. "Portis was always crazy about big-name people, even as a boy, always writing away for autographed pictures. The Monkees, I remember. The Incredible Hulk."

"You mean he devoted fifteen years to meeting celebrities?"

"Oh, he worked for a while," says Mother. "Worked off and

on for a theatrical agency, his grandmother told me. Worked a few weeks for a newspaper."

"His college major was journalism," I put in, "before he dropped out. Before we dropped journalism."

Lunch, in the breakfast nook, is Caesar salad, chicken sandwiches, sherbet. I sit there with half my mind still back at the office, apparently, for Claudette asks, "What's eating you, Leland? You're so different than you were in Nebraska."

My response is an evasive chuckle. I hate to be called different. I strive always to be the same.

She probes, "Tough morning on campus?"

Mother tells her, "He looks fretful like this every August and January, just like his father before him. You'd think they were embarking on a space voyage, when actually it's only a new semester."

"He's kind of cute when he's worried."

"So was his father."

"Lay off, you two."

They snicker like conspirators, while I try to ignore my mental picture of L. P. Connor sneering at me from across the cafeteria.

Over dessert, Mother backs up and comes at the Bridges family again, by way of ancient history. "Portis's Uncle Leopold wanted to be a senator. He ran three or four times and never made it. It wasn't until his Uncle Peter began selling furniture that the family got prominent around here. What started up as a two-by-four operation on Twelfth Street—remember, Leland, it's now the tanning booth next to the theater?—has become the seven-city chain of stores you see today. There's one Bridges or another managing each of the seven."

"If only there were an eighth, for Portis," I muse.

"Portis can't hope to be president," says Mother. "I told that to Viola when she called. He hasn't got a degree."

"But he's dumb enough to *think* he can."

"I don't believe he's dumb, Leland. Whatever the family lacked, it wasn't brains. No, it's not the presidency he's after, especially not with *you* in the running."

"You have to face it, Mother. I'm not in the running."

"Oh, Leland ..." Her expression, for Claudette's benefit, takes on its crestfallen look. "Only a few years, till you're sixty-five. It's such a plum, retiring as president, just think."

"I'll retire as a classroom teacher, Mother. We've been over this."

She sighs, and turns again to Claudette with a look that says, *See what a renegade son I have?*— this being the second time in my fifty-eight years that I've defied her. The other time, when I married Sally, she sighed the same sigh of disappointment.

And so, on our wedding night, did Sally.

While Sally claims that our wedding is foggy in her memory, I can call up every detail. I remember coming into the vestry of St. Blaise out of a chilly October mist and being surprised to feel underfoot the thick rosy carpet newly installed over the oak flooring. I remember the flickering candles, the smell of damp raincoats, the quiet strains of Bach on the organ. Despite the convention of divorcées marrying in relative anonymity, St. Blaise was fuller that day than ever before or since. Mother's radio fans, our friends from Rookery State, and a great influx of McNaughtons and O'Kellys vied for seating. Cousin Wesley and Bernadine, I seem to recall, were late arriving and had to stand at the back.

Some were surprised at my choice of best man—Sally's brother Otto—but Sally was pleased, and what friend or relative did I like well enough to honor with that role? None of the Icejam Quintet saw fit to return for the wedding, not that I blamed them, they all lived so far away: Victor Dash and Neil Novotny were in Ohio (Victor having recently changed labor unions and moved with his family from Milwaukee to Cleveland; Neil writing novels in Dayton), and Connor had taken root in New Hampshire, never once returning to visit his problematical wife and daughter. Now, of course, I have a truly close friend, but I'm describing a day many years before Angelo Corelli turned up on campus.

When Otto McNaughton and I stepped out of the vestry and took our places at the front of the church to await the bride, I heard a raised voice and what sounded like a momentary scuffle in the vestibule before the organist shifted into high gear, booming out the wedding march, and Sally appeared on the arm of her father. She wore a creamy calf-length dress with a low neckline and a pearl choker. She carried roses. I see her radiant smile coming toward me down the aisle. I recall Mother in the front pew, her teary smile, her notepad in hand. They were tears of joy, I tried telling myself. Some months before, having discovered how invincible was my will to marry Sally, Mother wore herself out pretending to approve, and the moment we left on our Canadian honeymoon, she checked herself into Mercy Hospital with the first of her recurring attacks of stress-related bronchitis.

Her ostensible objection, strange to say, was the eccentric nature of Sally's former husband. Ordinarily she viewed people's oddities with good-natured tolerance, but she was outraged—or pretended to be—by Roy Spang's laziness, by his well-known habit of spending most of a social evening napping in his RV while his wife lingered over dessert, by his reputation for disguising faulty automobiles with new paint, lowered odometer readings, and additives in the gasoline.

"What does Roy Spang have to do with anything?" I demanded. "She's been divorced from Roy Spang for the better part of a year. Roy Spang is history."

"Nobody is ever divorced a hundred percent," she replied mysteriously. "There's always a residual effect."

In retrospect, I believe what grieved Mother most was the fact that Sally was employed in Owl Brook, the dying county seat of poverty-stricken country north of Rookery. Mother never brought it up to me, but Hildegard Lubovich did, one day when I was filling in for an absent member of their bridge foursome. I've always suspected Mother of putting her up to it.

"Sally is nonetheless a professional," I pointed out to Hildegard, recalling how fondly she always spoke of professional people as opposed to the lower orders who took care of our lawns, remodeled our breakfast nooks, papered our walls, fixed our leaky toilets.

"But *such* a profession," she replied. "It's so self-defeating and dismal what she does." And to this, because Sally's job was a creation of Lyndon Johnson's Great Society, Hildegard added her ultimate condemnation: "It's so Democratic."

When the time came for Mother to announce our engagement on the radio, she referred to Sally simply as a government administrator working out of the courthouse in Owl Brook. This, though an accurate description on the face of it, did not take into account the tremendous patience and varied talents Sally brought to her all but impossible job as mother hen to a ragtag bunch of people known as the Concentrated Retraining-for-Employment Workers. The aim of this federally funded program, called CREW for short, was to turn lives around, no less. Of course the underlying goal was economic—to make self-sustaining wage-earners out of those on welfare—but that was only part of it, the measurable part. Before you could turn the down-and-out into responsible citizens, you had to instill self-esteem where before there had been despair, you had to create law-abiding citizens out of ex-convicts, you had to take indolence and teach it ambition and pride. In other words, you failed a lot.

Even Sally, the tireless caretaker, failed a lot. For example, the trouble with finding a cigarette-smoking CREW-worker a job as housekeeper for an antismoking family was that she shut herself in closets to smoke on the sly and was fired when the family discovered all their clothes imbued with the stench. The trouble with sending unskilled workers to blow particle insulation into the mayor's attic was that when you lost your balance while walking the attic floor joists, there was nowhere to put your foot except through the mayor's living-room ceiling.

But despite the difficulty of making carpenters out of ex-druggies, secretaries out of aging alcoholics, gardeners out of recovering hippies, Sally's work was not entirely "self-defeating." During her decade on the job, the Owl Brook CREW program achieved a success rate in the thirty-third percentile, which meant that for every two failures, one worker found self-sustaining employment—the highest ratio among all the eighty-seven counties in Minnesota.

On the other two counts, however, Hildegard was entirely correct. Sally's office in the dampish basement of Owl Brook's deteriorating courthouse was truly a "dismal" venue. You were urged by a handlettered sign, for your own safety, to enter the courthouse through a rear door, because the brick veneer, never tuck-pointed, had begun to fall away from the wall over the front entrance. Now, twenty years later, the building stands empty, all county offices having moved across the street into three vacant stores and a remodeled filling station. And of course Hildegard was right about Sally's work being "democratic." In the sense I most admired.

Needless to say, the fact of Sally's divorce did not go unremarked. Nowadays divorced people are married practically every Saturday in the churches of Rookery, but twenty years ago it was a rarity, particularly among Episcopalians, and more particularly under the rigorously high-church rectorship of Worthington Pyle. When Father Pyle challenged me about my marriage beforehand—possibly at Mother's behest, though she claimed not—I had to point out to him that I wasn't the Prince of Wales, for goodness' sake—didn't Anglicanism begin with King Henry's divorce? He capitulated finally, glad to be reminded, I think, that he wasn't going to scandalize the entire United Kingdom by officiating at our ceremony.

Father Pyle, in the event, looked the part of the estimable rector in his white and gold vestments, tried his best to be gracious, and said and did nothing embarrassing, unless you noticed, as I did, that he refused Holy Communion to all the O'Kellys and certain other guests he knew to be Irish Catholics. Well, why not? In those days I'm sure non-Catholics would have been snubbed by the Catholic priest in the same situation.

The reception, I'm sorry to say, which included a sit-down dinner at the Van Buren Hotel, was marred by the disorderly presence of Roy Spang. As the meal was being served, and the string quartet paused between movements of Mozart, Roy Spang stood up at his place at the far end of the dining room and proposed a toast. I was astonished to see him there. Mother and Hildegard were flabbergasted. I turned to Sally beside me, assuming she'd need consoling at the sight of this party-crasher, and sure enough, there were tears of anger in her eyes.

"Damn!" she muttered under her breath, "he promised me he'd behave himself."

At this I was further astonished, and a good bit irritated as well. "You mean you invited him?"

She confided then—while our guests rose to their feet, raised their glasses to us, and sat down again to address their plates of chicken and rice—that Roy, three days before the wedding, had asked her to meet him in his RV parked in the Spang Auto lot. She went, and found him still grieving over the divorce. He begged to be asked to the wedding. Out of the question, she told him. But for closure, he said. No, she said. But closure, he insisted, was what his therapist claimed he needed. If only he could see Sally married again, and happily, he could achieve closure.

"Was he drunk or what?" I asked.

"Not drunk, but he'd been drinking. He was so pitiful, Leland, I had to give in."

"Were *you* drunk?"

For this, I got a stabbing look from my bride. The first ever. Not the last.

Wounded, I leaned close and whispered, "I suppose if he'd asked you to join him in his bed, you'd have gone."

"Oh, he did," she said.

I drew back, frightened to hear more. I tried to eat but my fork shook off its load of rice. Her radiant smile returned as her brother Otto got to his feet, proposing another toast.

There were more toasts and speeches before and after the cutting of the cake, and then the string quartet resumed their Mozart. Later, when the dancing began, Roy Spang reappeared on the scene, presumably from a nap in the Motor Grove he'd parked in front of the hotel. The quartet by this time was playing Cole Porter, and Sally and I were among the half dozen couples moving across the small area of terrazzo where tables had been moved away.

"Roy's back," I whispered in her ear, and saw her turn to him with a long-suffering look on her face, and then saw her expression change to horror when he came toward us carrying a bar of metal about three feet long, with a length of bright blue nylon rope tied to each end of it. The musicians continued playing, thank God, and the dancers pretended not to notice Roy bowing to us with a drunken flourish and then holding the aluminum bar out to me. I refused to take it, whereupon he tried fitting it under my arm. I backed away. He handed it, then, to Sally.

"Thank you, that will do, Roy," she said sternly.

He bowed once more, nearly losing his balance, and left the room. Sally laid the bar on the floor, under a table. It was a trapeze, she told me later, which they had installed over their marriage bed for use during sex. She told me, too, that the shout and scuffle I'd heard in the vestibule of the church was her father and other relatives fighting off Roy's attempt to give the bride away.

So Mother was right, as she reminded me that night, telephoning our hotel in Winnipeg from her hospital bed. It was a brief call consisting mostly of coughs and wheezes, but this much was clear: "Didn't I tell you every divorce leaves a residue, Leland?"

"Who was that?" asked Sally sleepily, in the dark. We had wasted no time getting into bed, where I discovered married sex, as unmarried had been, stupendously satisfying. So had Sally, trapeze or no trapeze.

"It was Mother," I said.

She came fully awake. "Is she crazy, or what? It's our wedding night!"

"She's in the hospital."

Sally lay in restless silence for a time, then asked, "How did she know where to reach us?"

"I told her."

"Are *you* crazy?"

After lunch, I take Cousin Claudette on a tour of the campus. Not having been here since my wedding, she marvels over the changes. Our new Simon P. Shea Teaching and Learning Center she says is handsome. Our nondescript music building appeals to her as well, for reasons I don't understand. Our new art building, we agree, looks ugly enough to be arty, and we forgo the exhibit currently on display—twenty-nine blocks of wood painted black and studded with nails. Driven inside by the wind, we tour McCall Hall, recently remodeled for the third or fourth time in its long life. I introduce her to Viola Trisco and Angelo Corelli, interrupting their work on this morning's irreverent limerick. When President Zastrow appears in the corridor, just back from the Elks, I invite him to meet Claudette.

"Pleased," he says, squeezing her hand. "They play pretty good football down your way."

"The best," she agrees. "We're looking for the Cornhuskers to go undefeated this year."

"Yes, sir, pretty good football."

Judging by this unusually chatty exchange I can only conclude that the Elks outdid themselves today, for Zastrow's afternoon mood often depends on the quality of what he's eaten. Angelo apparently comes to the same conclusion:

"How was your lunch, sir?"

"Pretty good lunch. Beef."

"Sounds delicious."

"Spuds. Gravy. Elks are known for their beef gravy."

"So I've heard you say."

"You ought to be an Elk, Corelli. Edwards here's an Elk."

"But for my wife, I would be, sir. She resents it that women can't join."

The president frowns. "One of those, huh?"

Angelo nods sadly.

The president brightens. "She can come to lunch as a guest."

"Not good enough, sir. Gloria says full membership or nothing doing."

The president's eyes narrow—an idea crossing his mind. "Shrimp tomorrow. You and the wife both come as my guests. Women like shrimp."

"Thank you, sir. I'll ask her, but I can't promise."

We take our leave, Claudette (prompted earlier by me) telling Zastrow how impressed she is by the cleanliness of the hallways. He takes her hand a second time, wishing good luck to the Cornhuskers.

Resuming our tour, Angelo tagging along, we move downhill against the wind. Claudette says, in Zastrow's favor, "There's a man with no pretensions."

"Nor any brain to speak of," I add.

"Oh, you could have it a lot worse, Leland. You could be working for a man of limited talent, as I've done more than once, who thinks he's the last word in leadership. Being a little dumb is one thing, being dumb and believing you're brilliant is quite another."

"Well, I guess that's true," I reply, feeling a sudden twinge of guilt. Should I have viewed my president with more charitable eyes all these years? I turn to Angelo. "Do you ever think maybe we've been too hard on our president?"

" 'We'?" he asks, coyly. "What's this 'we'?"

"Forget it."

Our tour comes up against the new hockey arena, a mammoth, nine-million-dollar cube of windowless concrete on the riverbank. The architect's single concession to aesthetics is the double stripe painted around it—the college colors, navy and white. A three-tier parking ramp has gone up beside the arena, and fixed to the top tier is a sign flashing messages to drivers crossing the Eleventh Avenue bridge. The three of us stand in the brisk sunshine squinting up at the letters as they form and blink and disappear:

BLUE HERON HOCKEY

HAPPY NEW YEAR

2:22 PM

17°

The longer messages move from right to left across the board:

NEXT HOME GAME JAN 9: EASTERN MICHIGAN

COMING IN FEB: ARENA GRAND OPENING

"Isn't that classy?" says Angelo, I think sincerely.

"First class," Claudette agrees.

"It puts us way over budget," I tell them, turning away, regretting not only the expense but the spoiled view of the Bad-battle. Feeling my blood pressure rise as it always does when I cross over into Coach Hokanson's domain, I ascend the ramp to the main portal, and just as I'm pulling open the heavy door for a look inside, I hear Angelo exclaim, "Hey, Leland!" I follow his eyes up to the sign and stare in disbelief at the two words blinking on and off for a full ten seconds:

HEIM'S BEER

"Campus dynasties come and go," says Philosopher Kahlstrom, slowly following me down from his high office in McCall Hall. "Next time it could be a musician, it could be a sociologist. Who knows, it could be some upstart in metal shop."

"Don't give me that," I rage. "Nobody can spend a campus down to poor like an athletic coach gone haywire. No musician or sociologist will ever require a nine-million-dollar building all to himself. Hokanson's a dangerous man, Emeric. He's tied up every penny of our building money, and now he flaunts our rules. Two weeks ago he played an ineligible goalie, now he makes a deal with Heim's Brewery."

"Don't forget VanderHagen and his expensive sound system in the theater. You were up on your high horse about that, too."

"VanderHagen! That sniveling runt? VanderHagen is small potatoes compared to Hokanson."

I stand waiting for the old philosopher at the bottom of the staircase, breathless from having gone rampaging through the building in search of allies. Emeric Kahlstrom is my only recruit, this being winter break. Sandor Hemm and Madu Bhandi are working in their offices, but they're not sympathetic. Whenever she's asked to exert herself on behalf of the faculty, Madu Bhandi, our blue-eyed linguistics professor from Bombay, has the habit of pleading ignorance. Just now, when I explained the impropriety of a brewery taking over our new message board, she claimed not to understand American ethics. As for Sandor Hemm, my longtime colleague in English, he considers himself elevated above all campus strife because he now chairs the Division of Language and Fine Arts. Dr. Bhandi I can put up with, for I do believe she hasn't a clue as to how the American campus is run, but Dr. Hemm gets my goat, he's so everlasting supercilious. There I stood in his office doorway, fulminating about Heim's Beer and asking him to accompany me down to President Zastrow's office, and he turned me down without a word, conveying his refusal through his infuriatingly superior smile. I haven't yet heard his opinion of Richard Falcon, but I can predict it will be contemptuous.

"Hokanson's gone behind our backs on this," I remind Kahlstrom as we enter President Zastrow's outer office, where Angelo awaits us.

"He hissed and he spat, like a dumdiddy cat," Angelo says, trying out his limerick on April Ackerman, who finds it difficult to laugh, having just returned from the dentist, her upper lip stiff and fat from Novocain. I'm about to lead Kahlstrom through the president's open door, when April detains us, saying he's momentarily occupied.

"The Heim's Brewery people came to us when the new arena was nothing but a figment of Hokanson's imagination," I go on. "They offered to pay for our message board, and Hokanson kept pestering me, pleading their case. I told him to lay off. Colleges can't be mixing commercialism with education, I told him."

"Some do," mumbles Kahlstrom, stifling a yawn. "Shoe companies will sometimes pay a basketball coach to make his whole team wear their shoes."

"That's bad enough," I cry, "but mixing hockey and beer?"

"Better than cigarettes," he drones wearily.

"The outrageous thing is that in order to appease Hokanson, we told him *we'd* pay for the sign, and it's one of the reasons we went way over budget."

"Seventy thousand over," specifies Angelo.

"Dynasties come and go," says Kahlstrom.

Zastrow's flushing toilet alerts April Ackerman to his availability, and she nods us inside.

Standing with us in the doorway, as though fearing we'll come in and make ourselves comfortable, the president says, "Heim's Beer on the message board?" He frowns at Kahlstrom, smiles a little at Angelo, and then looks blankly at me. "What's the problem?"

"Ten seconds every minute we're advertising beer, is the problem."

"Not the best beer either," says Kahlstrom. "Heim's gives me gas."

"Look, O. F., didn't we tell Hokanson we'd pay for the sign
out of capital outlay?"

"We did."

"So why didn't we?"

"We did."

I'm mute with astonishment. Angelo takes over:

"You mean Heim's Beer didn't buy the sign, sir."

"Just bought ten seconds a minute, is all."

"Who from, sir? Not from you."

Zastrow shakes his head. "From Coach."

"No!" I cry. "Behind our backs!"

"Not behind mine," says O. F. calmly. "Coach informed me."

It takes me a moment to absorb this: the Athletic Department
has sold its soul to a brewery. I step past the others, going over to
the window and looking out at the shrubbery moving in the
wind. Fingers of drifting snow reach across the sidewalk.

"All right, O. F., what did they pay?"

"New uniforms" is his immediate and shameless answer. I'm
still facing away from him, watching a pack of hatless students
come up the walk leaning into the cold wind, the tails of their
open jackets flying behind them, yet I can tell from his tone that
my president is wearing his smug expression.

"And what's printed on the uniforms, if I may ask? 'Heim's
Beer' instead of 'Blue Herons'?"

"No, nothing like that—don't get so huffy, Edwards. They're
just very nice quality uniforms. No commercialism involved."

Speechless, I turn to Angelo and Kahlstrom for help—to no
avail. Angelo shrugs and Kahlstrom mutters, "Gassy, second-rate
beer."

Words come to me then, angry and disjointed. "Angelo, can't
you do anything but stand there and shrug? Emeric, for God's
sake, second-rate beer—is that the best you can offer? You're our
philosopher! When was the last time you put your philosophy to
work in the service of Rookery State College? Can't you say
something about professional ethics for a change? Educational
integrity? For God's sake, Emeric—second-rate beer!"

Angelo is obviously humbled. "Sorry, Leland."

Kahlstorm isn't moved, of course. He's in love with being our contrary senior citizen. "Always tastes a little on the green side to me, but that's just one man's opinion."

"We had a good brand of beer in Fargo the other day," says the president. "Real rich, in a greenish-brown bottle."

"Foreign?" inquires the philosopher.

"I guess so. Made in Denmark or Delaware or someplace."

My voice comes out soft and controlled, and I do my best to look pleasant. "O. F., I'll arrange a meeting with Coach Hokanson as soon as he's back in town. We've got to sit down with him and the athletic director and go over just what's ethical and what's not. If we don't, if we let this man keep expanding his hockey empire, we'll end up fighting the Napoleonic Wars all over again."

I leave then, doing my utmost not to appear huffy, smiling at April Ackerman as I pass through the outer office, even trying to smile at Sandor Hemm, whom I meet in the hallway. Cousin Claudette, whom I left sitting in one of my brocaded visitors' chairs, is involved in an animated conversation with Viola Trisco and a stranger sitting in the matching chair, an elderly man whose pocked and all but expressionless face strikes me as vaguely familiar. Standing at Viola's phone, waiting for Hokanson's secretary to answer, I study the old man. His blue suitcoat has gone threadbare at the cuffs, and his narrow tie hasn't been in fashion since the Kennedy era. He has a lot of gray-white hair, tousled in a way that puts me in mind of Hal Holbrook playing Mark Twain. Although his eyes are young and alert, his wrinkles tell me he's at least seventy years old; his throat is deeply ribbed with dewlaps and the backs of his hands are discolored with wisdom spots. He's a little shaky getting to his feet and the hand he offers me has the same pill-rolling tremor I associate with Parkinson's disease. His voice is very soft, asking, "Is this the man himself?"

"In person," Viola replies, giggling as though holding back a sweet secret. "Leland J. Edwards, dean of the college."

The hand I shake is cold and moist.

"Leland," says Claudette, her eyes alight with glee, "I'd like you to meet Richard Falcon."

I am dumb with astonishment. Richard Falcon, too, is wordless, tightly gripping my hand and looking deep into my eyes as though to determine if I'm trustworthy enough to be allowed to look deep into his. Evidently I am, for his little smile fades, graduating to an expression of great seriousness and then to anxiety.

He finds his tongue before I do. "We must talk, Dr. Edwards. I have to apologize for being here."

"Not at all, Mr. Falcon. If you only knew how thrilled we are to have you."

"No, no, I have to explain myself." His eyes turn insistent. "If you'll spare me a minute in private."

"Of course, of course." I indicate my door standing open.

Crossing the outer office, he pulls a wrinkled pack of very long cigarettes from his suitcoat and asks, "Do you mind if I smoke?"

"Not if you do it outside" is Viola's prompt reply.

"Nonsense, Viola, he can smoke."

"What?" Of all her expressions, Viola now gives me the one I'm least fond of—mock amazement, her mouth hanging open in perfect imitation of a drooling, dumbfounded cow.

"He can smoke," I tell her. "He's a poet."

Sitting at my conference table and shaking his ashes in the general direction of a crystal ashtray I've brought out of retirement, Richard Falcon draws from his shoulder bag a large gray notebook, a sturdy hardback with a sewn binding. He places it between us. Though he doesn't open it, I can tell it's had rigorous use, the edges of its pages ripply and soiled, its cover discolored and worn. The poet, too, seems hard-used. In the bright light off the river, I notice a scar on his chin. When he speaks I see gaps among his lower teeth. His long nose appears to have been broken; he breathes as though through a deviated septum.

"I'm working on something quite lengthy, Dr. Edwards. I'm expanding *Fording the Bee*."

"Yes, I know."

His eyebrows go up in surprise; then his shy smile returns. "Ah, of course." There's a brief rumble of a cough, shakily covered by his cigarette hand, before he takes another deep drag. "Peggy has told you," comes out with the smoke.

"How *is* Peggy these days?"

His eyebrows move in from the sides and gather in a frown.

For a few moments he appears to be choosing between a long answer and a short one. "Fine," he says flatly.

I wait to hear more, but having obviously decided on the short one, he drops his eyes to his notebook. To cover the uneasy silence, I declare, "She was a good friend of ours. Mine and my mother's, that is."

Head down, he directs his next voluminous steam of smoke at his lap, and says, "She still is. She speaks of you both with great praise and pleasure."

"Well, we do hear from her now and again, but we think it's strange she's been back to see us only once in a quarter century."

"It's understandable, isn't it? Connor's wife and daughter living here?" The fumes of his smoke, having crossed under the table, rise to my nostrils and burn my eyes. "Sorry," he says.

"You knew Connor?" I ask, blinking.

He directs his next exhalation at the ceiling. "Not an easy man to know." To this he hastily adds, as though to allay suspicion, "It was only after Connor died that Peggy moved neighbor to me in Tipton, you know."

I'm quick to say, "I do know," indicating I never suspected him of taking her away from Connor. What I do suspect, however—indeed, what seems confirmed now by seeing the poet in the flesh—is that he and Peggy are, or have been, romantically involved. This man exudes the same complicated mix of sensitivity and toughness that she fell for in Connor. On the one hand he seems fragile, and yet his presence is commanding. *I'll always need a genius to love,* Peggy once admitted to me, one uncontested non-genius among her acquaintants. I imagine her falling in love with the poet's reputation first, then with the poet.

"See this, if you will, Dr. Edwards." He opens the gray notebook at random and studies a page filled to the margins with very small handwriting. After a few moments, he turns it for me to read, and I make out something about river current and swampgrass and prayer books. The writing is incredibly tiny.

"Micrographia. Do you know what that is, Dr. Edwards?"

"I can guess."

"It comes, along with a dozen or more other curious symptoms, with Parkinson's disease."

"You have Parkinson's disease?"

"My doctor hasn't decided. But surely you noticed."

I nod sadly. "Is it painful?"

"Not particularly. Only fatal."

I look away.

"No, let me start over. I'm sorry for bothering you about it at all, but it's pertinent, you will see." He takes the book back, flips open a page near the end, reads silently.

"Is all of that *Fording the Bee*?" I ask, wanting it to be so. I know from Part One, dealing with his forebears and his early childhood and published twenty years ago, how marvelous the language is. I want it to go on and on. I want it to be the *Leaves of Grass* of this century. I want the readers of America to be stunned by its length as well as its gnarled and rigorous beauty.

"All of this and more."

I'm overjoyed. "It will be another whole book then!" The excitement in my voice causes his eyebrows to twitch and rise into arches. He looks up at me, closing the book and gently patting it.

"This is only Part Two."

"Good Lord." Giddy with pleasure, I watch him draw from his shoulder bag three more notebooks: green, blue, and brown. "Good Lord," I repeat softly, more reverently. "Is it finished?"

"It's mostly written." Again he frowns. "But far from finished."

He indicates that I may open the blue notebook. I do so, glimpsing,

A sultry night in Tipton Town,
The moon climbing over High Street
Like a ballooning bag of sweat,
The stars Leo Gorcey and the Bowery Boys
Projected on the west side of the grain
Elevator, in "Spooks Run Wild"...

The rest of the page is illegible.

"Mostly written but now comes the difficulty of arranging it, finding what it means, copying it out in legible order. The very task of deciphering the penmanship, page upon page, will be monumental." He opens and closes the green book, as though to make sure his words are still in there. "The structure is proving difficult. Ordinarily the structure of a piece unfolds with the writing, but not this time." Again the slight smile, the cough, the drag on the cigarette. "It's my life, and it's hiding from me."

I turn the page. He watches me read

the sound track moaning screaming
hooting, frightening my ancient
and unstable Aunt Patsy the other side
of town, despairing on her deathbed . . .

"That's how movies came to town when I was a teenager. We'd stand in the street looking at the big flat wall of the grain elevator."

"And Aunt Patsy?" I make bold to ask.

"Maybe I'll find it's not even poetry," he says, ignoring my question. "I mean, it may turn out to be prose, and that will not disappoint me in the least. Indeed, I sometimes suspect all the poetry I've produced in my life has been the result of trying and failing to make myself clear in prose."

"Oh, no, Mr. Falcon, all your work—"

"However, be it poetry or be it prose, I will publish it in poetic lines because that's what my public expects of me. All my life I've been mortally afraid of causing confusion. All my life I've striven to be predictable."

"Good Lord, and haven't I, as well!" I am overcome with a surge of fellow-feeling, as though I'm getting to know a soulmate, a brother, a friend. "Haven't I said those very words about myself!"

"Yes, you've said them to Peggy actually, in letters, and that's why I'm here, Dr. Edwards." He inhales more smoke, blows it into the beams of pale sunlight falling through the window. "I've come to an intersection in my life, you see, and I'm looking for someone to help me through it. Partly, it has to do with my Parkinson's, if that's what it is. Lately the effect of my medication's been wearing off."

"But you haven't been diagnosed?"

"That's not my fault—my doctor's an ass. I'm now beginning to have more 'off' days than 'on.' "

"I don't like hearing this," I tell him.

He shrugs his right shoulder. "It happens. It's the nature of the disease." He stubs out his cigarette with a spastic, spark-scattering motion, then slides the fuming ashtray away, brushes ash from his necktie, and retrieves the ashtray. "My doctor advises staying off the medication for a time. Let myself stiffen up and vegetate for a month or two or three, he says, and then start taking it in lesser doses again. That way, he says, it might regain its effectiveness. Might or might not, he says. Not a sure thing, he says, not at my age." He searches my eyes for understanding.

"But it would seem that you have no choice," I tell him. "I mean, if the medication isn't working anymore."

"Ah, but I've found a way to *make* it work. I'm 'on' today, you see, because I've taken more than I'm supposed to take."

"You're overdosing?" The word causes him to smile, perhaps at the alarm he reads in my face—I who never take as many as two aspirin at one time. "A large overdose—if I may ask?"

He shrugs. "Double, triple, I don't know, a handful."

"Isn't that dangerous? I mean in the long run?"

"Aha, that's just it, Dr. Edwards, I can't care about the long run, can I? I have a poem to finish." His voice rises. "Take my medication away, and I'll be planted in a chair or bed somewhere, quivering away like a leafy bush in the breeze."

Watching him stack and reshuffle the four notebooks, I ask how many "on" days he'll gain for himself at this rate.

"There's no telling. Overdosing has been tried with differing results. Some people went on functioning for quite a long time. One of the odd things about Parkinson's, you see, is that hardly any two people are affected at the same rate. You can even find pairs of Parkinson's victims whose *symptoms* aren't even very much alike." He removes another bent cigarette from his pack, puts it to his lips, but doesn't light it. He leans toward me, lowering his voice. "If I can get three months of steady work on this poem—till April, say—I will finish it. So!" He leans back in his chair, like a prosecutor resting his case. He brings the flame of his Bic tremulously up to the tip of his cigarette, then he turns and stares out my broad window. After a minute of smoky silence, he asks, "Any fish out there?"

"Yes, indeed—do you fish?"

"Trout?"

"No trout, I'm afraid. Northern pike mostly. Perch. Now and then a walleye. Panfish in the summer."

Another drag, another cloud of smoke roiling in the sunlight. "Aren't you curious to know why the most predictable man in the world should turn up in Minnesota a full three weeks before his speaking date?" He looks a little embarrassed.

"We're entirely honored to have you, Mr. Falcon. You needn't explain a thing. Please stay as long as you—"

I'm interrupted by the door swinging open and Viola Trisco barging in with the coffeepot and paper cups.

"Thought you two might like a shot of this. Just made it fresh."

"Ah, thank you," replies my guest.

Viola, who can't stand not knowing what's going on behind my seldom-closed door, pours, then remains standing at the poet's side, looking down at the notebooks. "You guys need anything else? I can send out for cookies."

"Thanks, Viola, this will do."

She scowls at me. On her way out, she cranks open the small window behind my desk and asks, "Want me to leave the door open?"

"No, please close the door, Viola."

"Pretty smoky in here, but suit yourself."

As she pulls the door shut, I see Angelo and Cousin Claudette seated side by side in my brocaded chairs, paging through a magazine together.

"Sorry," I tell him, "my secretary is sometimes overattentive." And then it dawns on me: "But she's efficient, she could help you put your work in readable form. I'll find you an office, or at least a carrel in the library, and you must feel free to dictate to her at any time—"

"A desk to work at is my only need, Dr. Edwards, apart from a place to sleep. As for secretarial help, it would only slow me down—I work out my poems alone."

"Ah, I see. Now let me be frank, Mr. Falcon. It would be a great privilege to put you up in our house, but my mother, you may be aware, suffers from serious lung disease as well as congestive heart failure, just out of the hospital as a matter of fact, and I'm afraid cigarette smoke is among the worst—"

"No, no, I wouldn't think of invading your house. I'd be afraid to, in fact, because staying with people often carries with it certain social obligations, and you understand that at this point in my life . . ." He stands a notebook up between us.

I protest, insisting that he would be left absolutely alone in our guest quarters, but his smile tells me he doesn't believe me. Nor do I, completely. Mother would surely have her eight or ten closest friends in to meet him.

"A bed and a bathroom, Dr. Edwards. Someplace simple and cheap. Clean would be nice, but not essential."

"How about clean and simple and free of charge?" I ask him, picking up the phone and calling Sally at the Hi-Rise.

Riding with the poet in the capacious backseat of Angelo's ancient and restored Buick Roadmaster, I try to prepare him for the Hi-Rise. I warn him about Worthington Pyle's arrogant nature, and I describe Hildegard Lubovich as insatiably nosy. I advise him not to take Johnny Hancock's every statement for truth, nor to leave any of his possessions lying around where Johnny might snitch them. And though I probably have no business doing so—my only evidence is her uncommon boldness as a newcomer—I tell him that the New Woman is aggressive and might try to seduce him.

"Leland, I can't believe you're saying these things," says Cousin Claudette from the front seat. "Why would you want to predispose Mr. Falcon against these people?"

"Who's against them? I'm just saying what they're like."

"You've sure got *me* curious," says Angelo, guiding his titanic automobile carefully through narrow streets made narrower by snowbanks. "I want to have a look at this New Woman."

"You've seen her, Angelo. She was at our Christmas party, on the love seat, under the big mirror. She was drinking vodka as if she were dying of thirst."

"That's her? God, who'd want to be seduced by the likes of her?" Waiting at a stoplight, he studies the poet in his rearview mirror, as though judging the man's susceptibility. "Don't worry, Mr. Falcon, she might be aggressive but she's homely as a mud fence."

"Will you two please shut up," demands my cousin without humor.

The poet looks a little dismayed despite Angelo's reassurance. "Do these apartments have kitchens?" he asks me as the light changes and we rumble off toward the west end of the city.

"Kitchenettes," I tell him.

"And private bathrooms?"

"Yes, of course."

"Well, then." The poet looks relieved. "I'll be able to shut my door and never come out."

"Oh, I wouldn't advise that."

"Leland, please let the man alone."

"Well, he's certainly welcome to do as he pleases. I'm only saying that when you're living in close quarters with a lot of small-town elderly people, the one sure way to attract attention is to make yourself scarce." Dot Kropp, our librarian friend, had the same intention when she moved in—didn't want to mix, wanted to stay aloof and read books—and before long her neighbors were listening for life signs outside her door—she could hear them breathing out there. "I'm just saying Mr. Falcon ought to come down for morning coffee so they get used to seeing him. Come down for his mail. Pass through the lobby two or three times a day. That way the lobbyists will leave him alone."

"Lobbyists?" inquires the poet.

"Whoever's sitting in the eight rocking chairs in the lobby. That's Sally's name for them."

"Who's Sally?"

"Sally McNaughton, manager of the Sylvan Senior Hi-Rise."

"And Leland's former wife," my cousin puts in.

"I'll be fine," says the poet softly, more to himself than to the three of us, Claudette's remark seeming not to have registered with him. "As long as there isn't a smoking ban, I'll be fine."

"No worry there," I assure him. "Not as long as Nettie Fire-hammer lives and smokes and has her being."

Pulling into the drive, we see eight faces looking out the broad front window, and the poet asks, "Is there a back door?"

"Sure thing. Angelo, would you drive around?"

At the back entrance we find Nettie Firehammer, bundled up in her muskrat jacket and her sagging sky blue sweatpants, blowing smoke into the wind. She watches us roll to a stop in a visitor's slot.

"I'm sorry, I hate looking a gift horse in the mouth," says Richard Falcon, "but do we have to smoke outside?"

"Only when you're downstairs in the lobby or dining room. Smoking's permitted in your apartment."

"God, that's a blessing," he says, climbing out with his shoulder bag.

I point to a corner window on the fifth floor. "That will be your apartment up there."

He looks up, then down along Court Street. "Not the greatest view," he complains, his eyes settling on the Rookery Rendering Plant. "It would have been nice to be afforded a panorama of countryside."

"You never know, maybe an apartment on the other side will open up. It looks down on a shopping mall. This is Mrs. Fire-hammer, Mr. Falcon. Nettie, this is Mr. Richard Falcon." She frowns warily at our approach. "He's taking a room for a few weeks. He's a famous poet."

Transferring her cigarette, she offers him her nicotine hand.

"Pleasure," he says, giving her thin fingers a gentle squeeze. "Such a rare thing these days, meeting a fellow smoker. I happen to be out of cigarettes at the moment—that is, I have a carton in my bag, but . . ." He looks longingly at the suitcase Angelo is lug-ging in through the door Claudette is holding open. "Would you have a spare one, Mrs. Firehammer, just until I unpack?"

"Not on me." She examines the mouth end of her filterless Camel, pulling out a stray shred of tobacco before handing it over. "Here, take a drag off this."

"Thank you. Just one, until I unpack."

But it's several drags each, down to the tiniest butt. I remain at their side discussing the weather and watching the gusts of wind toss and tangle the poet's long hair, watching Nettie's sweatpants flap and wrap around her birdlike legs.

"This isn't unusually cold for Minnesota then?"

"I'm afraid not," I answer apologetically. "Actually it's the wind today, rather than the temperature. . . ."

"Real sting to it," says Nettie.

"Sting is exactly the word, Mrs. Firehammer."

Encouraged, she elaborates, "Real icy feel to it."

He agrees. "Icy, all right."

After years of sharing the lobby with such disagreeable men as Pyle and Hancock, she's obviously thrilled by his positive responses. "Real nasty," she specifies further.

"Nasty indeed, Mrs. Firehammer."

"Real . . ." She gropes. "Cold."

"Yes, that too."

We enter through the laundry and pass through the furnace room to the hallway leading to the elevator. Sally is standing at her office door chatting with Claudette and Angelo. She beams at the poet with the warmth of a devoted reader, which she's not. To me she gives the hesitant kiss of a woman with a divided heart, which of course she is. When I introduce her as my former wife, Mr. Falcon steps back to give her a top-to-toe look of appraisal, and she and Claudette laugh hilariously. What have they been saying to one another while I stood outside? I recall the one occasion when these two women met before—our wedding—and how they hit it off like a couple of giggly old friends.

"Sally, Mr. Richard Falcon is perhaps the greatest writer of our time."

"Oh, please," he modestly chides me.

Worthington Pyle clears his throat, calling attention to the favor he's doing us by pressing the elevator button. He's waiting, no doubt, to preach to the New Man on the way upstairs.

Mr. Falcon turns to me. "Dr. Edwards, how could you have let a woman this lovely get away?" He appears not to be jesting. He's looking back and forth between us with true wonder in his eyes. Around the corner at the far end of the hallway come the lobbyists, the noisy laughter having tempted them out of their deep padded rockers.

"Yes, tell us," says Claudette. "We in Nebraska have had our theories, but we've never heard exactly."

My reply is "It's all rather complex."

Johnny Hancock provides a timely interruption, coming up to Richard Falcon and asking if he'd like to own a bat house, twenty-five dollars, reduced from forty-nine, all brass hinges and galvanized nails. "Holds seventy-five bats, or I can build you one that'll hold a hundred."

"Mr. Falcon, this is Johnny Hancock."

"Pleasure, Mr. Hancock."

"Got my tools here with me in the furnace room. I could go to work on a big one this afternoon yet."

Five or six women surround us, inspecting the New Man. The New Woman appears to approve of him, judging by her manner of taking him by the lapels and giving him a little shake, then standing back and laughing. Hildegard Lubovich, hoping to impress him with her authority, stamps her foot and barks, "Shame on you!" at the New Woman, who only laughs harder. "You too!" says Hildegard to Johnny Hancock. "Nobody wants one of your dirty old bat houses." Johnny backs away, looking sly and guilty and gratified that she paid him this much attention.

Sally leads the New Man into the elevator, introducing him to Father Pyle, and as the door closes on them, I hear the rector say, "Television's where it's at, Mr. Falcon. If I was young again, instead of serving the Lord I'd sell my soul and go into television."

In a few minutes, Sally returns to tell us that Mr. Falcon would like to take a nap and be picked up and driven to the campus library around four o'clock.

Claudette and I exchange a look of wonder, both of us suspecting, I guess, that we might have a very demanding genius on our hands.

"I'm on trial at three-thirty. Angelo, will you come and get him?"

"If you insist." An oddly uncooperative remark. My quizzical look prompts him to explain, "If you're not taking a lawyer in with you, at least you ought to take me."

"Nonsense." I turn to the two women and explain about L. P. Connor and her sexual harassment charge.

Claudette says it sounds open-and-shut.

Sally, familiar with L. P. Connor, disagrees. "She's out to bring you down, Leland. Take Claudette in with you as well."

"Yes, I want to have a look at this woman," says Claudette. "I picture an amazon."

"She's not that big," says Sally. "I'll drive Mr. Falcon to campus, so both of you can go in with Leland and get him off the hook."

"Picture a snake," says Angelo. "A killer water moccasin."

Angelo lets us off in front of our Simon P. Shea Teaching and Learning Center, where, on the second floor, we find Faith Crowninshield waiting for us in her conference room. "Ah, the dean's on time," exclaims Faith with satisfaction. Dr. Faith Crowninshield is a tall, broad-shouldered ex-nun for whom punctuality is next to godliness. She's wearing a tailored purple jacket today, over a silky yellow dress. "Sure, an O'Kelly cousin," she says, shaking Claudette's hand. "We probably met each other twenty years ago at Leland's wedding."

Faith goes back a long way at Rookery State. When she came to us as one of the earliest convent dropouts of the 'sixties, I had my misgivings. She doesn't think fast on her feet, and students complain of her tedious lectures. Then too, her idea of a perfect social evening consists mostly of entertaining you with her guitar. At faculty meetings, from the start, she was loud, bold, demanding, and overmeticulous. However, she has long since earned nearly the entire faculty's trust and respect, if not their affection, by taking on a good many difficult duties and accomplishing them all in a deliberate and tidy fashion. Being human rights officer isn't the first, by any means. She's our perennial representative on the Minnesota College Athletic Commission, and twelve years ago she led the faculty through an arduous self-study to restore our accreditation, which President Zastrow and Dean Patnode had carelessly let slip away.

She indicates that Claudette and I should sit side by side facing her across the table. "Sorry I couldn't be at your Christmas party, Leland."

"You were missed," I tell her, untruthfully.

"As you know, Sacred Heart Convent welcomes back its lost sheep every Christmas, and I like to be there to add my guitar to the liturgy."

"Of course, we understand."

It's her guitar that makes Faith so obtuse at parties. Instead of providing background music, she assumes that you want to listen closely to the New Age non-melodies she loves. I, for one, find her in-your-face method of string-plucking very tiresome.

I begin speaking of Richard Falcon's arrival on campus when the complainant in this case—who else but L. P. Connor?—comes slinking into the room and takes the chair next to Faith. I clam up, imagining my nemesis trying somehow to spoil the poet's reading. Her fixed, ungiving expression doesn't change as Faith shakes her hand, saying, "Thank you for being here, Ms. Connor. It will be so much easier to negotiate with your identity out in the open."

"Even if it wasn't me, he'd think it was me," she responds sourly. She's thinner than last time she haunted our campus, paler, more emaciated; the tendons of her neck stand out. Wearing a black cape over a black T-shirt, she puts me in mind of a giant bat. Her dyed black hair is blond at the roots. Her eyes and the line of her mouth, which have always registered a variety of unsavory attitudes—despair, haughty indifference, anger—are fixed today in an expression of cynical bitterness.

When I introduce Claudette to her, not as my cousin but as my adviser in human rights, she turns scornfully away from us and stares out a window as Faith explains to Claudette that a complainant is entitled to remain anonymous through Step Two if revealing her identity would put her at a disadvantage—this being one of several details I don't remember from the handbook, though I helped write it. But Ms. Connor is confident, says Faith, that because of my long reputation as a fair and compassionate administrator I will not be vengeful nor seek retribution.

Of this, I'm not so sure. After years of pitying this awful creature, I've come to the end of my patience. I feel like suing her for libel. I address Faith: "I'd like to hear the accusation, if you don't mind, straight from my accuser."

"Wait!" Faith closes her eyes. "This being my first sexual harassment hearing, I'm going to ask the Almighty for guidance." She makes a fist on the table and rests her forehead on it.

L. P. Connor raises her eyes to the ceiling. "Sheeeesh."

In the half minute of silence that follows, I picture Laura Connor as she was in the fall of 1968, the year she moved to Rookery with her parents, thirteen or fourteen years old, a gangly, potentially pretty girl with stringy blond hair, an alert mind, and a penchant for mischief. You could sense, underneath her shell, a crying need for security and love—a need partially fulfilled in our house whenever Mother was in a cooking or bread-baking mood, the two of them spending hours in the kitchen together, trying out recipes that KRKU's listeners had phoned in to "Lolly Speaking." Laura's mother, a woman immobilized by chronic depression, tried to take her own life in the spring of 1969.

I picture Laura growing thinner and even more hard-shelled through high school until her senior year, when her digestive system gave up waiting for nourishment and temporarily shut down altogether. She was hospitalized with symptoms suggesting appendicitis, an injured spleen, a bowel obstruction, gastritis, peritonitis, and everything else in the medical books under "Abdominal Pain," but it was none of these. What it was, beyond hunger, was depression. Her parents had divorced and she despaired of ever getting her father back from Peggy Benoit, with whom he was starting a new life in New Hampshire. Since puberty Laura had been confused about the role a daughter plays in her father's life. She saw her part as that of a wifely caretaker. She thought that it had been for her sake alone that her father had remained sober for long periods of time (in this, I think she was more or less correct), and she feared that under Peggy's permissive

influence, he'd take up his awful binge-drinking again, and ulti-
mately drink himself to death. Which he did, driving off a mountain road one drunken winter midnight.

I picture Laura at the funeral in Plymouth, New Hampshire,
stony-faced and frowsy. Mother and I were there, representing
Rookery State. This being the first time I'd attended a funeral
with no body, only ashes in a copper container the size and shape
of a book, the ceremony struck me as rather horrifying and
incomplete. I was glad the rest of the Icejam Quintet showed up
to help us console Peggy. Victor Dash flew in from Cleveland to
read a passage from Teddy Roosevelt. Neil Novotny was there
from Dayton to play "Just a Closer Walk with Thee" on his clarinet. Peggy herself, like the professional musician she is, sang "I'll
Get By" in spite of her tears, with me accompanying her on the
piano. Laura Connor, twenty-two that year, sat through the ceremony apparently unmoved. She avoided Mother and me until we
were leaving the cemetery, when she asked if she could ride home
with us. She'd flown out on a one-way ticket and didn't want to
ask Peggy for plane fare home. I hesitated, home being half a con-
tinent away, but Mother said of course. It took us three days. She
rode in the backseat sucking on Popsicles, racing through the
romance novels of Delphinia White, painting her toenails black,
and saying not a word to us all the way.

I picture her next in Petey's Price-Fighter Foods, shopping
with her mother and her mother's companion, Eldora Sparks.
This was during one of her recurring attempts at being a college
student and not long before Eldora Sparks died of a stroke. She
was calling herself L. P. by this time. She came up to me in the
freezer aisle to ask how to get her money back for a course she'd
decided to drop because she disliked the professor. "What a dud,
what a deadhead!" she said to me. I read in her black, blaming
eyes the accusation of fraud before she said it. "You're responsible, Dr. Edwards, you hired the creep! What a scam you run on
that campus!" On her left stood her mother, looking vacantly on;
on her right, Eldora Sparks smiled proudly. Eldora Sparks, a gruff
yet grandmotherly woman, had more or less saved Mrs. Connor's
life by taking her into her home after her suicide attempt. "Please
come to my office and we'll straighten it out," I told Laura,

backing away and doing my best to smile my farewell at the two older women. She came in the next morning and I appeased her, against state-college policy, with a full refund.

It's her mother I remember most clearly from that confrontation in the grocery store, this having been one of Mrs. Connor's rare appearances in public. She wore an old coat of gray, curly fur, and over her head a nubbly knit scarf knotted under her chin. It was apparent to me that she'd grown placid and quite fat since moving into Eldora's little clapboard house at the east edge of the city, a house identified as far back as I can remember by the dozens of large, white-painted stones lying about the yard. L. P. Connor and her mother live there to this day, I'm told, having been willed the house by Eldora. Her mother owes her untroubled demeanor, I've heard, to medication. Their income, I've also heard, is gained from a stash of Connor's paintings, which they sell off one by one as their taxes and other bills come due. Museums buy most of them. They never turn up on any wall in Rookery that I know of. It is said that Mrs. Connor passes her days, spring and fall, gathering stones of a certain size from the fresh-plowed fields bordering that side of the city, and takes them home and paints them white. I never drive down their street, preferring to avoid the Connor women altogether. The painted stones in the yard, according to Angelo Corelli, now number around five hundred.

Faith Crowninshield, having finished communing with her Maker, opens a folder and hands us copies of the Human Rights booklet. "Page three," she says, and while she reads aloud from the section on policies and procedures, I wonder how I could have allowed language this stilted to be set in print. I take out my pocket notebook and turn to a fresh page, where I write surreptitiously.

1994
#1. L. P. Connor is nuts.
Mary Sue Bloom is on the edge.
Mother plans her wake.
Coach Hokanson is deceitful.
Heim's Beer is in lights.
Jeffy Todd was in goal.

What a dismal list! Over against these perturbations I write Richard Falcon's name, and my spirits immediately soar as I begin another list:

> *Finalize date and time.*
> *Clean arena of construction debris.*
> *Prepare TV, radio, and print advertising.*
> *Alert motels, hotels, B&B's.*

Claudette nudges me, indicating that Faith has stopped reading and my nemesis is leveling her charges against me, speaking in a raspy, low monotone that's hard to understand, as though she hadn't used her voice in a long while. Faith then summarizes the charges, reducing them to their simplest legal terms. Number one, I abused my position of power in a sexual manner by kissing and hugging Carol Thelen in Room 208 of McCall Hall on December 18, 1993, at 11:57 A.M. Number two, I have habitually exhibited gender bias and have demeaned and humiliated my female students by excluding female writers from courses I teach.

I refute the first by explaining once again how the hug came to pass, adding "And a hug it was, not a kiss. Let's at least get that much straight." Trying to keep my voice down, I feel my neck heat up, my ears redden.

This prompts a consultation, *sotto voce,* between Faith and Ms. Connor, concerning the location, around noon of December 18, of my lips. It is determined that the complainant's case will be stronger if the questionable word "kissing" is withdrawn from the accusation.

"Thank you, thank you, you're both so very kind. Now, as for my so-called habit of excluding female writers from my courses, if Miss Connor is referring to English 337, History of the English Language, which she took from me a number of years ago, I admit that there were only two female names in my syllabus, but I have to point out that most of the experts in that field, at that time, were male. And while I admit that since becoming dean I've fallen behind in my scholarship and Miss Connor may have discovered studies by females I haven't heard of, I assure you my motives were—"

"I'm not talking about History of the Language," says L. P. Connor sneeringly. "I'm talking about Midwestern Lit. You always slight women writers."

"Ah, I see. And that's where you're absolutely wrong." Here I'm on firm ground, for this morning I cleverly thought to find the evidence in my files. "Numbers, Miss Connor, are you talking numbers? Because if you're talking numbers, I can show you . . ." Leaving this statement unfinished, I draw from my breast pocket and unfold my five-page Midwestern Literature syllabus, lay it on the table, and let it speak for itself.

They look it over. Faith totals up the names by gender, and seems satisfied. My nemesis, not impressed, says, "The females in your course are all poets."

"Not all." I point out the prose section. "Meridel LeSueur, Willa Cather, others."

"But *most* are poets."

"Tell me this, Miss Connor. *So what?*" This last is an angry shout.

She drones evenly, "Poems are shorter than fiction. The longer pieces are mostly by men."

"Because more fiction is written by men."

"That's a myth, Doctor Edwards. Don't you look at the paperback racks in Petey's Price-Fighter Foods? It's women four to one."

"That's because Petey stocks romances." This is scarcely out before I regret saying it, for I suddenly recall a classroom argument with this woman concerning reading taste, which I'd just as soon not repeat.

But repeat it we must. "And romances are trash, right, Dr. Edwards?"

"I don't say they're trash. I haven't read enough of them to call them trash. What I'm saying is, they're not literature."

"Like, how do you know if you haven't read them?"

"I do open one now and again. I read a page. The writing is . . ." I'm letting myself in for trouble, but I say it anyhow: "The writing is inferior, the stories are contrived."

"Inferior to what?"

"If you have to ask, then you haven't learned very much from all the English courses you've taken."

"Women can't write up to your standards is what you're saying."

"I'm not saying that. What I'm saying is that writers of romances don't take much care with their prose style."

"You mean *women* don't."

"Women, men, whoever writes them."

"Well, for God's sake, don't you even look at the covers? They're all written by women."

I'm about to point out that some are pen names for men. Surely she remembers Instructor Neil Novotny neglecting his classes in 1969 while he toiled away at his first novel, a romance entitled *Losing Lydia* which he planned to publish under the guise of a woman named Cornelia Niven. But I decide to shut up. It's useless to argue.

There follows another whispered conference, during which I glance at Claudette, whose expression is surprisingly pensive and neutral. I realize, then, that I don't know this cousin quite well enough to be sure that she hasn't come down on the side of my enemy. Rather than contemplate such a desertion, I open my notebook and add

> *Alert college bookstore to demand for Richard*
> *   Falcon's backlist.*
> *Prepare introductory remarks.*
> *Invite English departments from all*
> *   Minnesota high schools and colleges.*
> *Wake up, if possible, Sandor Hemm and the rest of*
> *   of the RSC English department.*
> *Where is Angelo?*

"All right then," says Faith Crowninshield, placidly shuffling papers in her folder. "We seem to be at an impasse. Unless, Leland, you're willing to take responsibility for some of your actions."

"Responsibility? *I* take responsibility?" I can't keep the lid on my anger. "What about Miss Connor taking responsibility for putting forth allegations with no foundation in fact?" I'm shouting now. "What kind of an inquisition are you running here,

Dr. Crowninshield? Do you realize you're asking me to admit to offenses I didn't commit?"

"I am not!" she fires back, scowling, slamming her folder shut. "I'm only saying that since you will admit to no guilt and Ms. Connor will not withdraw her charges, we have therefore achieved nonresolution at Step Two, and we'll have to proceed to Step Three." She stands up to leave.

"Hell's bells! How are we going to achieve resolution at any step if neither of us backs down—tell me that!"

"Read your handbook and find out," she says, striding from the room.

L. P. actually laughs at this—not the sneering laugh of ridicule I've watched her cultivate over the years, but a laugh of genuine amusement. It's amazing to see this chink in her armor of resentment.

"So much for policies and procedures," I say to her, hoping to draw her out a bit further. "Now perhaps you can tell me—"

"I love seeing you guys at each other's throats." Her laughter subsides, but a smile remains.

"Yes, well, now that we're alone perhaps you can tell me what motivates you to be so antagonistic."

"Who's alone?" she says, glancing at Claudette.

Claudette gets up to leave. "I'll see you in your office, Leland."

"No, wait, this will just take a second." Frankly, I'm afraid to be left alone with this woman. Who knows what further libelous charges she might concoct?

"All right, I'll be out here in the corridor." She leaves the door open.

Turning back to L. P. Connor, I see her smile fading, the line of her lips tightening into bitterness once again.

"Tell me now. Why are you doing this?"

She ponders my question for a few moments. "Bring you to justice," she drones, her eyes going dead. "See justice done in the world for a change."

"Ah, I see, an altruistic motive then. For the good of mankind."

"*Man*kind! God, don't you ever learn?"

"Miss Connor, I'm inquiring—why do you always choose *me* as your target?"

She shrugs.

"What have I ever done against you?"

Again she shrugs, raising her dead eyes to mine.

"I mean, those letters you wrote to St. Paul. You could have lost me my job."

At this, her eyes come suddenly alive. "How close did I come?"

I say nothing more. I hold her in my steady gaze, hoping she'll reveal some clue to her twisted motives. But she doesn't. Suppressing her curiosity, she clears her throat and turns aggressive again. " 'Attitudes of condescension and stereotyping are detrimental to campus life,' Dr. Edwards. It says that in your own handbook, page one."

I stand up, slipping the Human Rights booklet and my notebook into my pocket, and wishing I could leave with a dramatic barrage of words to convey my disgust. Good-bye is the only word that comes to mind. "Good-bye, Miss Connor."

"And if you don't stop calling me *Miss*, I'll add *that* to my complaint. 'Stereotyping based on age, race, physical appearance, or marital status,' section one, page four."

When we tell her the poet's in town, Mother insists that he be sent for and fed at our table this very evening. "We'll make it a gala dinner by inviting only the happiest people we know. We'll put on the dog."

"Not tonight, Mother. Dr. Kim said rest, remember."

"Rest! Rest is all I've been doing. Rest is too stressful." Leashed as she is to her oxygen tank, which stands in the archway between the living room and dining room, Mother has set up housekeeping on the living room couch, surrounded by magazines, trays of medicine, Kleenex, snacks, notepaper, cosmetics.

"It's nearly dinnertime now," says Claudette. "How could we possibly get a meal together?"

"We get on the horn to Helen Walker is what we do. At Christmas she brought in the best party food we've served in years, didn't she, Leland? The best dips and sauces and things."

"But, Mother, if you have a relapse—"

"Who's having a relapse? Here's my insurance against relapses." She fingers the tube running into her nostrils. "I tell you I haven't felt this good since I was seventy-eight—and to think all I've been needing was a teeny bit more oxygen than the Lord supplies in the air."

Claudette asks, "Isn't it awfully short notice for a caterer?"

Mother laughs. "Listen, dear heart, for the money I pay Helen Walker, she'll be here in ten minutes to draw up the menu. You see, when I started feeling decrepit a few years ago, I decided I had to put three people on retainer to make my old age tolerable, a lawyer, a hairdresser, and a caterer, and Helen Walker's been doing my food *and* my hair. I tell her now if only she'd get her law degree." More hoarse laughter from Mother, an admiring giggle from Claudette. "Leland, will you fetch me the phone? We'll invite Sally, of course—she'll bring our honored guest. You saw Sally at the Hi-Rise, did you, Claudette? Isn't she just the best-natured person you know? And the Corellis, of course, Angelo's so *up* all the time, and Gloria's such a dear."

I can tell from the speedy way her words come spilling out that Mother's been fiddling with her oxygen dial. I turn it down a notch, as Claudette tries to talk her into putting on the dog tomorrow evening instead. She's sitting there with her eyes half shut, nodding, as Claudette gently reminds her that Cousin Lucy arrives tomorrow. What a shame it would be if Lucy missed out on dinner with her favorite poet.

"Oh, Claudette, you're so sensible, I should put *you* on retainer to come in every so often to save me from myself, but honestly, where's your spirit, you young people?" Mother's voice grows thick and slow. "Where's your sense of fun? Where's your spontan . . . spon . . . where's your . . . ."

It's a curious sight, watching her drift off—the first sentence in her eighty-two years she's failed to finish.

Dinner is pizza in the kitchen with Claudette.

Mother takes to the poet on sight, and this confirms me in my fondness for him. What she likes best, I suppose, is the fact that he's well-spoken and radio-ready. Over the years she's watched so many hundreds of guests on "Lolly Speaking" struggle and fail to express themselves correctly that she grows very excited when visiting with someone like Richard Falcon, who advances precisely from the beginning of an idea to its end, then stops. He's scarcely seated in front of the roaring fire I've kindled in the fireplace before she elicits his promise to appear on KRKU. "Oh, that's *marvelous*," she exclaims huskily, sitting forward on the couch and reaching out to him as far as her oxygen tube allows, which would be just far enough to touch his hand if he would extend it, but he doesn't. Though he sits facing her, his eyes are turned inward. "Isn't it just *marvelous*, Leland? Would you fetch my calendar from the kitchen?"

"It *is* marvelous," I agree, although I hadn't imagined his *not* being on the radio. No celebrity passing through Rookery in the past forty-four years—from Miss Butter and Milk of 1950 to the newly appointed State Gaming Commissioner—has ever turned down the opportunity to appear on her show. Whatever you're merchandising, groceries or automobiles or the American Cancer Society, "Lolly Speaking" is your most effective platform in Rookery. Anthony K. Steadman credits Mother with single-handedly raising him from dogcatcher to mayor, and our Blue Heron basketball coach, jealous of hockey's sell-out crowds, is continually on the phone with her, pleading for airtime.

Richard Falcon doesn't drink. One gets the impression, teaching English, that American literature has been afloat these last hundred years on a sea of alcohol, and so I'm delighted when he turns down my offer of a cocktail or beer and asks for ice water instead. When I bring him the glass he's ready with a large blue capsule, which he pops into his mouth and swallows with difficulty. His complexion is quite red this evening, the alarming color of hypertension, it seems to me. His eyes have a recessive or glazed look.

"I can't promise, however, that your listeners won't desert you, Mrs. Edwards," he drones. "Poets are not proven media stars." He has the strange habit of making his eyes turn outward when he speaks, then making them recede inward the moment he falls silent.

"Oh, go on, Mr. Falcon. The public will be ordering tapes of the show." Again Mother, a toucher, reaches out unsuccessfully to pat his arm. "Please call me Lolly."

"Fair warning is all I'm saying, Mrs. Edwards, don't get your hopes up. If it's small talk you broadcast, you'll find I dry up awfully fast, and if it's political opinions, I have only one or two, which I express in the briefest of profanities."

She laughs. "It's fifteen minutes of whatever you want it to be. Leland, my calendar please." She slaps the air near his hand. "But no profanities, you naughty poet."

I leave the room reluctantly, for I'm fascinated by the way this guest of ours almost imperceptibly shrinks away from her each time she reaches out to him. Is it fear of being touched or is it a kind of majestic aloofness? Fear is my guess, because how can anyone who has offered his readers a lifetime of reading pleasure be truly ungiving and aloof?

In the kitchen I find Sally and Claudette discussing my sexual harassment session. Following Mother's instructions, they're helping Helen Walker get out our best silver and china and our scrimshaw napkin rings. Under their aprons, they're dressed to the nines, Claudette in a long red dress and on her feet what is surely the last pair of patent leather spike heels in existence—or do short people still wear them in Nebraska? Sally wears blue and brown with a paisley scarf at her throat. There's no telling what goes through her mind as she handles the Haviland and silver that might have been hers one day. Probably nothing. If she regrets what the divorce cost her in terms of property, surely she wouldn't come calling, as she does, at the slightest provocation.

"Can you imagine it, Sally?" asks Claudette. "Making sexual overtures in his classroom?"

"My God, no." Sally's laugh and look of disbelief seem to mean I'd be incapable of making sexual overtures anywhere—an unfair implication, coming from Sally of all people. Turning to make eyes at me, she adds, "He's *so* innocent."

I unpin the calendar from Mother's wall of cork and leave them snickering like girls.

In the front room I find Angelo and Gloria Corelli removing their coats and the poet putting his on. There's a terrible moment when I fear he's fleeing our dinner in a huff, but it turns out he simply needs a smoke.

Mother, whipping her oxygen tube out from underfoot, warns the Corellis, "Careful, don't trip on my lifeline." They kiss her and Gloria sinks into the couch beside her. Gloria, looking snappy in black and pink, wants to know all about the quality of health care in her native Nebraska, while Angelo, too young and antic for the pinstripe suit and vest and grandfatherly tie he's wearing, wants to know how I like the poet so far, how the poet likes Rookery, whether the president and his wife have been invited, and whether I've yet come up with an adjective for the "dumdiddy" cat.

"I'm keeping Zastrow out of his way as long as possible, Angelo, for fear he'll darken Mr. Falcon's view of Rookery. As for my opinion of the poet, I've never before met anyone I've admired so much."

"But I mean in person, how does he measure up?"

"Just fine," I tell him dismissively, not wanting to get into my suspicion that Mr. Falcon may be something other than the gentle-hearted gentleman the world makes him out to be.

"How about the dumdiddy cat?"

"Leave it in, you'll never do better than 'dumdiddy.' Excuse me, Angelo, I hear voices." Opening the front door, I find, under the lamppost, my cousin Lucy laughing with the poet. No one laughs quite like Lucy O'Kelly. Her eyes go shut, and out of her wide-open mouth comes a scream like a siren. I'm heartened to see Mr. Falcon amused as well, except you don't really *see* his amusement. You hear it in his nose—a subdued kind of snuffle.

"What's so funny?" I want to know, embracing Lucy and catching a whiff of her scent, a mixture of perfume and rubbing alcohol.

"Oh, I'm so embarrassed, Leland, you haven't got any business springing my favorite poet on me like this. Here I come up the walk introducing myself, and when he tells me who he is I'm so flustered I tell him how my favorite poem in all the world is the one about the man on the train to Omaha—you know, in the club car?—and I even recite the last couple lines for him, and he says yes, it's one of his favorites too, and he wishes he'd've written it." Again the piercing laugh. "It's by Carl Sandburg. Embarrassment city, right?"

Of course she's not embarrassed in the least, being the most self-possessed person I've ever known. "Ta ta, Mr. Falcon," she says, "I'll see you inside when you finish your smoke." I pick up her suitcase and usher her inside. "How is she?" she asks in the entryway, removing her coat. "Is she good about her medicine and oxygen?"

"Very good. She knows they're the reason she's still living."

Mother gets to her feet to embrace Lucy and introduce her to the Corellis. Gloria and Mother rave about her outfit, a kelly green outfit, sweater and billowy slacks. Angelo looks on amazed. Did I forget to tell him that Lucy is African-American? Mother then leads her into the kitchen to meet Sally. Gloria follows, wheeling the oxygen tank.

"What's the protocol, Angelo, when your guest of honor is outside smoking? I mean, do I put on my coat and cap and stand out there with him or stay indoors feeling guilty?"

"Depends whether you've got an assistant," he says, stepping into the entryway and wrapping his scarf around his neck.

"No, I can't let you freeze, Angelo. I'll go." I reach for my coat, but he won't let me put it on.

"I need to cool off," he says. "Your fire is too hot."

"Don't be silly, it's nearly zero out there."

Our little skirmish at the coat closet is settled by the poet, who comes indoors with his eyes teary and his nose running. "Christ, it's cold."

"Sorry," I say, apologizing in behalf of the weather system that's been parked over Minnesota since before Christmas.

"But it's a dry cold," says Angelo. "I was in Boston once. Ten above felt like twenty below."

Richard Falcon gives him a scathing look, as if to say he can't abide such stupidity. Angelo smiles weakly and turns away, visibly wounded. I pray the poet will never turn such a deadly expression on me.

Our honored guest needs three or four more cigarettes before we go in to dinner, by which time he's chilled to the marrow and shuddering.

"I can get you a cold tablet," I offer, ushering him to the foot of the table.

"What for?"

"Ward off a cold."

"I don't get colds."

The Corellis and Lucy sit on his right, their backs to the windows, which have been transformed into mirrors by the blackness of this midwinter evening. I sit facing them, between Sally and Cousin Claudette. Mother insists on taking her place at the foot of the table, so as not to trip up the rest of us with her lifeline, and I sense the poet stiffen and suppress his anger when he's asked to move to the head.

Sally, Mother, and I recite an Episcopal grace, and Helen Walker comes in with the serving dishes—walleye, zucchini, and a baked Hubbard squash. I'm eager to get the table talk around to *Fording the Bee*, but before I can do so I have to answer an endless train of questions, set in motion by Sally, about my human-rights predicament. Yes, we're taking it to Step Three, a confrontation which is sure to be a disaster, what with O. F. Zastrow presiding. Yes, L. P. Connor is definitely unhinged. No, the woman I hugged, a Miss Thelen, is not involved in the case, was not in the least offended, has not been consulted; nor, according to our bylaws, is there any need for her even to be kept informed about the proceedings. Yes, it's obvious that our bylaws were drawn up by idiots, myself chief among them.

Throughout this discussion I see Richard Falcon pay close attention each time L. P. Connor's name comes up, and I wonder if Peggy Benoit has sent him to Minnesota on a fact-finding mission.

"Has anybody tried horsewhipping her?" blurts Claudette.

Lucy flinches at this, and so does the poet. Gloria Corelli looks aghast.

"Sorry," she continues, "but you'd have to see her in action, as I did this afternoon. She's a horrible person."

"I was thinking just the opposite," Gloria puts forth rather timidly. "I was wondering if it might be time to try kindness."

"We did that," I remind her. "Years and years we were kind to her."

"And it paid off," says Mother.

"For a short time."

"Nearly five years," she corrects me. "From the age of thirteen to seventeen she responded to our kindness. Don't tell me you've forgotten how helpful she was around the house all that while. What good company she was."

"Who wouldn't forget, in view of the twenty years of trouble she's caused us since?"

"She changed at seventeen?" inquires Lucy, as if the number might be significant.

Mother nods. "Right after graduating from Rookery High, she had a kind of breakdown."

"Schizophrenic?"

"Her doctors thought so for a time, but decided no, they can't put a name to her trouble."

"I can," says Claudette, my ally. "It's called bonkers."

"Now, now," says Mother, as though gently calming an obstreperous child.

"Listen, Aunt Lolly, you better keep your distance from this woman. She's got a heart like a cinder."

Mother reaches behind her to adjust the dial on her tank, upward apparently, for I watch a faint flush spread over her cheeks. "But just think of her side of it for a minute. She's been knocking around town for twenty years . . . with nobody showing her any kindness. Who wouldn't be making trouble? Leland, I really believe Gloria's right . . . we must see what we can do for the poor thing."

I open my mouth to protest.

"I know, I know, she did those awful things to us, but we can't give up on people. It's in the Gospels. Seventy times seven times and all that."

"Listen, Mother, we passed our 490th forgiveness years ago. Now what I think—"

We're interrupted by an awful clatter of silverware on china—Richard Falcon either losing control of his knife and fork or ringing for attention. "I knew her father, though not well," he says, clearing his throat. "I dare say nobody knew him well. He was a complicated man. Kept doing unexpected things."

"Like dying," I blurt. I'm suddenly lonesome for Connor. I

resent his dying. After twenty years I still get this occasional pang of longing for him and the other absent members of the Icejam Quintet. Such music we made. The few combos I tried to put together after that were never as lively, never as interesting, never so much fun.

"Oh, his dying was no surprise," says Mr. Falcon. "Not the way he was drinking at the end. No, I'm talking about the way he made those sudden, impetuous turns in his art."

"His troubles, Mr. Falcon," says Mother. "He had more than his share of troubles."

"Troubles! Don't tell me about troubles." He glares at Mother in a withering manner such as I'm sure she's never been glared at before. She responds with raised, inquiring eyebrows directed at Lucy, with a sideways nod toward the poet: *Well, what's eating his highness tonight?*

He goes on: "I'm talking about the way he'd change course in his painting. You see, when he moved to New Hampshire . . ." The poet's voice grows faint, and he stops to draw a deep and labored breath. "At first he was painting mothers and daughters, and then about the time they started to catch on, he started on still lifes . . . flowers and crockery . . . wouldn't paint a mother-daughter portrait no matter what he was offered, don't ask me why . . . and he was offered plenty, let me tell you. . . ."

He keeps outtalking his breath. I imagine running a second tube off mother's tank. This idea amuses me, and when I catch myself lowering my head so he won't see me smile, it dawns on me just how intimidating is our honored guest. I'm disappointed—all right, I'm devastated—to realize that if he weren't the best talent now writing in English, I'd probably consider Richard Falcon nothing but a domineering ass.

He continues. "Then it took awhile, but his admirers started to come around, started to buy up his pots and daisies, and then what do you suppose?" He looks from one face to another, angrily, it seems to me. I am about to reply when Sally answers for me:

"Derelicts." I used to show her my letters from New Hampshire.

The poet's eyes soften as they settle on my former wife.

"Right you are, Ms. McNaughton. Tramps and bums. He'd set up his easel in soup kitchens and pay some poor homeless bum to sit for him." Next, he focuses on Claudette—again a tender look. "I remember one time he made a special trip down to Worcester, Mass., because he heard about this interesting panhandler living out of a grocery cart in the city square. Came home with a portrait so big it hardly fit in his car. Nobody bought it. Who'd want it?"

Lucy speaks up. "Well, you have to admit that's pretty darn interesting. Pursuing a vision like that."

"Oh, I do indeed." On Lucy he bestows not only his kindly expression but the hint of a smile as well. "More than interesting. Enviable, I'd call it. Nothing short of inspiring. I credit Connor with giving me the courage to shift styles wherever I please in the poem I'm working on."

"*Fording the Bee,*" I announce to the other guests, glad to have arrived finally at the topic of my desire. "Could you give us some idea, Mr. Falcon, of the length of the poem and how it's structured?"

It's a question I regret the moment it's out of my mouth, for he shoots me the same searing, chastening look that wounded Angelo and Mother earlier, the sort of intensely dark expression that can only be achieved through a lifetime of unhealthy feelings like anger, frustration, and despair. Or—I regret to say this—a lifetime of hate.

Sally and Lucy both come to my aid, speaking lightly of studying poetry in school, and Mr. Falcon is immediately captivated by their happy voices. He actually smiles. That's when I figure out that Richard Falcon is the sort of man who sees the human race as divided into two types—good-looking women and the rest of us stupid wretches.

Helen Walker comes in with dessert. From poetry, the talk shifts to campus personalities, Angelo's speciality, and I watch the poet's attention turn inward again. A discussion of burnouts ensues, burnouts in many a field of endeavor. What is there about young people these days, Mother wants to know, that keeps them from sticking to things? Announcers and radio engineers, she says, have been passing through KRKU like itinerant fruit pickers. In nursing, says Lucy, it's the stress and low pay, at least that's the case in Grimsby, Nebraska. Sally supposes that in her own field, gerontology, it's the strain of being surrounded by senility and drool all day, with death always waiting at the door to sneak in. Angelo, it turns out, now has thirteen people signed up for the next meeting of his support group. Of course Mother wants to know who these burnouts are, and despite my protest he begins naming them. At the mention of Mary Sue Bloom, I bring up Francine Phillips's trip to Bismarck, which prompts the poet's eyes to come suddenly alive. He says, mysteriously:

"Is there enough gas in the pickup, Phillips?"

"I beg your pardon?" says Angelo, for it seems to be Angelo he's addressing.

"We'll never make it to Kilmer Pond on half a tank, you know that."

"Sir?"

"Oh, never mind," he mumbles with disgust, and he sinks back into himself.

What am I in for? Is dementia a symptom of Parkinson's? Kimberly Kraft, whose father had Parkinson's, will be able to tell me how to handle this man. I'll have Richard Falcon on my hands for a mere thirty days, I remind myself, whereas Kimberly took care of her father for years.

"Oh, oh," says Gloria Corelli under her breath, getting suddenly to her feet and helping Mother up out of her chair. Lucy, too, rises and comes to her aid.

"What's the matter?" I ask, imagining a silent coughing fit coming on, or a kink in the oxygen tube.

Sally nudges me, her eyes looking past me at the head of the table, where the poet has pushed aside his uneaten pie and is lighting a cigarette.

"Mr. Falcon, Mother's terribly allergic to smoke, I'm afraid."

Taking the cigarette shakily from his lips and blowing smoke down the table, he says, "Make sure Phillips puts gas in the pickup."

Sally uses her Hi-Rise voice of command on him: "It's a no-smoking house, Mr. Falcon. You'll have to put it out."

He looks up at her with a fond smile, grateful, it seems, for her attention, and takes another drag.

I go to him and urge him to stand up, gently lifting one of his arms, but to no avail; he can't seem to take his eyes off Sally.

"Come along, my dear," she says, taking his hand in both of her own. "I'm driving you home."

He stands stiffly up. He wedges the cigarette into the corner of his mouth and rests his other hand on the chair for a moment, then allows himself to be led away from the table, warning Angelo as he passes behind his chair, "Remember what I said, Phillips."

"Sir," says Angelo obediently.

In the living room, Sally's firm grip prevents him from moving toward Mother, whom Cousin Lucy is settling on the couch. Gloria Corelli stands over her fanning the air with her hand. "I'm much obliged, Mrs. Edwards," he says with surprising cogency. "If you're sure you want a live poet on the radio, I'm your man."

"Oh, I want you all right, but I won't trouble you to come down to the station. We'll do a phone interview."

Ashes fall to the carpet as I help him on with his coat. Outside, hit by the cold, he mutters, "Christ almighty." His walking seems impaired. He shuffles over to the Hi-Rise van, shaking off my attempt to support him, accepting Sally's arm instead.

"It's a no-smoking van," I tell him, adopting her authoritative tone.

Waiting for her to unlock his door, he stands looking up at the moon through the branches of our maple. "I'm not going to Kilmer Pond in weather like this," he says.

"We're not either," says Sally. "We're taking you home."

He tries to climb into the van, but Sally stands in the way. "Put out your smoke," she tells him.

He takes a last long drag, exhales in the direction of the moon, and flicks the cigarette into a snowbank.

By asking him a few leading questions on the way to the Hi-Rise, we determine that he knows more or less where he is. He's already mapped out the days ahead. Having found the library suitable for writing, he will require a ride early each morning. He wants me to meet him for his coffee break around 10:30 or 11:00. He'll work through the lunch hour, eating at his desk. He asks us to recommend a scenic area for a walk if the weather warms up. He likes a little exercise in the late afternoon. Because it will be March before we can count on warmer days, I suggest he go fishing with me in Roman's spearing house. He's never speared fish. He says he'd like to try it.

We stop at Petey's Price-Fighter Foods for cigarettes, breakfast rolls, and coffee. We stop at Stanhope Pharmacy for a prescription confirmed by a phone call to New Hampshire. Pulling into her parking place at the back of the Hi-Rise, Sally further tests the poet's sanity by asking what pickup he'd been talking to Phillips about.

Sitting beside her, he snuffles with laughter and turns his head a bit to the left, in order to throw his voice back to me. "That assistant of yours, Dr. Edwards, that Corelli. He reminds me of a flunky I had working for me one time. Name of Phillips. Dumb as a doorpost."

SPRING TERM

A new semester doesn't immediately find its legs and move from one hour to the next without considerable support from the dean's office; therefore nearly a week passes before I find a large enough lull in my schedule to leave campus in the early afternoon.

"Viola, I'm going to pay a call on Kimberly Kraft."

"Creepy," she says, without lifting her eyes from her computer screen.

"Would you call and tell her I'm coming?"

"Good luck," she says, reaching for the phone with an expression of distaste. She knows how tricky it is getting in to see Kimberly Kraft since her retirement. Kimberly will never open her door to an unexpected caller, nor will she pick up a ringing telephone, so the best I can hope for is that she's listening to her answering machine as Viola announces my visit.

"Better be back by three, for your sex meeting," she tells me as I slip into my new gray overcoat (a gift at Christmas from Mother) and my new tartan scarf (a gift from Sally).

"Sexual harassment, Viola."

"Then there's Corelli's support group at four. He says a couple of them are real shaky. Dr. Bloom is—"

"I'm leaving that alone, Viola. Burnout's contagious."

She shrugs. "I wouldn't know, I'm sure." Viola's bulk is contained today in a navy blue sack her husband Bud gave her for Christmas, a loose nylon pantsuit cinched with drawstrings at the neck and ankles.

"Also Dr. Hemm wants to see you. He's got his undies all in a twist because you're putting off tenure for Dr. Bhandi."

"Dr. Bhandi will have to show a bit of interest in campus affairs and show up at faculty meetings before I approve her for tenure."

"Hemm's sore about your poet, too."

"*My* poet! Please, Viola, he's America's poet."

"Yeah, well, Hemm says he's third-rate."

"Does he say why?"

"Says he's a rhymer." Wisely giving me no time to fulminate against Sandor Hemm's narrow taste in literature, she goes on. "Also you might go up to third and find out why Kahlstrom's been skipping classes."

"Again, Viola?"

She nods vigorously. "Two this week already."

"Well, we know why, don't we. He's lazy."

"If that's the case, I'd go up and set him straight if I were you."

"And exactly how would you accomplish that, Viola?"

"I'd exactly kick butt."

Ringing the doorbell of 400 Bellwether Drive, an enormous old house of chipping paint and sagging porches front and back, I am struck once again by President Zastrow's brutal and wasteful effect on the lives he touches. Kimberly Kraft, always a bit of a neurotic, has perversely decided to spend her retirement in seclusion in order to show the world she's been wronged. What does the world care? Nobody but Mother and me and maybe her next door neighbor gives her a thought from one month to the next. Although I didn't know her as a child, I can picture her flinging away her croquet mallet and going off to pout while her playmates go happily on with the game.

Since last July, by federal law, it's been illegal to force employees into retirement by reason of their age alone. That's why O. F. Zastrow fired Kimberly in May, claiming she was too old to drive safely to the schools where her interns were teaching. Which might have been true. There'd been two citations from the state patrol, one for a minor accident caused when she sped through the village of Osage at sixty miles an hour, and the other—the very next day—for refusing to drive over twenty-five miles per hour on the open road.

A traffic citation is the very sort of thing that makes a deep impression on the dim mind of our president. He has no concept, despite my pleading, of what a priceless faculty member we've lost. Kimberly Kraft, at sixty-eight, knows more about classroom management than anyone in the department, and she spent her career establishing invaluable connections with almost every public and private school in our service area. Had it been left to me, I'd have taken her off the road and given her less demanding duties on campus. We have no one left with her savvy. Who will now inform our graduating teachers, for example, which schools are essentially run by their principals, which by their department heads, which by their janitors and secretaries? Where will they learn the subtle little tricks of classroom discipline if not from Kimberly Kraft?

I ring the doorbell again and wait. I should have telephoned earlier. Most of her window screens, I notice, have not been replaced by storm windows. Drifted snow has not been cleared from the porch.

Minutes pass before the deadbolts slide back and the door creaks open a few inches. "You may come into the foyer if you're chilly, Leland," sings the delicate soprano voice I recall from perhaps fifty weddings and funerals during her thirty years in Rookery. Her repertoire consisted of only three pieces. For brides she invariably sang "Oh Promise Me," while the bereaved got "Rock of Ages." She could go either way with "Ave Maria."

"Thanks, Kimberly," I say to the crack in the door. I give her a moment to flee, then I step inside and close the locks. Standing in the chilly foyer, I converse with her unseen presence upstairs.

"How are you?"

"You *have* to give me more *warn*ing, Leland."

"Sorry, Kimberly. I'm stealing time from the office."

"You can't *always* expect me to drop what I'm doing."

What she's been doing, I know, is sitting in her rocking chair with her stuffed owl in her lap and her eyes fixed on Bellwether Drive, watching for the occasional car or pedestrian to pass by.

"You'll see for yourself soon enough, Leland. Unless you manage your time, retirement will wear you right out."

The rise and fall of her delivery brings to mind the way her untrained but serviceable voice, in church, used to start off shaky and perhaps half a tone off-key, but grew in confidence and volume as she went on. Who will ever forget the time she belted out "Oh Promise Me" at a funeral, and never realized her mistake? At least she was not visibly mortified. It was the funeral of C. Mortimer Oberholtzer, for many years my chairman in the English Department. She was singing *a cappella* with no introductory organ tones to guide her. Even a few of the mourners, though not Mrs. Oberholtzer, had to smile.

"How's Lolly? She hasn't called me since I don't know when."

Since last summer, actually, because Kimberly never answers her phone. "Mother's not been feeling up to par," I tell her.

"I thought so. She hasn't been on the radio."

"She had a setback in Nebraska. She's on oxygen."

"Oh, what's the use of living!"

Styles today are plainer than the dress she returns to the foyer in—it features appliquéd flowers of purple and green—nor have I seen anyone her age in saddle shoes for at least thirty years. Her shoulders are wrapped in the ancient knit sweater she acquired on the trip she took to Ireland several years ago with a view to getting acquainted with distant relatives—cousins who went by what she took to be the aristocratic Anglo-Irish name of Harrington; but when she discovered them to be impoverished farmers barely eking out a living among the stones of Connemara, she fled and never responded when their letters followed her home. As she explained to Mother, "They're very friendly and all that, but their clothes smell of peatsmoke, they can't spell, and their teeth are extremely crooked."

A small and demure woman all her life, she appears to have lost weight and height in retirement, as well as the ability to look me in the eye. Smiling not at me but at my buttons, she squeezes my hand, saying, "Well, now that you're *here*, you might as well *sit* for a minute." She quickly turns away, leading me into the kitchen, where I am offered a seat at a wobbly antique table and she busies herself at the stove, making tea. Her thinning white hair is tightly curled. Her wrinkles are those of a smiler, someone who's spent a lifetime hiding her loneliness under a happy appearance and telling people to look on the bright side. But now, in old age, she can't keep it up. Her smile is a grimace.

"What is it, her breathing again?"

"Yes, it's worrisome, Kimberly. One of these times I'm afraid it will be fatal."

"*Living* is fatal, Leland." She's always been ready with this sort of snappy answer, making conversation difficult. "I've been going through pictures," she says, submerging a single teabag in her pot of boiling water. "Boxes and boxes of pictures. What do you do with a lifetime of pictures, Leland?—three lifetimes really, many go back to my grandparents' time, pictures of people nobody will know the names of when I'm gone, half of them I don't know myself."

"Write their names on the back."

"I'm sick of them. I'm on the point of throwing them out."

"Oh, don't do that. Give them to our history department. They've started a collection of old family photos."

"Next garbage day I'm throwing them out with the trash."

I groan, which causes her to smile wickedly, pleased with the power of her wayward petulance. She pours pale tea into two cracked cups from her parents' set of antique china. Some years ago, her parents, who'd grown wealthy selling farm machinery on the fertile plains of southern Minnesota, got rid of the business in a timely manner, just before the farm recession, and moved north to join their daughter in Rookery. They bought this large house for the three of them to live in, which, until Mrs. Kraft died and Mr. Kraft became incapacitated, was one of the showplaces of Bellwether Drive—green lawns, flower gardens, trimmed hedges. But Kimberly, a penny-pinching apartment dweller most of her adult life with no sense of property, has let it go downhill. She's confessed to Mother that there are rooms upstairs she hasn't entered for years. The kitchen smells musty.

"I've come to talk about your father, Kimberly. To ask you about his Parkinson's."

Disappointment appears in her eyes, as though, despite her protestations, she'd hoped that this might be a purely social call.

"We have this very distinguished visitor on campus, the poet Richard Falcon, and he requires special handling, so I've come to ask—"

"Not *the* Richard Falcon."

"The same Richard Falcon," I state auspiciously. I love saying his name. Despite his self-centeredness and his cigarette smoke, my pride in hosting the great man has not diminished.

"I thought he was dead."

"Very much alive, and working furiously away on his big autobiographical poem. *Crossing the Bee,* he's calling it."

"*Fording the Bee,*" she corrects me scornfully. "It was published years ago."

"*Fording the Bee,* of course you're right. But only the first part came out. It's going to be book length."

"It was book length then."

"Yes, but a very thin book. It will be at least four times as long when he's finished."

She drills me with her eyes, scowling as she reprimands me. "Honestly, Leland, must you contradict everything I say?"

I look into my tea, thinking how sad to witness the delicacy of Kimberly Kraft hardening into brittleness. How unexpected and unjust that a woman who used to cling to fading styles of dress with such a flair that they actually looked stylish again should now fall so far out of date that she looks dowdy, maybe a little goofy. Until recently it hasn't been painful to watch Mother grow old, but Kimberly, fifteen years her junior, makes advancing age seem tragic.

"Richard Falcon has Parkinson's?" she asks in a softer tone. "I never heard he had Parkinson's."

I nod. "One hasn't heard *anything* about the man for years."

"No, I guess one hasn't."

"I thought you could tell me about the symptoms, Kimberly. What's typical. How you handled it."

"He has the tremor?"

"Yes."

"Loses his balance?"

"I haven't noticed that."

"Father used to lose his balance so easily." Kimberly looks past me with a tender, nostalgic expression. "Remember how nice he was, Leland? Father was so *nice*. I brushed past him here in the kitchen one day and knocked him over, just the slightest *touch* and down he went, and what was the first word out of his mouth? 'Sorry.' I knocked him down and he *apol*ogized, consoling me because he knew how bad I felt. It was right there behind where you're sitting, Leland, he was lying on his *back* and looking up at me and saying, *'Sorry.'* "

I expect a break in her voice at this point, and maybe a tear or two, but no, her reprimanding scowl returns and her eyes are drilling me again.

"It's a shame that nice doesn't *count* anymore, Leland."

"What do you mean?—of course nice counts."

"Not at Rookery State it doesn't. Not with you!"

"Nice counts," I repeat, but uselessly, for I know what's coming.

"Does May nineteenth, last year, have any meaning for you, Leland?"

I sip my tea and brace myself.

"Last spring, on May nineteenth, you weren't nice, Leland. That was the day I was evicted from my office, as if you didn't know."

"That was Dr. Zastrow not being nice, Kimberly."

"Who *expects* Dr. Zastrow to be nice? Dr. Zastrow's never been nice in his *life*. I'm talking about you, Leland, you never came to my aid."

"But I did, I pleaded with him. I've told you that."

"Ha! Lot of good *that* did."

I meekly hear her out, and we're on our second cup of tea before we get back to the poet:

"It's not his physical disability I want to know about, so much as his odd behavior. Did your father act strange sometimes?"

"Don't we all? Honestly, Leland, you are being so difficult."

"I mean was he irrational. What I'm thinking of is the other evening Mr. Falcon came to dinner and said some irrational things. And then, having been told of Mother's condition and thus having gone out on the doorstep to smoke three or four cigarettes before dinner, he lit up a smoke at the table, over dessert, and when I hustled him out of the house he seemed perplexed."

Kimberly casts her eyes about the kitchen, cocking her head left and right like a wren. I recall this habit from faculty meetings; it signals her weighing two or more intemperate responses. She settles on this one:

"Leland, you're so innocent. Didn't it occur to you that he might be simply a heartless bastard?"

"Well, yes it did, actually."

"You're such a babe in the woods."

At this I'm afraid I raise my voice slightly. "Be that as it may, my question is, was I seeing the disease the other night, or was I seeing nastiness?"

"How should I know?"

There's an edge in my raised voice. "Because you know more than most people about Parkinson's. Now don't be difficult, Kimberly. You took your father to that support group for years. All I'm asking is how the disease affects the mind."

"Father only got nicer as time went on. It saddens me to think you've forgotten how nice he was."

At this I'm afraid I lose control. "I have *not* forgotten how nice your father was—your father had to be a *saint* to put up with you all those years, I know that." I stand up, button my coat, pick up my hat. "Talk about nastiness. I only came here to ask a civil question, and you—" Here I stall, interrupted by shame. There she sits, huddled over her cooling tea, visibly wilting under the heat of my anger. Regret sweeps over me. "Forgive me, damn it."

The face she turns up to me is wet with tears. "Oh, Leland," she cries.

I kiss a wet cheek and leave.

"Urrr," says President Zastrow, standing at my office door, snapping his gold watchband and wearing a look of sad impatience. Kimberly Kraft's tears have made my heart heavy and prevent me from trying to lighten his spirit. I'll leave that to Angelo.

"Your office or mine?" I ask him.

"Mine."

"Just a second, I'll hang up my coat."

"Urrr," he replies.

"How was she?" Viola wants to know.

"Difficult. Is Angelo in there already?"

"Corelli went home. Said he'd be back but he isn't."

"Home!"

"Emergency. Bloom flipped out."

"Mary Sue?"

"Cried like a baby."

"Good Lord."

"Ever seen an honest-to-god breakdown?" Viola, seldom moved by anything outside the wrestling arena, makes big eyes to show how impressed she was. "Boy, that dame's a regular screaming meemie."

"So he took her home?"

"She sounded a lot like a pickup we had one time with vapor lock."

"He can't just take her home and leave her there. He should take her to a doctor."

"No, no, *his* home. Figured his wife could get her fixed up and back on the road."

"Urrr," says my president, waiting at my door.

"Coming," I tell him. "Has Miss Connor brought someone to represent her?"

He nods curtly. "A woman. C'mon."

I step into my inner office and get Gloria Corelli on the phone. "What's going on? Viola says she flipped out."

"Nothing like that, Leland—she's just having herself a good cry."

"Can I talk to her?"

"Just a sec, I'll ask." A moment later: "No."

"Okay, I'll see her later."

In the mirror, I straighten my tie, comb my hair. On the way out, Viola offers to come with me, in Angelo's place. "You need a mouthpiece," she tells me.

I thank her. "No, Viola, you can't leave the office unattended."

"I can get a girl to come in."

"It wouldn't be worth the trouble."

"Don't be so sure."

"I'll call for you if I think it's necessary."

It's no surprise that O. F. Zastrow is unprepared to preside over Step Three, and Faith Crowninshield has to guide him, paragraph by paragraph, through the pertinent pages of the Human Rights handbook, which he silently and arduously reads with his lips moving, his right eye squinted, his nostrils flared. He gives his thumb a thorough licking before turning each page.

L. P. Connor, sitting on my right with a fresh glossy coat of black paint on her fingernails and a smirk on her white-powdered face, remains silent. Sitting beside her, at the corner of this small conference table, is her defender, a gray-haired woman with steel gray eyes who keeps putting forth platitudes intended to aid in the president's instruction, such as "Learning is impossible in a pervasive atmosphere of sexual harassment." She's a Legal Aid attorney whose name, Callie Horner, I've seen in the *Morning Call* as the defender of certain homeless men and women who keep defying city ordinance by sleeping under highway bridges. When Zastrow finishes reading, Callie Horner asks a chilling question in her client's behalf, directing it at Faith but with her humbling eyes on me. "How long has Doctor Edwards allowed an atmosphere of sexual harassment to pervade his classroom?"

"That's undetermined at this point in time," says Faith. "We're still in the fact-finding phase of this case."

"Has Dr. Edwards been known to indulge in humor or jokes emphasizing gender-specific traits such as breasts?"

"No, not to my knowledge," replies Faith, "but as I say, we're still gathering information."

"Are Dr. Edwards and Ms. Carol Thelen involved in a consensual amorous relationship?"

All eyes, including the president's, turn to me.

"Ask Miss Thelen," I mutter.

And that's my only utterance during the entire meeting. At first my silence is caused by disgust. I mean, why should I waste my breath on this nonsense? But after further questioning of my moral fitness plus half an hour of haggling over handbook policies, mention is made of Steps Four and Five, and my mouth dries up with fear.

#10. An enormous cloud of murk is descending on us. One thinks of Kafka. Of Orwell. Of Bleak House. We could spend the rest of our lives at this fiasco and never emerge from the fog.

Eventually Callie Horner looks at her watch and says, "Excuse me, I have to be at the courthouse in fifteen minutes."

"And I have a class coming up," says Faith, snatching the handbook away from the president like a mother not trusting her child with books—he might chew it or scribble in it.

"Urrr," he says, looking at the space where the book had been. "Meeting adjourned."

I return to my consoling view of the Badbattle in time to see Coach Hokanson and the athletic director trudging uphill from their offices in the old arena. They breast the cold wind without coat or hat. I see them pause at the door below me while the athletic director, Ernie Burr, finishes a cigarette, and then they pause longer, checking their watches, spitting, shivering, gazing out over the river, neither of them willing to enter McCall Hall a moment before the meeting I've called. Unless summoned, they never show their faces along Administration Row.

Their faces are similar. I'm struck by this as I welcome them into my office and pour coffee—their wide jaws, squinty little eyes, and receding hairlines. It's their coloring that sets them apart from each other. Coach Hokanson is pallidly Scandinavian. Ernie Burr has a swarthy Mediterranean look. Their bodies, in their snug sweaters, are similar as well—the stocky, top-heavy build of the athlete going to pot. They grew up in neighboring towns on the Iron Range, both of them high school stars who never got over it, lettering in three or four sports apiece. Hokanson, according to his *curriculum vitae*, went on to play hockey for the Bulldogs at the University of Minnesota–Duluth and then had a brief career in the National

Hockey League. Ernie Burr never tires of pointing out the injustice done him by a certain Twin Cities newspaper when it named him All-State in football as a high-school junior and not—in 1961—as a senior.

"Just three of us today?" asks Hokanson, looking rather desperately about my office for a friendlier face than mine.

"Right, Coach, just us."

"How about Corelli?" Ernie Burr asks.

It's my sad duty to inform them that Angelo, formerly a high-school infielder, is occupied elsewhere this afternoon. Were Angelo here, we could ease ourselves into this meeting with a discussion of walks, balks, and errors. As it is, we can't get any friendly banter going. Besides having no facility in the language of sport, and no athletic background to brag about, I am, as dean, not to be trusted. I'm coaching the opposition, so to speak—let's call my team the Administration Bugbears—and if these two guys aren't on their toes I'll emerge from this meeting—horrors!—the winner.

"Two things—Jeffy Todd and Heim's Beer," I begin, sitting down to face them across the table. "But first I have good news. The contractor will turn our new arena over to us at the end of January. He's guaranteed it."

Both men swell with pleasure while trying not to show it. "Long overdue," says Hokanson. Ernie Burr consults his pocket calendar. "We're on the ice February fourth against Duluth," he tells his coach. "What a great way to break in a new sheet of ice. We'll have hockey fans up the gazoo." He turns to me then, and says, as though I didn't know it, "The place has got forty-four hundred seats."

"Ah yes, and I hope to fill every one of them on the first of February when we inaugurate the building with our poet's presentation. I hope you're both planning to be there for it."

"Our poet?"

"What poet?"

"Richard Falcon. You've had two memos on him."

Choosing not to witness their sour expressions, I gaze out at the sunshine glaring off the river ice, the jackpines on the far bank bending in the wind. Though I've asked for suggestions of a celebratory nature, no one in Physical Education has responded to either memo. I suppose they're hoping that without their support, my plan will come to nothing.

"Well now, Dean, as far as poetry, right there in the arena," Burr begins, and I sternly interrupt him:

"First I want to talk about Jeffy Todd and Heim's Beer."

I sit back then and watch their reaction, which I suspect has been rehearsed. While Hokanson feigns perplexity, Burr gives me a worried frown and says, "Jeffy Todd? Don't tell me that kid's doing bad in class again."

"He's been doing bad right along, Ernie. He's been ineligible to play hockey since his sophomore year. Current grade-point average of one point eight."

Coach Hokanson feigns disgust. "Jeffy Todd's no athlete. I don't know why a kid like that even comes out for hockey, can't skate worth a damn, can't handle a stick."

"Comes out because his parents pressure him," Burr explains to his colleague. "Hockey parents can be real demanding."

Hokanson looks amazed, as though at a newly discovered truth.

"Hell's bells, Hokey," says Burr with a hearty roar of false laughter, "hockey parents can get coaches fired."

Hokanson next feigns trepidation, which causes Ernie Burr to turn up the volume of his laugh. "Just joking, Hokey, just joking."

I then put forward my accusation. "You had Jeffy in goal for seven minutes of the second period against St. Albert's."

At first Coach Hokanson looks wounded. "Dean Edwards, what kind of hockey coach would put an ineligible player in a game?"

"An opportunistic one."

"Well, Jesus, don't look at me." '

"Are you saying this guy's dumb enough to bring the Minnesota College Athletic Commission down on his head?" asks Ernie Burr.

The answer is yes, but I don't say it. Instead I tell them I've been expecting a letter from the Commission saying we'll have to forfeit three games.

"But no letter ever came," Burr declares.

"You never got a letter because Jeffy Todd never played,"

Hokanson lies. "Jeffy Todd's a third-string goalie with no hope in hell of ever playing Blue Heron hockey. My whole third string's a bunch of stumblebums. They played a fair B-game against North Dakota, then they went and lost to Berrington *Junior* College, for God's sake. They been erotic like that all year."

"Jeffy played, it's a matter of record," I tell him, pulling open a drawer of my table and taking out the sport section of an old *Morning Call*. "His grandmother brought this to my attention."

At the sight of the newspaper, Hokanson's fear is unfeigned. He knows all about the stringent regulations of the MCAC. Break an eligibility rule once and forfeit your last three wins; do it twice, forfeit the season.

Burr, the better actor of the two, shows no concern. He gives me a soft, long-suffering smile, asking, "Now, Leland, tell me, who you gonna believe—your athletic staff or somebody's old grandma in a old-folks home?"

"I've decided to believe the newspaper." I open it to the hockey page.

"Jesus," sighs Hokanson, studying the box score as though for the first time. He points out Jeffy Todd's name to Burr, who asks me, still smiling:

"You gonna make something of this?" By which he means, will we kill this little secret within these four walls?

"You know what a dean has to do, Ernie."

"I know. I'd say go ahead, except it's not true."

"It's not true," Hokanson echoes, nodding energetically.

"Tell you what," says Burr. "We'll have the *Morning Call* print a correction, how's that?"

"You bet," says Hokanson, risking a little smile of relief.

"That satisfy you, Leland?"

"You're forgetting . . ." I examine the box score for the attendance figure. "You're forgetting that two thousand and nine people saw him play. The radio announcer saw him play. His grandmother heard it on the radio."

Burr chuckles. "You mean they *thought* they saw him play."

Hokanson comes in on cue. "Got their jerseys mixed up, is what happened. Jeffy Todd and our second-string goalie name of

Hauser had on each other's numbers by mistake." Evidently sensing my skepticism, he adds, "It happens."

"But his parents were there. Wouldn't Mr. and Mrs. Todd know their own son?"

Burr, sensing my anger, broadens his smile and states delicately, "Not when he's a goalie, Leland. Goalies wear masks."

"Then how about his teammates? How about Jeffy himself? I talked to all of them."

Here they stumble over their lines, not having rehearsed this part.

"Maybe he played," admits Hokanson. "Maybe I sent him in by mistake. Different jersey. Different number."

"Nonconference game," says Burr.

"You know your players only by number, not faces?" I ask.

"Heat of the game," Burr suggests.

"Yeah, heat of the game," Hokanson agrees.

"Besides, nonconference, who cares who plays?"

This I ignore—Burr knows very well there are no exceptions. Hokanson too I ignore when, eager to change the subject, he warns me that unless the state eligibility rules are liberalized, the quality of Rookery hockey will go into decline. "We already had two defensemen drop out and go across to North Dakota."

It's time to move on to Heim's Beer. "I overruled you on selling space on our message board, remember?"

Burr looks blissful. "Wait'll you see the uniforms the Heim's people bought us, gold, dark blue, and teal green, snazziest in the league."

Hokanson, too, is transported. "Socks, pads, the whole ten yards. They even threw in a bunch of sticks."

Burr: "You know how much a new uniform costs, Dean? You can pay upwards of six hundred bucks not including skates."

Hokanson: "Why'n'cha come to a game once, Dean? Catch an eyeful of our new uniforms, I guarantee you'll be very enhanced."

Burr: "So we saved the college . . . let's see, six hundred times eighteen."

Hokanson: "Just for flashing Heim's Beer once a minute on our signboard."

Burr: "Well, figure this way, six times nine is fifty-four, so four times eighteen is twice that, that's a hundred-some, so we just saved the college budget over a hundred thousand dollars."

Hokanson: "And all them sticks besides."

"Ten thousand, not a hundred," I point out.

"Just come and see one game," Hokanson insists. "Happened to Zastrow, he came to a game a few years ago and he's been an invertebrate fan ever since."

These guys drain me. With what feels like my last bit of energy, I tell them the purpose of this meeting is to notify them of my intentions. I'm going to report them to the eligibility committee of the Athletic Commission, and I'm going to pull the plug on the message board.

Humbled and angry, they quickly depart the scene of their defeat. They cross the corridor to the president's office, surely to lodge an appeal.

#11. I'm beginning at last to understand the minds of our athletic director and hockey coach. Their minds consist of two parts fear and one part regret.

Their fear of losing has become an obsession, extending beyond hockey games to every facet of life. Jeffy Todd. Heim's Beer. Right now they're seething, having lost on both counts to the Bugbears.

They also fear that a poetry reading will contaminate their new arena.

What they regret is this arrangement whereby athletic departments are attached to larger entities, like degree-granting institutions. Physical Education, in their minds, ought to be totally independent.

In mine too, actually.

Viola puts through a phone call from Angelo, who says Mary Sue is better, it's the support group that depresses her. I ask if I might speak to her.

"I'll ask her." A moment later: "No."

"Will she see me if I come over?"

Another moment. "Maybe."

"Angelo, I just learned something from Coach Hokanson.

Did you know that a single hockey game turned our president into an invertebrate fan?"

"Don't you believe it, Zastrow was a reptile from the start."

"I'll be fine, Leland. Right now I want to die but I'll be fine."

Mary Sue Bloom, sitting in the parlor of Corelli's restored manse on Rookery's oldest street, addresses me through the steam rising from her Sleepy Time tea, the cup held up to conceal the tear that now and then runs down her cheek. "If I can just take some time off, I know I'll be fine. In Bismarck last spring they gave me some time off and I got my confidence back to the point where I was able to go out looking for another job. You can't go out job-hunting if you don't have a whole lot of confidence. Didn't I seem extremely confident at my interview last spring, Leland?"

"Of course you did, Mary Sue."

"Of course I did. If I were just better able to control myself. I hate making scenes like this. If only I could get a little of that confidence back."

"I wouldn't call this a scene, Mary Sue."

"What would you call it then? I'm crying my eyes out in front of my dean."

"I'd call it a talk over tea. By the way, I wonder if I could have a cup."

"Sure, Gloria's in the kitchen, go and ask her." She kicks off her blanket and rises from her chair. She's wearing a blue silk blouse that invites the eye to admire her lovely breasts. I've never before seen her in jeans. "Why can't our lives go on as smoothly as they did the first fifty years?" she asks, following me into the kitchen. "I went to grade school in Mott, North Dakota, and then we moved to Bismarck and I went to high school to the nuns, and I got my undergraduate degree from another order of nuns, and after a few years teaching primary grades in Bismarck, I went off to the University of North Dakota and got my doctorate and returned home to Mother and a job at Mary College, which now goes by the name of the University of Mary. It's the only four-year college within a radius of hundreds of miles and it's a wonderful school. There were a couple of years when I actually lived in the nunnery because my mother was going through some stuff at the time. How's Lolly, Leland? I heard she was sick."

"She's improving, thanks."

Gloria puts the teakettle on the range and we stand listening to Mary Sue.

"Do you realize what similar lives we've been leading, Leland? My dad died when I was twelve. He was in the army but it wasn't war that killed him, it was a car accident in Maryland. If he'd have lived to a ripe old age, I might have lived a more normal sort of life, but I stayed home because my mother seemed to need me. I have two sisters and a brother, but they were quite a bit older and married, so it naturally fell to me to stay around home. Not that Mother was incapacitated or anything, but you know how mothers are, they like to hang on to as much of their family as they can, and since I obviously wasn't all that eager to try my wings, she didn't kick me out of the nest. To me, it seemed like the natural thing to do, you know, to just be around. You were fourteen, right, when your father was killed?"

"Fourteen."

"And it's not a bad life, right? I mean for about the first fifty years? It's so comfortable, I mean, living there at home with your mother and sharing her life, knowing her next move, knowing *your* next move, never being challenged, never altering the same smooth pace day after day, going to church with her, driving her to the beauty salon, the garden store, the post office when she needs stamps. It would be easier, of course, to buy the stamps for her on your way home from work, but it wouldn't be as enjoyable, would it, because you know how much she enjoys going in and visiting with the postmistress and the clerks and catching up on the gossip along the Rialto. I suppose there's a lot of people who couldn't stand that sort of life, but if you're cut out for it, it seems sort of perfect, the way one day follows another with no unpleasant surprises. You're a homebody like me, aren't you, Leland? You're cut out for it."

"I guess I'm cut out for it, yes."

"So was I. But only for fifty years or so. Which is only

natural, of course, because everybody has to break away some-time, has to cut the apron strings and try out a bit of real life for a change, has to go through a period we call adolescence which doesn't necessarily occur during your teenage years. I mean look at me. I'm in the middle of adolescence and I'm nearly fifty-four. You've obviously been through it already, Leland, otherwise you'd never have married Sally. It takes a mighty strong force to press you into adolescence when you're the sort of responsible homebodies we are, and there's no stronger force in the world than sexual attraction. You develop this grand passion and it puts everything else in the background, even loyalty to your mother. Sally must have been your grand passion, Leland. Maybe she still is, for all I know. I'm very curious why you divorced and went back to your mother. Not that you have to tell me, I'm just curious is all."

"Some other time."

Gloria pours me a cup of Sleepy Time, tops off Mary Sue's. The two of them stand leaning against the kitchen counter, facing me. Whenever the sunset draws their eyes out the window behind me, I steal glances up and down Mary Sue's shapely form.

"It took me forever to get my doctorate," she goes on. "I did it long-distance because my mother didn't want me to leave Bismarck, so it took me twelve years. Sometimes I'd think, Screw it, by the time I get this thing it'll be time to retire. But I went ahead, you know how you do, because I sort of liked the routine of working on my dissertation, comparing test scores of kids nationwide to the test scores of the kids in Mott, North Dakota, and trying to figure out why the Mott kids always came out way ahead."

"Did you figure it out?"

"I did. I finished my degree and then along came this handsome guy wearing these great shoes of Italian leather and I decided if and when I ever got around to marrying anybody, I'd marry him, but by this time my mother was failing—she had a weak heart—and I figured if I got married she'd die. I mean, how could she stay in the house if I moved out?"

"How indeed?"

"And besides, this guy in the great shoes, I thought he wasn't interested in marriage. He was only interested in what most men on the road are interested in."

"And that is?"

"Sex in the motel. But I was wrong. The third time he came back to Bismarck he asked me to marry him. So I did, and my mother died."

She leaves an opening here but I'm stumped for a response, perhaps because I'm preoccupied by lust. I can't take my eyes off the contours of her body in denim and silk.

"You know, I feel four hundred percent better than I did in that support group. I mean, it helps to talk things out, but to a friend, not a support group. I say, Screw support groups. I'm so glad to think Lolly's better, Leland. Francine said she was real sick, but she must be basically very strong. Well, you can tell that over the radio can't you. It's the only thing I missed about Rookery over Christmas, hearing Lolly on the radio."

MEMORIAL
for
LOLLY EDWARDS
Sunday, February 1
5:00–8:00
Service at 7:00
The Gathering Room
Church of Saint Blaise
12th and Tailrace
Rookery

Next week this quarter-page display ad will have appeared for the third successive Sunday on page two of the *Morning Call*, for Mother has decided to be honored on the day of Richard Falcon's reading, thus saving out-of-towners a second trip to Rookery. Most of the weeklies in KRKU's listening area are also carrying the ad. It's been engraved as well on creamy bond and mailed to friends far and wide. Into many of these envelopes Mother has slipped a note of explanation, but not, despite my urging, into all of them. "Heavens," she exclaimed as we addressed them, "I don't know when I've had this much fun making a decision." Who should be forewarned and who will be shocked to find her alive and present for her own wake—that was the decision.

Not that anyone who listens to KRKU will be shocked. Her memorial service became the main topic on her talk show as soon as she returned to the air. Radioland, it seems, is divided.

"Lolly, this is Toni over at Bonnie's Botique, just calling to say you got a super idea there, being around to hear your own eulogies. Makes a lotta damn sense, and I hope it catches on."

"Hey, Lolly, are you pulling our leg, or are you really and truly off your rocker? My wife always used to say you Episcopalians was about the most bigheaded people in town, and this goes to show it. I mean, you must have an ego the size of a house to sit there and hear your own praises sung."

"You know what I say, Lolly? This is Gloria Corelli. I say go for it."

"Lolly, listen to me, this is Father Pyle. You obviously haven't looked into church regulations on this. Go ahead and carry out this harebrained scheme if you must—live and let live has always been my motto—but don't, I repeat *don't*, do it on church property. It flies in the face of Anglican tradition because it's disrespectful of all the people who've gone ahead and died before their funerals."

"Hi Lolly, say, this is Sara Sexton from Hamburger Heaven. If the guy who called Episcopals pigheaded would please call back and identify himself, I'd like to tell him a thing or two. Some of my best friends are Episcopals."

"Better make it pretty soon, Lolly. You don't sound so hot."

"We'll be there, Lolly, my husband and I, and we're bringing a carload down from North Siding."

"Hey, Lolly, would you tell that dame over at Hamburger Heaven she better get a hearing aid? This is Arnie Carlson. I didn't say Episcopals was pigheaded, I said they was *big*headed, and nobody can argue with that."

"Go for it, Lolly, just go for it."

RICHARD FALCON IN MINNESOTA
The poet in person
Reading his poems
2:00
Sunday February 1
New Hockey Arena
ROOKERY STATE COLLEGE
Rookery, Minnesota
Free Admission

This ad, along with a photo of the poet, was sent to virtually every newspaper in the five-state area, and Angelo and I have been on the phone every day, strong-arming editors into printing news items about the poet's backlist, about *Fording the Bee*, about the peaceable union of literature and athletics on our campus. Mailings and posters have gone out to schools and colleges. I wish Mr. Falcon had permitted us to use a new mug shot, but he insisted on that curious photo from his last book jacket, the one I never cared for in which he's wearing a sort of bib or towel tucked into his shirt and looking quizzically up and to the left as though listening to a waiter run through a puzzling menu.

Most newspapers, large and small, including *Fargo Forum* and *Des Moines Register*, have printed a short essay I wrote concerning the need in our lives for the poems and stories we grew to love as youngsters, the consoling and stabilizing effect of that literature in these chaotic times, and its likely demise unless we who value it pass it on to the twenty-first century. We can demonstrate the importance of these poems and stories to our families and younger friends, I concluded, by making the effort to come and hear Richard Falcon, the last surviving poet of my youth.

Response has been overwhelming. Every day Viola answers a dozen letters and takes two dozen phone calls asking about the nature of the poet's address and inquiring about accommodations in Rookery. I myself have had a dozen calls inviting the poet to other campuses when we're done with him. He's instructed me to turn them all down. Almost every day some high-school teacher calls for reassurance that his or her busload of students will get tickets. Come one, come all, I tell them—no tickets, no charge, our new arena holds well over four thousand people.

Meanwhile the poet works away at his poem. His routine begins every morning at 7:30, according to Sally, when he appears in the lobby to wait for his ride. He stands at the window ignoring Johnny Hancock and the New Woman—the only other early-prowling residents—and with the split-second timing of a prison break he steps out the door as Angelo pulls up in his Roadmaster.

Angelo says they don't talk on their way to campus; the poet smokes and jots things down in a notebook on his lap. At the library Angelo hands him the thermos of coffee Gloria has prepared for him, and he gets out of the car mumbling something that might be thanks.

The librarians tell me he scarcely acknowledges their greetings as he crosses to the elevator and rises to his tiny windowless room on the third floor. Our chief librarian, Miss Weisgram, has complained to me about his cigarettes, and I've had to overrule the smoking ban with my illogical decree—he can smoke, he's a poet. Miss Weisgram took her complaint to the president, who dismissed her with the statement, "Leave that to Edwards, he's the port tree expert around here."

Mr. Falcon doesn't emerge from his tiny room for about two and a half hours, or until he runs out of coffee, and that's when, if my schedule permits, I meet him in the student center for thirty minutes of what has become the most stimulating experience of my life. Richard Falcon actually shows me the lines he's working on. He actually wants to know what I think of them, and I actually tell him.

> When at nine he lifts his gaze
> Up the mountainside to these
> Yearly falcons in migration
> Circling the topmost crag as though
> For a last look at the northern slope
> Of their upbringing, then vanishing
> Down the misty coastline, he decides

He loves his name, but who in school
Will call him any name but Quitter?

    He's a quitter by nature,
A solitary only child,
A potential anchorite at twelve.
He dreads the cheering adulation
Of the vast holiday population
So he quits the gunny sack race
Two hops ahead and four from the tape.
Too high-strung for first-string first base
He retires, at sixteen, from the diamond
Rather than face the beery fans
Gathered gaudy and throaty in the stands
Blurting and burping his name, "Quitter,
Hey, Quitter." They're the reason
His ardor ends before the season.
    (January 16, 1994)

This is part of what he showed me yesterday. I hold passages like this in mind until I get back to my office, where I write them down and date them. I have over a dozen. I show them to no one. I carry them in my pocket for only one purpose: the pleasure of taking them out and reading them now and again.

Not that I actually need to read them. So far, coming away from our late-morning sessions, I've discovered every syllable etched permanently in my memory. I'll sometimes wake in the middle of the night and find myself murmuring certain lines. I'll lie there maybe an hour or more, testing the sound of each phrase against some aesthetic standard I didn't know I had, and occasionally I'll astonish myself by coming up with a better sequence than the master did. At first I was hesitant to suggest any changes—his defiant streak is so forbidding—but now, after two weeks of these get-togethers, he's begun to see the wisdom of some of my choices. I feel a kind of heart-stopping elation whenever he incorporates one of them into his poem, and I wonder, Am I dreaming?—the greatest living American poet taking me seriously?

Today's lines follow from yesterday's:

>   As young as seven or eight we forded
> The Bee on stones upstream from the mill,
> And shame it is in Tipton Town
> Not to have swum by the time you're twelve
> The booming Bee below the mill
> That grinds in the sun that grinds in the fog
> That grinds round the clock, not to have swum
> To the gasworks on the far, too far, bank,
> Forty rods of swift cold water
> Where one of Preacher Samson's daughters
> Drowned emulating her brothers
> Jim and Ted, who to this day swim,
> Though in condo pools not rivers,
> Like otters. Quitter Falcon saw Jim
> The younger Samson brother swim
> it blindfolded once, and the other, Ted,
> swim it drunk.
>   Quitter never swims it, afraid he'll sink.
>   (January 17, 1994)

This passage at first strikes me as unimprovable, but on second reading I begin to feel that the opening isn't quite as strong as the rest of it.

"The two lines about the mill, Mr. Falcon. I wonder if they might have too many *that*'s in them."

"Repetition is a poetic device," he replies rather testily.

"I know, but a word like *that*—is it worth repeating?"

He nods, making a note in the margin.

Next I venture to tell him that "swift" and "cold" might not be his two best modifiers for water. Being predictable, they aren't quite up to his standard description.

Again he defends himself. "The water was swift, Dr. Edwards, the water was cold. Those are facts."

"But let me remind you, for comparison's sake, of yesterday's 'gaudy and throaty' baseball fans. Those, too, I assume, are facts, but so unexpected as to be the perfect adjectives."

He nods again and makes another note.

That's the extent of my help—nothing very imaginative, no designing or tailoring, no adding any strands to the weave, only ironing out a wrinkle here and there. But whenever I remind myself that down through the ages *Fording the Bee* will contain my little emendations, I experience a thrill quite unlike anything I've ever felt before.

Another day, another passage:

> Added to "Quitter" are "Sissy" and "Chicken,"
> So-called friends calling, "Ain't you odd!
> There's girls with more guts than you, child."
> One midnight alone he steals to the river,
> Strips, steps into the chill swirl,
> Swims to the gasworks and back to the mill,
> Defying the ghost of the Samson girl,
> Dresses, sneaks home, catches cold, smiles
> Next day at "Chicken!" "Sissy!" "Child!"

Leaving the cafeteria this morning, he surprises me by gripping my hand and thanking me.

"No, no, Mr. Falcon. *I* thank *you*."

"What for? It's you doing me the service."

"But it's you doing me the honor."

"Well, anyhow . . ." He pauses to look deep into my eyes, and when he finally lets go of my hand and speaks, it is to say, mysteriously, "I'm beginning to trust you." And off he goes to the library.

Isn't it strange, I ask myself on the way back to McCall Hall, that a poetic talent of this man's magnitude should allow a phrase as expected as "swift cold water" to slip into his verse? Did his earlier poetry contain lapses like this and was I simply too awestruck to notice, or am I witnessing an old man's natural weakening of judgment?

In my office I open his *New and Selected Poems, 1940–1970* and examine it for carelessness in diction and style. Nothing of the kind anywhere. Each line clean and shapely as a new leaf. Each poem perfectly irreducible. Reading at my desk, I lose myself in their loveliness, until Mother phones to say I'm late for lunch.

On the Friday before his public appearance, a Federal Express letter arrives in my office for the poet. Hurrying over to the library with it, I see that it's from Tipton, New Hampshire. I angle through the stacks on the third floor, following my nose to the source of cigarette smoke, until I'm stopped by a student worker shelving books, a young man who warns me that I'm encroaching on the poet's preserve.

"It's all right," I tell him. "I have a message for him."

"But he says no interruptions between two and four especially."

"And why is that?"

He shrugs. "Who knows?"

"Well. I'll take my chances."

The young man follows me deeper into the smoky haze and waits at a distance to see what sort of confrontation my lightly rapping on the door will bring. It brings no response. I don't knock a second time—it's only a six-by-ten-foot carrel after all—but as I turn to leave I hear something like a snore. I put my ear to the door and listen to the unmistakable sound of a man deep in sleep. I slide the letter under the door, and with a finger to my lips I make a shushing gesture to the young man.

I return to my office, where little else but plans for the poet's reading is accomplished these days. I phone the Van Buren Hotel and find that all rooms are booked for Saturday and Sunday nights. Two college faculties from Iowa have chartered buses, and River Falls, Wisconsin, is sending a large delegation of students and townspeople. I phone half a dozen motels—all booked. I'm told that motels as far away as Berrington are filled. I'm also told, by the chamber of commerce secretary, that, except for Richard Falcon's appearance, it's a dead weekend in Rookery—no ice-fishing contest, no cross-country ski meet, not even a hockey game. "Only poetry," says the secretary, laughing incredulously.

I'm thrilled. I have the strongest urge to summon Chairman Sandor Hemm to my office and say to him, "See, what did I tell you, you narrow-minded philistine? Metrical, rhymed poetry still counts!" But of course I resist the impulse. Merely imagining it brings me pleasure enough. Sandor Hemm's latest objection to Richard Falcon's poetry, he told me in the men's room the other day, is that he capitalizes each line. "So quaint," he said, wrinkling his nose as though at a bad smell. Wait until Sandor Hemm sees the turnout Sunday.

From the backseat of Angelo's car, I ask, "Do you have an editor, Mr. Falcon?"

The poet turns and looks at me as though astonished to find me there, even though I've accompanied him to the Hi-Rise whenever he's left campus late enough for me to lock up the office and ride along. The clock on the dashboard says five-thirty.

"Someone who goes through your work with you before it's published?" I'm curious to know who, if anyone, helped him to such perfection of phrasing in New and Selected Poems. Perhaps the editing I've done on Fording the Bee, though minimal, is unprecedented.

He looks thoughtful then, staring past Angelo and out the driver's window at the small houses along Court Street. He says nothing and I don't press him. He's in a strange mood in the late afternoons, preoccupied, restless, easily distracted from conversation. And he gets stranger, Sally tells me, as the evening wears on. Sometimes, after ten o'clock, he'll come down from his room in his robe and slippers and talk nonsense to anyone who happens to be sitting in the lobby. He might describe a bus trip he's just returned from, or a sailboat belonging to somebody named Virginia which he considers unseaworthy. His hallucinations, Sally has noticed, are always built around some form of transportation.

"I had a fellow named Green at Houghton Mifflin," he says after a time, his eyes still out the window. "He was good with jacket design, that sort of thing. I had a fellow at Harcourt I couldn't stand. He wanted to change things."

"What things?"

"My *poems*, for Christ's sake! My *words*!"

We fall silent then for a block or two, until he turns abruptly to Angelo and says, "Watch where you're going, this isn't the way to the Connecticut River."

Sally has begun to doubt my theory about Parkinson's dementia, and so have Angelo and Mother's doctor. Both the doctor and Sally, who have seen plenty of Parkinson's in their day, say he speaks nonsense with too much energy; he's too contrary, too aggressive. The doctor, from what we've told him, suspects either a bi-polar mood disorder or a lesion on the brain. Sally wants to have a look at the medicine he's so secretive about; she thinks he might be a drug addict. Angelo's diagnosis is simpler. "He's just a complete asshole," says Angelo.

We pull up at the door of the Hi-Rise, and the poet asks me to step out with him for a private word—which I'm glad to do, for I want to speak to him about Sunday and make sure he's prepared for an audience of thousands. I follow him into the vestibule, where I greet Johnny Hancock, who's pinning up a new notice. "Nobody wants bat houses these days," Johnny mutters.

"That's too bad," I tell him.

"So I'm calling 'em purple martin houses." He presses in a final thumbtack and stands back to admire his printing. "Hee, hee."

"It might work, Johnny. Purple martins eat mosquitos."

"Yeah, so do bats." He drops a stream of spit into his pocket, draws his sleeve across his mouth and adds, "Bats are better, they ain't so spendy to house. You can get fifty bats to live in a house that only ten or twelve martins'll live in."

I signal to Angelo and he drives off. Sally will take me home.

Upstairs the poet leads me into 506 where he's living a life stripped to its essentials. Indeed, even the essentials seem to be missing. No pictures on the walls, no TV, no radio, no newspapers, no plants. Nothing on any tabletop except dusty lamps and full ashtrays. On the counter in the kitchenette stands a salt-shaker, a toaster, and a roll of paper towels. In the sink I see a table knife, a wine-bottle cork, and a plate of toast crumbs.

"I'll be right back," he says, stepping into the bedroom and beyond. I hear the toilet flush. I hear the rattle of pills in a plastic vial. Running water. Silence. A sigh.

He emerges from the bathroom with his tie loosened. "I have to talk something over with you," he says. Something pretty serious, judging by his scowl. He huffs and puffs, pulling a straight chair over to the window—I assume for me to sit on. "No, not here," he orders as I am about to settle myself onto it. He indicates a soft chair so low that when I sit down my knees are in front of my face.

"Good luck standing up," he says, snickering. "First night here it took me a minute and a half to get up out of that sinkhole."

He sits down at the window and lays the letter from Tipton shakily on his lap. He stares down at the traffic on Court Street for a few moments, then he removes the letter from its envelope and says, "There's people chasing after me, Dr. Edwards."

Good Lord, I muse—paranoia on top of everything else. "Who?" I ask.

"A woman."

"Peggy? Chasing you?"

"Not Peggy—some loony dame from Italy. She's been trying to track me down for months, and now she's finally zeroed in on Tipton. On Peggy. Peggy says she's been on the phone with her. She's coming to Tipton."

"And she's insane?"

The poet shrugs. "Sane, insane, the point is I want nothing to do with her."

Taking the letter with him, he goes into the kitchenette for a fresh pack of cigarettes. Returning to his chair, he makes a lot of tremulous work of opening it and lighting up.

He says, "The IRS is after me as well."

"Oh, dear."

"Have you ever been audited by the IRS, Dr. Edwards?"

"Yes, years ago."

"If you have nothing to hide, it takes days. If you have, it takes weeks, maybe months, am I right?"

I nod.

"You could end up in jail, am I right?"

I shrug. "I had nothing to hide."

"I don't have a single day to waste on G-men, Dr. Edwards. Nor do I have any money to pay them what they claim they have coming. They've made an appointment to see my account books a week from Monday." He snickers. "What account books?" He lays Peggy's letter on the windowsill and takes another from his suitcoat pocket. This is from a law firm in Boston—he shows me the envelope. "And now Lambert Hall Publishers is taking me to court."

"Good Lord, what for, if I may ask?"

"They want to publish *Fording the Bee*, and I won't give it to them. Warren and Styles has promised me a better deal."

"Isn't that your free choice?"

"It's complicated. Years ago I told Lambert Hall they could have it."

"You told them in writing."

"A contract, evidently."

"Oh, my. Doesn't the mail ever bring you any *good* news?"

At this he smiles inwardly and he sets the letter aside. "And my grandson," he murmurs. He turns to see if I understand. I nod. Ronald J. Kampmann, in his monograph on Richard Falcon, mentions his mentally disturbed grandson. He must be thirty years old by now.

"A sad case. I used to take him fishing. Stream-fishing for trout. He was a sweet child . . . good . . . happy. Now he's still sweet, but . . . he troubles me."

In the corridor I hear suppertime voices gathering at the elevator. Two or three residents who haven't yet lost their sense of smell are speculating about the aroma from the kitchen. The consensus is meatloaf.

"Therefore . . ." Mr. Falcon draws in a deep breath and bores into me with his eyes. "Perhaps you already know what I'm about to say."

"That you had good reason to turn up in Rookery a month early. And I couldn't agree more."

"I can trust you, Leland." I don't recall his using my first name before. He intensifies his penetrating gaze. It intimidates me.

"Yes, of course you can trust me," I reply, hiding behind my knees and wondering, What does he think—I'll grow tired of going over his poem with him? Though he hasn't said so, I foresee my editorship continuing after he's returned to New Hampshire. I like to picture his lines coming into my office each day by mail or fax.

"I can trust you to help me hide, is my meaning."

"Hide? You mean continue on, here in Rookery?" I'm elated.

"That depends." On what, he doesn't say.

"It's possible you'll have to give up this apartment. Sally's obligated to give priority to Minnesotans, and ordinarily there's a waiting list of local people, so it's unusual, actually—"

"I'm moving out," he says grimly.

"Well, in that case, I was about to say we shouldn't have much trouble finding you a room elsewhere."

"Sunday, the world takes notice of me in Rookery."

"Yes, that's true."

"And learns I'm living here."

"A good many, I suppose."

"Anybody could find me here."

So he means it. He's going underground. "I could get you into a dormitory, of course, but I'm sure you'd want your own bathroom."

"Dormitory's the next place they'll look."

"They?"

"G-men. Lambert Hall's lawyers. My grandson. The German woman."

"You mean the woman from Italy?"

"Whatever."

"Well, there's the Van Buren Hotel. Register under another name. It's pricey, but very comfortable. The rooms are all newly redecorated."

"No, no, no, no, I'm not looking for comfort, I'm going into hiding, don't you understand? A hotel! I can't afford a hotel!" He gets to his feet and stands over me. "What makes you think I could afford a hotel?"

"It was just a suggestion. I thought perhaps your royalties—"

"Royalties! What royalties for God's sake? How many people do you know who've bought a book of mine in the last twenty years?"

His anger arouses me to skepticism. I gaze up at him, trying to analyze his sincerity. Is he truly planning to disappear, or is this a wild idea hatched out of late-afternoon lunacy?

His heavy breathing subsides. "Leland," he says softly, leaning over me, supporting himself with a hand on my shoulder.

"Please, Leland." He says this with such feeling that my doubts evaporate. "My life has come down to one thing, Leland. A poem to finish. If I delay, if I don't turn my back on the mess my life has become . . . Do you understand?"

"Yes, I see that."

He takes his weight off my shoulder, returns to the window.

I struggle up out of the low chair. Standing behind him, looking over his shoulder, I'm straightening my tie in the dark glass when I blurt, with no premeditation, "If it's secrecy you want, Mr. Falcon, I know a place."

He starts toward his bedroom. "I'll get my things."

"No, not now. I'll need time to arrange it."

He stops. "Tomorrow then."

"Sunday."

The poet comes over and stands too close to me for comfort, takes my lapel in his shaky fingers. "Sunday the world will know where I am."

"Your new landlady—she's very . . . Let's say nobody springs surprises on her. She'll need a day to get used to the idea and to get your room ready. Sunday afternoon, after your reading, while everybody else is transferring their attention from the hockey arena to Mother's memorial service at St. Blaise, we'll spirit you away." I visualize Kimberly Kraft's back porch—the poet going in under the cover of dead grapevines and dusk.

He's hanging on to my lapel, begging with his eyes. "We?"

"There are others we'll have to tell about this, Mr. Falcon. Your new landlady obviously. She's a retired professor, a reclusive type, entirely trustworthy. Sally McNaughton will have to be in on it, otherwise she'll put the authorities on your case when she finds you gone. And of course Mother."

His supplicating expression is replaced by a scowl. "Mrs. Edwards, no."

"Oh, I always confide in Mother. She will sense something's going on. She'll worry."

"Let her worry!"

I remove his hand from my lapel and count to ten lest I say something angry. I explain, then, that anyone who trusts me trusts Mother. We are of one mind.

Turning to the dark window, he says, "We'll tell Sally, if we must. We won't tell Mrs. Edwards."

I am about to remind him that he's in no position to bargain when he clears his throat and explains, slowly, evenly, cogently, to the darkness outside, "I'm trying to empty my mind of this overload of worries I've left behind in New Hampshire. Right now I can't take on one more worry. Mrs. Edwards . . . the voice of Rookery, well-meaning as she is . . . accidentally she lets slip what she knows about me and it's all over town in an instant. Next thing I know, I'm being hauled back home in shackles by G-men and lawyers from Boston . . . it won't happen, I suppose. I'm not saying it will happen. I'm only saying I'll *worry* it'll happen, and I don't have room in my head for one more worry . . . I have a poem to finish."

I can't argue.

Still gazing outside, he says, "Tell your mother and I will not give my reading." So he *is* in a position to bargain.

"Okay."

He turns to me then, a haggard, shrunken old man. He's aged ten years in two minutes. He lowers himself to his chair and sits there shaking.

I lay a hand on his shoulder, chagrined to think that I've forced him into such an energy-draining argument. "Are you hungry, Mr. Father? Can I make you something to eat?" Mr. *Father*? He's shaking his head no, while I'm wondering what this slip of the tongue might mean.

"What can I do for you, Mr. Falcon? What do you need?"

His head is lowered so that I can't see eyes. He speaks in a broken voice:

"Somebody I can trust."

Waiting at a stoplight on Division, Sally taps her lips with her forefinger and stares thoughtfully into the exhaust billowing up from the car ahead. "Do you believe him?" she asks.

"Believe him? Of course I believe him!"

She turns and peers at me. "Well, I mean, he does hallucinate."

"Not about this he doesn't!" I enumerate his reasons for

going underground—the woman from Italy, the angry publisher, the unstable grandson, the Internal Revenue. In order to conceal my excitement, I make light of the scheme, chuckling and saying, "So it looks like we'll have five-oh-six to ourselves again."

She lays a hand on my arm. "I'll do it for you, Leland, but just keep in mind he's not always coherent." The light changes and she drives ahead. "And what makes you think Kimberly will have him?"

"Good Lord, she's been reading him all her life." Snow has begun slanting across the headlights. The streets are wet with it. "Sally, if you could have been in his room just now, if you could have heard him, seen him." I hesitate before telling her, "Tonight he's a broken man."

"The poor dear, he's not nearly so strong as he'd have us believe, is he?"

"And you know what else? He called me Leland."

She doesn't respond. The van purrs past the snow-dusted campus and turns down Sawyer.

"He said his life has come down to one thing. A poem to finish."

She turns into our driveway, pulls up to the garage door, leaves the engine running, the headlights on. "Sleep on it, Leland, is all I'm saying. See how it feels on Sunday morning."

Her caution irritates me. "Sally, you weren't there. If you could have seen how he trembled. And then, you know, I made such an embarrassing slip of the tongue. When he called me Leland, I called him Mr. *Father*."

She peers at me. "Mr. Father?"

"Slips like that aren't really accidental, you see. The last time I felt this worked up about anything was the night of the Christmas party when Father Pyle drove into the Coopers' patio room. I was subconsciously linking the poet up with Father Pyle."

"Oh, Leland." She's looking at me with the same sweet smile she first bestowed on me as a child, the day after her brother sawed my thumb. *You're so cute,* she told me then. "You're so unaware," she tells me now. "Don't you see?—Mr. Falcon *is* your father."

"He's my father?"

"Just think about it. You've built up a lifetime of devotion to your father with no father to lavish it on, and now along comes this man about the age your father would be, a man you've respected at a distance all these years, and you're immediately bonded."

It's a revelation that takes my breath away. My missing father! No wonder his autobiographical poem has taken over my life. No wonder I feel like weeping.

"Here." Sally touches my cheek with a hankie. My God, I *am* weeping.

"Sorry to embarrass you," I say, dabbing at my eyes.

"Who's embarrassed?"

"I don't know why this should hit me like a ton of bricks."

"Well, it's not every day we find a lost parent."

I button my coat, pull my scarf snug, but I don't get out. Melting snow runs down the windshield and off the hood of the van. The light over the front door comes on and Mother peers out a window.

"There was a moment tonight, in his room, when I almost blew my cork," I tell her. "He was telling me not to let Mother in on our plan—you know how demanding he can be—and I was about to tell him, 'Look, I'm handling this—you need me more than I need you.' I had it on the tip of my tongue."

"And?"

I shrug. "That's it."

"You didn't say it?"

"No, luckily."

"I wouldn't call that blowing your cork."

"But it's not true, don't you see? I'm the needy one. I keep needing to be near him, to keep helping him with his poem. . . ."

"Sure, I see that." She pointedly looks at her watch.

"Thanks for the ride." I get out and stand looking in. "I keep needing to be worthy of him. What I feel for Richard Falcon is so strong . . . it's as strong as my allegiance to the college."

"And how does it compare to your allegiance to Lolly?"

"It's stronger than that."

She smiles and looks askance, not believing me.

"I'm not telling Mother about our plan."

Her skeptical smile remains.

"Believe me."

"I'm not sure I want to."

What an odd thing to say. She leans over and pats my cheek and then backs out of the drive.

She's not sure she wants to believe it? I stand in the snow for a minute, trying to figure this out.

Next morning I'm back on Bellwether Drive. "Kimberly, why can't you come to the door when I knock? I told your answering machine I'd be here at precisely eight-thirty, and so I was, freezing my fingers and toes."

"Come in, you poor thing," she sings mockingly, throwing the door open and bending her knee in something of a curtsy. She's wearing an elaborate snood or maid's bonnet. "I heard a noise and thought it was the wind." She leads me into her front parlor where I see she's been sitting with her stuffed owl, her teapot, and a clear view of my car under the street lamp. "I'd ask you into the kitchen but I've been cleaning it and everything is topsy-turvy."

"This is fine," I assure her, although this west-facing room is the coldest in the house, its picture window being a single, ill-fitting pane of glass with no double glazing. The purple velvet drapes, held open with ties, move in the draft. "I'm here to ask a favor of you."

"I'll get another cup," she says, slipping out of the room. I sit down in my coat on her threadbare couch, facing Owl, who stares wisely back at me from the arm of Kimberly's chair.

"I clean and clean, and there's always another room to look after," she calls from the kitchen. "I'm thinking of selling the house and moving into the Hi-Rise."

I don't respond. I'm imagining Richard Falcon coming in through the back porch—an ideal location, hidden from view, nothing but woods behind the house.

"What do Lolly's friends pay at the Hi-Rise, Leland? Is it still a percentage of their income, or is it a flat fee?"

"I think it's a percentage." If Mr. Falcon needs a breath of fresh air he can walk out the back door and never be seen. I can show him trails through the woods to the river.

"Because if it's a flat fee, I probably can't afford it. A house

this size is fine for a family, but for one person it's an albatross."
She reappears with a small white cup and half fills it with colorless
tea. "Sugar or cream?" she asks.

Feeling mischievous, I answer, "Cream."

"Oh, I don't keep cream *or* milk, it sours so fast."

I knew it. I watch her settle herself into her easy chair and
touch her teacup to Owl's beak. Only after Owl declines does she
take a sip.

"Can't you see my point, Leland? When Lolly goes, surely
you'll sell your house and move into the Hi-Rise."

"Never."

"Goodness, you're old enough right now to qualify."

"No, Kimberly."

"Just wait till you find yourself rattling around alone on
Sawyer Street, you'll see."

"I intend to die on Sawyer Street."

"Oh, God, don't be so *morbid*. A house is only sticks and
shingles."

"Not if you've spent a lifetime in it."

"Fiddleshit."

We sip our hot water.

She emits a bitter little giggle. "Is Lolly in her right mind? Is
she well enough for her wake?"

I nod. "She's hoping you'll be there."

"Well, I don't know," she says evasively. She begins relating
her several excuses for seldom leaving the house, but I don't want
to hear them.

"Kimberly, I'm here to ask you to take in a roomer
temporarily."

She gasps, fingertips to her heart. "Oh, no."

"You'd be doing yourself a great favor, as well as the lodger.
When you hear who it is, I'm sure you'll be honored. I'm talking
about Richard Falcon."

"Oh, no ... Richard *Falcon*?" She can't conceal a smile of
pleasure. She raises her eyes to the ceiling, as if hearing his footfall
upstairs. "A night, a week? What?"

"Two months anyway, starting Sunday afternoon. His revi-
sions aren't coming along as speedily as he'd hoped."

"Well, I . . . no, I can't possibly."

I tell her about the four furies pursuing Richard Falcon across the northern tier of states. Because of her strict sense of morality, I make light of his tax evasion and the contract he signed years ago with Lambert Hall. I play up the woman from Italy and his clinging grandson, and I finish with what I consider my strongest argument, apart from our opportunity, hers and mine, to be good Samaritans—namely Rookery State's reputation. Our own dear campus, where Kimberly spent virtually her entire career, will go down in literary history as the place where Richard Falcon was allowed to finish his *magnum opus*. "Think of it, Kimberly, your house remembered as his refuge."

She shrugs off the honor. "Sticks and shingles."

"But I mean you yourself as his landlady."

"Leland! I, a full professor of education, remembered as a *landlady*? You *are* a fool."

"Okay, so you remain anonymous, but think of the college."

"*You* think of the college." She sets down her cup and crosses her arms. I see by her dark look that I'm in for it. The attack, when it comes, is withering. "You're so caught up in hero worship, you haven't given a thought to the consequences. First of all, where do you get this 'temporarily' bullshit? What makes you think a man with problems like his will *ever* want to come out of hiding? Admit it, he hasn't actually told you how long he'd like to disappear for, has he?"

"It all hinges on the poem."

"Because take it from me, you starry-eyed groupie, problems like his don't go away. He comes out of hiding and there they are, waiting—the IRS, the publisher, the nutty grandson, and the woman from Italy."

"But he's a poet, Kimberly. To him, it's only the poem that matters. Once the poem is finished, he can face those things."

"Don't kid yourself. Once you go into seclusion wild horses can't pull you out of it—I ought to know. And then what? Just *think* about it."

I shrug, at a loss what to think.

"Because at that point, what you have is a real live missing person on your hands, and not only that—a missing celebrity.

We'll have the FBI, the county sheriff, and a whole fleet of newscasters going through your house and my house and the rest of Rookery with fine-tooth combs. Rookery State's reputation—*ha!*"

"Kimberly, listen."

"You listen, damn it. The longer you succeed in hiding this old guy, the more firmly Rookery State College becomes planted in everyone's mind as the campus that lost the greatest poet in the land."

"Kimberly, I—"

"And what sort of news release does the dean's office put out then? 'Oops, sorry, we misplaced him, I guess.' "

"Kimberly, I don't really think—"

"Or he dies. Yes, he dies, in hiding. Why not? Old people die, you know. And then what? Do we bury him in the woods out my back door? Or maybe we bribe some crematorium to dispose of him."

"Kimberly, will you stop it? We're only talking about providing a poet with the time and the place to finish a poem. You take a plain fact like that and blow it up into a secret burial in the woods."

"Yes, and let's say we get away with it, and Richard Falcon is never heard of again. If you think Rookery State College has a reputation for being remote now, just you wait. Instead of Paul Bunyan's Alma Mater, your precious little campus will be known all over the world as the Black Hole of Higher Education."

I stare out the window, dejected. I should never have come here. I should have asked Angelo and Gloria to take in the poet— they have a big house. But Kimberly's place is so perfectly situated for secrecy. And Kimberly, of all people, understands the need for seclusion. Nor did any professor, during her tenure, display a stronger allegiance to Rookery State.

"Kimberly, can I trust you to keep this a secret?"

She doesn't reply.

"I mean if you can't take him in, will you at least let us proceed? Not tell people?"

"Who would I tell? I'm a recluse." I detect a humorous tone in her voice and I turn to see if this is said in jest. She does indeed appear to be hiding a smile behind her teacup.

"Mother, to start with," I reply. "I've heard you on the radio with her. Mother doesn't know anything about this."

Her eyes enlarge above the cup—an expression of wonder. "You're not telling *Lolly*?"

"I'm letting Mr. Falcon decide who to tell. You and Sally are the only ones."

"Not telling *Lolly*?" she repeats, emitting the first whole-hearted laugh I've heard from her in a very long time. "But, Leland, you always tell Lolly *everything*." She continues to laugh, squeezing her eyes shut and spilling a few drops of tea. "I'm tempted to do it, Leland, just for the sake of watching you try to function without Lolly pulling your strings."

Ignoring this insult, I stand up and button my coat, wondering if, during her years as my ally on campus, she was carrying around the seeds of all this bitterness.

"Oh, what the hell," she says, setting down her teacup and getting to her feet. "I *will* do it."

"You will?"

She settles Owl comfortably in her warm chair, covers him with an afghan, then removes her maid's bonnet and pats her wispy hair. "If you promise two things, I'll do it." Her voice has lost its sarcastic tone, has turned sweet.

"Tell me."

"First, you must never, *never* admit, even if treasury agents put you in leg irons and throw you in a dungeon, that you *ever* breathed a word to me about Richard Falcon's tax evasion."

"That's easy, I don't know any of the facts."

"I'm simply Richard Falcon's stupid, hoodwinked landlady, remember that."

I agree. "And second?"

"You'll never tell Lolly."

"I already said I'm not telling her, at least not till the poet's gone home."

"Leland." She gives me a stern, level stare. "I said *never*."

It seems little enough to promise. "Okay."

"Because it's going to be such a *hoot* watching you operate on your own for a change."

THE EVE OF ST. BLAISE

I'm up at dawn and relieved to discover the neighborhood covered with scarcely a two-inch blanket of snow. I was
awake until three o'clock imagining a blinding blizzard, blocked
roads, motorists stranded on their way to hear Richard Falcon.

I shave and dress and put my ear to Mother's door for a
minute. The faint hiss of inhaled oxygen is slow, regular, reassuring. Downstairs I switch on the coffeemaker, and then step
out into a lovely morning, chilly and still. A pair of chickadees
peep happily at our feeder. A pair of itinerant geese, having
doubtless spent the night in the open water below the power
plant, pass overhead on their way to breakfast. I shovel the walk
until the paperboy arrives. In the living room I settle onto the
couch with my coffee and paper and fall instantly asleep. I dream
about a family of six found frozen in their snowbound car, lured
to their deaths by literature.

I'm awakened by a rare phone call from President Zastrow.
He wants me to come in for a meeting.

"It's Saturday, O. F. I've got a hundred things to do. I
promised Father Tisdale I'd decorate the church, and I have to see
everything's ready for the poet's reading tomorrow. I have to
pick up a chapbook we're having printed—"

"It isn't me calling the meeting, Edwards, it's the chancellor."

"The chancellor? She's in Rookery?" Our previous State College Chancellor, an ineffectual man named Eddie Almquist, came to town twice during his five years on the job. His successor, Dr. Gail Ann Suderman, was appointed scarcely a month ago.

"Came last night on the plane. Wants to meet in half an hour."

"Who with, besides you and me?"

"Bunch of people."

"Any idea how long?"

"Give her the morning, she says."

Of all days to be under scrutiny from St. Paul. I call Father Tisdale and delay until this afternoon our preparations for tomorrow's double celebration—our Patron's feast day in the morning and Mother's memorial service in the evening. I call the Hi-Rise to delay our fishing excursion, but Angelo has already delivered Mr. Falcon to campus for a rare Saturday session at his desk. I phone the library and ask Miss Weisgram to convey the message. "Please tell him it's better fishing later anyhow. I'll try to pick him up by two o'clock." Now, how do I get a message to the phoneless Romans that we'll be late using their fishhouse? I take out the car and drive to the birch grove across the river.

The Romans aren't home. From the hilltop above the railroad pier, I see smoke puffing out of the darkhouse chimney, and I call their name but my voice doesn't carry that far. I haven't brought boots for slogging across the snow and ice. Besides, I'm already late for the meeting. I write a note and slip it under the door of their house.

Chancellor Gail Ann Suderman, sitting at the small table in Zastrow's office, scarcely acknowledges my apology, so involved is she in a conversation with Angelo. The president scowls at me, as I take the chair opposite him.

Angelo, trying his best to bring a concerned expression to his naturally optimistic face, is speaking of burnout. "And furthermore I hear from personnel we've got a bunch of profs taking early retirement this spring."

"It's a plague," says Chancellor Suderman. "Campuses across the nation are going through it. You don't see burnout this bad in any other profession."

"In my forty-two years as a schoolman," brags President Zastrow, "I've never burned out."

"Because you probably never caught fire" is Dr. Suderman's immediate reply, which Zastrow evidently interprets as a compliment, for he breaks out in a self-satisfied smile.

#17. I can't help staring at our new chancellor. I'm struck, first and foremost, by her frumpy appearance. A keen-minded administrator, *said the newsletter that crossed my desk when she was appointed by the State College Board. I must not have looked closely at her photo, otherwise why did I expect to meet this morning a keener-looking woman, someone younger and wearing perhaps a stylish, dark blue business suit? Dr. Suderman has taken no pains to look a minute younger than her sixty years. She's dressed today in a wine-colored suit with a food stain on the carelessly tied bow of her frilly pink blouse. She resembles that brusque, industrious, singleminded, wide-bodied teacher all of us had at least once as a child, the one whose buttons and gray hair came undone while she concentrated on our progress through the fourth grade. Or she might be one of your grandparents, if yours—like my Grandmother O'Kelly—grew large and muscular and genderless from years of helping with outdoor work on the farm.*

Seated as I am with my back to the door, I don't see who enters the outer office and interrupts their discussion of burnout.

"She's early," says the chancellor. "Mr. Corelli, would you shut the door."

He does so.

"We'll get to her in a minute, but first I have to compliment you, Dr. Edwards, on bringing Richard Falcon to Minnesota. He's the reason I'm here ahead of schedule. What a coup."

"Thank you, though I can't take credit for—"

"All my life, living in the East, I wanted to meet Richard Falcon, and to think I had to come west to do it. Will you have his reception before or after his presentation?"

"Actually there's no reception planned. The man's health, you see, isn't the best. He tires very easily."

"But just for a few of us. O. F. tells me not even *he* has yet had a chance to meet him."

"Uhhhmm?" says O. F., coming alert at the sound of his initials. Whenever he's not presiding, he tends to drift.

I lower my voice and reverently utter the diagnosis. "Parkinson's disease."

"Well, then, I'll just thank him personally, after the reading."

"I have to take him to his plane immediately afterward," I lie, avoiding her eyes. Out the president's window, I watch the first stiff breeze of the morning make its way down Sawyer Street, brushing snow off the boughs of the bare trees.

"Plane?—what plane?" she asks. "Noon is your only plane in or out of here on Sunday."

"I'm driving him to a plane in Duluth." This falsehood slips out with amazing and guiltless ease.

"Perfect," she says. "Take me along. I need to get back to the city myself tomorrow."

I haven't time to realize how impossible it will be to worm out of this proposal before she nods Angelo to the door and—I'm shocked, I actually flinch—he ushers in L. P. Connor.

Dr. Suderman slides sideways and draws another chair up to the table. "Here, Ms. Connor. Sit here."

L. P. Connor sits down and places a stem of tiny yellow forsythia blossoms on the table. She slides it in my direction. This can't be a peace offering, surely it's a joke. Do I detect the hint of a smile playing across her lips? And why do her eyes seem less dead than usual?

"The sexual harassment issue, Dr. Edwards," says Chancellor Suderman, looking forcefully into my eyes. "Let's put it behind us."

Who has drawn the chancellor into this ugly little spat? L. P. Connor might well have done so, but on the other hand, I recall the many times President Zastrow has dumped his more onerous problems on anyone from the State Office who happens to be passing through town. It can sometimes be his one strength— knowing when he's out of his depth and needs rescuing.

"I understand you hugged a female student, Dr. Edwards."

Once again I plead innocent; once again I tell the story of the December embrace. When I finish, the chancellor turns to L. P. Connor for her response, but she remains silent, her eyes cast demurely down as she fingers the stem of forsythia.

"Come now, Ms. Connor, tell us your view. We want to get this settled."

I break in, overcome with anger. "That's exactly what she does *not* want to do. This woman has been needling me and pro- voking me since forever, and I can predict she's going to try to string out this sexual harassment tangle for years to come." I stand up and pace to the window. "She's very clever, Dr. Sud- erman—be careful, she's a calculating sneak."

Undeterred by my outburst, the chancellor repeats, "Now please give us your view of this matter, Ms. Connor."

Does my nemesis sob? I turn from the window and look at her. Can those be tears in her eyes? Her odd expression draws me back to the table.

"I understand your meaning, my dear," says Dr. Suderman, patting Ms. Connor's hand. "For the record, however, you have to say out loud what you told me earlier."

Earlier? They've been conferring? Conniving?

The younger woman's voice comes out timidly, her eyes averted. "I just want to be friends again, Dr. Edwards, with you and your mother."

Zastrow and I look on, amazed, as Dr. Suderman pulls rumpled tissues from her pocket and Ms. Connor applies them to the tears running down her powdered cheeks. We look discreetly away as she leans over and rests her forehead on the older woman's shoulder for a moment. Is this rehearsed, or is my man- hating nemesis actually capable of tenderness? Impossible. It's either a nervous breakdown or a ploy.

She addresses me again, but without taking her eyes off Chan- cellor Suderman. "I'm sorry, Dr. Edwards."

The chancellor lays a gentle hand on the woman's cheek and

turns her head toward me, saying, "Look him in the eye, my dear, and say it again."

"I'm sorry, Dr. Edwards."

"For what?" I ask. Then to the chancellor: "Has she any idea how many separate offenses she's asking forgiveness for?"

"I just wish I could bake bread again with your mother."

Pathetic as she looks—her tears have cut pink rivulets down her white face powder—I can't allow myself to take her seriously. I have to believe that the tremulous smile she's offering me is calculated to win my trust so she can violate it again.

The chancellor puts me on the spot. "She's asking forgiveness, Dr. Edwards."

I stall. I look at Zastrow, who has lapsed back into his distant mode. On his desk I see my volume of Thurber, bristling with bookmarks. I look out at the sunny morning, ideal for spotting fish from Roman's darkhouse.

"And I'm asking you to sign this." The chancellor slides a two-page document toward me. "For the permanent record."

I read it carefully. It's an account, thickly strewn with Faith Crowninshield's commas, of what has transpired thus far: L. P. Connor's accusation. My rebuttal over the phone. Step One leading nowhere. Likewise Steps Two and Three. Zastrow's appeal to the chancellor (as I suspected), and the chancellor's meeting at 7:30 this morning with Faith and Ms. Connor, "at which time, the Said Accuser was judged sincerely eager to reach a compromise with the Said Accused, and a happy conclusion is anticipated, as soon as the Said Accused signs Page Two of this document, which will, then, be filed Confidential, in the Personnel office."

Page two enflames me all over again. It says, in effect, that I'm guilty. I shake page two in Miss Connor's face. "You're asking me to sign a confession? You take me for a fool? What a ludicrous miscarriage of justice! What an insult!"

I tear the page in half.

The president leaves the table and goes into his private toilet.

"Now, now, Dr. Edwards," says the chancellor, quickly retrieving the halves. "Isn't this a true account of what you just told us?"

"Yes, but the language. Quote, 'The College Dean then took a young female student in his arms.' Where's the explanation of what led up to it? Where's the part about the classroom skit, the embrace in the story we were dramatizing?"

"It's Ms. Connor's viewpoint, Dr. Edwards. All she's asking is validation for what she saw. You may add another account, for the record, of your own viewpoint."

"Why does this need to go on record at all? Why must everyone looking in the Personnel files learn that in December of 1993 I took a young woman in my arms?"

"It's a provision in your very own handbook, Dr. Edwards. And if there is no further accusation against you, the document will be destroyed in seven years."

"Upon the occasion of my retirement, I suppose. What'll we have, a little ceremony at the shredder?"

For this I'm given a swift look of reprimand. It's the same look I used to get in the fourth grade when I whispered. Says the chancellor, in a voice as deep and forceful as my Grandmother O'Kelly's, "I repeat, is the account not true?"

"As far as it goes, yes."

"Then I suggest you sign it and avoid bringing further attention to it. I mean out*side* attention. You see, Ms. Connor is not without recourse. She can go to civil court—it's Step Four in your handbook."

"Then why *doesn't* she?" Not that I doubt for a minute she might. "Up until now, a court of law is about the only thing she hasn't dragged us through, Mother and me."

"Because she wants to put it be*hind* her, and all she asks is that her viewpoint be validated. That you did what you did, and she saw what she saw."

I'm momentarily distracted by her phrasing. I imagine Angelo fashioning a bit of doggerel beginning "You did what you did, and she saw what she saw . . ."

"Will you do this for her, Dr. Edwards?"

"Who sees it after I sign it?"

"Only the chairman of the Personnel Committee."

That's Sandor Hemm, no friend of mine. I'm on the verge of refusing, on the verge of asking what Ms. Connor ever did for me, when Chancellor Suderman plays her trump card, uttering the only phrase that could possibly give me pause. She's obviously done her homework on me; it must be well known in St. Paul—I hope it is—where my heart lies. "For the good of Rookery State College," she says, and sits back, resting her case.

I feel my resolve weaken. It's true, a civil suit would doubtless draw negative attention to our campus, erode the goodwill generated by Richard Falcon's appearance. Even if I were to plead my case successfully in court, proving Ms. Connor to be the deranged crank she is, who would remember anything but the hint of scandal—Rookery's dean linked forever in the public mind with something indiscreet having to do with a female student?

I pick up the torn document and ask the chancellor, "I have your word this will never be made public?"

"Never."

Would I doubt my fourth-grade teacher's word? My Grandmother O'Kelly's? I look into the chancellor's narrow, weathered, trustworthy eyes, and try to disregard the fact that her office lies 250 miles south of Rookery and she can't possibly guarantee what I ask.

I turn to Ms. Connor. "And your assurance?"

In her eyes is a gleam of brightness that's hard to look at, and I wonder if it's drug-induced. Her speech is amazingly coherent. "I'm going to be thirty-eight in April," she says. "I need to make connections with people again, my counselor says, like I did as a girl."

"What people?" I ask.

"I need to get back in your kitchen and bake that delicious bread with Lolly."

Instead of pointing out that her bread, when she was a girl, came out underbaked and heavy as lead, I uncap my pen and am about to scribble my name on the bottom half of the page I tore in half when she says softly, "Please notice I haven't brought up anything else but the embrace."

"Such as?"

"Well, what I said before, you know? About how you ignore women writers in your courses?"

I swear to God, this woman, once she stabs you, never stops

turning the blade. "Ms. Connor, you haven't been in a course of mine since the spring of 1987. You have no idea what you're talking about. This past semester in freshman English we've read book-length works by Willa Cather, Jane Austen, Meridel LeSueur, and Alice Munro."

"I don't mean that. I mean, where is that whole class of women writers that women are *really* reading?"

"Romance writers."

Her little smile has not left her face. "What's *wrong* with romance writers? Why does it always have to be *serious* writers nobody'd read if teachers didn't make us?"

The chancellor interrupts. "Ms. Connor, I think we should move along. We're pressed for time."

I overrule the chancellor. "No, let's hear her out." For a wonderful idea is dawning on me.

"I mean, Richard Falcon is fine if you dig poetry, but for the average person . . ."

"Ms. Connor, how would you like to meet a romance writer in person?"

"Really?"

"How about Delphinia White, Ms. Connor? Would Delphinia White do? Would you like to meet Delphinia White?"

"Oh, God, *Bride of Tiberius.* I'd die."

"Done! I shall bring Delphinia White to Rookery for a reading, and you will meet her."

"Oh, God," she repeats with unction so untypical that I have to ask:

"Ms. Connor, has your medication been changed?"

"You can tell."

I nod, signing my name to the document.

Ms. Connor is scarcely out the door when Coach Hokanson and Athletic Director Burr eagerly enter the office. Their presence causes a bit of an inflation in my meager respect for Zastrow. What a good idea to have Gail Ann Suderman put these jocks in their place, bring the hockey program under control, nip message-board advertising in the bud. I just hope she's brief about it, or I'll be too late to wrest control of St. Blaise Church decoration from the rector's wife.

Both men are unusually jovial as I introduce them to the chancellor. Their Saturday outfits consist of multicolored sweatsuits and shoes of ankle-caressing white rubber. Hokanson carries a duffle bag, from which he draws out a purple athletic jersey. He holds it up for our inspection. It has gold stripes across the shoulders and under the arms, gold chevrons on the sleeves. Across the back, above gold numerals, is stitched a player's name, *JOHNSON*. A stylized bird, green and beaky, appears on the front; a vulture or hummingbird in flight, it's hard to tell.

"What a tasteless rag," I declare, laughing, believing that it's being held up for ridicule. "Who wears this?"

"Cory Johnson," says Coach Hokanson proudly. "He's a shoo-in to make all-conference this year."

"But I mean, what school?"

Both the coach and the athletic director give me a quizzical look, wondering, I'm sure, how any self-respecting man can remain unaware, halfway through the season, of hockey heroes around the conference. I sense Angelo chuckling behind his hand.

"It's ours," says Ernie Burr, a bit wary of my reaction.

"Rookery State," says Hokanson helpfully, in case I've forgotten.

"Ours? But the colors are wrong."

The president ventures to say he likes the colors.

"But our colors are blue and white."

"This is blue," says Hokanson.

"This isn't blue, it's purple." Grabbing the hem and stretching out the shirt, I point out, as though to a child, "This is purple, this is gold, and this is green!" I look to the chancellor for support. "Our colors have been blue and white since 1929."

Her support is slight. "A little on the ostentatious side, I'd say."

"And what have you done, changed our logo? We're not the Rookery State Buzzards or whatever this needlenosed creature is supposed to represent. We're the Blue Herons, remember?"

"That's a blue heron," says the coach.

"That's no blue heron, it's a travesty! Why would you want a hockey player skating around with a cartoon on his chest? What do the pants and socks look like?"

Hokanson to Burr, accusingly: "I told you we shoulda brought the whole uniform."

"Pants are the same," admits Ernie Burr. "The gold stripes."

"On purple?" I ask.

He nods. "Dark blue."

"Good Lord, our team must look like a bunch of ..." I'm about to say "clowns" when it hits me—purple and gold and teal green are the trademark colors of Heim's Beer. "A bunch of beer cans!"

Since Chancellor Suderman hasn't taken up my cause, I explain about the Heim's Beer connection. "Please, let me show you," I offer, and she kindly accompanies me across the corridor to my office, where I point out the window: time, temperature, next home game, and then, flashing boldly,

BE SOMEBODY'S VALENTINE
HEIM'S BEER

I turn from the window in disgust, resting my case. But I have no case:

"Nothing wrong with corporate sponsorship," says the chancellor, leading me back across the hall. "Indeed, we're out seeking it."

"Since when?"

"Since I took over. I've made it internal on each campus. Each advertising proposal is judged on its merits by each president."

We rejoin the three men. Zastrow gloats, snapping his watchband and smiling victoriously as she explains, "O. F. has decided to go with Heim's Beer on the message board, and I don't see anything wrong with it. The shirt, as I say, does strike me as maybe a little too splashy, but I'm always years behind in matters of style."

"But what about ethics? What about good taste? Beer and athletics? What sort of mix is that?"

She gives me what I'm afraid is a pitying look. "Yes, Dr.

Edwards, your anti-hockey bias is well known, and your feelings are hurt. I understand that. So I've asked these two men to come and show you what you can sometimes get for selling space—"

"For selling out, you mean."

Hokanson complains, "I just wish we had Moorhead's mascot."

"A potato?" asks our president, familiar with the Fargo–Moorhead area as his favorite vacation spot.

"No, no, the Spuds are the high school. I'm talking about Moorhead State College. The dragons!"

"What *is* a blue heron, anyway?" asks the chancellor. "Are they indigenous to this area?"

"They are," says the president, in a rare show of intelligence. "We see herons out on the river by our house."

"Their nesting areas are called rookeries," Angelo explains. "That's how Rookery got its name. The largest rookery in northern Minnesota once occupied this very spot of earth where the campus now stands."

"Ah," says the chancellor in a way to indicate waning interest.

"Think what you can do with a dragon," says Hokanson. "You can have fire coming out of his nose."

"Come now, everyone, I want to talk about other sources of corporate income," says the chancellor, and we all sit down like the obedient fourth-graders she makes of us. "Now first, we'll brainstorm. We'll forget about public-relation parameters for the moment, and I'll write down whatever creative things come into our minds."

I take out my pen and notebook.

Prexy search. Q-A for candidates:
What's your stand on corporate contributions?
On advertising beer on campus?
On changing school colors?
On our guilty-till-proven-innocent sex-harassment policy?
On the poetry of Richard Falcon?

The brainstorm, difficult to sustain in such austere surroundings, blows itself out in a mere ten minutes. The name "Bridges"

draws me out of my notebook. Dr. Suderman is saying, "I understand he's already struck out on several celebrities, O. F."

"Oh, Portis isn't one to give up easily," says the president
fondly. "The reason he isn't here, he's in Minneapolis making
contact with a famous band. I've asked my executive committee
to come in. They ought to be here any minute."

"In that case, let's find ourselves a bigger office," says the
chancellor. "It's getting stuffy in here."

"Only two more. Phillips from Chemistry and VanderHagen
from Speech." Zastrow casts a blaming look at me, adding, "Kahlstrom from Philosophy says he doesn't come in on Saturdays."

"Ah, here he is," announces Ernie Burr, as Reggie Vander-
Hagen advances through the doorway wearing a smirk and a new
dangling earring. Teacher's pet that he is, his greeting to Dr. Suderman is at once fawning and hearty. Though he's not quite the
spectacle he was after Christmas, January having paled his face
and drawn a half-inch stand of hair out of his follicles, the chancellor can't hide her expression of amazed curiosity, which Vander-
Hagen accepts with a satisfied laugh. We enlarge our circle of
chairs, making room for him. I'm prepared for another battle
such as we fought over Addison Steele. Pray God our new chancellor, having already taken a wrongheaded position on L. P.
Connor and Heim's Beer, won't come down in favor of rock
stars.

We enlarge our circle once again, our backs to the walls, in
order to accommodate Francine Phillips, who comes in looking
perky and impatient, wearing jeans and a portrait of Einstein on
her sweatshirt. "Hi, guys," she says, and then, shaking Dr. Suderman's hand, wastes no time in pleading for an enlarged lab
budget. The chancellor evidently concurs, for, jotting down the
needs Francine enumerates, she nods her head so vigorously she
throws a hairpin.

A resumption of brainstorming is called for, but it leads
nowhere. The meeting deteriorates. Without the stupidly stabilizing presence of Portis Bridges, Reggie VanderHagen can't
settle down, can't bring his high-pitched, chaotic nervousness
under control, and soon the rest of us are infected by it, all of us

speaking at once, throwing out the names of celebrities there would be no hope in hell of attracting to Rookery. I suppose Dr. Suderman's choice of Frank Sinatra is no more surprising than my piping up with, "Well, if we're going after a singer, I nominate Linda Ronstadt."

Francine Phillips too, it turns out, favors Linda Ronstadt. VanderHagen, of course, sides with the chancellor, claiming that, note for note (whatever that might mean), Sinatra is the finest male singer ever recorded. The men from the hockey arena come out in favor of Dolly Parton—based, I'm sure, on the busty calendar photo of Parton I've seen in Hokanson's office—while Angelo insists, despite VanderHagen's scorn, that we try to get Bob Dylan to do a benefit concert. It's a pipe dream, says Vander-Hagen; Dylan has vowed never to return home. Thus we find ourselves stuck in a senseless four-way debate, which I'm about to stand up and walk out of when the chancellor herself, thank God, stands up and declares the meeting adjourned.

Each visitor she dismisses with a handshake and a word of advice. She promises Francine all the financial help she needs, and then, conversely, she stuns me by telling Burr and Hokanson, "You fellows are way over budget in athletics this year, so lie low for a while, will you? Any purchase over five dollars, ask Dean Edwards for approval."

Hokanson unwisely corrects her. "The president handles the budget."

"Not anymore he doesn't."

Ernie Burr says, "You mean *five hundred*, don't you?"

"Didn't I say five dollars?"

Hokanson is about to object when Burr takes him by the shoulder, turns him and leads him away, speaking earnestly into his ear, advising him, I'm sure, that the chancellor ranks higher in the scheme of things than even the Rookery State hockey coach.

President Zastrow, abruptly divested of this vital component of his authority, scowls at me as the chancellor, lowering her voice, tells him, "Get your act together, O. F., you aren't quite out to pasture yet. You *do* keep a tidy campus, and until this year you *did* keep a lid on spending, but there's more to running a college than making sure there's toilet paper in all the rest rooms. Have you set up interactive TV instruction for your outlying communities?"

The answer being no, he says nothing while continuing to glower at me. Stronger than my pity for Zastrow is my respect for Gail Ann Suderman. On the job less than two months and pre-occupied, I'm sure, with our larger sister campuses to the south, she's nevertheless had time to do her homework on Rookery. "Above all, O. F., get a grip on your expenditures. You went sky-high on your new arena."

Zastrow retires to his toilet, and I am about to leave when the chancellor says, "Hang on there, Dean, I need to have a word with you." She gathers up her coat and purse and extra pair of shoes in a Kmart bag, and we cross to my office. I place a quick call to Miss Weisgram in the library, to make sure Richard Falcon is still there. Yes, he got my message, and will be ready to go fishing whenever I call for him. "Thank God it's his last day here," says Miss Weisgram. "That whole section stinks of tobacco." Out my window I see Hokanson and Burr scurrying downhill in the chill wind like a couple of whipped dogs.

The chancellor sits down to take off her heels and slip on a pair of flats. Then, glancing at her watch, she stands up and gets into her coat, saying, "I'm due across campus to meet with your student government, but I need to know what's holding up your presidential search."

"We're on track," I assure her. "We've advertised the position, with an April fifteenth deadline for applications."

"April fifteenth! Fat chance you'll have of getting it filled by the end of May."

"Actually, there's no hurry. President Zastrow has kindly agreed to stay on until he's replaced."

"No, no, no!" She shakes her head, dislodging a curl that springs out and dangles over her right ear. "You can't afford to keep O. F. around here even five minutes longer than necessary." She tugs at her blouse collar as though it's choking her. "He's a drag on progress, don't you see that? He's a nonentity."

Music to my ears. I try to look impassive, concealing my satisfaction. "Well, he can't drag us down very far in the summer. Summers are rather sleepy around here."

"Not anymore they're not. I expect your next president to start up a full schedule of summertime activities. You had a thriving summer music program once upon a time, Dr. Edwards, what's become of it?"

"Yes, I know. In my father's time—"

"And you've lost ten percent enrollment over the last three years, why is that?"

"Actually, although the population of Rookery itself has been holding its own, the surrounding rural areas—"

"Because you haven't been out recruiting, that's why. You've got that beautiful new education building sitting there with half its classrooms empty."

"There's more teachers than jobs these days, Dr. Suderman."

"Then turn out more really *good* teachers. If they're dedicated enough, they'll find their way into classrooms. We had a saying where I come from, 'The cream of the crop will rise to the top.' "

She strides across the room to pick up my desk calendar. "You've got an activity calendar, except for sports, that makes it look like everybody's on vacation around here. Mankato's growing, Winona's growing, Moorhead's holding its own, so why is Rookery falling behind? We used to have this saying on the farm, Dr. Edwards, 'The runt's a runt because it sucks the hind tit.' "

I turn away to conceal a surge of anger. I want to explain that I haven't had time for any sort of visionary improvements, that my deanship's been devoted almost entirely to keeping the ship from sinking. I've been down in the hold plugging holes while the captain allows the superstructure to rust away and the deck to cave in. But I hold my tongue, afraid of sounding like a self-serving bureaucrat protecting his turf.

And she's right, of course. Rookery State's been on a downhill slide for years. The truth hurts. I feel much as I did the day Mother's doctor told us the unsurprising news that her emphysema was irreversible and terminal. While I'd long suspected this fact, I resented an outsider confirming it.

"You *will* have summer music again, Dr. Edwards. And what's more, you'll have summer theater and summer workshops for writers, for artists, for tax accountants—you name it. Don't forget this is vacation country. You've got thousands of tourists fishing and hiking and floating in boats and sunning themselves on beaches all around Rookery, and whether they know it or not, they're hungry for mental stimulation."

"Yes, I suppose."

"Of course, they are. It's a misconception that vacationers leave their brains at home with the dog, don't you believe it. Give them reasons to come to campus, and I guarantee you'll be overrun with summer people and they'll keep coming back year after year."

She goes on in this vein, inspiring me with feelings I didn't know I still had, emotions long suppressed, such as pride in my work, hopes beyond the quotidian, ambitions for a more vital campus. I create in my mind's eye—or did I actually see this as a child?—three clarinetists rehearsing on folding chairs in the shade of a giant white pine. I construct in my imagination a broad deck overlooking the Badbattle and place upon it our college orchestra playing Vivaldi for an audience seated on the sloping riverbank and anchored in boats on the water. Will Richard Falcon come back in the summer to address a writers' conference? Will our Drama Department be up to establishing a vital summer theater?

"Is your search committee in place?" she repeats.

"Oh, yes, we have a standing committee, which I chair." I withhold the fact that it has served primarily as a search-and-destroy committee.

"It's about time you informed me then, because I'm on it."

"You are?"

"As chancellor, *ex officio,* in any presidential search."

"I didn't realize. It's been twenty-five years since—"

"So is a State Board member."

"Which one?"

"Whoever the Board appoints. We've been waiting for your input."

"I'm sorry. I had no idea. Administration, you see, isn't my strong suit. Actually I think of myself as dean by default."

"Well, you better get over it. O. F.'s term ends with spring commencement, and until his successor takes over I'm appointing you interim president."

At the printer's I carry out seven cartons, each one containing a hundred of the little books we've designed. The poet and I sit in the car examining its glossy, dusty blue cover.

THE ROOKERY CHAPBOOK
TEN POEMS BY
RICHARD FALCON

A student of mine has contributed two sketches. I'm so proud all I can do is sigh. From this day forward, Rookery State is on the literary map.

"What's this?" I ask, showing him the back cover:

LIMITED EDITION, $10

We had agreed to charge five dollars.

"I authorized them to raise the price," he says. "I can live twice as long on seven thousand dollars."

"But what if there aren't seven hundred people with ten dollars to spend?"

"Then we'll do this." The poet takes out his ballpoint and draws a light wavery line through the ten dollar figure, writes five above it. "You can't go up, but you can always come down."

I find the title page. "May I have your autograph?"

"Sure." He takes a few shaky moments to write something; then he closes the book and we drive off to church.

Our church, nearly eighty years old, stands at the corner of Tailrace and Twelfth. Although you can't call it imposing—it's surrounded and dwarfed by gigantic white pines—I've always thought it beautiful, with its square-topped tower, its fieldstone facade, its unusually wide and welcoming front door.

As a parish trustee I'm expected to help decorate for feast days. For me it's a pleasure; I love putting the best face on dear old St. Blaise. Since the deanship doesn't allow me time for the piano, arranging flowers and banners is about as close to artistic expression as anything I do these days. I love St. Blaise, whence the two Josephs, my son and my father, were carried to their graves, where I someday will follow them.

I try to explain this to the poet, how I must stop here for an hour today, particularly since I'll miss tomorrow's service. "Then we'll go home and change clothes and go fishing."

Mr. Falcon nods agreeably. He carries his tote bag of notebooks into the church and sits in a back pew working on his manuscript.

Mrs. Kahlstrom is already on duty in the sanctuary. With Father Tisdale's help she's unrolling our heavy old Norfolk banner while the rector's wife looks on with disapproval. Trustee Edna Kahlstrom and I used to have an easier time decorating before the Tisdales came to town. Whereas Worthington Pyle, who had no eye for aesthetics, gave us a free hand, the thrifty and overscrupulous Mrs. Tisdale takes a very officious stand where banners and flowers are concerned. It seems that she alone was the decorator in their previous parishes. She's nuts about geraniums, for instance. "So beautiful and cheap," she says each time she carries in a pot of geraniums from home. Now it's true that reds and pinks can do a lot to brighten up the shadowy corners of our small-windowed, underlit church, but the nurseries of Rookery won't be showing geraniums until late March, and so the only ones available for our patron's festivities are the pale and dying specimens the Tisdales have been struggling to keep alive through the winter in the south windows of their condo on Riverside Drive. Today's contribution is five more unhappy plants. You can see by their elongated and droopy stems how tired they're feeling, how overwatered and underfed they've been, how desperately they long for a few more weeks of dormancy.

And then there's the matter of the Norfolk banner, a faded yet precious roll of purple velvet sent to us some sixty years ago by our sister church in the north of England, depicting in word and symbol the martyrdom of our saint and bishop. I can remember when the gold and sky blue stitching used to stand out so brilliantly you'd swear it was lit by neon, but that was before the advent of Father Pyle, who insisted that it be hung outside during the entire octave of our patron's feast day. Twelve Februarys of sleet, sun, and snow, as well as punishing winds and coal smoke from the power plant two blocks upwind, produced the soiled and broken threads and the tattered edges that Mrs. Tisdale finds so offensive today.

Climbing the stepladder I attach one end of it to a hook high on the wall behind the gospel side of the altar. I then move the ladder to the other side and am about to mount it when I hear her mutter, "What a ghastly rag." I'm suddenly enraged. Instead of saying so, I drop the banner and stalk out of the church by the sacristy door. In the floral shop at the end of the alley I place an order for eighteen baskets and pots of fresh begonias, carnations, fuchsia, and roses, together with assorted greenery, all of which I pay for out of my own pocket because after tomorrow's service we'll move it from the church into the Gathering Room for Mother's wake.

I return by way of the snowy churchyard, enter by the main door, come up behind the poet and startle him in his shadowy pew. I help him gather up his notebooks and we're on our way out through the vestibule when I turn and see Father Tisdale on the ladder trying to hang the other end of the banner. He's a short man with short arms, and the hook is beyond his reach. I go back and help him hang it, then leave again. "Where are you going?" his wife calls after me, "we aren't done."

"Fishing," I shout.

Driving home, I tell Richard Falcon that unless I submit a letter of refusal to the State Board, I'm going to become interim president of Rookery State College.

His response is the chancellor's. "Why would you refuse?"

I explain about my need to teach, and he says I'll have to weigh this against the college's need, and I think, How do you know what the college needs, stuck in your six-by-ten room in the library? Well, it seems he's picked up a good bit of campus chitchat from the library staff, some of it overheard, some of it told to him directly in the hope (he speculates) that he would convey it to me. To wit: Edwards for president.

"Let's not mention this to Mother just yet," I tell him as we park in our driveway.

In the back entryway, Mother and I help the poet on with my storm coat and warmest boots, and I find older garments for myself, left over from winters past.

What a strange foursome we make. Roman leads the way out to his fishhouse, making sure we avoid the places where the current keeps the ice pretty thin. His wife is next, walking practically backward in order to gush her adoration at Mr. Falcon, who, engulfed in my storm coat and with my stockingcap pulled down to his eyes, trudges through the snow on my arm. I'm reminded of a time years ago when St. Blaise was a higher church than now, and we used to have Corpus Christi processions in which a deacon or two would backpedal up and down the aisles, censing the Sacrament. Mrs. Roman's devotions take the form mostly of imperfectly memorized lines shouted over the wind. When she goes wrong, I hear the old man correcting her under his breath; I hear him chuckle with pleasure when she's right.

Roman lights a fire in the fishhouse stove and goes to work with his hatchet, chopping open yesterday's hole in the ice, while the three of us stand outside in a tight little circle shielding the poet's Bic from the wind as he tries and fails to light a cigarette.

We spear no fish, see none to spear. Although the house is only a two-seater, a third person can squeeze in if he stands, which means that I spend most of our hour-long excursion alone outside, flapping my arms and running in place to keep warm, and wishing I'd brought my angling line. The Romans keep putting their heads out the door and offering to change places, but I tell them no, I need the time to think. (Being uneducated in the formal sense, Mr. and Mrs. Roman naturally overestimate my power of thought; they've expressed an unfounded admiration for my professorship a number of times.) What I'm thinking, mostly, is how I'd rather be outside shivering than staring down into that hole in the ice. I've never cared for spearing. For one thing, in order to see into the water the house must be completely dark, and if you're going to spend time in the elements it seems perverse to shut yourself up in a box. Then too, there's an element of fear involved; the hole is so big you could easily slip down through it and drown.

It's hard to make out their words through the wallboard, so I listen for nuances of tone, trying to judge the mood in the fish-house. At first there's a good deal of laughter and joking, mostly from Mrs. Roman, the men lighthearted as well. This subsides into a long period of silence broken by a yawn, a cough, the shuffle of a changed position. Then they grow noisy again, but it isn't a happy noise. Arguments, accusations and denials, grumbles of irritation. That's why we leave after scarcely an hour of fishing.

I drive Mr. Falcon back into the city a changed man. Whereas earlier, leaving the house wearing my warm fishing clothes, he spoke to Mother so graciously that she risked another invitation—would he like to stop in, after fishing, for homemade soup and bread? "Yes, of course, how kind of you," he said. Yet, in the event, he can't sustain his civility, and supper ends as the last one did, with his lighting a cigarette and blowing smoke in Mother's direction.

THE FEAST OF ST. BLAISE

I'm out walking very early, too nervous to stay indoors reading the Sunday paper. Sunrise, pink and gray over the Badbattle, is partially clouded and worrisome at first, but before long a westerly breeze scatters the overcast and allows the sun to beam a bit of warmth across the land—not the sort of heat that melts snow or lengthens icicles, but warmth enough to be felt on my east-facing cheek as I head north along the Badbattle. I walk three miles upstream and back, and then I phone the Hi-Rise to make sure Mr. Falcon hasn't done something drastic, like disappear.

"He's fine," says Sally, on Sunday duty today, at my request. "I just checked on him, under the guise of taking him a tray of breakfast, and he's just fine."

"No funny behavior?"

"None. He's never weird early in the day. We had a nice talk."

"Still I worry. Who's with him now?"

"He said he wanted some time alone, so I stationed Marigold up there, waxing the corridor."

"Angelo's picking him up at one-thirty."

"He'll be ready."

"Can we check into room five-oh-six later tonight?"

"Maybe."

Sitting in the breakfast nook, nibbling toast, I try to concentrate on the front page of the *Morning Call*. It's a day for finding men. A man has been found alive in L.A. after two weeks trapped in the earthquake rubble. A man has been found in Phoenix who disappeared from his job and family seven years ago in Iowa City; his wife is remarried. A man—no one she knew—was found in Queen Elizabeth's bedroom.

Mother comes down in her violet robe and her red, pointy-toed slippers. I haven't seen her looking this vigorous for months. Whereas I grow pale with anxiety on occasions like this, Mother is bright with anticipation, her eyes clear, her breathing nearly wheezeless. While she settles herself on the couch with her coffee and clipboard, I go up to her bedroom and bring down the oxygen tank. I make toast and boil an egg for her, then descend to the basement to iron the laundry creases out of my best oxford-cloth shirt. Then it's upstairs once again to put on my new olive suit and my forty-dollar necktie. My farewell peck on her cheek startles Mother. "But, Leland, what will you do on campus for four hours?"

"Pace, probably. I can't sit still."

"Suit yourself," she says absently, her mind on her notecards.

"Have you decided when you'll go?" I ask, curious to know whether she'll station herself at the parish center early to receive her guests, or make a delayed and dramatic entrance.

"I want to be there early. When you're dead, you're not wheeled in like a liquor cart, are you? You're there from start to finish."

"But you're not dead, Mother—have you forgotten?"

I hear her laughing as I go out the door.

Ah, February. Walking to campus I detect a higher slant of ten o'clock sunlight than last week. Frost is turning to beads of water on cars left out overnight. Icicles *are* lengthening, drop by drop. Nearing the college, I'm struck at first by all the traffic on Sawyer, so untypical for Sunday morning, and next I'm astonished to find dozens of strangers already milling about the campus. I introduce myself to a family of five named Mockler from Milner, North Dakota, who left home at 4:30 A.M. Among them is an elderly Aunt Hilda, who, having read her first Richard Falcon poem in 1943, has been reading him aloud in the car all morning, much to the delight of the two Mockler children, who've memorized his "A Brace of Dreams" and recite it to me in unison, taking particular pleasure in

> ... and jerked about
> Like a chopping-block chicken.

Their father and mother, on the other hand, wear the squinty, withered expressions of people who've been force-fed an over-dose of verse.

In the student center, I find a busload of hungry teenagers and their chaperons from Fosston waiting at the door to the cafeteria, which doesn't ordinarily open till noon on Sundays. From a pay phone, I call Dorcas Muldoon at home and ask her to send a couple of employees to work early. I phone the manager of our bookstore and gift shop with the same message. I summon the custodial staff as well, promising them overtime wages to open all classroom buildings to browsers, and I ask Librarian Weisgram to come in early.

I then unlock McCall Hall and go to my office. Standing at my office window watching a caravan of schoolbuses cross the Eleventh Avenue Bridge, I'm caught up in a wave of excitement. This day will be a success, by God. No matter what happens to him after the reading, Richard Falcon, today, belongs to Rookery State. My euphoria is accompanied by a surge of affection for Sally. I phone the Hi-Rise. "Sally!" I shout.

"What is it?" she says, alarmed.

I want to tell her how crucial she is to the poet's plan, but there isn't time to go into all that. I hear visitors approaching along Administration Row. "Thanks for everything," I say, and hang up.

I spend an hour showing people through McCall Hall and handing out admissions material. By eleven-thirty, my thoughts have shifted to Mary Sue Bloom. I phone the convent in Bismarck, where she's been living since Christmas, and reach a kindly voice: "This is Sister Corinthia saying God bless. How may I help you?"

"I'm calling for a Mary Sue Bloom, please."

"Who is calling, sir?"

"Dean Edwards of Rookery State College. In Minnesota."

There is a moment's pause before Sister Corinthia decides she must be exacting with me.

"Is 'Dean' your first name or your title, Mr. Edwards?"

"It's my title."

"All right, if you'll leave me your phone number I'll give it to Mrs. Bloom. She's at Mass and then there's breakfast, so it may not be right away."

I leave my number and thank her. I turn and see Francine Phillips advancing through my outer office, wearing her customary lab apron, accompanied by Brooks Dumont of Industrial Arts, who wears a suit and carries a two-year-old grandchild in his arms.

"Leland, there's people prowling through Science trying to see into my lab, and Brooks says they're over in his building too. What's going on?"

"Open house—I ordered all the buildings unlocked."

"When? Why didn't we get a memo?"

"I did it on the spur of the moment because I found all these people on campus with nothing to do."

"Okay, as long as you know about it. I thought it was a break-in—the Revolt of the Taxpayers, that sort of thing."

"Would you mind showing them around, Francine?"

"Not at all. And while I'm at it, I'll give them my appeal for funds." I make a sour face, so she adds, "The short version, don't worry."

I step over to Brooks Dumont and take his granddaughter Melody from him. She howls, but I need to hold her for five seconds, gauging her weight as compared to Joey's. Brooks understands this about me. Having served on our faculty for nearly thirty years, he witnessed my brief, happy fatherhood. Melody seems lighter than Joey. She has ruddy cheeks, a tiny mouth, long fingers for her age. She screams bloody murder as I set her on her feet. She seems not quite Joey's height. Brooks picks her up, putting an immediate stop to her crying.

"Did you open up our house?" he wants to know.

"No, I wasn't sure it was safe."

"Flooring's in. No danger." He's talking about the modular, solar-heated house his students are putting together behind the football stadium. "Guess I'll go and show some people through it."

"Good idea, Brooks."

He departs. I follow him out, calling to Francine, who's hurrying out the door. To his granddaughter scowling at me over his shoulder, I wave and smile and sing, "Bye bye, Melody," whereupon she begins to cry again. Melody is the age Joey was when he died.

"Francine, I tried to get ahold of Mary Sue. What in the world is she doing in a convent?"

"Staying there with friends," she tells me over her shoulder.

I hurry after her. "You mean it's like a hotel? She and her friends check in for the weekend? What's the deal?"

"No, it's not a hotel, don't be obtuse. Her friends are the nuns."

"Well, why?"

"What kind of question is that?" She stops to face me in the chill sunshine.

"Well, I guess I never imagined a nun as a friend."

She glares at me. "Sisters are women, Leland. Women are people." She softens her expression. "They've been her friends forever. It's where she went to college."

"So when she talks about going home, it's actually this nunnery."

"Right. Incarnation Priory."

"She isn't considering . . ."

Francine's hesitation before answering is answer enough, and quite depressing. She turns and looks out across the river and says, "Possibly." She gives my arm a little pat. "Good luck this afternoon."

Back in my office, I see Ernie Burr unlocking the main door of the hockey arena and calling to a group of wanderers to come and inspect it, though what there might be to inspect is beyond me. Apart from its size, which is rather astonishing when you first step inside, the arena is no more interesting than an empty warehouse—a vast oval floor surrounded by 4,400 seats with blue backs. He holds the door open for a long stream of people, while above him, the disgraceful words HEIM'S BEER are flashing on the message board.

I watch a long line of cars move slowly across the bridge and turn in at the college. Ordinarily our audiences show up for campus events at the last minute, yet nobody wants to stay home on the first mild day of the year. In the parking lot I recognize a gratifying number of faculty cars, though very few belonging to English professors. I can't forgive Sandor Hemm for condemning the work of our honored guest.

I'm standing at my window timing HEIM'S BEER with my watch when it occurs to me that the stream of people entering the hockey arena does not produce a matching stream coming out. What is the Athletic Department up to now? There's an awful moment when I imagine the crowd being entertained by two teams from the local Peewee hockey league. Has Ernie Burr disregarded my memo forbidding him to ice the arena until Monday at the soonest? I put on my hat and coat and hurry downhill to find out.

Pulling open the arena's heavy door, I step into a cluster of two hundred people staring up at the images on an enormous scoreboard screen, my own image being one of them. Ernie is climbing the bleachers toward the pressbox where a cameraman, no doubt at Ernie's behest, is aiming his long-range lens at everyone who enters. The floor of the arena has not been iced, thank the Lord. It's covered, according to my instructions, with fifteen hundred folding chairs. The place still smells like wet cement.

I will not complicate my day by climbing after Ernie and demanding to know by what subterfuge he acquired a Spect-O-Cheer scoreboard. Instead, I step up onto the podium where the poet will speak, switch on the microphone and count to ten. The numbers roll around the arena and return to me in diminishing echoes. "Welcome to Rookery State College," I say to the growing number of visitors filing in the door, many carrying picnic coolers and sack lunches. "My name is Leland Edwards, Dean of the College, and I just want to say how heartwarming it is to see you turn out in such numbers for our distinguished

guest. You're welcome to tour any and all of our campus buildings, including the student center where you will find the bookstore and cafeteria and art gallery open for your convenience.
Anyone interested in our brochures or talking to our admissions
people . . ."

I let my message trail off into silence when I realize no one is
paying the least attention to me. I am struck, not for the first time
in my life, by the power of moving figures on a screen, for
everyone is gaping and pointing above my head at their enlarged
images on the scoreboard.

I shake a few hands on the way out and return to McCall Hall
to make another phone call.

"Something very big is happening at Rookery State College,
Angelo. People all over the place and it's almost three hours till the
reading. There're already eighteen school buses in the parking lot."

"Wow! Is our prexy there?"

"Are you kidding? On Sunday morning?"

"I'll call and tell him. He'll want to be there to show off his
new toilet."

"Don't you dare, Angelo. We don't want to put Zastrow on
display until absolutely necessary."

I phone Sally again. Marigold answers and transfers me to
room 506.

"Hi, Leland. We're just getting his things together."

"Remember, nobody sees that stuff go out."

"Don't worry. We'll go out the back door with it and stash it
in the van."

"Not in the van! Your residents will see it there, the ones you
bring to the reading."

"No, they won't. It's only two bags and a briefcase, behind
the backseat. Don't be so fretful."

"How is he, Sally?"

"He's fine. Relax."

"Nothing strange?"

"Here, I'll put him on."

Richard Falcon's raspy voice: "Hello, what is it?"

"Just calling to say good morning, Mr. Falcon."

"Hello, Leland."

"Your audience is already gathering. I expect you'll be reading to five thousand people."

I don't hear his reaction to this because there's a racket in the hallway, and a crowd surging into my office—my Nebraska cousins.

"Where's the president of this place? I want to speak to him about giving Leland a raise."

"Where's the can? I gotta go to the can."

"Leland, your campus is absolutely beautiful. It's expanded so much since we last saw it. When did we last see it, Maylene?"

"We saw it when Leland got married."

"I know, but what year?"

I say good-bye, in case the poet is still on the line, and I hang up.

"What year did you get married, Leland?"

"When did you put up that Simon Shea building? It's a beauty."

"When did that godawful art building go up?"

"Where's the hockey arena?"

"Where's the can, I gotta go to the can."

I shake hands with Cousin Ron, Cousin Maylene, and Maylene's inscrutable husband Detlef. I'm kissed and hugged by Lucy and Claudette. My left shoulder is patted and pounded by Cousin George, while George's son Scott comes up on my right to ask if he can join our Social Science Department; his high school position in Omaha is being terminated.

"We don't have Social Science as such," I tell him. "There's Government and Sociology and History."

"Anything will do," he says, "unless you can get me into politics. I'd like to be a politician."

"In what capacity?"

"As a congressman to start with."

Meanwhile, Scott's pretty sister Georgia is handing me a manuscript tied with a red ribbon—her college term paper on the family tree—and her seven-year-old sister Bridget is jumping up and down and pulling at my arm, shouting, "I read twenty-eight books since Christmas, I read twenty-eight books because I'm gifted."

I catch sight of one of Maylene and Detlef's sour-looking

twins cutting through the crowd in my direction, his hair longer and dirtier than a month ago, his repellent sneer, if possible, more pronounced. Putting his mouth to my ear and reeking of marijuana, he says he needs to find a rest room in the next ten seconds. Glancing into the hallway, I see President Zastrow unlocking his door and leading the other twin into his office. I point this out to the one at my ear, and he hurries after his brother. What possible interest these twins might have in Richard Falcon, or any other of the finer things in life, is beyond me. Surely they've been coerced to accompany their family north, perhaps by a parole officer.

"Where are the others?" I ask, scanning the room. I'm told that the bus, driven by George, stopped at our house to let out Uncle Bill, Aunt Mary, and Uncle Jack. When I express apprehension concerning Mother's stamina, they assure me that Bill and Mary are due for their daily two-hour nap, and Uncle Jack will be absorbed in my library.

When the twins reappear in my office, President Zastrow comes trailing after them, and it's one of those moments when I can't help feeling sorry for the simpleton, standing there at the edge of this warm family gathering looking genuinely bewildered by the sight of people laughing and chattering and enjoying themselves. I do believe the man has never in his life experienced for himself the O'Kelly brand of camaraderie. I quickly introduce him as we sweep past him on our way to the student center for lunch.

The cafeteria is packed. There can't be thirty days of life left in Dorcas Muldoon. Seated on her high stool raking in cash, her bent and emaciated figure seems to be hanging from its shoulder blades. Pulling rank on a couple of students, I usurp a table for eight, and draw up more chairs. I am just about to sit down and join them when someone calls out, "Leland, Leland, my dearest!"

It's Peggy Benoit, come from New Hampshire.

"Good Lord, Peggy."

"Hi, Leland." She stands before me, older yet radiant, her dark eyes larger and deeper-seeming than ever before, her smile pretty if not quite the heart-lifting expression I haven't forgotten from a quarter century ago, her moss green coat trimmed in mink, her jeweled hand lifting mine and squeezing it tightly as she informs me that she's flown in for Richard Falcon's reading because it's the rarest thing in the world; he's never appeared in public like this in all the time she's known him. She feels partly responsible, having practically forced the poor man on Rookery State in the first place. Moreover she feels sad—here her smile turns winsome—that it's been so long since she's seen Mother and me. "How is she, Leland? You said she was on oxygen."

"Her health is variable, day to day. The oxygen's a constant."

"I feel terrible not having come sooner. It's been years."

"I know."

"Oh, Leland," she gushes, throwing her arms about my neck. "Please, *please*, don't turn stuffy on me—I can't stand it." She bends me down for a hard kiss on the mouth. Her scent is musky. Her fur cuffs tickle my ears.

"Who's the old bag hangin' on Leland?" I hear one of the O'Kelly twins ask the other. Maylene's response is a shushing finger to her lips. Detlef shrugs and closes his eyes to convey his boredom.

Removing her coat and revealing a loose, two-piece black dress designed to make her seem thinner than she is, Peggy whispers harshly, while holding her smile in place, "Be the Leland I knew on 'Bye Bye Blackbird.'"

I smile at the memory—better to smile than take offense. Carrying her coat to the coatrack, I picture a cold winter night in 1969, the music room in McCall Hall warm and brightly lit, Peggy and Connor and I, three-fifths of the Icejam Quintet, rehearsing a long, bluesy version of "Blackbird." We played ourselves into a kind of transcendent state that tied us together as never before—the way a musical performance will sometimes do, allowing you to anticipate your partners' every note and change of tempo and mood. Peggy scat-sang the parts she didn't know, then she blatted out the melody on her sax for a few minutes, then fell silent and moved her body to the rhythm of Connor's string bass, arms out as though for balance, hips swaying, head bobbing. I picture the young, lovely, dark-eyed woman she was, so light on her feet, so clear of voice, so tightly bonded, I thought, with Connor and me.

But not with me. I was fooled. That was the night, I learned later, that they discovered their love for each other. I was odd man out.

I introduce Peggy to the O'Kellys and steer her to the chair between Lucy and Claudette. I sit down opposite them, next to Detlef, whose silence allows me a minute to wonder at my attitude toward Peggy. Mother used to worship Peggy. I used to thank God that she turned up in Rookery, not only as the guiding force behind the Icejam Quintet, which provided me with one of the most joyful experiences of my adult life, but also because of her peerless skill with the college chorus and chamber choir. No one we've hired since 1970 has been her match as a teacher of voice. It was Peggy who brought about my one brush with creativity, inspiring me to write the only piece of music I've ever composed. And yet, what I'm feeling at the moment is guarded and leery, put at a distance. Is it caused by the falseness I see in her smile? Hardly—her smile is the automatic one most of us wear in late middle age when asking inconsequential questions of people we don't know:

"Is Nebraska anything like Wyoming?—I had a sister in Wyoming. Do you come to Rookery often?"

"Oh, no," says Claudette. "Twice in the last twenty years."

"Boondock city," says Lucy, smiling devilishly.

"To think I lived here once," says Peggy, calling up a nostalgic expression. "It seems like another life."

Claudette goes on to tell of her first trip north, as George's bride in 1971, but Peggy pays little attention. Her eyes dart around the cafeteria and then settle on the entrance.

"Mr. Falcon will be here at one-thirty or so," I tell her, assuming she's looking for him.

"*Mister* Falcon. What has he been here, a month? And you still call him mister?"

"You'll just have time to say hello before the reading."

She doesn't jump at the chance. "After," she says complacently.

"He'll no doubt be flattered to think you came all this way."

She smiles at me with a flicker of doubt in her eye; then she turns away to scan the room. "My God, is that Dorcas Muldoon?" Her smile disappears.

I nod. "Cancer."

The O'Kellys turn and examine the woman on the stool. "Jesus," says Ron.

"Really a funny color to her," says George.

Even the twins are impressed, staring slack-mouthed at the haggard figure.

"She used to be chubby," says Peggy.

"Hell of a way to lose weight," says Maylene. "Come on, let's eat."

"Lunch is on me." I lead Peggy and my eleven cousins and cousins-in-law to the cafeteria line.

At precisely two o'clock, we enter the arena, unnoticed, from the visiting team's dressing room, Mr. Falcon, Angelo, and I, and we find the folding chairs reserved for us next to Angelo's wife. I look up and around and find the arena about 80 percent full. It occurs to me that this is probably the largest gathering in the history of Rookery State College, larger than our largest spring commencement, larger even than our homecoming crowd in those rare seasons when we've had winning football teams.

"Poetry did this," I comment to Viola and Bud Trisco, who brush past me, having also come in through the dressing room.

"Poetry and publicity," she reminds me.

I nod at Walt Cruthers of Cruthers' Construction, who climbs the two steps to the podium, and he's joined there by O. F. Zastrow, Ernie Burr, and Coach Hokanson. Walt Cruthers looks uncomfortable in a brown suit and wingtips instead of his customary hard hat and boots. Having quieted the crowd by directing his chronic cigarette cough into the microphone, he presents the college with the keys to the building and asks for a winning hockey program in return.

Athletic Director Burr responds with a pointless description of what we've bought with our nine million dollars—the arena's dimensions in square feet, the length of its electrical wiring in miles, the number of lightbulbs. Mild applause. Then it's Coach Hokanson's turn. He promises a victory over Duluth in the home opener on Wednesday and, come March, nothing less than the league playoff championship. His voice rises to a shout at the end of his message in order to transcend what he expects will be a deafening ovation, and this leads to his looking embarrassed and a bit miffed at the subdued applause, apparently discovering for the first time in his forty-odd years that there are other hearts besides mine that don't beat with athletic fervor.

Then it's our president's turn. I cringe for fear he'll say something monumentally stupid, but he doesn't. I should have known he's incapable of rising out of his level-eyed, shortsighted view of things. With O. F., it always comes down to what he likes to call logistics, and his advice today on how best to leave the campus parking lots and avoid traffic jams is actually quite helpful.

Then it's my turn. I begin—since the other three failed to do so—by thanking the architects, the contractors, the laborers, and the taxpayers of Minnesota for this enormous structure, and I glide from that into my introduction of our guest speaker, all the while disoriented by the sight of my listeners looking not at me, but at my image magnified to the eighth power on the screen high above my head. "Today's guest comes to us from New Hampshire, where he's spent his life—" I begin and am interrupted midsentence by a sudden burst of applause. I turn and look up at the screen, confirming my suspicion that the camera is now trained on the poet. I boldly request that the camera be shut off. This brings my image back on the screen; I'm shown glaring sternly up at the pressbox. I assume that the photographer is so engrossed in the Spect-O-Cheer scoreboard that he hasn't heard a thing I've said—which is precisely the phenomenon I hope to spare the poet from: the audience's admiration directed not at his poetry but at the technological marvel up there under the rafters. I repeat my order and wait until the screen finally goes dark. There are groans of disappointment among the motion-picture-addicted, but they quickly die away when I plead, "Focus on the poet himself, and listen to his poetry."

Then I return to my prepared introduction, which has mostly to do with the importance of a college campus, a place set apart, in the creation of art; indeed, in the continued well-being of the human race. I then go on to describe how today's poet has been on our campus for the past month, finding here the solitude necessary for the completion of *Fording the Bee,* which, down through the ages, will be considered one of the major literary works of the late twentieth century. Saying this, I'm astonished to discover a tremor in my voice. I'm scarcely able to get out the words, "I give you now Richard Falcon," before my voice deserts me altogether.

As I turn to guide the old man up the two steps to the platform, the arena fills with applause so sudden and deafening you'd think the Blue Herons had scored a gamewinning goal. Oh, the thrill of it. The intoxicating pleasure. The heart-stirring sight of this giant of American literature stepping unsteadily toward me, book in hand, smiling at me, gripping my arm as he steps up to my level, and saying something I can't hear because of the wild ovation.

The ovation continues as I adjust the mike downward and he creases open *The Rookery Chapbook* and arranges his dog-eared copy of *Selected Poems* and several loose sheets of manuscript on the lectern. It grows in volume as I leave him there and step over to my folding chair, which is behind and a little to the side of the podium, and I am about to sit down next to Angelo when I notice the entire audience rising as one to its feet—and I weep. I can't help it. I'm overcome with happiness. Were I Richard Falcon himself I couldn't feel more gratified. Picture it—this little old man standing there in the natty new pinstripe suit Sally helped him choose, trying and failing two or three times to speak over the PA system, and finally giving up and bowing his head to his book, his white hair falling forward and glistening in the spotlights. *Wait, we need a full minute or more to do this,* the audience seems to be telling him. *We'll give you the floor all right, but not until we've conveyed our thanks for what you've spent your life giving us.* To think I had a hand in creating this spectacular moment. I stand there clapping with tears running down my face.

The ovation dies away and the reading begins. I look at my watch. Two-fifteen.

First, at the poet's invitation, the audience recites a familiar piece along with him, the simple and lilting "Squatters' Rights," which begins,

Over needles
Under norways
I know a path
To the doorless doorways
And warping walls
Of a weathered house
Surrendered to
A covey of grouse . . .

The audience, timid at first, gets into the swing of it by the end, and so he asks them to do it over again. He's a showman. He knows what he's doing. Having thus drawn us into this early, highly accessible work, he goes on to recite a number of denser, less rhythmical poems, and a reverential hush falls over the arena. "Time, You Treefarmer." "Shoes in the Stocktank." "Boston, 1941." Everyone seems captivated by the rise and fall of his husky voice, by his pauses, by his eyes sweeping the audience whenever he recites from memory. At one point, he stumbles midline, and he has to back up and come at the stanza again with his eyes closed. This happens, if I'm not mistaken, when his eyes first fall on Peggy Benoit sitting front and center. Next to Peggy sits a brutish-looking young man who keeps falling asleep.

I scan the house. Who are these thousands of strangers? I see clusters of hometown faces, a fair number of teachers from Rookery High, for example, and even more from the local grade schools. Paul Bunyan Elementary is represented by the fourth, fifth, and sixth grades sitting together behind the penalty box. I pick out Sally sitting with a vanload of Hi-Rise ladies. I see quite a number of St. Blaise parishioners. I don't see a whole lot of our Rookery State students, and those I do see are mostly freshmen— easier to coerce than upperclassmen. I'm sure that my own freshman class, under threat of expulsion, is here in its entirety; I spot most of them standing or sitting near the exits I assigned them, with *The Rookery Chapbook* for sale. Which leaves about four thousand people I've never seen before. Most are either quite young or getting on in years. Early middle age is not well represented.

Angelo leans close to my ear and says, "He was wondering if Peggy-somebody would be here. Somebody from his hometown."

"There." I point to Peggy, and as I do so, she raises her hand and wiggles her fingers at me. I'm afraid my response, meant to be a smile, is more like a grimace of shock, for this is the moment when I realize that the sleepy, brutish young man at her side has accompanied her from New Hampshire. If he were a stranger to Peggy, he wouldn't be sitting between her and her old friend and colleague Georgina Gold. Surely this is the poet's autistic grandson.

"This poem came to me one noon on the porch of the old L. L. Bean store in Freeport, Maine," says Richard Falcon, by way of introducing "Moon Over Merchandise." Not one of my favorites. Nor his either, judging by his lack of involvement as he reads. I listen then for a change in his tone, signifying a change in commitment. Some poems he glides over without penetrating a single word or line, others he reads as though he were making a study of them.

"I wrote this next one when I was in love—so long ago it's the only evidence left of that love." He scans the audience. "Did you ever carry on an absorbing correspondence with somebody, and then watch it gradually grow stale?" He then recites "Postal."

Next, he gives us two lengthy parts of *Fording the Bee*, the adolescent section we've been working on all month, which now strikes me as definitely containing some of the most wonderful poetry written in my lifetime; and another, shorter section, new to me, about his service as a Seabee in World War II. I'm afraid he loses me on this; I'm too busy picking faces out of the audience. Sitting with Benny Smith of KRKU radio are the rector and his wife from St. Blaise. My O'Kelly cousins exhibit various degrees of interest, Ron and Lucy and Claudette looking spellbound, one of the twins and his father dozing, the other twin nowhere to be seen. President Zastrow has brought his distracted wife. Viola and Bud Trisco are sitting with April Ackerman. And, my God, isn't that Emeric Kahlstrom sitting high up under the roofbeams, and doesn't he appear to be paying attention?

I'm drawn back to the poetry by familiar lines, the poet having returned to his earlier work. He rattles off three or four short pieces from memory, then opens his book again and reads "Tipton in the Rain." It's rather long. He reads it slowly, and when he finishes he steps backward as though startled by it, and says, "Why, that's a good poem," and then, charmingly, humbly, he apologizes for this unguarded self-congratulation, admitting that he hasn't read it for many years and had forgotten its merits.

Then he thanks me and President Zastrow and the library staff for our help in what he calls one of the most sustained periods of writing he's done in twenty years. Applause. Next, allowing his business sense to take over for a minute, he's happy to announce that Rookery State College has a commemorative book of ten poems for sale at the exits for ten dollars. To this, he adds shamelessly, "A lot of money, God knows, but whatever income this brings me"—he holds the chapbook high, twisting his wrist—"will be the first money I've made on my poems in twenty years."

"They're all gone," comes the voice of Mrs. St. George from on high. "Sold out," cries another of my freshmen. Mr. Falcon turns to me with a smile of profound satisfaction. I step over and confer with him for a moment, then return to my seat. He assures the audience that a second printing of the book will be available, by mail, through the dean's office.

"And now, finally, to wrap this up, if you'll please join me on a few jingles." What? He's quitting already? I look at my watch expecting to see that it's about twenty to three. It's twenty after. He's been up there for over an hour.

"Reflection on the Water" is first, followed by two or three other poems for children, and as we recite them a strange and stirring thing happens. All five thousand of us rise spontaneously to our feet, as though for Our National Anthem or the Lord's Prayer. Our voices gradually drop away, and we stand there in silent tribute to the little man at the lectern, committing to memory his scratchy monotone as he comes to the end of "Contrast."

An oak leaf in flutter,
A bluejay in flight.

He closes his book. Nobody claps. More stirring than applause is the utter silence of these adoring readers. Not a cough, not a murmur, not the scrape of a foot. It's a silence so complete that you can actually hear the rustle of his loose pages as he gathers them up and the shuffle of his shoes as he turns away from the microphone. I step forward to guide him down the two steps, and as our fingers touch, the spell is broken by the sudden flash of our images on the scoreboard, and the arena breaks out in a thunderous ovation.

Through the dressing room, out the back door, and there's Sally waiting in the van. I help him up into the seat behind her, which she has already lowered to a half-reclining position, and I slide the door shut without a word of farewell. Standing there alone in the chilly breeze off the river, I watch the van move slowly away, bouncing along the trail the contractors have worn into the riverbank and then climbing the slope to Eleventh Avenue where it merges into a line of cars. Sally will return for her charges, whom I've asked Viola to round up at the front door. Why didn't I have the presence of mind to tell the poet *Good luck* or *I'll be in touch*, or at the very least, *Good-bye*? Because I was struck dumb by the look of terror he turned on me as I shut the door.

I don't go back inside. Shivering in my new lightweight suit, I walk along the riverbank trying to recover the euphoria I felt in the arena. Daylight is dying an early death, forks of streaky clouds have moved over the city, and the colors of evening— pink, purple, gray—are already playing over the icy mirror of the Badbattle. It's no use. What I'm feeling instead of joy and excitement is a sense of foreboding. Richard Falcon is now a fugitive from justice. Sally, Kimberly, and I are now accessories to his crime.

It's a good thing we arrive at the Gathering Room before anyone else, because, as Mother points out, we're a laughable sight—I wheeling the oxygen tank up the sidewalk and leading her, as though on a leash, by the tube in her nose. Father Tisdale, a man much too solemn for his august vocation, is perplexed by our laughter as he greets us at the door and helps us inside. The room, with its low lights, rust carpet, and lots of expensive new furniture arranged in formal clusters along the peach walls, is chilly. From the CD player sounds a lugubrious version of "All Through the Night," a violin and organ duet. I'm more certain than ever that this wake is a bad idea.

The Gathering Room, next door to the church, is actually a two-story house. It's the manse, remodeled. The Tisdales don't live here. No rector or rector's wife in the history of St. Blaise has ever felt comfortable in this house, which was overbuilt and underinsulated in 1914. Its conversion took place during the rectorship of Worthington Pyle, a bachelor, who never used half the rooms and who convinced the trustees that we needed a church hall for wedding receptions and meetings and religious instruction. Thus a contractor was hired to knock out the interior walls downstairs and to convert the upstairs bedrooms into offices and classrooms. Worthington Pyle, meanwhile, lived out the rest of his rectorship in a pricey room of the Van Buren Hotel, and when he retired, the parish bought a condo on the river for Father and Mrs. Tisdale. Money has never been a problem at St. Blaise, thanks to the founder of the hockey-stick factory and several well-to-do widows, including Mother.

"Let me assist you, Mrs. Edwards," says the rector sanctimoniously. "Where would you like to situate yourself? Will you mingle or sit?"

"Or lie down?" calls the rector's obtuse wife from the kitchen. "I mean it's her *wake*, after all."

Ignoring her, Mother says, "I'll sit, thank you, Father. My mingling days are over." Mother is not fond of the Tisdales, particularly Mrs. Tisdale, whom she views as a competitor in the field of radio chatter, for not only do they have matching senses of mordant wit (*Or lie down* is precisely what Mother would have said, had their roles been reversed), but the rector's wife also has begun her own once-a-week talk show on KPLG (Praise the Lord God), Rookery's new station featuring evangelists and so-called sacred but treacly music.

Mother tries out a wingback chair, finds it comfortable, and asks us to move it out to the center of the room. We do so, though it weighs a ton. I then go out to the car for a guestbook and a fresh box of Kleenex, while the rector rearranges other furniture to Mother's liking, drawing three side chairs into a semicircle facing her.

Gloria Corelli soon arrives and replaces the rector's syrupy, funereal taste in music with the CDs Mother has chosen— Vivaldi, Purcell, and the Carpenters. "Where's Angelo?" Mother asks, and Gloria replies that he's still at the arena looking for the poet in order to chauffeur him back to the Hi-Rise.

"But he finished speaking an hour and a half ago," says Mother.

"I guess anybody that famous is mobbed by fans." Gloria faces me and adds, "Somebody said they saw him leave with you, out the back door."

"Just for a minute, he needed a smoke" is my excuse.

Next to arrive is our caterer, Helen Walker. Her mourning outfit includes a black hat and veil. Mrs. Tisdale grudgingly oversees the placement of food trays around the room. She's let it be known that it's *outré* to serve food at wakes, but Mother has overruled her.

Next comes the delivery man from Spangler's Floral, and I help him transfer the baskets of flowers from the church. The bus from Grimsby pulls up across the street. Uncle Bill and Aunt Mary are first through the door of the manse, followed by the dozen other O'Kellys. Father Tisdale stands just inside the doorway, his customary post at wakes and funerals, and welcomes them with a vigorous handshake and the assurance that he's as sorry as he can be. Mother has urged him to lighten up tonight, but he's obviously not one to change his habits. Next to him, as usual, stands Mrs. Tisdale, repeating her husband's words in exact imitation of his sad tone of voice and his facial expression of blissful resignation. Mother and I, having attended perhaps a dozen funerals since the Tisdales came to town, have decided that she does this in earnest, that she's not making fun of her husband. More than a little embarrassed by the whole affair, I retreat to a far corner and watch.

But for Detlef and one of his twin sons, the Nebraska cousins take turns sitting down in pairs or groups of three to pay their respects to Mother, exchanging a few words with her and signing their names in the registration book she holds on her lap.

Detlef and the reluctant twin drift over to the bouquet I pretend to be improving upon. They stand silent for a few moments, one on each side of me, and then—lo!—Detlef starts a conversation. "I didn't know she wasn't dead," he mumbles in a way to indicate his feelings are hurt.

I'm astonished. "But we wrote it on the invitation."

"Maylene opens the mail."

"Didn't she tell you?"

"Just said Lolly's wake, is all."

"Then you must be mighty surprised."

He nods. "Mighty."

"You seen *Naked Gun Two* yet?" asks the twin.

I shake my head. "Nor *One*," I tell him.

I grow more and more uneasy watching the O'Kellys and Mother in conversation. This isn't working. Everybody's too stiff. Leaving Mother's presence, each pair or threesome makes a beeline for a snack tray and they stand over it, eating silently and hungrily and (I can tell) pondering an excuse to round up the family for an early departure back to our house, where the elders are assigned beds and the younger two generations will unroll their sleeping bags in our enclosed sleeping porch.

I venture to ask Detlef, "Why is everybody on pins and needles? What's missing?"

"Booze."

"Really?" I had thought to provide wine, but the Tisdales said no.

"Booze," Detlef repeats wearily. "O'Kellys like their booze."

"Seen *Robocop*?" asks the twin.

"No, I haven't."

"How about the *Slasher* flicks? Any of them?"

"Nope."

"Wow," he says in his father's monotone. "They're radical."

The conversation at the center of the room becomes more animated when it's Lucy's turn. She sits facing Mother with her seven-year-old niece Bridget on one side of her and her husband

Ron, who holds Baby Detroit, on the other. Lucy's high-pitched laughter and the sight of her slapping Mother on the knee, as well as Mother's obvious pleasure at being called "the most downright party animal in captivity," has the effect of booze on the family, loosening their tongues and setting them in motion from table to table, sampling the vast variety of cheeses and coldcuts. The arrival of certain friends helps as well, among them Viola and Bud Trisco, Mayor and Mrs. Steadman, Professor Francine Phillips, and several members of the Bridges family of furniture tycoons. I'm relieved, at first, to see that Portis Bridges is not among them, but a moment later he comes through the door, accompanied by Rookery State's chief exhibitionist. Reggie VanderHagen, who—out of respect for this solemn occasion?—has reduced his display of jewelry to a glinting diamond ear stud. The room is too dark to reveal, at this distance, whether he's painted or bronzed or gilded his face.

It's fortunate that this first wave of townspeople includes so many gregarious types, otherwise the second wave would surely have sunk the party. I'm talking about the likes of President Zastrow, who comes in leading his wife by the hand. He looks around for a fireplace to park her in front of and, finding none, brings her over to stand at my right hand with Cousin Detlef. Meanwhile, Edna Kahlstrom shows up with her doom-saying philosopher husband, and delivers him to me as well. "Do you mind?" she says, leaving him in my care (what am I, the Dean of Misfits?) while she joins Professor Faith Crownin-shield and Benny Smith of KRKU on the three chairs facing Mother.

And then—to my astonishment—Cousin Wesley of Omaha comes solemnly forth with his tiny wife Bernadine. Their moss-green satin jackets say *Ducks Unlimited*. Wesley mumbles a greeting, "Har doin'," and his effervescent wife takes me by both hands and exclaims, "Hey, Leland, your mom sure gets some screwy ideas, but when you think them over they usually make sense, like this one, I mean." She turns to her husband. "I mean any excuse for a party, right, Wesley?"

"Right, Bernie," he replies without enthusiasm.

Detlef's twin, who has been studying the president's wife, asks her, "You ever seen Sylvester Stallone?"

Her eyes, amazingly, flicker to life as she turns her head to him, robotlike, and speaks. "What a hunk."

Detlef himself ventures another opening, saying to Wesley, "You're a duck hunter."

This brings Cousin Wesley to life and sets the two of them off on an exchange concerning shot and powder, teal and mallard, the daily bag limit on the Missouri flyway. My father, a hunter, would have enjoyed this conversation, but I, strictly a fisherman, find it incomprehensible. Ten-gauge versus twelve. Four-shot versus six. They ignore Philosopher Kahlstrom's pronouncement:

"All hunters ought to be taken out and shot."

This attracts the twin's attention, however. He asks Kahlstrom, "Hey, man, you seen *Naked Gun*?"

Kahlstrom gives the boy a look of utter distaste before shaking his head.

"Which one?" asks the twin.

"Which one what?"

"Ain't you seen? The first one or the sequel?"

Kahlstrom turns his back on him.

Bernadine, meanwhile, has moved over to the president's wife, whose eyes have gone out of focus again. Unaware that the woman is stewed or drugged to the gills, she inquires, "How long have you known Lolly?"

I take Mrs. Zastrow's part. "Since 1969, I believe. Her husband's been at the college nearly as long as I have."

The twin beckons his brother over to us, his mouth full of carrot. I venture a guess, saying, "Hello, Karl."

His reply, "Hey man," indicates I'm correct.

Kurt, his brother, nods his head sideways, indicating Mrs. Zastrow, and the twins study her with keen interest, doubtlessly recognizing a dead and kindred spirit when they see one.

Misfit corner grows more crowded with the approach of Reggie VanderHagen, whose watery eyes are shining with pleasure or medication or street drugs or sheer insanity. Portis Bridges, too, joins us, and I stiffen, prepared to be insulted for my stand on Addison Steele. Bridges has put on a necktie for the occasion, a wide display of Peanuts characters at golf.

"Dean Edwards, wonderful to see you," says VanderHagen, grabbing my hand and shaking it.

"Ditto, just marvelous," says Bridges, grabbing my lapels and adjusting the hang of my suitcoat. His own sagging outfit is the closest thing I've seen to a zoot suit since I was about seven, the pegged black pants ballooning out at the knees and the single button of the coat located at crotch level. "Dean, we've hatched this marvelous idea, now please hear us out."

"Wonderful get-together," says VanderHagen, whose eyes are traveling in jerks about the room. He wears a tight black T-shirt under his tailored sportcoat. "Lolly's looking so nice."

"Yes, isn't she just precious!" says Bridges.

"And you yourself, Dean, you're looking pretty spiffy yourself."

"Yes, isn't he? Just marvelous."

Friendliness this false can mean only one thing: they have yet another outrageous name to foist on the president's committee. Mike Tyson comes to mind. Saddam Hussein.

But no, I'm wrong—Bridges is trying to insinuate himself deeper into the workings of the college. It's not only his duty but his fondest desire, he says, to serve on the Presidential Search Committee. I try not to look stunned at the prospect. He's presumably read the State College Handbook, where it specifies that all administrative search committees must include at least one member each from the alumni and the local community. "I'll be happy to add your name to my list of nominees," I tell him. Actually there is no such list.

"Don't forget now," he says happily.

"First thing tomorrow."

"I'll be in touch about it," he says, giggling.

"I'll bet you will."

Sally is late arriving with her first load of residents. I fly to her side and follow her about the room as she deposits her seven charges, including Nettie Firehammer and Hildegard Lubovich, on chairs and settees. She's wearing high heels and her dressy coat—black, straight, ankle-length. Her anxious expression I take to mean something went wrong. My own anxiety must be equally obvious, for she answers my questions before I ask them:

"No problems, Leland. Nobody saw us. Kimberly was waiting at the door."

"I worry about Kimberly," I tell her. "Whether she's stable enough to be involved."

"It's Peggy Benoit who worries me."

"Oh, you've seen her then."

"She's been at the Hi-Rise for over an hour, waiting. I told her you'd be along soon, that you might know where he'd gone."

"You didn't tell her?"

"Of course I didn't tell her." She turns on me, looking wounded. "Did Mr. Falcon say we should tell her?"

"No, but wouldn't she be an exception? Being his friend and neighbor and all."

"It's the 'all' that bothers me. What's she doing in his life, anyway?"

"I don't see why that should matter. Is there a boy with her?"

"His autistic grandson, in his thirties. Come with me, will you? I'm going back for another load."

Hildegard Lubovich, insisting on an immediate audience, rises out of the chair Sally assigned her to. "I'm Lolly's best friend," she declares, shooing others off the three chairs facing Mother. This causes at least four of her fellow residents—the competitive ones—to stand up and move to the center of the room, all vying for Mother's attention, claiming, "No, *I'm* Lolly's best friend." "No, I am." "Lolly, tell them—Aren't I your best friend!"

Mother sits in their midst, laughing at the fuss. Of the seven residents, only Nettie Firehammer remains humbly seated where she was put. Following Sally to the door, I pass Nettie's chair and hear her moaning, with tears in her eyes, "Lolly was *my* best friend."

"Mother isn't dead," I assure her, leaning down to pat her bony shoulder.

"I know, but it won't be long and she will be. That's the point of our being here, isn't it?"

This remark stops me in my tracks. I stand there for a few moments imagining more vividly than ever Mother dead and gone. The void in Rookery. In all of radioland. In me.

"I could just weep," says Nettie, weeping copiously, "when I think how short life is."

"It's just a feeling I have about her," says Sally at the wheel of the van, moving us swiftly along the deserted Sunday-night streets. "The way she came rushing into the Hi-Rise asking for Richard Falcon and looking sort of desperate, telling me, 'I know he's staying here, I've been told he's here.' She strikes me as dangerous, Leland. I think she's a golddigger."

I chuckle in disbelief. Here and there a snowflake goes whizzing by.

"Don't forget how she squabbled over Connor's paintings."

"But she was Connor's . . . helpmeet."

"Yes, and she fought tooth and nail to deprive his wife and daughter of his work."

They've met only once before tonight, during Peggy's brief visit to Rookery many years ago, and yet Sally, for a reason I guess I'll never understand, has always been rankled by her.

"Look, Sally, a golddigger knows where the gold is. Richard Falcon's broke."

"His manuscripts, Leland. He's sitting on a treasure of paper."

"Is that so? How do you know some college doesn't have them? Boston University goes out aggressively seeking manuscripts. Or Harvard—he gave a series of lectures at Harvard, and they surely—"

"He told me."

"He did?"

"His papers, going all the way back to his first book, are in a bank in Plymouth, New Hampshire. He told me this morning when I took breakfast up to him. That's why he's being pursued by that law firm and that woman he told you about. And why would the IRS be after him if he was truly impoverished?"

"So that makes Peggy a golddigger?"

"Well, the golddigger part is a theory I've put together from the way she looks, from the way she behaves. She's self-serving. You don't see it but I do. I see it in her face. Her eyes are cold. She came into the lobby and you could feel the temperature drop."

"Does she know who you are?"

"I didn't expect she'd know me. She's a show-off, with all that fur and gold and makeup. And her eyes are not only cold, they've undergone some deeper change."

"Suffering can change a person's eyes, I've noticed."

"Suffering? What suffering?"

"Well, that whole business with Connor—he died, don't forget."

"But that was ages ago, Leland. You never got over your crush on her, did you? I can always tell it in your voice, this undying crush. She's the last person in the world I'd have predicted you'd get interested in. Flashy isn't something I'd expect you to fall for."

"Sally, please. There's more to Peggy than flash. We had this musical combo—"

"And her hair. Is that the style in the East? It looks stupid."

This bitter little skirmish goes on all the way down Division Street. I try to give Sally the whole picture, what it was like, in 1969, to be playing in that quintet, how proud I was to hold my own on the piano, with Peggy on sax, Neil Novotny on clarinet, Victor Dash on drums, Connor on string bass. I've played with others since. Before I became dean I put together trios and quartets that played better and certainly lasted longer than the Icejam Quintet, but it was the Icejammers who showed me, for the only time in my life, what it must feel like to have brothers and a sister. All of this I explain to Sally, but jealousy of course speaks louder than reason:

"I dread seeing the two of you together, Leland. Please don't fawn over her—promise?"

Irked, I don't respond.

"Leland?"

Jealousy, as I've said, is about the only vice Sally is susceptible to.

"Leland, you're upset, aren't you."

"No." But I am.

Nearing the Hi-Rise, she resumes her account: "I told her Mr. Falcon wasn't back yet, I said she was welcome to wait, so she plunked herself down in the lobby between Nettie and Hildegard and quizzed them. Was he friendly toward them? Was he seriously working on his poetry? Did he ever act odd?"

"Hildegard must have remembered her."

"Not at first. It was Dot Kropp, coming down from her room, who recognized her. 'Dr. Benoit,' she said, 'you're the lady with the pipes,' and of course this started up quite a little discussion among my lobbyists—who remembered her, who didn't, what she taught, where she was teaching now. With the tables turned on her, she clammed up. Sat there trying to ignore them. Giving one-word answers to their questions. Sat there with her fur coat drawn up over her shoulders and staring out at the driveway, waiting. One look at her and you could tell she was trying to hide how tense and worried she was."

We pull up at the front entrance. Through the window I see the next load of residents sitting in the lobby with their coats on. I see Peggy stand up and start toward the door.

"Leland, we're not telling her a thing until we're sure Richard Falcon wants her to know. I mean, it could be Peggy Benoit he's running away from, couldn't it?"

This strikes me as so preposterous I can't help laughing. "He'd be the first man ever to do *that*."

The first thing Peggy does, coming out the door with Jonathan in tow, is hug me. She won't let go. We stand pressed against the van while the others climb slowly in and take their seats. "What is it?" I ask, patting the thick fur of her coat collar.

A shudder. Then a whisper: "Where is he?"

"Angelo must have taken him to Mother's wake." This falsehood flows out of me so smoothly that I risk another. "Mother made him promise he'd be there."

She stands back and looks at me with a troubled smile. "Oh, Leland," she gushes, and pulls my face down for a kiss. I have no idea what any of this means. If she's trying to be romantic, she's twenty-five years too late. It's a melancholy fact that what I find attractive is the memory of her, not the woman herself.

Father Pyle, on his way by, taps her on the shoulder and says, "Tut, tut, girl." I steel myself for some asinine remark from his sidekick, Johnny Hancock, but Johnny is not among those boarding. Johnny, in fact, hasn't been seen since lunch. We learn this from Sally as we pull away from the Hi-Rise, nine of us stuffed into her seven-passenger Caravan. I'm sitting next to Jonathan, who keeps repeating a syllable that sounds like "Gug."

"He didn't come to the arena with us," says Sally. "And when we got back, Twyla Todd said she saw him heading down Skidder Street." She turns to Peggy riding beside her and explains further, "Since Twyla Todd became immobilized by arthritis, her window's become our watchtower."

"The dear soul," says Peggy tenderly.

"Oh, do you know Twyla?"

"No, just the idea . . . an old woman like that, a prisoner in her room."

"She keeps a pair of binoculars on the windowsill."

"Oh, how quaint, the poor dear."

I never knew Peggy to be sentimental. These remarks of hers, like her kiss, strike me as a little false. Each time she speaks, Jonathan says "Gug."

Sally goes on. "Between her lookout window and her police-band radio, she doesn't miss a speck of local gossip."

"The dear, dear soul."

"Lolly even consults her for news." She throws her voice back to me, along with her side of the conversation. "Doesn't she, Leland?"

"That's true."

Peggy turns to me with a burst of joyous laughter. "Honestly, Leland, isn't Lolly a piece of work? Who else would think of having her wake before she died?" She shifts her expression from light to dark, changes her voice to a low, confidential register. "But it has to be a very sad occasion for you."

I shake my head, indicating otherwise.

"Not sad?" she says.

"No," I tell her.

"What is it then?"

"Goofy."

"Gug."

Sally turns south on Skidder, and into the parking lot of Petey's Price-Fighter Foods, Johnny Hancock's favorite hangout when the lumberyard is closed. Petey will sometimes give him a bunch of grapes or a small pack of chips to munch on as he wanders the aisles reading labels. I volunteer to go in and look around. Stepping out of the van, I hear Father Pyle grumble, "Where will we put him? You don't have a trunk in this contraption."

Petey's interior lights are momentarily blinding. "Hey, Edwards," calls a fat young man I don't recognize. He's standing at Carol Thelen's till, lifting currency and checks out of the drawer and stuffing them in a deposit bag. Miss Thelen, my freshman dropout with the mismatched eyes and off-center chin, is the only checker tonight. Three customers are waiting in line behind their carts. The store, as usual, smells vaguely of raw meat and ripe fruit.

Miss Thelen beams me a confident smile such as she never displayed in Freshman English. "Dr. Edwards, this is Brian. He's our new manager."

"So you've been passed over," I joke, causing her to giggle and Brian to look threatened.

"I been in groceries since I was sixteen," he claims defensively.

"Tell him, Brian," says Carol, laying a hand on his soiled shirtsleeve.

"I wrapped meat for a year to start with, then—"

"Not that, Brian. Tell what else."

"Oh, yeah, we're getting married."

Whereupon she puts her arms around his thick middle, lays her head on his barrel chest, and gives me a dreamy smile.

I'm slow to reply, convinced it's a mismatch. Brian looks unpromising to me, and Miss Thelen is going to require tenderness.

"Hey, congratulations," says one of the customers waiting in line, a woman in a black jogging outfit. The man behind her says, "Yeah, congratulations, now can we get a move on?"

"Isn't it super, Dr. Edwards?"

"Wonderful news, Miss Thelen." I glance sideways, down the cereal and cracker aisle.

"Isn't it super?" she asks her betrothed, looking up at him with a smile that becomes pitifully uncertain, lovesick.

"Dynamite," says Brian, without emotion.

"Has Johnny Hancock been in?" I ask, moving over to look down the soap aisle. All the stock in this store is displayed in high stacks of cut-open cartons.

"Ha!" says Brian. "Tell him, Carol."

"We called the cops on him, Dr. Edwards."

"The cops?"

She releases her hold on Brian and gets busy with the groceries before her, pulling them across the bar-code reader. "I said not to, but Brian has to follow the rules."

"Why? What did he do?"

"Shoplifted," says Brian, zipping his money bag shut and piercing me with his icy, defiant eyes. His face, framed in a circle of pasty flesh, looks more comical than frightening. "Petey said the next shoplifter we catch, no matter if it's a Councilman's kid or somebody's mother, we're calling the cops and making an example of him. Petey's fed up with shoplifters. We lost seven cartons of cigarettes since Christmas."

"Where is he?"

Simultaneously, Carol says, "At the police station" and Brian says, "In the clink."

"Good Lord, you can't do that to an old man who's losing what few brains he had."

"We do what Petey says," Carol repeats, rolling a ragged head of cabbage across her scale.

"Petey wouldn't do that to Johnny Hancock. Let me talk to him."

"He ain't here, I'm in charge," says Brian.

"He's away for the weekend, Dr. Edwards. He flew out to Montana to see his mom."

I hurry out to the van and announce Johnny's fate to the passengers.

"Musta been a sex crime," declares Dot Kropp, causing the New Woman to giggle. Worthington Pyle says, "Good riddance," and a woman in back echoes, "Good riddance." The old woman beside me mutters, "Good riddance all right, let him start feeling up some fellow jailbird and see what happens to him."

Sally speeds down Division Street, passing the outdoor ice rink (three skaters) and the Paramount (*Mrs. Doubtfire*), and turns down Tailrace toward St. Blaise.

"Hey, ain't we stopping for Johnny?" asks the New Woman.

"Let him be," two or three women advise.

Pyle says, "Out of Christian charity, Sally, I believe it's our duty to spring him."

"There isn't time," she says. "I've got another load to deliver before the service starts."

By seven o'clock it's standing room only, the Gathering Room packed to the walls. Father Tisdale begins the ceremony by stepping up to the lectern and recommending Mother to God the Father, to Jesus, to the Virgin Mary, and to all the saints in heaven.

"What about the Holy Ghost?" complains Worthington Pyle at my side. "Don't tell me Tizzy has stopped believing in the Holy Ghost."

I defend Father Tisdale. "It's hard to personify the Holy Spirit. I mean, you can't picture a spirit."

"Bah, you're all heretics!"

The eulogies begin. First is Hildegard Lubovich, Mother's oldest friend. She steps forward and speaks fondly of bridge opponents outplayed and outlived by Mother and herself. The names call up faces long dormant in my memory. Madge Welter, our high school principal during my youth. Alice Demitrius, the wife of the pharmacist who owned Demitrius Drug until he lost his license for taking pity on a stranger and selling him, without a prescription, something the stranger used to take his own life. Eddie Todd, the unmarried older brother of Twyla, who shunned the company of men, socialized only with women, and died of heart disease at the age of forty-four. Back and back go the names, to a faceless time when all I remember is some random detail to go with each name—Adeline Zellner's gauzy scarves, the old

Hudson Hornet driven by Beatrice Peterson, the rumor that Margaret Annunciation was related to Indians. What's it like for Mother, I wonder, to have it pointed out to her that the vast majority of her friends are in the grave? She appears unmoved, nodding and smiling as each name is spoken.

Benny Smith, of KRKU, is next. He takes us through five decades of "Lolly Speaking," starting with her first program in 1947, an interview with Phil Anderson of Our Own Hardware on the labor-saving features of the new postwar models of wringer washing machines. He tells about her two on-air phone conversations with the White House; she chatted with Lady Bird Johnson thirty years ago about highway beautification, and with Hillary Clinton just last fall concerning health care. He recalls her two on-the-spot reports that were rebroadcast by CBS: the forest fires of 1976 and her interview with Senator Humphrey, in which he first revealed his fatal illness. I expect Mother to join in at any moment, adding her own favorite tales from the studio, but she sits deep in her wingback chair with her eyes closed for minutes at a time, opening them now and again to check the mourners' reaction to some particularly amazing memory of Benny's. The rapid rise and fall of her chest indicates either excitement or blocked-up breathing. I step over and make sure her tube of oxygen isn't kinked.

There is a break of about five minutes while Mrs. Tisdale packs us closer together to make room for a dozen newcomers, who are followed by two dozen more, including Sally and her last load of residents. The front door is left open, for the room has grown very hot.

The next eulogist is Mayor Tony Steadman, a man incapable of speaking without political implication. He praises Mother for her lifelong support of the Steadman family of officeholders. He forgets or glosses over the years when Mother was on the outs with his brother Harry the state senator. (It was Mother who announced on the air the news of Harry's bankruptcy and the reason for it—he was addicted to playing the horses in Winnipeg.) The Harry Steadmans owned a mother-daughter portrait by Connor, which Mother, to atone for blabbing, tried to sell for them, again on the air, but the highest local bid was only nine hundred dollars. So Mother bought it herself, for fourteen hundred. (Some years later we sold it to a gallery in St. Louis for twelve thousand.)

Everyone knows it's potentially dangerous to give Worthington Pyle an audience, but of course there's no way you can leave your former rector out of a memorial service if he wants to participate. Tonight, however, instead of harping on heresy and the downfall of humanity, he surprises us all with his civility. He pays tribute to Mother as "the staunchest pillar of St. Blaise. Without the Joseph Edwards trust fund," he says, "we might very well be one of the many parishes reduced to mission status in recent years. We thank you, Lolly Edwards, for the time, the talent, and the financial help you've blessed us with."

He's about to return to his place when he sees that I'm next, and last, in line. He scowls at me with what I assume to be anger, but the words out of his mouth are solemn and true. "It isn't often that a son or daughter can say publicly what he feels for a parent. This is a rare opportunity, Leland, make the most of it."

It's a good thing I prepared my eulogy beforehand—I didn't expect to feel quite so emotional. For the second time today I'm fighting back tears. "My mother's life is a list," I begin, my voice aquaver, and I take the mourners through a recent notecard from Mother's bulletin board.

```
 9:00   Mercy Hosp—blood test
10:00   KRKU—healthy veggie recipes w/ Helen Walker
11:30   clinic Dr P
12:45   lunch w/ Fr T—funding summer youth camp
 2:00   nap damn it
 3:00   tour sheriff's office & jail w/county commissioners
 4:00   answer letters esp Lucy's
        Rsvp Henderson–McNally wedding
        Call potential regrets to Tuesday bridge in case
        breathing not better.
 6:00   dinner w/Corellis
```

Not bad for a woman going on eighty-three, what? Then, for contrast, I summarize a few notecards from years ago, when a typical day consisted of eighteen or twenty items, including speaking engagements, meetings of service clubs, and classes in flower arranging, chair-caning, china painting. She keeps all these cards in decks, tightly bound with rubber bands and packed in boxes in the garage. There are approximately ninety cards to a deck, and four decks for each year of her life since 1948, tan cards for autumn, pink for winter, yellow for spring, green for summer. Her biography.

I also tell the mourners about her lifelong habit of jotting down lists at random, in the margins of books, on shirt cardboards, on deposit slips—lists of blessings hoped for, schoolgirl songs and poems memorized, the birthdates and deathdates of ancestors and cousins, favorite recipes. Is it any wonder that I, too, became a listmaker?

I read my favorite list to the mourners. I've copied it off the flyleaves of our family Bible, where it appears under the heading, *Questions for God*. It's a list of conundrums, and I interrupt myself halfway through it to say to the mourners, "What this amounts to is an account of the light and darkness we all experience in this vale of tears.

"Can an unsaid prayer ever be answered?" I read. "Or unanswered?"

"Yes, certainly!" Mother calls out, startling everyone in the room, especially me. I always considered these questions unanswerable by any mortal.

She clears her throat and continues. "I never prayed that I'd meet your father," she says. "But if ever there was an answer to a girl's prayer, it was Joe Edwards, let me tell you." Her voice, though weak, is clear if you listen, and everyone does, in hushed respect. "I married Joe, it'll be sixty years ago in June. He was twenty-three and I was twenty-two. He died at thirty-eight. Leland was fourteen."

There's a whimper from Nettie Firehammer. Here and there hankies and Kleenex appear.

"I can't speak for Leland, but I know that not a day has gone by in these forty-five years that I have not thought of Joe." Here she falls silent, but with her hand raised to indicate she's not finished. More whimpering from Nettie, more dabbing at eyes. Mother's shoulders heave the way they do when she's repressing tears or laughter. To everyone's surprise, this time it's laughter. It comes out with her next statement: "Lately I've been apologizing to Joe for taking forever to join him."

She goes on in this vein, reminiscing about my father, until I realize that she intended this to be his memorial service as well as her own. Very little of what Mother does is unpremeditated. She recalls picnics, dances, trips to Nebraska. Finally his death.

"And that was a case of unsaid prayers unanswered," she explains. "I certainly never prayed for Joe to come in safely from fishing on August 15, 1948. Joe was out on the water two and three times a week, fishing was like breathing to Joe. But if I'd known an electrical storm was about to come over the horizon, I certainly *would* have prayed, and who knows, my prayer might have saved him. Or it might not. But either way it would have been a *said* prayer, and I'm talking about *unsaid* prayers. It was my *unsaid* prayer that went unanswered that day."

Nettie Firehammer tries to suppress a howl of sorrow.

"Murky theology," calls out Worthington Pyle. "Very murky."

Ignoring the old rector and reproving Nettie with a friendly frown, Mother sits forward in her chair and sweeps the room with both arms in a kind of all-inclusive embrace. "Thanks for being here," she says. "You're all very kind to show up. Now let's get back to the eating and drinking."

And with that she falls back in her chair and accepts a plate of brie and crackers from Cousin Claudette, a plate of cookies and chocolates from Cousin Lucy. For all her attention to diet over the radio, Mother's been eating the wrong food all her life. Nobody seems to realize that I hadn't finished my tribute. Oh well, it was going to be mostly about me anyway—how I'd inherited her habit of making lists, but of a different sort and for a different reason. My list of random musings—up to nearly three hundred items per year—has been my aid to sanity during the dreaded and tedious meetings a dean must attend.

When Lucy and Claudette finish fussing over Mother, I expect Peggy Benoit to step dramatically forward and embrace her, but Peggy seems to have vanished. I circle the Gathering Room and peer into the kitchen and cloakroom. I inquire of

Angelo and Sally. Angelo says he never saw her come in. Sally has already scanned the room and found her gone.

We go to the phone in the kitchen and I call Kimberly's number. I get her answering machine, of course. Listening to her longwinded greeting (Owl is indisposed today, has eaten a mouse) and waiting for the go-ahead tone, I rehearse my warning that Peggy's in town looking for Richard Falcon and Sally suspects she's a predator. It's possible Peggy will deduce his location, for surely she will remember Kimberly as an ally of mine in those early days. I'm on the verge of recording this when it occurs to me that Kimberly keeps her answering tape turned up to its highest volume so she can hear it throughout the house. I picture Peggy standing in her front doorway, listening to my warning.

"Sally and I are going to drop in on you" is all that I say.

By continuously ringing her doorbell, we manage to rouse Kimberly out of her reverie in a mere two or three minutes. First, the dim porch light goes on overhead, then there's the locks opening, and finally the door opens four inches and she sings, "What is it?"

"It's about your houseguest. Can we come in? Sally's with me."

Unhooking the chain, she says, "We're in the kitchen," and she spins around on her oversized woolly slippers (no doubt her father's) and shuffles hurriedly away. She's wearing a lavender dress of some coarse, brittle fabric that rustles loudly in the hallway as we follow her into the kitchen. I expect to see Mr. Falcon sitting at the wobbly antique table, sharing the bottle of apricot brandy she likes to uncap when darkness falls, but there's no sign of him. Only one brandy snifter half full, one coaster, one chair pulled out from the table.

"Who's we?" I ask.

Busy with tea things, she nods at Owl, standing on the table, propped against a sugar bowl.

"Please don't bother with tea," I tell her. "We only came to say Peggy Benoit's in town. If she shows up at your door we wouldn't want you to tell her anything, because—"

She casts an angry, damaged-looking expression at me. "Honestly, you college administrators are all alike. You don't even trust your best friends." She pointedly avoids facing Sally, whom she decided to dislike many years ago.

"Kimberly, all I'm saying is, she might try to make you think Mr. Falcon wants to see her."

"And how do you know he doesn't?"

"Well, it's a suspicion we have. We wonder, or I should say Sally wonders . . ." I hand it on to Sally:

"What we mean is, what if Peggy Benoit's the person he's trying to get away from, don't you see?"

There's a renewed flash of anger in Kimberly's eyes. Her resentment of Sally goes back to the days when Mother tried to involve me romantically with Kimberly. In fact it was Kimberly—long on insight and short on tact—who, by means of the scathing remarks she used to spit out concerning Sally, first made Mother aware of her presence in my life.

I attempt to distract her. "Peggy might make you think, because she's come so far, that she deserves to see him."

"Yeah, yeah, I got it," says Kimberly, plunking herself down on her chair and taking Owl into her arms.

"I'd like to go up and see him for just a minute," I tell her.

She gulps down a slug of opaque, thick-looking brandy. "See who?" she asks.

I laugh at what I suppose is a joke. "How many men do you have upstairs?"

"None."

"None?"

"He came in and I made him a cup of tea. He drank it, then asked me to call him a taxi. He left by the front door."

"A taxi? He took his things with him?"

"Never let go of them—sat here drinking tea with his bags at his feet."

"Good Lord, he can't have run away!"

She gives me a smile at once joyful and vicious.

Sally is on the phone. She's standing at the counter, next to the sink, facing away, head down, as though meditating on the many rings that finally bring a response. It's Billy Swan at Badbattle Cab—I can tell by the pleasantries she exchanges with him.

Billy Swan is one of Sally's successes from the CREW program in Owl Brook; when he got out of treatment she took him in hand and made a cab dispatcher out of him. Swan is a common family name on the Basswood Reservation. She hands me the receiver.

"Hello, Mr. Swan."

"Who's this?"

"Leland Edwards. I was wondering—"

"You need a cab?"

"No, I have a question."

"Good thing. Cabs are all tied up at your mother's shindig."

"One of your drivers picked up a man on Bellwether Drive around four o'clock, and I need to know where he was going."

"I'd have to look it up."

"An elderly man carrying bags."

There's a pause, with staticky voices in the background. "One of them Hi-Rise types on the loose again?"

"Right."

Another pause. "Nope. Nothing here on Bellwether. What time you say?"

"Around four."

"Nope. I was here at four. Nobody called from Bellwether."

"Is there another taxi service in town?"

"Nope. Badbattle's all there is. Hey, give Lolly my best."

"I will."

"Some of my relations are there for it."

"Good of them to come."

"She's always stood up for us, you know, on the rezz."

"I know."

"I'd of been there myself if I wasn't on duty."

"Good of you to think of her, Mr. Swan."

Sally has left the kitchen. I turn to face Kimberly, who has placed Owl flat on the table and is examining him for lint, picking at specks of it here and there.

"Where's the poet?" I ask angrily.

"I have no idea, I'm sure."

"He's here in the house, isn't he!"

She raises her eyes to the ceiling, raises her voice and sings, "You're calling me a liar!"

I go into the foyer and start upstairs, but meet Sally coming down. "Nobody there."

I return to the kitchen. "Kimberly, no taxi came for him."

"I didn't say it did, did I?" Now she's trimming Owl's furry chest with a manicure scissors.

"You said—"

"I said he *asked* me to call him a taxi. I didn't actually *call* one. You said he was to stay here, so I couldn't very well help him leave, could I?"

"Well, what did he do, just walk off into the night?"

"I couldn't very well hold him against his will, could I?"

"So he *did* walk off into the night!"

"Honestly, Leland, must you be so goddamn melodramatic?"

Sally is on the phone again, this time to the Hi-Rise. She asks Marigold to check and see if Mr. Falcon is there, authorizing her to unlock the door and look into 506.

We stand there awkwardly, silently, waiting for Marigold to call back. Finally, to evade Kimberly's glowering gaze, I leave the kitchen, saying I intend to follow the poet's footprints along Bellwether. Snow has been falling lightly and intermittently ever since the reading.

"No, I'll go," says Sally, following me to the front door. "You stay," she whispers. "She spooks me."

So I go back to the kitchen. Kimberly seems relieved to have me alone. She asks me, quite civilly, to sit down. The tension has gone out of her voice.

I sit. The table rocks as I fold my arms on it.

She says she feels sorry for me, having this troublesome man on my hands. She advises me to forget him. She says I can't win. "It can't end well, Leland. Either the poet is found and forced to go back to the life he's screwed up, or he *isn't* found and you get blamed for it." She giggles. "I can see the headlines, Leland: *Famous poet vanishes after reading in Rookery.*"

"So what!" I shoot back. "At least it gives us a bit of name recognition." Not that I mean it.

Renewed giggles. "Black Hole College."

I pick up the phone on the first ring. Marigold tells me that 506 is empty. I thank her and hang up.

I put my face close to Kimberly's. "Call me if he comes back here." I say it twice. Then I leave her there, muffling her giggles in Owl's linty breast.

Enough snow has fallen to obliterate all footprints but our own. Now sleet is pelting down. The two of us stand shivering under a lamppost, debating what to do next. Sally says this confirms her suspicion about Peggy. The poet saw her at the reading and panicked.

I'm panicked. "We'd better call at some of these neighboring houses, or talk to the police."

Sally cautions me. It's too early to draw public attention—as well as Peggy's—to the poet. Richard Falcon is shrewd; he knows what he's doing.

"But he gets nutty at nightfall," I remind her.

"It's an act, Leland. I've thought that from the beginning."

"What if you're wrong? What if the poor man's disoriented, carrying his bags through the city, not knowing where he is? What if he's in the woods down there behind the house?"

"He's shrewder than that. He's outsmarted us, don't you see?"

"What if they pull his body out of the river next spring?"

"Stop it, Leland!" She's looking down Bellwether toward Division Street. "Let's ask at that convenience store. He may have called a cab from there."

Which he did. The clerk behind the counter, a long-haired young woman wearing a Tom Thumb blouse and a tiny gold ring through the outside of her left nostril confirms it. "An old guy came in with bags and asked me to call a taxi," she says. "I was busy, so I pointed to the pay phone back there by the rest rooms. I figured he got off the Greyhound from Bemidji. The Greyhound'll let people off out here, but you gotta go downtown to get on."

"And was it a Badbattle cab?" I ask her.

She shrugs. "There's another brand?"

"But you saw him leave?"

She shrugs again. "I was busy."

I go back to the phone and feed it a quarter. I check the men's room while waiting for Billy Swan to answer. I look into an adjacent storeroom as well. Both are empty.

"Mr. Swan, it's Leland Edwards again. You sent a driver to the Tom Thumb on West Division."

"Yup. Did. Couple hours ago."

"Where did he take his fare?"

"Never said. Never reported in."

"Why not? Don't they always report?"

"When they remember. Cab drivers get sloppy, you know—they aren't geniuses."

"Well, it's rather urgent. Can't you raise him on your two-way?"

"Sure, but give me a few minutes, I'm busy."

"Call Sally at the Hi-Rise when you find out, okay? Leave a message on her voice mail."

"Yup, will do. Say, you and Sal aren't married anymore, I hear."

"Divorced."

"When'd that happen?"

"About twenty years ago."

"Well, I'll be damned. Tell her hi anyhow, will you?"

"Okay, Mr. Swan. Thanks."

It's nearly eight, time for Sally to take her charges home. As we make our way slowly back to St. Blaise on icy streets, we try to imagine possible hideouts. Sally suggests the campus library. I doubt it.

"McCall Hall?" she suggests.

"Not likely, all offices and classrooms are locked."

"The hockey arena then."

A possibility. The arena has doubtless been open for cleanup since the reading. I picture the poet finding a secret place down in its bowels, among the twisting and cavernous shower rooms and equipment rooms. I'm wounded to think he planned to deceive me. I say nothing.

At Tailrace and Twelfth we find a traffic jam, mourners by the dozen encountering icy walkways as they come pouring out of the Gathering Room, hanging for dear life on to railings and lampposts and gripping the door handles and hood ornaments of cars halted in the street. In the glare of headlights I see at least two people fall down. While one rises, laughing with embarrassment, the other lies shrieking the shriek of a broken bone. Before a crowd of people close in on the wounded figure, I glimpse the flailing arms and one leg of an elderly woman wearing four-buckle overshoes. Good Lord, it's Aunt Mary.

I leave Sally jammed in traffic, and make my slippery way over to the cluster of Nebraskans blocking the street. Aunt Mary lies flat on her back in the glare of Benny Smith's headlights. Cousin Claudette is kneeling there cradling her head while Cousin Lucy gingerly examines her left leg. Her face is covered by a hankie, her torso by a red Cornhusker blanket. She's not making a sound. Cousin Ron, I'm told, has gone back inside to call an ambulance. Mary's brother Jack, standing over Lucy, coos reassuringly. Uncle Bill, her husband, is pacing fretfully about, keeping his balance with an arm around the shoulder of one of the derelict twins.

"What can I do?" I demand of the family.

"Tell Lolly she's got company for another couple days," says Lucy. "No doctor's gonna let her ride a school bus home tomorrow with this broken ankle."

"Lolly's in there waiting for you, boy," says Uncle Bill sternly. "Best you go in and see to her."

I obey, making my way carefully up the walk.

"Leland, honey." It's Lucy following me. "Leland, I took a phone call for you." She takes my arm as we climb the steps to the Gathering Room. "There was this call for you and the funny thing was the caller wouldn't talk to anybody but me. The preacher's wife came and got me. I went into the kitchen and it was Richard Falcon."

In the Gathering Room, Mrs. Tisdale comes at us with a roaring vacuum cleaner. We step into the quiet of the kitchen.

"He said he'd trust me to give you a message and not tell anybody else. It was kind of a kick, Leland, like I was in on something."

"What did he say?"

" 'Tell Leland I'll be in touch.' "

What a relief. I stand there pinching my forehead and taking deep breaths.

"How does he know me?"

"I told him all about you."

"What's going on? Or shouldn't I ask?"

"No, please don't ask," I tell her, embracing her.

"Oh, Leland, there you are," says Mother, lumbering into the kitchen on the arm of Cousin Ron. "I couldn't imagine where you'd run off to, right in the middle of my obsequies. Wasn't it splendid? Wasn't everybody just full of praise for their favorite old windbag? Isn't it just horrible about your Aunt Mary lying out there in the street? Ron says she won't be going home with the rest of them—"

She's interrupted by an elderly woman edging timidly into the kitchen and touching her sleeve. "I beg your pardon, Mrs. Edwards, we're from Loomis, and Lowell has something to say." A bleary-eyed man, presumably her husband, slips into the room behind her. They're both dressed in stiff new clothes for their excursion into Rookery, she in a quilted black coat that makes loud rasping noises when she moves her arms. Lowell wears a zippered denim coverall.

Lowell's voice is thick and weak. "Them in Loomis asked me to say a few words."

"Your listeners up home," his wife explains.

"But I never got the chance to say 'em in there."

"I'm sorry," says Mother. "Say them now and give me a rush, I feel a slight wheeze coming on."

From a deep pocket Lowell takes a number of papers folded small. While he studies them, looking for page one, Mother addresses Lucy:

"Do you realize by the end there were three hundred people jammed into that room, and fifty or sixty more standing out in the side yard listening on speakers? Did you know that, Leland? Did you know Father Tisdale had outdoor speakers set up, the ones we use at the fall bazaar?—and those dear souls stood out there listening to the eulogies, and afterward, when they filed through to shake my hand, they were covered with snow and ice, the poor dears. I told them we'd do it again next summer when the weather's fine."

"Mother, where's your oxygen?"

"Who needs oxygen when you're full of the fresh air of praise and respect? I feel like I can go six months on what I've heard tonight. Take that ugly tank back where you got it and tell them to start bottling praise and respect and we'll all be a lot better off. You hear me, Leland, Lucy? You two from Loomis? Praise and respect, I tell you. It's such a tonic I'm calling my doctor this very night and telling him to spread the word among all his patients with lung disease—gather up the praise and respect you've got coming and your pipes will clear up in no time."

Lowell's wife, helping him with the papers, discovers that page one is missing. They look hopelessly at Mother.

"You'll have your say," she tells them. "I've decided to have another wake on my birthday."

"When's that?"

"In June. We'll have live music."

The Loomis woman looks relieved, but Lowell is troubled. "What if you're dead by then?" he asks.

"Dear God!" says Mother. "I never thought of that." She looks at me and laughs. "Well, either way, we'll be here for it, won't we, Leland."

With this reassurance, the Loomis couple leaves. And prompted by Mrs. Tisdale's slamming cupboard doors and sweeping around our feet, so do we.

The traffic is unjammed by this time. We hear the ambulance siren fading away in the direction of Mercy Hospital.

"I told Bennie I'm making praise and respect the main theme on my show tomorrow," she declares to figures in the darkness, several of whom may be O'Kellys. "Throw away your pills and start collecting on some of that praise and respect you've been earning all your life."

If I'd thought to warm up the car, she might not have needed oxygen until she got home. As it is, I have to pull off Division and hook her up to her lifesaving tank.

GROUNDHOG DAY

I'm up early, brewing coffee and cutting seven grape-
fruit in half when the phone rings. Assuming it's Richard Falcon,
and not wishing to disturb our guests, I rush to pick it up on the
first ring.

"I didn't wake you?"

"You know me, Sally—rise and shine."

"Well, I'm calling from jail. I stopped on my way to work to
pick up Johnny, and—"

"Good Lord, I forgot about Johnny. He was there overnight?"

"Could you possibly come down to the police station and
vouch for his character?"

"Of course—and what a character he is."

"Arly Quist wouldn't release him last night because Petey
wasn't back from Billings, and now that Petey refuses to press
charges he still won't release him without two character witnesses. Arly Quist is so arrogant he makes me sick."

"Yes, he's basically a pretty stupid man." Arly Quist is
Rookery's new chief of police, a redneck appointed by the slim
majority of reactionaries on the city council. "Did you know he's

been taking college speech courses with a view to running for governor?"

"I'd vote for him for president just to get him out of town."

"Can you give me fifteen minutes, Sally? I hear the first of our fourteen guests stirring upstairs."

"They're all at your house?"

"Thirteen adults and a baby."

"Forget it, Leland, I'll send Marigold down."

"No, no, I have to go out anyway and pick up an oxygen tank."

"All you need to do is sign for Johnny. Then drop him off at the Hi-Rise, would you? I've got to run."

"How's he taking captivity?"

"He couldn't be happier. 'Room service and a spittoon,' he keeps telling me."

"Fifteen minutes."

"Leland, any word from you know who?"

"I'm going over to Kimberly's and see if he's gone back there."

"You know what I think? I think we've seen the last of Richard Falcon. His next call, when it comes, will be from New Hampshire."

Of all the eventualities that passed through my head last night, this one hadn't occurred to me. "Sally, that's very depressing."

"Depressing! Look, Leland, Richard Falcon is a great writer—I'll take your word for that—and you've had this wonderful month with him, but at this point in his life, he's big trouble, and I'm afraid if you get involved . . ."

"Not you too, Sally. That's Kimberly's line."

She tries then, at length, to make me see the folly of clinging to the coattails of a man pursued by furies. I see her point, of course. She succeeds, better than Kimberly did, in scaring me. But my fear of Richard Falcon's furies is nothing compared to the fear that I'll never see him again.

On Bellwether Drive, instead of waiting forever at the front door, I walk through the ankle-deep snow to the back of the house and startle Kimberly—she drops Owl and spills a spoon of tea leaves—by appearing in her kitchen window. With an expression of inquiry on my face I point upstairs. Instead of indicating he is or isn't there, she springs to the window like a cat, cranks it open and cries out in the most humiliating manner, "You're nothing but trouble, Leland, now get away from my house and don't bring me any more *shit*!" Adding to my abasement, my oxfords are full of snow, and by the time I reach the law enforcement center my feet are wet and frigid.

The center is the old Great Northern freight house remodeled, criminals at one end behind bars, and lawmen at the other, in mostly windowless offices. Arly Quist, a swarthy, chesty young man with the customary lawman's mustache, occupies an office with two windows looking out on half a mile of abandoned railroad track. Along with his diploma from Gopher Prairie High School, his two-year degree from Berrington Junior College, and his honorable discharge from the Marine Corps, there is displayed on the wall behind the chief's desk an enormous poster of Kojak. Chief Quist, on duty or off, is never seen out of the uniform which the city provides for him, and to which he's added a twist of gold braid around each buttonhole (Mrs. Quist, one hears, is a seamstress) and pinned a pair of tiny gold pistols to the points of his collar. Angelo asked him one evening last summer at a neighborhood lawn party—he lives near Angelo—if he didn't want to take off his uniform and stop sweating; to which his reply was, "Law enforcement in Rookery is a twenty-four-hour job."

When I tell him I've come for Johnny, he goes to the door and shouts down the hallway, "Bring the old guy in here." Waiting for Johnny to appear, he stands behind his chair lecturing me on shoplifting. "A big huge problem, Edwards. I told Petey last week it's about time we made an example of these stealing bastards, and Petey agreed with me. Petey, he'd been losing cigarettes and candy and pop by the carload. So we decide the next shoplifter over eighteen, we're gonna fine the bejesus out of him and spread his face all over the front page of the *Morning Call* and see if that don't scare off the rest of the lightfingered buggers. Under eighteen isn't no use to us, you can't publish names of criminals under eighteen, and if that isn't the god-*damned*est law ever passed by that bunch of yokels in St. Paul. So anyhow we catch this old guy Hancock from the Hi-Rise and we're all set to throw the book at him and Petey goes soft on me, says the old guy's harmless, says he's not worth prosecuting."

"I've never known Johnny to steal. What did he take?"

"Hey, bring the Hancock evidence in here," the chief calls out.

Comes a voice from an adjacent room. "Where is it?"

"In the freezer."

Johnny is ushered into the office at this point, ruddy-faced and healthier than he's looked in months. He's wearing a T-shirt and a pair of jeans with the cuffs rolled up—obviously a change of clothes provided by Sally. "Nice place," he tells me. "Want to see my room?"

"I'm here to take you home, Johnny."

"But I only been here one night."

"You can't live here. It's jail."

"I know it's jail. I like jail. Toilet's real handy, right by the bed. Plus they got this brass spittoon left over from the Great Northern days. It's got 'Great Northern' carved right in the brass."

Chief Quist tears a page off a tablet and slides it across his desk. It's a form releasing prisoners from captivity. I sign it.

Another of Quist's underlings enters the office carrying, in his right hand, a small sack of Johnny's belongings, which he dumps out on the chief's desk—mostly nails—and, in his gloved left hand, a small Minute Maid orange juice can, which he sets down with great care, presumably so he won't smudge finger-prints. It's covered with frost.

I have to laugh. I'm about to pick it up and hand it to Johnny when the chief says, "Leave that alone. It's what he stole."

"Johnny didn't steal this, it's full of tobacco juice."

The chief looks astonished and his lieutenant looks sour as I explain what I imagine happened in the grocery store. "Petey's new manager, the fat boy, saw a bulge in Johnny's pocket, the middle pocket of his overalls, right here." I point to my sternum. "Johnny always carries an orange juice can there for spitting his juice into. Especially in winter, so he doesn't have to go outside."

I look to Johnny for a nod of verification, but he's busily gathering up his nails.

Arly Quist gazes at the can for a moment and then responds to my laughter with a little smile of his own, on one side of his mouth. He's relieved, I suppose, to have been spared an embarrassing session before a judge. I don't expect a thank you, but I do wish he had something more civil to say than "Get out of here."

In the car, I hand Johnny the cold can. He wears no gloves, and drops it at his feet.

"Careful," I tell him. "It might start leaking."

"It won't," he says, tucking and tamping a fresh chew along his lower gumline.

By this time ℞ Medical Supply is open, so I stop there and rent a second oxygen tank. Though she hasn't complained, I'm sure Mother would like more freedom to move about the house when I'm not home to carry her tank up and down the stairs.

On Court Street we're slowed by rush-hour traffic. My attempts at conversation come to nothing.

"You missed a great reading yesterday, Johnny."

"Yuh."

"Mr. Falcon read a poem about a covey of partridge that set up housekeeping in an abandoned farmhouse."

"Huh."

Two stoplights later, I try again. "Didn't you feel violated when they hauled you off to jail?"

"Yuh."

"What a shame. You missed Mother's wake."

"Yuh."

"I didn't like the idea at first, but it turned out fine. I mean, it made you rethink our system of memorializing people after they're dead."

"Yuh, they got a spittoon right by your bed, left over from Great Northern days."

When I turn slowly in at the Hi-Rise, Johnny opens his door to dribble spit along the driveway, and he's stepping out of the car before I come to a complete stop.

"Here, take your spit," I call after him, picking up the can.

"Keep it," he says, slamming the door and hastening inside.

I see that the opening tab of the can is intact, the cover tight. It *is* orange juice.

At home I find Detlef and both of his twins stripping pinecones and birchbark off the trees in our side yard. "You can have all the pinecones you want," I tell him, "but birch trees die without bark."

"Tell that to Maylene," Detlef replies acidly. "She needs it for her Christmas crafts."

"We're only taking the loose stuff," claims Kurt, tugging vigorously at a tight strip and pulling it away from the moist inner wall of the tree. His brother Karl giggles stupidly.

"Come in for breakfast, while I talk to Maylene."

Kurt, eager, I'm sure, for the chance to light up his first toke of the new day, elects to stay outdoors. "We already ate."

"Yeah," giggles Karl.

Detlef hands them his sack of cones and follows me inside.

I've missed seeing Wesley and Bernadine off, and this amuses Mother. "You know how they are, Leland, chafing like ponies to get on the road." Her laugh is supposed to convey to the O'Kellys how eccentric she finds my Omaha cousin and his wife. "Wesley kept saying, 'Eight hours to Omaha,' and Bernadine kept saying, 'Wait, we've got to say good-bye to Leland,' but what choice does the little lady have, with her bossy husband practically wetting his pants to get back to his hammer and nails? And why are they fixing up that old place anyhow? It wasn't all that fantastic a house to start with, even when your grandparents were living there, sitting on that busy corner with its foundation shivering every time a truck goes by. I tell you, that Wesley . . ."

Mother is very jolly this morning, enlivened by her houseful of blood relatives, who have collected themselves and their duffle bags in the living room to say good-bye. "Let's hit the road," Uncle Bill gruffly urges, moving among them, pointing at his watch. "Give Lolly a kiss and we'll hit the road."

Uncle Bill and Lucy have already been to the hospital, where

Aunt Mary, I'm told, is mildly sedated. Her ankle proved to be broken in a nasty way, requiring surgery and screws and a seven-pound walking cast. She'll be released later today and will rest here for a time. "Leland will drive her home over the weekend," Mother volunteers.

No one protests, or even offers to meet me halfway. The trip must seem twice as far, twice as tiring, in a school bus.

"I simply can't believe that none of you ever met them before," Mother goes on. "Grimsby isn't all *that* far from Omaha. Aren't they a stitch? Isn't Bernadine the funniest little creature on two legs? I tell you, it breaks me up whenever I see them together, she's so happy-go-lucky and Wesley's exactly as interesting as a mud fence. Remember him as a boy, Leland, such a glum little thing? Not a speck of humor about him, the poor child."

One by one, the O'Kelly clan files out the door, pausing in the entryway to embrace Mother and promise to return for her next wake. Outside I draw Cousin Lucy around to the street side of the bus, where I satisfy her curiosity about the phone call she took last night. Breaking my vow of secrecy, I reveal the poet's plan to escape the life he's been living. "After his poem is finished, he's on his own, but until he's written the last word of *Fording the Bee*, I'm going to assist him any way I can. Can you understand that?"

I needn't have asked. Lucy's eyes dance with excitement. She says, "Leland, go for it!" Sensing her exhilaration, her effervescence, I realize that Lucy is the accomplice I need at this point. A new scheme occurs to me.

"He can't stay in Rookery, Lucy. They're closing in on him."

"Who?"

"His enemies." It hurts to call Peggy an enemy, and likewise the pale and pathetic Jonathan, and yet what are they but adversaries, standing in the old genius's way to fulfillment? "When I show up in Grimsby with Aunt Mary, I may have Mr. Falcon with me. Can you find him a sanctuary, someplace he can work in peace?"

"You bet. How long, a month?"

"Maybe more."

She snaps her fingers. "Claudette and me, we can do anything."

"Remember, it's a secret. If Claudette has to know, okay, but she's the only one you can tell."

"My lips are sealed, Cousin." She plants them on both of my cheeks then, and boards the bus as Benny Smith pulls up in his car to take Mother downtown.

Lucy puts her head out a window. "Except I gotta tell Ron," she says. "I tell Ron everything."

It's another pleasant morning of high clouds, dripping icicles and puddles underfoot. I stroll to campus with my Walkman plugged into my ears, tuned to KRKU.

"Hi, Lolly, just calling to say we *adored* your wake last night, such a neat idea, so fun."

"Me too, Lolly. Say, why don't you get St. Luke's chamber choir to sing at your next one in June? And don't have quite so much cheese next time, would you? It's bad for cholesterol."

"Lolly, Portis Bridges here. What a beautiful idea, Lolly, and you looked just gorgeous. I'm going to call the Lasky–Postern Mortuary and see if they'll arrange a wake like that for my grandmother. We'll pretend somebody died and take her to the mortuary and when we get inside all her relatives and friends will be there with balloons. Grandma loves surprises."

"Lolly, this is Twyla. Did you know Richard Falcon has turned up missing? Right here in Rookery. It came over my shortwave radio. Nobody knows where he's got to, and the cops are looking high and low."

"Zastrow said I had to let 'em in," says Viola Trisco, tipping her head toward my inner office. "Two cops and a dame."

Keeping my distance, I look in. Seated at my conference table are Police Chief Arly Quist and Rookery's other leading lawman, Sheriff Reuben Gresser. Quist is playing with the braid down the front of his uniform; Gresser, dressed in a jean jacket over a flannel shirt, is reading the *Morning Call*. I jump to the ridiculous conclusion that they're here to see me about Johnny's can of orange juice, but then I see Peggy Benoit standing at my window, looking out.

"Well, well," I say, announcing myself.

Peggy, turning from the window, her coat draped over her crossed arms, speaks demurely, with seductive sweetness. "Leland, where's Richard Falcon?"

No lies are necessary, unless playing dumb and worried is a kind of falsehood. "Good Lord, you mean he's missing?"

She nods, busily brushing dandruff or powder from her coat collar. "He was last seen leaving the arena—with you." She looks to the two law enforcers for support.

"The lady says you acted suspicious," says Arly Quist, "the way you hustled him out the door."

Peggy gives me a pained look, as though to apologize for tattling. Behind her, in my desk chair, sits Jonathan Falcon, unconscious of his surroundings, his eyes focused on a point six inches in front of him.

Chief Quist continues, "Why did you feel you had to take the guy through the shower rooms and out the back door, like the lady says, unless you thought he was in danger or something?"

"We took the quickest way out of the arena in order to escape the hordes of fans bearing down on him."

"Fans? What fans?"

"The poet's fans. They love his work. He's an old man, he was exhausted."

A *likely story* is what the chief's sneer says to me. He clicks his ballpoint and asks, "Where did you take him?"

"Out to the van parked behind the arena. Sally drove him back to his room at the Sylvan Senior Hi-Rise."

"Sally who?"

"Sally McNaughton. She manages the Hi-Rise." I sit down at the table and watch him print *Sally* on his notepad. I turn to the sheriff. "You know Sally, Reuben."

The sheriff nods, his eyes on the notepad as well. "Nice lady—Sally." When he sees the ballpoint stop at the "c" in "McNaughton" he patiently spells it for him.

Sheriff Gresser and I were classmates through high school. He's by far the longest-standing elected official in the county,

having served twelve consecutive two-year terms. He credits
Mother's support with putting him over the top in the early days
when the vote was close. By now, of course, he's become an
institution and undefeatable. Last November he beat Stonewall
Hancock, Johnny Hancock's grand-nephew and Arly Quist's
ally, 4,007 votes to 920. Reuben's wife Betty, an expert flower
arranger, is a frequent guest on Mother's show.

"Who discovered him missing?" I ask, feigning urgency.

"I did," says Peggy. "There's not a trace of him left in his
room at the Hi-Rise."

"We'd better check the college library," I suggest. "He has a
desk there."

"We did that," says Arly Quist. "Now, what would be the
motive for kidnapping a poet? His bank account's down to
nothing, we called his bank out East."

So they've decided it's a kidnapping. This is fascinating. What
does Peggy know? Is she aware that RF is running away? And has
she planted the concept of abduction in the lawmen's heads, as a
method of enlisting their aid?

"No rich relatives to give a ransom," the chief goes on. "No
relatives period, except a daughter about as broke as he is, and a
crazy grandson."

"Autistic," I tell him. "Not crazy."

"It's his papers," Peggy raises her voice in irritation. "I told
you it's his papers."

"Papers?" Quist looks to Sheriff Gresser to explain this difficult concept. Gresser looks at me.

"The papers—that is, the manuscripts—of famous writers can
be worth quite a bit of money," I tell them. "And Richard Falcon
is the most famous poet in America."

Chief Quist murmurs, "Papers," apparently trying to absorb
the truth of this.

At Sheriff Gresser's request, I enumerate the people the poet
has become acquainted with in Rookery. Besides Mother and
Sally and the Hi-Rise residents, there's Viola and the Corellis and
the library staff. The African-American woman who's been
selling him cigarettes at the 7–Eleven on Court Street comes to

mind as well—more than once I've waited in Angelo's car while the poet took a minute to chat with her while he lit up and took a few puffs—but I don't mention her because it's well known that Arly Quist suffers from Afro-phobia. Let's face it, we live among a vastly white majority here in northern Minnesota, and Arly Quist's suspicion that most people of color, including Indians, are either deviates or criminals fits the mind set of the councilmen who appointed him.

The two law enforcers turn to each other and carry on a mumbled discussion.

"There must be other people on campus he knows," says Peggy.

"I can't say who else he met," I tell her. "I only saw him once a day for a brief visit."

The police chief inquires suspiciously, "What did you visit about?"

"His poem-in-progress."

He follows this up with more mumbled remarks directed at Peggy as well as the sheriff.

Glancing out the window, I see a curious sight across the river. I squint, trying to make out the identity of the figure fishing through a hole in the ice at some distance from the Romans' darkhouse. I believe it's Roman himself. Roman is a spear-fisherman, I've never known him to angle through the ice. This intrigues me, so that I'm only vaguely aware of my visitors getting ready to leave. Is the poet in the darkhouse with Mrs. Roman?

Sheriff Gresser invites me along. "Come on, Leland, you can buy us a snack in your cafeteria."

"Glad to," I tell him. I help Peggy on with her coat. "I'll be along in a minute, I've got to have a word with my secretary."

Chief Quist, full of mistrust, wants to wait for me, but Sheriff Gresser, as though gentling a mustang, eases him out of the office with assurances and pats on the back.

Peggy, rousing Jonathan out of his dream, says, "If something's happened to him, Leland, I'll never forgive myself. I realize now that I should have flown out here with him, but how could I leave my job for a month? Do these cops know what's at stake? Have they any idea how much even one sheet of paper could be worth—say his autograph of 'A Brace of Dreams' or 'Reflection on the Water'?"

On the way out, I stop to murmur instructions to Viola. She must call Billy Swan, the cab dispatcher who never got back to me. I want him to confirm my suspicion that Richard Falcon fled last night to the Romans' house.

Jonathan follows us dreamily down the corridor and outside, where we find the two lawmen standing on the walkway with President Zastrow, their heads bent, their eyes on the ground. They are discussing whether the dark areas at their feet are shadows or merely discoloration in the concrete. If it's not discoloration, then the weak sunlight filtering through the overcast is bright enough for groundhogs to see their shadows.

I hate to foist them unexpectedly on Mother in her breathless condition, yet what can I do with Peggy and Jonathan during the noon hour but invite them home with me? Where else can I leave them relaxed and unsuspecting while I slip away to the hospital, to Roman's fishhouse, and then on to Grimsby, Nebraska?

I restrain myself from outpacing them as we make our way slowly along Sawyer, a leisurely heel-scuffing saunter being Jonathan's natural pace. Peggy speaks admiringly of Chief Quist, how quickly he jumped on the case after she called him (which she apparently did within minutes of my leaving the old Great Northern freight house this morning), how he went directly to the Hi-Rise to grill the residents, and then to the college library to talk to the staff. Meanwhile, she says, his officers, patrolling the streets and alleys all over town, turned up a breakthrough piece of evidence. Someone living near the corner of Division and Bellwether, having heard he was missing on Lolly's radio show, recalled seeing, last night, a man fitting Richard Falcon's description get into a taxi and head east toward the center of town. He was carrying suitcases.

"It doesn't sound like an abduction then, does it, Peggy? I mean if he called a taxi."

"God, who knows? Maybe it's temporary insanity. I didn't

tell the police, but sometimes when Richard's tired he behaves in odd ways. You've witnessed it, surely."

"His conversation does wander a bit, evenings."

"It's natural aging, his doctor says. Mild senility. Hurry up, Jonathan."

The young man has fallen behind, strolling dreamily along with his hands in the pockets of his poplin raincoat, opening it and closing it like doors. Outdoor light accentuates his paleness, makes his skin seem almost transparent, except for the dark pouches under his eyes and cheekbones. With a trusting smile, he allows Peggy to link arms with him and propel him along. "We're almost there," she tells him. "See this pretty house with the big trees? This is Leland's house."

Jonathan looks at me and his smile fades to uncertainty. "You remember Leland's mother, the lady we met last night, in that house with all those people in it? She's very nice."

He halts, an expression of terror crossing his face, and Peggy looks to me for help.

"Very nice," I concur.

He refuses to proceed. He looks shrewdly from Peggy to me, and then proves, with one word, to have understood more about last night's gathering than I thought: "Dead," he says, in a voice of surprisingly deep register.

I try nudging him along, but Peggy scolds me. "Jonathan doesn't respond to force. It's only reason, isn't it, Jonathan, that interests you?"

"Reason interests me," he replies clearly and emphatically, with a sly smirk, like that of a con artist, a look you will some- times see on the face of a spoiled child when others are dancing attendance on him.

"Lolly's a radio personality," Peggy tells him. "Last night was just a pretend wake, for her radio show."

At this, his smirk expands into a horsey, wide-mouth smile exposing his gums, back teeth, tongue, and throat. He allows himself to be steered along our front walk, up the steps, and into the house.

I hang up their coats but leave mine on. Settling them on soft chairs in the living room, I offer them a drink. Peggy declines, telling me that she hasn't touched liquor since Connor died. Jonathan asks for a beer. In the kitchen I phone Helen Walker, asking her to come over and help Mother entertain. I give Jonathan a can of beer, with a glass. He opens the can and drains half of it, it seems, in one gulp.

Upstairs I find Mother, home from her show, napping. I wake her with the news, "Peggy's downstairs."

She smiles even before her eyes are open. "Just like old times."

"Jonathan's down there, too. The poet's grandson."

"Oh the poor thing," she says, sitting up. "What did you say his malady was, anemia?"

"Autism. He needs watching round the clock."

"*And* anemia. Last night he looked the color of my table linen."

"I'm going to the hospital now, Mother, and argue for Aunt Mary's release in time for dinner. Helen's on her way over."

"You go right along, Leland. While you're gone, Peggy and I will plan a show for Wednesday. Such a lot she'll have to tell radioland about her career."

I go into my room for socks and underwear, and then into my bathroom for razor and toothbrush, all of which I stuff into the pockets of my coat.

I call to Mother, referring to the downstairs cannister of oxygen, "You can hook yourself up all right?"

"Go right along, Leland. Tell the nurses not to dillydally."

I phone Viola; no word yet from Billy Swan. I hurry downstairs to find that Peggy has moved over to Mother's place on the couch and is dialing her phone, while Jonathan is rocking back and forth in his stationary chair and gazing at the crushed beer can in his hand. I breeze through, saying I'm on my way to pick up Aunt Mary. Backing the car out of the drive, I pretend not to notice Peggy open the front door and gesture for me to come back.

Already, turning down Eleventh, I find myself rehearsing what I'll tell Mother when I return. Shall I blame my twenty-four-hour absence on Aunt Mary, her need to be at home in the consoling arms of Uncle Bill? Besides which her pain was such that she feared upsetting Mother? Yes, Mother would believe that of the self-effacing Aunt Mary, whose devotion to Uncle Bill has amazed even his own sister over the years.

I'm able to sail swiftly across the Eleventh Avenue bridge, oftentimes a bottleneck—an answer to an unprayed prayer, Mother would call it. I'm turning off East Riverside before it occurs to me that maybe I should have gone to the hospital first. What will I do with Mr. Falcon while I'm trying to get Aunt Mary released? But on the other hand, I have to get the poet out of the fishhouse before anyone else figures out where he is. Could that be what Peggy was trying to tell me—the poet's been found? I bump across the abandoned railroad yard and pull into the grove of birches, relieved to see no other cars, no tire tracks in last night's thin layer of snow.

I run to the riverbank and spy Roman dragging his ice auger out toward the middle of the river, fifty yards beyond the darkhouse. It's windy. Skidding downhill in my smooth-soled oxfords, I steady myself by grabbing Sheriff Gresser's no-dumping sign and I pause there to catch my breath. Today's additions to the trashpile include a broken baby crib, a toaster, and a number of well-worn paperback books. I resist the urge to pick up *Death in the Afternoon* and take it with me, the only Hemingway I haven't read. I can't waste a second. Letting go of the sign, I continue my slide down to the river level.

Trudging through the drifted snow and slipping and sliding on the windswept bare spots, I make my way awkwardly across the ice to the windowless fishhouse and pound on the flimsy wallboard. "Mr. Falcon, it's me, Leland." I go around to the small door on the lea side and find it locked from the inside. "Mrs. Roman, will you please open up? It's urgent."

No response. I check the chimney—yes, there's a fire. Two northern pike, stabbed in the back, lie nearby on the ice. "Mr. Falcon, I'm ready with my car. I know the perfect hiding place, but we've got to hurry."

Perfect silence.

"Four hundred miles from here," I shout, confident that the Romans will keep our secret.

Again no sound, except the whine of the wind across the chimney in two or three flutelike tones. I set off toward the middle of the river and come up behind Roman. He's drilling another hole. Either he hasn't seen me, or pretends he hasn't. I touch him on the shoulder and he turns. It's not Roman. It's Mrs. Roman, wearing his parka. "Hello, Leland, what's up?" No surprise or curiosity on her upturned face; we might be meeting in a grocery aisle.

"I'm here to take the poet off your hands."

"Who?"

"Richard Falcon, inside there, with your husband."

Her expression is so blank it can't be authentic; it has to be willed.

"Look, I realize he's sworn you to secrecy, but I have to talk to him. I have to help him get away."

She squints up at me. "What's wrong, Leland, are you on the sauce?"

My confidence draining away, I return to the darkhouse, and speak through the wall. "Mr. Falcon, you aren't as safe as you think, living here with the Romans. Word is out that you're missing, so it's only a matter of time before somebody will see you here. If we leave now, we can be in Nebraska before midnight. My cousin Lucy has a place ready for you."

I stand waiting, tipping my head into the icy wind, my feet freezing to numbness, Mrs. Roman gaping at me from a distance. If I am mistaken and Richard Falcon isn't here, why has one or the other Roman been fishing outside all day?

I call to her. "Why are you drilling holes? Walleyes don't bite here in the winter."

"It's Roman's idea. Says we can scare some northerns over toward the house. Fishing's been lousy."

I point to the fish at my feet. "These are northerns."

"Too small."

So I *am* mistaken. Chagrined, I run gingerly across the ice toward the bank, worried now that my toes might be truly frozen. At the pier, I hear a shout. Looking back, I see Roman standing at his fishhouse door and calling to me. I ask him to repeat what I think he said. "What about Peggy?"

"Tell him I've given Peggy the slip," I shout, running back.

At this, the poet himself comes stooping out the low door. He's wearing his overcoat, suit, and a stocking cap. He's clutching his tote bag of notebooks.

"Mr. Falcon, we can't wait." I'm panting like a dog. "The police are combing the city for you, we've got to get out of town."

His response is a single nod of assent.

Mrs. Roman comes over, drops her auger, and puts her arms around him. "Oh, Mr. Falcon," she says. "To think you slept in my house."

He stiffens at her touch, and steps back out of her embrace. "Thank you, Mrs. Roman, especially for the oatmeal. It was wonderfully oaty." To both of them he says, "Come to New Hampshire, I know a trout lake."

"We'll help you up the bank, Mr. Falcon," says Roman, leaning back inside to shut off his kerosene stove.

I need more help up the snow-packed slope than the old man does; he's wearing a pair of Roman's boots with treads on the soles. We pause at the sheriff's sign, where I explain that Aunt Mary will be riding with us. "We'll pick her up at the hospital on our way out of town."

"No, in that case, come back and get me," says Mr. Falcon, squinting across at the city. "I can't risk getting any closer to Peggy than I am right now."

I look at Mrs. Roman. "Will you keep him till I get back?"

"Of course."

"Gresser's deputies might come searching."

She shrugs. "They'll never find him."

We climb to the car. Getting in behind the wheel, I feel Mr. Falcon's hand on my arm. "Where's Jonathan?"

"At my house, with Peggy and Mother."

"How is he?"

Compared to what? I'm tempted to ask. "He's fine," I tell him.

Though she's dressed and sitting in a wheelchair ready to leave, it takes me an hour to get Aunt Mary released and down to the pharmacy and then over to accounts receivable, where despite my pledge of good faith, we stall for another twenty minutes over billing and insurance.

Wheeling her to the car, I pray for compliance from this most docile O'Kelly, and my prayer is answered. Settling her in the backseat with pillows and blankets borrowed from a nurse, I tell her about Mr. Falcon and the reason we're bypassing Mother. Either she doesn't care or doesn't understand, for she nods contentedly and sleepily and whispers, "Whatever you say, Leland." She's probably sedated.

"It will be a long ride, so you must tell me when you want to stop and change positions."

"I will."

"Or you need a rest room."

"I will, thank you, Leland."

"We'll have you home by midnight."

"Lovely."

"Mr. Falcon will be riding in front with me. Do cigarettes bother you?"

"Goodness no, Bill's been smoking since 1951."

"Well, they bother me. I'll urge him to keep it to a minimum."

The car is warm, but my feet are still numb. Crossing the bridge, Aunt Mary asks in a dreamy voice what time it is.

"Almost two."

"My watch is in with my things."

"Is your leg comfortable, with your cast up on the seat like that?"

"Lovely," she says, and by the time I park in the birch grove, she's fast asleep.

I signal, as agreed, with my horn, and in a few moments three figures materialize in the brush. I open my window to see more clearly this picture that will doubtless remain imprinted on my memory till the day I die—this reclusive, unlettered pair, a retired crossing guard and a former hobo, leading America's foremost poet through the trees. At first they're mere shadows moving soundlessly in the shadowy grove; among the white and gray trunks they might be bear or browsing deer; then they take on human shape, stopping and starting, seeking the trodden path, stepping over newly fallen branches blown down by the wind, and finally their faces become clear—Roman in front, carrying the suitcase and overnight bag and appearing anxious and impatient, then his wife leading the poet by the hand and displaying an open-faced smile of excitement, and finally Richard Falcon himself coming along with faltering steps. With the stocking cap pulled low to his eyebrows, and looking exhausted and bewildered, he puts me in mind of an idiot child.

We lay his two bags in the trunk and help him into the car. He drops his manuscript bag at his feet and emits a sigh of deep fatigue. I help him with his seat buckle, then I thank the Romans.

"He's sort of out of it," says Mrs. Roman.

"Like last night," says her husband.

"Last night it was the wine." Her laugh echoes in the woods. "We had a high old time of it last night, Leland."

"You'd better scoot," says Roman.

"Thanks a million, both of you. Not a word of this to anybody."

"That there's a promise," says Roman.

His wife repeats her laugh. "Come again, when you can stay a little longer."

By the time I turn the car around, they've vanished in the trees.

We're silent for fifty miles, both of my passengers dozing, the radio on low, tuned to KRKU for news of the poet's disappearance. At three-thirty Benny Smith comes on with the local news, and plays a brief recorded interview with Chief Arly Quist, who says he's following up a hot lead. That's it. Nothing more. Benny then segues into "Cliff's Obituaries," sponsored by Madge's Videos and Tanning Salon, and announces that Nettie Fire-hammer died this noon at the Hi-Rise.

I'm always jolted by news like this. Nettie, who prematurely grieved Mother's passing last night, is gone. Death among the elderly never shocks Mother anymore. Having stood at the graves of more than a dozen lifelong friends, she's come to think of death as the norm. The surprise, says Mother, is that anybody's left alive.

Mr. Falcon wakes up at a stoplight in Park Rapids. I tell him about Nettie's death.

He yawns and stretches and reaches down to make sure his manuscript is safe. Then he lights a cigarette and says, with a chuckle, "She smoked too much."

So he's shifted into his contrary mode. I feel myself heat up with resentment—even my feet grow warm—and I drive nearly a hundred miles into darkness, without saying a word.

By the time we get to Fargo, Aunt Mary is awake and needing a toilet, so I drive through the city to West Acres Mall, where I know we can find a wheelchair and clean rest rooms. A kindly security guard, a young woman wearing a holstered revolver, takes her in for me.

By this time, I've figured out how to break the news to Mother. I find a pay phone and call Sally's house.

"Leland, where are you? Lolly's been calling me."

"I'm taking Aunt Mary to the University hospital in Minneapolis. She's got seven broken bones in her ankle and foot, and there's a specialist at the University waiting to perform surgery on her. Would you call Mother and tell her? The doctors at Mercy thought they'd fixed it, but it isn't set right."

Sally is silent for a moment, apparently weighing the credibility of this lie, and then says, "Okay, but why don't *you* call her?"

"I've tried but her line's been busy. Tell her they were about to load Aunt Mary into an ambulance when I got to the hospital, and I volunteered to take her. At first they didn't want me to, but Aunt Mary pleaded with them, and they said okay if I drove nonstop. I'm in St. Cloud at a drive-up phone."

"Leland, is any of this true?'

"Of course not, I'm in Fargo."

"With Mr. Falcon."

"And Aunt Mary. We're on our way to Grimsby."

"Where did you find him?"

Before I can answer, before I can ask how the manhunt is proceeding, Richard Falcon comes wheeling my aunt over to the phone and parks it beside me.

"All right then, Mother, good-bye." I hang up. "Mother sends her love."

My aunt, clenching her teeth and closing her eyes, says, "Lovely."

"You're in pain."

"It's nothing," she says.

The mall is all but deserted. Mr. Falcon spies a coffee counter and says he wants a cookie. I suggest we take our snack to the car and keep driving, but he says he needs more time to unkink his cramping legs. We order muffins and coffee. Standing beside the wheelchair, Mr. Falcon, to my great surprise, takes an interest in Mary's broken ankle, comparing it to an ankle he broke as a young man, running across a hayfield and stepping in a wood-chuck hole. This happened to him, he says, in 1941, and this sets both of them off down memory lane, where they come up against the major historical event of that year. Richard Falcon was up on a shed, shingling the roof, when news of Pearl Harbor reached his town in the White Mountains. He says a neighbor named Chris-tenson shouted up to him that war had been declared. Aunt Mary was washing dishes when the news came over the radio. She would leave home the next morning and cross Nebraska on a bus, from Scott's Bluff to her cousin's house in Grimsby, where, in the Church of the Assumption on the day after Christmas, she would marry William B. O'Kelly.

They turn to me then, as if to say it's my turn. "I don't remember Pearl Harbor," I tell them, "but I do remember your wedding. I was seven. Somebody had a beautiful soprano voice."

"That was a friend of Bill's. She still lives in town, still plays the organ, but her voice is gone."

It's dark outside. Traveling south on I-29, the two of them continue visiting like a couple of old friends, the poet half turning in order to throw his words back over the seat, my kindly old aunt leaning a little forward to catch them. Mile after mile they spill out their hearts as though I weren't listening. It turns out that Uncle Jack is certain to be dead by summer. He's stopped his treatments and gone to painkillers, says Aunt Mary. He reads a book a day to keep his mind off his cancer.

And it turns out Sally was right about Peggy. She's been pur-suing Richard Falcon for a long time. He first made Peggy's acquaintance in the Tipton post office and general store some twenty summers ago, when she accompanied Connor on a sketching trip into the mountains. There was a spark of friendship there from the start, says the poet. They got to laughing about something or somebody in the store, he can't remember what or who, and they couldn't stop. They went out and sat on a bench in the autumn sunshine, the three of them, and had a conversation such as he'd had with no one else in years, an amusing, insightful talk about Plymouth State College, where Peggy taught in the music department and where the poet came in as a visiting lecturer now and then when he needed the money. He didn't recall Connor saying very much—he sat there sketching all the while. The spark kept glowing, says the poet, long after Peggy and Connor went down the mountain.

Peggy tried to lure him into Plymouth for dinner. Lots of people had been doing that for years. What surprised him was his desire to accept her invitations. But, despite her attractiveness, he declined, dinner parties being such ordeals, draining away his writing energy in trivial, late-night talk—late night to him being any time after seven-thirty. As a recluse, he'd developed the sleeping habits of a bird, bed at sundown, up before dawn.

He did consent, however, the following spring, to the occasional brookside picnic on a Saturday afternoon, and he took pleasure in these outings. So did Peggy. Their compatibility endured. He couldn't say whether Connor enjoyed these meetings in the wilderness. Connor was a hard man to read.

Then one night, very late, Peggy showed up at his house above Tipton, needing, she said, to talk to him about Connor, who was hitting the bottle again. At first, guarding his privacy, the poet was offended. Besides, he had enough problems of his own, the main one at the time being his daughter's growing neglect of her autistic son. He was tempted to turn Peggy away, and might have, had she not been so weepy and desperate.

"And that's how I fell into her clutches," he says, wrenching himself around in his seat and looking Aunt Mary squarely in the eye. "She stayed hours. Far into the night, talking, talking, until I fell asleep in my chair, and the next thing I knew she was leaning over me, kissing my forehead. 'Let's go to bed,' she said."

"Heavenly days!" replies Aunt Mary.

I can't believe this of Peggy, not with Connor still in the picture. "You've got to be kidding, Mr. Falcon. I've known Peggy since 1969."

He falls silent, irked by this interruption. Though I don't look at him, I can feel him glaring at me.

I go on to explain. "I mean, she went through so much with him, both here and in the East, how could she suddenly be unfaithful?"

"She couldn't. Not with me, because I resisted."

"But I mean, to suddenly turn like that."

"Nothing sudden about it!" he shoots back. Then softer: "One heard things in those days. There was a composer-in-residence at Plymouth State one year, a guy you might have heard of named Tillemans. His stuff sounds like jangling your keyring." His voice trails off. "And later there was a potter . . ."

He falls silent again. Eager as we are to hear more, my aunt is presumably too polite to press him, and I've learned he's unpressable. This is a flat, desolate freeway we're traveling now—six or eight miles between headlights, twenty miles between exits. "Jesus," he says at last, lighting a smoke and gazing out at faraway yardlights glinting like stars. "I'm lonesome for hills."

Aunt Mary, perhaps attempting to open him up on the subject of his grandson, tells us of a family named Atkinson in Grimsby with an autistic child. The boy wears a helmet all day because he beats his head against walls.

"There are degrees of it," says the poet. "Jonathan's case isn't that extreme."

And yet it's a poignant story he tells of his grandson, who turned thirty-three last month. His mother Renee, Richard Falcon's daughter, was a single parent long before it was the fashion. She'd been a theater major in college, but dropped out when she discovered herself pregnant. She works full-time in Plymouth as a legal secretary and lives with her son near Tipton. There's a day-activity center in Plymouth where she usually leaves him, but on his stubborn days when he refuses to go there, she leaves him with his grandfather. "He gets into things around the house, scatters my books, bangs kettles and pans in the kitchen. I can't write."

"But you love him," prompts Mary.

He weighs her supposition, then says, as though to himself, "I used to love him." Awhile later he adds, "I can't love anybody who gets in the way of my poem. At my age I don't have a day to waste."

"Oh, you still do love him," says my aunt with confidence. "The Atkinsons love their Bobby dearly."

"I dare say they're not poets."

"The Atkinsons?" A giggle from the backseat. "For heaven's sakes."

Though the night is moonless, I can pick out the O'Kelly farmstead the moment I come up over the last rise in the road. Their mercury-vapor yard light illuminates the house, the pines in the windbreak, the barn surrounded by several outbuildings, and the three enormous Harvestore silos. It's nearly midnight, yet as we draw closer, I see light in all the windows and the taillights of somebody's vehicle idling in the yard, its ghostlike exhaust rising and shifting in the chill air. I assume it belongs to either Lucy or Claudette. What with our being such kindred spirits, I imagine they've sensed my arrival without being told, and they've driven out to welcome Aunt Mary home and to spirit Richard Falcon off to his hideaway in Grimsby.

It's this very sort of dreamy, late-night imagining that can get you into trouble. I nearly drive into a trap. I'm about to turn in at the drive when I realize it isn't Claudette's Jeep Cherokee or Lucy's pickup pulled up to the kitchen door; it's a patrol car, probably the local sheriff's. I drive on by, speeding up, turning right at the next two crossroads and heading back to town. I'm parked in front of Lucy and Ron's house on Main Street before my passengers are quite awake. I spring from the car and run up the walk. The house is dark. I pound on the door so loud that I wake Baby Detroit—I hear him crying—before a light comes on upstairs. It's a long couple of minutes before I see, through the small window in the storm door, a lamp switched on and Ron carrying Detroit in the crook of his arm.

"Hey, Leland, what's up? We thought you were coming later in the week. You've got the whole family in an uproar."

The back door of the car opens and Aunt Mary calls out, "Ronnie, how's little Detroit?"

"Is this where I'm supposed to get out?" asks Richard Falcon, getting out.

Ron holds the door open for me, and I step inside, jabbering, "There's a deputy or somebody out at the farm. I didn't stop. The cops must be onto our plan, but that's impossible. How could they know I was coming?"

"Been a deputy out there since suppertime," says Ron. "Claims he's there to make sure Mary gets in the house all right."

"But how did he know?"

"Seems he was notified by your people up north that you were coming down."

"With the poet?"

"It's safe to say the poet's the reason, isn't it? I mean, this Falcon guy is running from the law, in case you didn't know."

"He's behind in his taxes. I told Lucy to tell you."

Ron lowers his voice. "Well, Christ almighty, you didn't say the cops were chasing him. You better come in and call the sheriff and get yourself a plea bargain." He looks warily past me at the poet, who is standing beside the car massaging his neck. "That's a fugitive you got there, Cousin Leland. Turn him in this minute, and they might let you off. Tell 'em you never knew."

"Is Lucy here?"

"She's on night shift."

"What does Lucy say?"

"Don't mind Lucy, she listens to Claudette too much."

"I've got to talk to her. Can you get her on the phone?"

"Except Claudette's finally coming around to my way of thinking."

"I need to talk to Lucy."

"Come on."

He leads me through to the kitchen. He dials a number and hands me the receiver. He lifts Detroit's bottle out of a pan on the stove. Discreet enough to leave me alone, he returns to the front room, turning on more lamps, and then I hear him open the front door.

A voice on the phone says hello.

"Could I speak to Lucy O'Kelly please?"

"Leland?"

"Claudette? Are you at the hospital?"

"No, I'm home. How's Mother?"

"I'm trying to reach Lucy."

"Listen, Leland, things are getting dicey, you realize that? Ron and I've been talking it over and decided you'd better turn your poet over to the authorities, otherwise you'll end up in the slammer along with him. I mean, cripes, Leland, they've got the sheriff out there watching the farm."

"Thanks for the advice, Claudette." I hang up on her.

I find a phone book on the counter. As I'm looking up the hospital number, a new scheme occurs to me. Before dialing the phone, I stand there for a few moments with my eyes closed, trying to foresee flaws in my plan. My vision is limited. I'm too nervous and excited to see past a picture in my mind's eye of myself and Richard Falcon speeding along a dark freeway in a pickup truck. "Dear Lord," I pray, "grant me the courage to see this through, and steer me to Omaha." I call the hospital.

I'm quickly put through to a nurses' station. Lucy answers.

"Hey, Leland, you're in town?"

"I'm in your house. Your husband says I have to give up if I want to stay out of jail."

She laughs. "Oh that Ron, he listens to Claudette too much. How's Mary?"

"She's fine, but I can't take her home—the farm's under surveillance. I'll leave her here with Ron."

"You got the man with you?"

"I have. Lucy, is your pickup at the hospital?"

"It's home, probably in the garage."

"I've got to use it, just for tonight, but I doubt if Ron will—"

"Never mind Ron. Just sit tight there one minute, Leland honey, I'm acomin' home." She hangs up.

Aunt Mary comes through the front door with Ron supporting her on one side and Richard Falcon on the other. She makes cooing noises at the baby lying on the couch as they let her down gently into an easy chair and lift her cast onto a hassock. Ron deposits the baby, with its bottle, in her lap, then leads the poet through the kitchen to a bathroom at the back of the house. I stand at the little window in the storm door as Aunt Mary speaks to Detroit, detailing her adventures since leaving home some forty-eight hours ago. The baby, sucking milk, looks up at her with the probing eyes of a rapt listener.

A minute goes by. I'm about to go out and move my Lincoln Town Car out from under the streetlight when I hear Lucy in the kitchen, arguing briefly with her husband. She then sails breezily into the front room, all in white, and kisses Aunt Mary, Detroit, and me. Ron follows, fuming.

"I'll drive Mr. Falcon over to—"

Before I get the sentence out, she leaps at me, covering my mouth. "Don't tell us where, Leland—you'll incriminate us." She flashes a wicked smile at Ron. He shakes his head in disapproval and climbs the stairs.

"Poor Ron can't stand knowing any more about this adventure than necessary," she says, drawing aside a curtain and looking out the front window. "Now bring that gas hog around to the alley, and see if it'll fit in the garage. I'll back out the pickup."

It's an unattached, single-car garage with crooked doors, through which I'm able to maneuver the Lincoln without a scratch. I transfer the bags to the pickup idling in the alley while Lucy leads Mr. Falcon across the dark backyard. Because the garage doors won't close tightly, my car being six inches too long, Lucy secures them with a bungee cord.

We boost the poet into the pickup. I tell her to get in and we'll give her a ride back to the hospital. "It's only over there," she says, pointing at a four-story building looming behind the bare trees. "When you want to trade vehicles, call me up and I'll meet you somewhere."

She stretches up and kisses the poet on the cheek. "Good luck with your writing now, Mr. Falcon." She slams his door and comes around to my side. "Four speeds forward," she tells me, reaching across and demonstrating how the shifting works. "Overdrive to the right and down." Then she kisses me on the lips and says, "You're making history tonight, Cousin, now get out of town."

We jerk along in a gear too high until we reach the end of the alley, where I pause a few moments, clutching and shifting until I get the feel of the mechanism. Then, turning into the street, I glance back to see Lucy standing against the darkness in her angelic white uniform, waving.

I'm awake before dawn, chilled and stiff, having slept in my clothes on the sofa. The thermostat on the living room wall produces no heat, which means that Cousin Wesley is still shopping for a furnace. I can see my breath; the dampish air in the rugless, curtainless rooms feels like forty degrees. Last night I carried the portable heater upstairs to my father's bedroom, where Richard Falcon is sleeping.

The kitchen is unfamiliar—new cabinets and appliances, new floor tile, a new window over the sink. All the tools and clutter of renovation have been moved out to the garage, where I gather up an armload of wood scraps and I carry them to the fireplace in the living room. No matches. Rather than bother Mr. Falcon for his lighter, I get a fire going with a rolled-up page of newsprint lit on the kitchen stove, and by the time I hear him stirring upstairs, the crackling lumber has produced a meager zone of warmth into which I drag two easy chairs for our editing session.

There's a jar of instant coffee on a cupboard, but the taps yield no water, so I go out into the drizzly morning and drive the streets looking for breakfast. From a Dunkin' Donuts I bring home coffee and rolls, and by seven o'clock we're delving deeply into Part Two, the Second World War section of *Fording the Bee*—Richard Falcon in the Seabees.

After about two hours of work, I interrupt the invasion of Saipan to call up Wesley and Bernadine and tell them their house is occupied. "Hey, super, Leland," cries Bernadine. "Wasn't I right? Isn't a few days' R and R exactly what you needed? Don't you feel better already? You took the heater up to the bedroom, I hope, otherwise you wouldn't be on the phone with me now, you'd be a frozen corpse. Sorry about the water, but we can't turn it on till the weather warms up or Hotshot here breaks down and buys a furnace. Here, I'll put him on."

Before I can stop her, my laconic cousin says, "Yeah?" I'd prefer to tell his wife what I tell him:

"I'm not alone here, Wesley."

"Oh?" I detect a modicum of interest. "You and what's-her-name back together?"

"No, another friend of mine. He'd like to rent your house."

Boredom again: "Too bad. Got another party interested."

"Price is no object with this friend of mine. He'll pay more than your other party."

A renewed spark of interest: "How much more?"

"How much do you have to have?"

"Eight fifty a month."

"He'll pay it."

Disbelief: "He will?"

"But he'll have to have a furnace and running water."

"No biggee."

"Today, Wesley."

"Mmmmm." A thoughtful pause. "Nine fifty then."

This brings Bernadine to life on another line: "Shame on you, Wesley, gouging your own cousin. Eight fifty will be fine, Leland."

"Hell it will, Bernie. You know what furnaces cost? You realize how much sales tax there is on a item like that?"

A quarrel ensues, which I break in on, urging them to come over to the house and meet their new renter.

"Give us an hour," says Bernadine. "We'll stop on the way and see about a furnace."

This gives us time to page through notebooks three and four and determine how much work lies ahead. Richard Falcon estimates two months. Glimpsing certain lines toward the end of notebook three, I grow fearful that the quality of the work is not consistent. I sense that a good many of his lines came not from the heart but from the need to make his life as a grown-up seem as interesting as his youth. Which it never is. Show me the memoirist who can sustain his magical hold on the reader (or at least on *this* reader) once he leaves the exotic country of childhood and crosses into the self-conscious and mostly flat landscape of adulthood.

We exchange notebooks. Oh my. Four is no better. I spend nearly a half hour reading it closely. Here he's dealing with the onset of his difficult old age. His moody daughter. His grandson. His poverty. His longstanding battles over publication rights and against writer's block. A more recent battle to stop smoking. Medical expenses. Since he hasn't allowed his talent for reflection to wash over them, none of these grievances shine with the freshness of the earlier events. I can't imagine anyone reading through to the end of the work without losing the respect that Parts One and Two command. This last part is boringly didactic until Peggy shows up in his life, and then it becomes mawkish and bitter. He doesn't name Peggy. He calls her the "pretty soprano," an epithet as dead as the language surrounding it.

Dare I tell him how pedestrian it all is? Dare I predict that the months he spends trying to improve it will be wasted time, that in the end he'll probably give it up and publish a shorter book? So what, I want to tell him, so what if *Fording the Bee* ends with your return from the war to your beloved White Mountains, where you take up your pen and write, *The fish that takes the fatal bite* . . . Subtract the rest and you still have an epic poem!

Then, as though I had told him, Mr. Falcon looks up from scribbling marginal notes and our eyes meet for a moment across notebook four. He reaches over and gently closes it and takes it from me. He clears his throat and says, "I know."

Wesley and Bernadine come in the back door then, still bickering. Their expressions—as I expected; they're not bookish people—betray no suspicion when I introduce the poet as Richard Anderson. I tell them the rather baroque tale we made up in the pickup last night, driving from Grimsby—Professor Emeritus Anderson, a member of our Geography Department for twenty-five years, is writing a book comparing four Midwestern states to four New England states, paying special attention to commerce, government, and topography, and he's finishing up with Nebraska.

Bernadine's curiosity seems not to extend beyond his personal life. Married? "Not for many years," is his cryptic reply. Children? "One, a daughter." Favorite food? Here his response—"Margarine"—causes her to shriek with laughter and hug his arm, and he's unable to stop a fleeting look of affection from crossing his face. God bless Bernadine, the poet will be in good hands.

"How'd you get in?" asks Cousin Wesley.

"I saw where you keep the key when you showed me the house. In the window well."

I ask Wesley, "What about heat? You can't expect him to spend all day sitting in front of this sputtering little fire."

"Oh, they're coming from Lennox Heating right away," Bernadine assures me. "He'll be toasty by suppertime, they promised."

The poet looks outraged. "You mean I can't shave or wash my face until suppertime?"

His tone makes Wesley mad. "Now listen here—"

Bernadine, giving her husband a neck rub, says, "You can turn the water on now, can't you, Hotshot? It's not going to freeze before suppertime."

While Wesley's on the phone with the water and light people, his wife invites us to dinner. When I beg off, saying I have to start home, she turns her full attention on the poet, planning lunches and dinners and tours of the city. She can't wait, she says, to introduce her bowling team to a real geographer.

"Some scholars, like Mr. Anderson here, require continuous solitude in order to concentrate," I tell her, hoping to spare him from her social circle. I needn't have bothered; he's so much more efficient, not to say hardhearted, at this sort of thing. Affection is gone from his eyes, and I see Bernadine's effusiveness quashed with his single question, delivered with withering scorn:

"Why should I waste my time?"

———

The furnace workers arrive. Bernadine drives off in the red pickup, leaving Wesley in the basement, overseeing the installation. The noise in the ductwork drives us upstairs, where we spread the notebooks out on my father's bed and pore over them until noon. Part Three, I discover, is not a total loss. Here and there certain passages of great beauty crop up, particularly in lyrical praise of the Tipton peaks and brooks and rocky fields that he returns to after the war. Seamus Heaney comes to mind—he's that good with landscapes. Less good with people, as it turns out. I resolve to tell him so before I drive away, but by the time Lucy turns up in my Lincoln and we close the notebooks and shut the door on my father's bedroom, my resolve has weakened. Lucy has brought lunch, but I dare not stay and eat. If I remain a minute longer in their company, I'll never want to leave.

IDES OF MARCH

Dear Chancellor Suderman,

This morning I have formally entered my name as a nominee for President of Rookery State College.

You said that taking this step would make me suddenly feel qualified. Far from it. I feel like a sky diver with a faulty parachute.

Yours truly,

Leland J. Edwards, Dean

Dear Administrators, Faculty and Support Staff,

Contrary to the refrain you've heard me singing these past several years, I've decided to run for president of Rookery State College.

I'm doing it for two reasons. One, many of the people whose judgment I respect more than my own are urging me to do so. Two, in the few years left before retirement, I want to repay the college, at least in part, for what the college has given to me, namely my reason for being.

I will greatly appreciate whatever support you can give me.

    Sincerely,
    Leland Edwards

Dear Annie and Victor,

Thanks for your letter at Christmas, and the newspaper clipping. I'll tell you something funny. I'm running for president. I have the support of our new chancellor and the old guard among the faculty. Laugh now, while there's still time. If I win and thus wade into the morass left behind by O. F., I'll no doubt sink in over my head, but at least I will have done my best to save the place for the next generation of students, and I can go back to the classroom to rest up for retirement.

On the other hand, what if I endure? To me, that's even more frightening. The chancellor tells me that any president still in place after the first year and a half is good for another decade. My consolation is that in six years I'll be 65 and can gracefully shrug off the mantle—after assigning myself *in perpetuum* to Freshman English. I love both English and Freshmen. Or rather, Freshpersons. See? I'm learning.

As for the *Plain Dealer* clipping, it was the bitter and intellectually diminished Kimberly Kraft who coined the phrase "Black Hole of Higher Education," long before the wire services picked it up. Meanwhile the poet remains at large.

    Yours,
    Leland

Dear Neil,

Happy 56th birthday. Incredible. To me, you will always be that 29-year-old clarinetist trying to keep his students at bay while toiling away at his first novel in that squalid basement at the corner of Seventh and Burl. Cornelia Niven was born that year, was she not? Which makes her 26. And Delphinia White is what—about 16?? Was she born with *Bride of Tiberius*, or earlier? As for Mary Magdalene Peterson, I'll be amazed if she sells half as many books as either of her predecessors. Her prose is much too pietistic for my taste and her choice of subjects is so blatantly meretricious. *Candlelight at Cana* and *The Gethsemane Ghost* were bad enough, but *Under the Upper Room* takes the cake. Not even Mother, your tireless promoter in Rookery, could finish it. Sorry, Neil. On every page I kept wishing you'd get back to your specialties—cruelty, gluttony, forbidden sex, and other such depravities.

Fifty-six, as I recall, was the only birthday I had a hard time with. When Mother asked me why, and I said it was discouraging to be on the downside of the fifties. To which she replied, "Well, I ought to be happy then, being on the upside of the eighties."

This may shock you, are you sitting down? I'm running for president. If I'm chosen I'll no doubt be at the helm when Delphinia and Mary Magdalene arrive for Writers' Week in June. Yes, I know, I've resisted the idea as far back as our Quintet days, but my resistance crumbled in an instant when, one night about a month ago, it came up against five little words.

I was driving home from Nebraska where I'd delivered my Aunt Mary after her visit to Rookery. I was alone in the car and sleepy, so I had the radio on and was just beginning to pick up KRKU's signal. We were playing our first hockey game in our new arena that night, and Al Shaverly, the unctuous voice of the Blue Herons, was going through the starting lineups. (Here I guess I should preface the five life-changing words he uttered with the fact that our ignoble Athletic Department, for some time, had been selling itself out, little by little, to the Heim's Beer people.) The radio signal faded away for a minute or more as Shaverly named the six starters for Rookery, so I turned up the volume just as they skated out of the dressing room and the signal returned and Shaverly's voice filled the car with a deafening boom: "Here comes the Rookery Six-Pack!"

Yours,
Leland

Dear Alumni and Friends of Rookery State,

For our FIRST ANNUAL RSC WRITERS' WEEK, June 19–23, we have lined up four of the most popular writers currently at work in the Midwest:

JIMMY OLSEN

AUTHOR of the incredibly successful Jimmy Olsen series. His latest thriller, *Things in Ditches*, is currently #4 on the Twin Cities bestseller lists, and threatens to outsell his last blockbuster, *Blood on My Chainsaw*. Mr. Olsen will deliver a public reading of his work on Monday evening, June 19, at 7:30.

"These days Jimmy Olsen sets the standard in the field of tough-guy fiction."

—Dave Wood,
Minneapolis Star-Tribune

DELPHINIA WHITE AND MARY MAGDALENE PETERSON

MEET both of these heart-stopping
romance writers in person:
Tuesday evening, June 20, 7:30, DELPHINIA WHITE, author of *Bride of Tiberius* and *Kept Women of Pompeii*, will read from her work.

"Wow, what a talent!"

—LaVyrle Spencer

Wednesday evening, June 21, 7:30, MARY MAGDALENE PETERSON, author of *Candlelight at Cana* and *Under the Upper Room*.

"What happens under the Upper Room shouldn't happen to a dog."
—Mary Ann Grossman
Pioneer Press

LANCE PALEY

Winner of seven grants and fellowships while working on his first novel, *Bygones* (T. Woodman Press, St. Paul, 1968), Lance Paley, visiting professor from Moorhead State University, will conduct a daily writing class (9:00 A.M.–noon) in the Fireside Lounge of the student center.

"This tome takes up where your grandmother's memories leave off."
—John Tesich
Twin City Pages

Call the Dean's Office for details, 218/823-2392.
Yours very truly,
Leland J. Edwards
Dean of the College

MAYDAY

Dear Leland,

Detroit loves his dad more than his mom, except when he needs nourishment, and Ron appears to be trying to cut off the nourishment connection. I came home from work yesterday to find Detroit in a high chair and Ron trying to feed him mashed carrots. Baby's too little for solids I said. No says Ron, gotta put some muscle on him cuz the Broncos have put out the call for free agents and this here boy's gonna be one hell of a pass catcher. No pass catcher I tell him, he's gonna be a rock musician and put us all on easy street.

The other day I dropped in on Luke Frieze who said he was stuck for ideas on remodeling, said everything above the second floor was pretty shaky and wished he had your opinion.

On the home place everything is copacetic with Mary. She limps around the kitchen in her walking cast and when I say Take it easy Mary let me do those dishes, she says Never mind you just set there and thank the good Lord I can even stand up. Uncle Jack's none too healthy looking—thin in the face—though he keeps humming Casey would waltz with the strawberry blond all day long, which irks Bill and causes him to bitch and pout, which means Bill's his same old self.

Ron and Detroit send love, George and Claudette too, they were over last night. Maylene is burned at Detlef cuz he keeps saying he guesses he'll go home for a visit by which he means Germany. This right here is your home don't you even know where you live? she keeps harping.

xxx&ooo's

Lucy

"Who's Luke Frieze?" Mother asks me, reading the letter in the car on the way to lunch at the Van Buren Hotel.

"He's somebody Lucy knows in Grimsby who works at the hospital," I tell her. "He's remodeling an old house. I met him when I took Mary home in February."

I should have known better. Mother says there aren't any old houses in Grimsby over two stories high, and I dig myself a deeper hole by saying "Maybe it's in a neighboring town."

"But you've seen it," she says.

"I have?"

"Well, why is the man asking your advice if you haven't seen it? Honestly, Leland, you've been so vague about that trip to Minneapolis and Grimsby that if I didn't know you better I'd say you were drunk the whole time."

Bennie Smith is waiting in the Van Buren lobby with Angelo. We're ushered to Mother's favorite table in a sunny window of the dining room, and the meeting begins the moment we're seated. I don't ordinarily accompany her to these KRKU lunches, but today's topic is radio coverage of the inauguration. Mother, in secret conclave with Chancellor Suderman, arranged for the ceremony to take place on Thursday, June 22, my parents' wedding anniversary. This is altogether fitting and proper, I suppose, since from that day forward, I'll be indissolubly bound, for better or worse, for richer or for poorer, with Rookery State College.

I dare say nobody's ever achieved high office with greater

ease. The day after I notified the chancellor of my decision, the State College Board met in St. Paul, approved unanimously of the chancellor's recommendation, and called in the reporters. Why didn't the Board bother to tell me? Why did I have to learn of my appointment from Viola Trisco, who, the next day, scanning the *Morning Call* headlines in the outer office, shouted, "Hey, Dean, what's a prexy?"

"Because it wasn't news to any of us," Chancellor Suderman replied to my inquiry. "I thought you, of all people, knew what a shoo-in you were. Didn't I say when I was up there for the poet's reading that you'd be our next president?"

"Interim president, you said."

"I had to say interim so as not to violate our equal opportunity regulations."

"I have to confess, Dr. Suderman, that I've been dreading this appointment. What if I don't have what it takes? Already I'm getting cold feet."

"Listen, Leland, you're everybody's idea of a president, so you won't have to do anything for the first six months except look like one. By the way, where's your poet got to? Any idea?"

"A hiding place somewhere is my guess, to work undisturbed on his big poem."

"That's what I tell reporters when they call. Papers are blaming Rookery State, you know."

"Tell them they're right to blame us. It was here that he got his first true taste of the solitude he needs."

"See? Spoken like a true president."

I went home for lunch that day, and found Mother in tears of ecstasy, pinning the *Morning Call* headline to her bulletin board: DEAN EDWARDS IS SHOO-IN PREXY.

And that's why I'm here at the Van Buren, planning Inauguration Day. The football stadium if the weather's fine, or the lawn in front of McCall? The auditorium if it's not, or the hockey arena? Are we permitted, in this secular age, to have a clergyman on the platform to read an invocation? I suppose, as president-elect, I might be expected to exert some influence at this lunch, but a meeting is a meeting and I can't break a habit overnight.

That's why I've brought Angelo along—to pay attention for me while I pretend to take notes.

> #102. *Dear Mr. Frieze, Sorry I have to agree—the plans I saw for the 3rd and 4th stories, while strong in color, aren't as interesting overall as the lower half of your new house; the materials struck me as inferior and your design allows for too much repetition. I still say, however, that the lower half is the closest thing to architectural perfection produced in my lifetime. Rather than risk ungainliness why not be content with your beautiful two-story dreamhouse?*
>
> *(Enclose above with letter to Lucy this aft.)*
>
> *No doubt I should have disregarded Mr. Falcon's wishes and told Mother the truth from the start. She smells a rat; she will give it no rest. But the important thing is that he's had 90 days of freedom in which to figure out—at last—where* Fording the Bee *ends. Never mind that on each of these 90 days I've expected the news of his disappearance to flare up again in the papers. Indeed, on many of these 90 nights I've had sweats and fears, both waking and dreaming. In one particular nightmare the woman from Italy, by now a Cosa Nostra insider, came busting into my office, shouting, "Tell me where the deadbeat went, or I'll see that you go swimming in the Badbattle with cement shoes." She looked a lot like L. P. Connor. And every day on my way to work—this is no dream—I've half expected to be hustled into a car by G-men and hauled off to the IRS office in St. Paul.*
>
> *And what about Peggy? Why, after all those daily phone calls, has she been leaving me alone of late? I pray God the rumor Angelo brought back from his conference in Boston is true, namely that Peggy has found herself another genius—a composer this time, somebody on the Harvard faculty named Arthur Tillemans.*
>
> *And what about Jonathan and Jonathan's mother?*

She's the true mystery in this case. Never a word of inquiry from her.

"Leland, you aren't paying attention to a thing we're saying."

"You're right, Mother."

"And you're not touching your salad."

"Sorry."

WRITERS' WEEK

By mid-June, thank the Lord, Mother is so energized by this longed-for, prayed-for event in her son's life that she's given up the idea of a second memorial service. For weeks she's spoken of nothing but Rookery State on the radio, interviewing its personnel, relating its history, laying out each new aspect of Inauguration Day as it's been fitted into place. This is pretty unsettling. It's as though she has decided to live my life rather than her own. She studies me. She reads my moods the way I, as a boy, used to read hers.

For one reason or another (the one being the presidency, the other being Mary Sue Bloom) my moods have been untypically changeable lately. I've been up and down like a kite in a fitful breeze. There is, in Mother's mind, no prospect of the downward plunge I keep imagining for myself. "Just like your father," she'll say whenever I appear less than sanguine about my future. "Your father could always find the tiniest thing to worry about."

But trading my beloved teaching for the onerous work of the presidency is no tiny thing, I've told her more than once.

"Oh, just think about it, Leland, your predecessor in office has been such a stupid man—how could you be anything but fantastically successful?"

By being hauled off to prison, for starters—I have all I can do not to say this. It's become my obsession. Last time I was in the Twin Cities I drove out of my way to have a look at the Federal Building and imagined myself summoned there for interrogation by the IRS.

As for Mary Sue, she returned to the faculty this spring, thanks to my prayers and the staff of a Bismarck mental health center and a refillable prescription of Prozac. And thanks as well, she claims, to the duets we play, though she's the one with the true mastery of the classics while I, primarily a jazz musician, rumble around in the bass clef trying not to add a syncopated beat to her stately and lovely progress through our favorite pieces for four hands.

Whenever Mary Sue veers into a black period, I can't help but go into it with her. I don't go as deep as she goes, fortunately, nor do I stay quite so long, yet it's unsettling. It's been a very long while since my days were marked by this sort of dent or depression—I'm thinking of the year or two following my marriage to Sally—and because her mood swings take me back to my younger, unhappier years, I've started going to counseling myself in order to get a bit of perspective on my past. As a by-product of these sessions, I'm also picking up a good bit of advice on how to live with a neurotic woman and discovering that, except for those two-plus years married to Sally, I've been living with a slightly neurotic woman all my life. At least that's my counselor's conclusion. I've been tempted to break this news to Mother, particularly when I find her in a jolly mood, but I haven't dared because I'm not sure it won't turn her suddenly resentful. Which proves his point, says my counselor.

He's a stern young professor of psychology fittingly named Cross, and he tells me that if I dropped Mary Sue I could probably drop counseling as well. I shrug this off as bad advice. Mary Sue means the world to me, I tell him. I've never known anyone so interesting, so bright, so straightforward, so funny and warm. "Suit yourself," says Dr. Cross. "It's your seventy-two dollars an hour."

"Sixty-two," I reply, reminding him of my faculty discount.

And Mary Sue *is* becoming more stable. Almost as helpful as Prozac, we find, is a Mozart sonata or Beethoven bagatelle or perhaps something by Schubert. I realize how simplistic this sounds, but the moment we sit down together at Mother's baby grand, which I'd hardly touched since becoming dean, or at the concert Steinway in the music wing of McCall Hall, our spirits take wing. Oh, the happiness of having someone to play with once again, the pure joy of harmony. It's so exhilarating to come trudging together up out of the adagio movement and go racing through the scherzo. And then, sitting with my hands in my lap, I feel at once proud and humble as I watch Mary Sue walk, then run, through the intricate cadenza she's worked out for herself. And finally comes the thrilling moment when we jump into the finale, shoulder to shoulder, and build to the explosion of the last measures which I insist on pounding out, never mind the musical notation, with all my might. Ta, TA, TA, TA / Tata, TA, TA, TAAAAAA! Oh, the ecstasy of it. I've decided that the next time we come to the end of a Mozart sonata I'm going to surprise Mary Sue with a propopsal of marriage.

The way I picture it is this: emerging from the final measures in a state of music-induced euphoria, I'm going to grab Mary Sue and tip her across my lap, look into those bottomless dark eyes and so help me God I'm going to say, "Will you marry me?"

I've already asked her, sort of. One evening, strolling among the campus lilacs, I said, "Mary Sue, would you ever marry me?"

Her eyebrows went up. "Pardon me? Are you asking me to marry you?"

"I'm just saying would you."

Her brows gathered in a frown. "I might . . . but . . ."

"But what?"

She shrugged. "I'd probably never marry anybody who puts it in such tentative terms."

"It's called the subjunctive mode," I said, losing my nerve, and I went on to talk of other things.

And so did Mary Sue:

"I was married for fourteen months, Leland. My husband's

name was Jerry Bloom. He was a lawyer, from Chicago. His firm sent him out to the convent in Bismarck where I was staying. He was collecting depositions from the sisters concerning a former student of theirs who was on trial for something or other in Illinois. It might have been mail fraud. Jerry's firm was handling the defense, and they were looking for character witnesses. He was in Bismarck over a weekend and I met him after Mass on Sunday and he asked me to show him around. We both fell in love at once, I guess you could say. The only trouble was, while I was falling in love with Jerry, Jerry was falling in love with Bismarck. I kid you not—the only person I ever knew who loved Bismarck without having grown up there. I remember we were standing on the west edge of the campus—where you yourself stood, remember?—and looking west over that great trench cut into the earth by the Missouri River, and he was entranced. 'Mary Sue,' he said, 'this is about as far from Michigan Avenue and Lakeshore Drive as it's possible to get in one lifetime. This is like the other side of the moon, and do I ever love it.' We didn't go together very long—four and a half months—before we decided to get married. He wasn't a bad guy, Leland. *Isn't* I should say."

"You loved him."

"Sure, who wouldn't? Love my city, love me. Here he was, a big-city lawyer in love with the entire state of North Dakota. He was absolutely knocked out by all that space. So sure, I loved him. And besides that, he was a very decent, kind, well-meaning guy, and not bad looking either, by the way. He reminded me of a young Perry Como. It wasn't till after we were married I discovered his problem."

"Which was?"

"We call it attention deficit. His attention kept wandering."

"Other women."

"No, no, not Jerry. Other *places*. See, he joined a firm in Bismarck when we got married and I kept teaching there, and then one day he had to fly out to Helena, Montana, on business and suddenly Bismarck wasn't good enough anymore. I guess he'd never seen a mountain before."

"So you moved?"

"Right. His firm let him set up an office in Helena—it's the capital you know—and he moved first and I finished out the school year, then joined him. Well, shit! Wouldn't you know, I no sooner got to Helena than Jerry said he'd found paradise and it wasn't Montana."

"Idaho."

"No, Washington. He was just back from a couple of days in Seattle. I blew up. I said to him, 'Why don't you check out the entire Pacific Rim while you're at it, Jerry? Let me know when you settle down, and I'll come and join you.' And I went back to Bismarck and waited."

I chuckled and said, "Good for you."

"Hey, I don't mean to make light of this, Leland. You can imagine what it was like parting there in Helena. I mean it wasn't like I hopped in my car and made a U-turn and went right home. We spent three days and nights talking, talking, talking. Oh, the pain of it. He felt it as much as I did. He pleaded and pleaded and I cried like a baby and waited for him to make the offer that would allow me to stay, namely that we'd settle in Montana, at least long enough to buy a house. Or at least take out a six-month *lease* on a house. I mean otherwise how could I ever be sure we wouldn't be spending the rest of our married lives traipsing around the entire world?"

"So you never did live together?"

"Later that summer I got a long letter from a small town in the redwoods, north of San Francisco. Here at last was what he'd been looking for. The ocean. The climate. The vegetation. There was even a mountain he could look at in the distance. I called him and told him, 'It sounds wonderful, Jerry—if you're still there in six months, I'll start packing.' "

Mary Sue fell silent, so I had to ask, "And in six months?"

"In six months, Singapore."

I have been to Bismarck. I went during spring break in order to see Mary Sue safely back to Rookery. Francine Phillips and Faith Crowninshield, who had planned to make the journey, were surprised and I think relieved when I offered to go.

"But you've always said you'd never drive across the Dakotas."

"I'm not driving out, Francine. I'll fly to Bismarck and ride back with Mary Sue."

"Oh, Leland, believe me," exclaimed our resident ex-nun, Faith Crowninshield, "you'll love Incarnation Convent. You'll love the sisters. You'll see how fond they are of Mary Sue."

"Yes, I'm sure it's altogether a peaceable kingdom, but my instincts fight against it. I'll stay in a motel. I'm not one to get up at four A.M. to pray."

"Neither are they, silly. They're modern women. They run a college. If you're passing up the convent, you might as well stay home. Why are you going anyway?"

Could Rookery be that unaware? *For love!* I was tempted to exclaim, before realizing that our love had blossomed since winter break entirely unwitnessed, entirely over the phone. "I want to consult with their college president" is my answer.

"You won't have a choice," said Francine. "Mary Sue will insist."

I flew to Bismarck, and there I found paradise. Angelo laughs when I say this, and so does Mother, and that's okay—let Bismarck keep its secret. In early April, North Dakota from the air was a vast, brown moonscape as far west as the Missouri River, but then, circling to land, we followed a few miles of the river valley and I was amazed to look down on the gold-green filigree of budding trees. Taxiing to the terminal I saw baggage handlers in short sleeves and a mechanic wiping his brow. Catching sight of these first signs of spring is ecstasy to any Northerner like me who hasn't seen a green leaf since early October and has been shoveling snow since Thanksgiving.

"It's *warm* here," I exclaimed, embracing Mary Sue at the gate.

"It's been sixty every day for a week."

"That's not fair. Rookery is the same latitude and we haven't seen fifty yet."

Hand in hand, we hurried out to the car for a second kiss.

"How are you, Mary Sue? You've been sounding wonderful on the phone."

"Full of pep."

Pointing out landmarks, she sped through the city and out the other side. There was a glow about Mary Sue, an attractiveness she hadn't shown me before, a happiness of spirit I prayed might be permanent. We were miles out in the country before I thought to ask for a hotel or motel.

"Are you kidding?" she asked, laughing and drawing up to a strange-looking bell tower. She parked between the tower and a colonnade and said, "Come on, bring your bag."

I followed her, without my bag, along the colonnade and into an airy foyer where I was introduced to a very small figure in pink slacks and a very old woman wearing a dark dress and the brief veil of a semi-modern nun. "Sister Emily, our prioress," said Mary Sue, "and Sister Hermione, who's in charge of our switchboard."

Having checked with Faith Crowninshield and memorized the protocol, I said, "Hello, Sister," to the small one, then turned to the old one and gushed, with a bow, "I'm very pleased to know you, Sister Prioress."

This was met with giggles of delight, which puzzled me until a buzzing sounded from behind a door and the old nun hurried to tend her switchboard and the younger one disappeared behind another door marked *Prioress*.

"A mother superior in pink slacks?" I said, following Mary Sue down a corridor of granite and oak.

"Why not? Here's your room. Look it over and decide if you want me to drop you at a motel."

I stayed at the convent. The room, the meals, the campus, the services in chapel—everything about the place had been exquisitely planned, and you'd have thought I was sent from the pope the way I was pampered by that sorority of women, several of whom I intend to add to my Christmas card list. When, next day, Mary Sue's car was packed and ready to go, I felt my spirit hanging back, unready to leave the only place in the world where, as far as I know, this pencilled note is to be found on your pillow:

Dear Guest,
    Making this bed this morning, I prayed for the happiness of whoever sleeps in it tonight.
        —A sister of St. Benedict

Sally has been jealous from the start. One Friday afternoon—I think it was April Fool's Day—she beckoned me up to her end of the table and said, over her strawberry parfait, "You have a girlfriend."

I didn't deny it. Instead, I went ahead and blurted the dumbest thing possible. "I'm sorry," I said.

"For what?" asked Sally, laughing a little.

"For making you jealous."

"Who says I'm jealous?"

"Nobody. It's just that you've never been indifferent to other women in my life."

Her laugh had an edge to it. "*What* other women?"

"Peggy, for one. When Peggy was here, remember? You seemed jealous."

"That wasn't jealousy, that was concern for you. I was afraid you'd fall for her all over again."

"And if I had?"

"If you had, I'd feel exactly the way I do now."

"How do you feel?"

"Jealous."

She must have gotten over it, because she later asked Mary Sue to her house for lunch. This was in late May, during exam week. Sally, ever the caretaker, needed to make sure Mary Sue knew the dimensions of the space Mother takes up in my life. They spent most of the afternoon together, and Mary Sue returned to campus looking thoughtful.

I asked no questions, preferring to wait until she chose to tell me what went on at lunch. There are no secrets with Mary Sue, only delayed reports. Pressed, she will sometimes minimize what's on her mind, whereas if she's left to mull over the facts and order her observations, she'll eventually spill out everything you want to know, and then some. This is what makes her so different from Sally, so different from me, so fascinating. Sally never bares her own soul. Sally, bless her, is too busy tending to the souls of others. Having been reared by a mother who broadcasts her every waking thought over the air, I turned out to be the type who conceals lots of stuff, the way Sally does, and yet at the same time a person who, like Mary Sue, needs to be confided in.

The whole truth came out yesterday, Sunday, after we had spent most of the day with Mother—church at ten, followed by brunch at the Van Buren, then reading the paper and dozing in the shady backyard—the day of perfect idleness I promised myself at the start of this complicated week. I'm driving Mary Sue back to her apartment when she comes up with this:

"Sally says you're a mama's boy."

"Damn her."

She turns to me with an intensely curious look, then adds, "She says you never gave her the attention she deserved because Lolly required so much of you. No man can be faithful to two women at once, she says, and you're programmed to be on call to your mother at all times. She says Sundays were the worst for her, Sundays like today at your mother's. She says toward the end she got physically sick as Sunday approached."

"She never told me that."

Mary Sue takes out an emery board and goes to work on her nails. "She told me about the day Joey died. The ice storm. How you promised you wouldn't go out."

"So now you know the worst of me."

"You wouldn't go out on the icy streets, you told her, but you went out anyhow, because Lolly needed a ride."

"I know, I know, God for*give* me, Goddammit! I've been living with that for nearly twenty years."

"So it's true."

"Yes, it's true, and isn't it enough that I lost my son?" Tears spring into my eyes. "Do I have to lose you too?"

"Hey, relax, Leland, I'm not going anywhere."

This produces in me a single, enormous, shoulder-heaving sob. Driving past the Division Street Park, I grab her hand and give it a desperate squeeze. The young and old are out, taking in the aromas of spring, warming themselves in the sun. At the corner I stop for two young mothers pushing babies in strollers.

"I'm just telling you what Sally said at lunch. I love Lolly. I don't mind going to your house and just sitting around. I told Sally that. Not every Sunday of the year by any means, but now and then it makes for a nice relaxing day. Sally said it would be every fucking Sunday of the year. Those were her words: every fucking Sunday of the fucking year. Boy, is she ever pissed. Was she that angry as your wife?"

"I don't think so. I'm not sure—it was a long time ago."

"Well, she sure comes to life when she's pissed. It wouldn't be *every* Sunday, would it, Leland? I mean, you know, if we actually got together, you and I?"

"No, of course not."

"Was it every Sunday back then?"

"It may have been, I can't remember."

"I said, 'Sally, sometimes I get real lonesome without Leland, and I know it's a package deal—take Leland, you get Lolly as well—so what?' I said. 'Everybody loves Lolly, you do yourself,' I told her. 'You've said so.' "

I turn off Division onto River Drive. Mary Sue wipes a tear from my right cheek, then takes her hand back and resumes work on her nails.

"She said of course she loves Lolly, everybody loves Lolly, but that doesn't mean that she, as your wife, didn't have to put up with a lot—Lolly's interfering in her marriage and causing her son's death. It doesn't mean—"

"Wait a minute! My mother caused Joey's death?—she never said that."

"Maybe not those exact words, but you get the idea. How it all came apart after Joey died. You know how it is, after a tragedy like that, you look around for somebody to blame. Remember what's his name, that student of mine that committed suicide? Lockheed, Locklear, Lock-somebody. I looked around for somebody to blame and decided it was me."

"But with Joey we're talking twenty years ago."

"Yeah, that's the real scary part, isn't it. Do you suppose in twenty years I'll still be going on about that student?"

"Not if you can't remember his name, you won't."

I pull up in front of the Badbattle Arms and switch off the ignition.

"I think Sally meant well," says Mary Sue. "I think she just wanted me to know what I'm getting myself—what I *might* be getting myself into."

"True, she's such a caretaker. It's kind of poignant actually, to think of one's ex-wife being solicitous of one's new girlfriend."

"Yeah, and in the process she gets mad all over again. Are you still in love with her, Leland?"

"No."

"A little bit?"

"No . . . it isn't love."

"What is it?"

"I don't know. Tenderness. Respect. It certainly doesn't feel like what I felt when I was in love with her."

"When did it stop?"

"When you came along."

"Really? When did it start?"

"Fifty years ago. I was nine or ten."

"Jesus."

Later, on the phone:

"You see, my love is a very ponderous thing, Mary Sue. It takes a lifetime for it to move away from one person and settle on another."

"And you're sure it's moved away from her?"

"I'm sure."

"But do you ever still see her—you know what I mean—upstairs in the Hi-Rise?"

"What?" Was Sally out of her mind—revealing our secrets? "She told you that?"

"Don't be silly—that isn't something a woman tells about herself."

"Who then?"

"You don't want to know."

"I want to know."

"Let's just say I first heard it last summer on the day I came for my interview."

"On campus? And more than once?" I feel strangulated.

"Do you still do it, Leland?"

"Lord no, never."

"How long ago?"

"Six months. Before Christmas."

"Well, it comes up now and then, like you hear about the great hockey team of 1988. It's part of college lore."

"Mary Sue! You're joking! I can hear you giggling."

"Old Dean Edwards, they say. Gets it off at the senior center." She can't hold back her laughter.

"You *are* joking."

She says, "The fifth floor lately, I've heard. Five-oh-six."

Dear God! Of course! Hildegard and Twyla and their ilk have been monitoring our lovemaking for years. It's all over town. Does Mother know? What a hell of a point to have arrived at in life—sixty years old, about to be invested with the presidency, and too ashamed to look any citizen of Rookery in the eye. College lore indeed!

Monday and Tuesday I spend in St. Paul, being briefed by the Board and the chancellor on the arcane policies and procedures of the State College system.

The Board part is easy. I already know most of what they have to say, and so we spend hours over lunch simply getting acquainted. I've met three of the five Board members before: a farmer, a banker, and a CEO of an HMO; the two I'm introduced to for the first time are a veterinarian from Rochester and a publisher from Minneapolis. The publisher and the farmer are both women, and somewhat younger than the three men. They, together with the CEO, are considerably more engaging than the other two. The banker and the veterinarian are blowhards, and it's during their discussion of fiscal responsibility I open my notebook.

#118. Have the last twenty years of a perfectly peaceful— not to say deadly dull—home life made me too stodgy for Mary Sue Bloom? Am I adaptable enough to be her husband? Is there resilience in these old bones?

Will Victor and Annie Dash show up for the Inauguration?

Will Neil Novotny be insufferable now that he has achieved fame, more or less, as Mary Magdalene Peterson and Delphinia White? Is he still planning to write his serious novel? Can he? Can anyone, after writing nothing but schlock for twenty-five years?

What is Richard Falcon doing at this moment? And where is he doing it? Wouldn't Lucy have told me if he moved? It's been weeks since she's written.

Dr. Gail Ann Suderman and her staff take up most of my Tuesday, and it isn't until midafternoon that we adjourn and I get to a phone.

Mother reports that Angelo and Gloria took her to last night's session of the Writers' Workshop where Jimmy Olsen made a spectacle of himself. "He's a physical wreck, Leland. His complexion is bad, he's flabby, and he wore jeans and a faded T-shirt at his reading."

"Not much to look at, huh?"

"I taped a few minutes of it for my show, but I can't use it. You wouldn't believe how he stumbles over words. Why, you were a better reader in the fourth grade."

"Thanks to Mrs. Wolf."

"He came to the word 'basketry' and was stumped. People walked out."

"How about the morning session?"

"You'd have to ask Angelo. I didn't go."

"And your breathing?"

"Clear as can be."

"Good, I'll see you tonight."

"Viola tells me you're not moving your office."

Oh dear God, I knew this was coming. "I like it where I am, Mother."

"But it's the dean's office. It's been the dean's office since your father's day."

"It's bigger than the president's."

"Size means nothing—it's location. People will think you're still dean."

"And the view—I need to look at the river."

"A president needs to be front and center, Leland."

"We'll talk when I get home. I've got to run."

"And you'd have Zastrow's private toilet, don't forget."

"Angelo, how many enrolled?"

"Twenty-eight; we lost two of our earlier ones."

"Lost them?"

"This Jimmy Olsen guy—what a pain in the ass. This morning he gets up there in front of the group and says, 'If I were a would-be writer and I'd taken a week out of my life to come to this conference, I wouldn't be *at* this conference, I'd be home writing.' And two people left and went home to write."

"They got their money back?"

"Of course. Satisfaction guaranteed is our policy, according to our incoming president."

"Has Neil Novotny shown up yet?"

"Neil Novotny's another pain in the ass. And a complete phony, if you ask me! There's no way in hell a guy that stupid can be publishing books."

"It's all a show, Angelo. He's strange, but he's not stupid. Tonight as Mary Magdalene Peterson he'll be different. He'll probably be pious and sappy."

"Tonight he's Delphinia White."

"Whatever. I should be home in time for his reading. I'll see you there."

"Hey, Leland, where do you find all these nutty writers?"

"So long, Angelo."

"Your poet Falcon was the prize nut of all. Kept calling me Phillips the whole time he was here. Whatever became of him anyway?"

"I never hear from him. Good-bye, Angelo."

"Hey, did you hear another Hi-Riser dropped dead?"

"Who?"

"The dumdiddy cat."

"Not Father Pyle!"

"Fell down dead right there amongst the lobbyists."

"Mary Sue, I'll catch the five-thirty plane home, so I will be in time after all for Delphinia White. When you get this message, would you call Mother and let her know if you're free to go with us? Then if you come back to the house with us after the reading, we can try out this new book of duets I'm bringing home."

"Sally, I heard Father Pyle died."

"This morning. In the lobby. One minute railing against *Roseanne*, next minute cardiac arrest."

"Funny, Mother didn't mention it."

"Your mother's got a one-track mind these days. Mama's boy is becoming president."

Oh, oh, she's decided to be jealous again. "When's the funeral?"

"Friday. At first they were thinking Thursday, but of course that's a holy day—I mean Inauguration Day—in Rookery."

"Sally, could you let up a little? You're not at your best when you're jealous."

"Who's jealous? You think I want to be president?"

"You don't want Mary Sue Bloom to be the president's friend."

"I wish I had time for more of your romantic chitchat, Leland, but we're pretty busy around here today. We've got to get Father Pyle's room emptied out and cleaned up."

"Who's moving in?"

"Your poet."

"What?"

"Richard Falcon."

"No! He's coming back?"

"Just got off the phone with him. He called yesterday to ask if I had a room for Inauguration weekend, and I didn't. But now I do, so I called him back."

"Where is he—still in Omaha?"

"Area code 402."

"That's Omaha."

"Gotta go, Leland. Marigold's waiting for me with her mops and pails."

Replacing the receiver, I have visions of detectives trailing the poet into Rookery.

I return from the phone to Dr. Suderman's office for my brief-case. My fretful look is apparently a dead giveaway. "What's wrong?" she wants to know. "Bad news?"

"Yes, our old pastor died." I try on a cheerful expression. "But the good news is, twenty-eight are enrolled for our Writers' Workshop. I had bet my assistant we wouldn't hit twenty-five."

"When are you going to start raising your sights? The whole northern third of Minnesota is all yours—all you gotta do is go out and herd folks onto your campus like cattle. Now before you leave, I've asked Mr. Stevens to come in and say a few words about economizing in the Xerox room."

"Gee, I don't know, Dr. Suderman, I have a five-thirty plane to catch."

"Plenty of time. Mr. Stevens will be brief."

#154. If I am arrested for conspiracy to defraud the IRS, pray God let it happen before the inauguration ceremony. I cannot go down in history as RSC's only president-felon. SHOO-IN PREXY SHOOED OUT.

Am I ready to propose marriage to Mary Sue? Sometimes when I haven't seen her for two consecutive days, I'm seized by doubt—not about her, but about myself. Am I fit for marriage a second time?

I catch my flight and as we grind north over the lakes and pine forests in a rattly old turbo-prop, I acknowledge to myself that my excitement at the prospect of seeing Richard Falcon far outweighs my fear of the law. Does it equal my eagerness to see Mary Sue? No. Nothing equals that. The plane sets down in St. Cloud and Brainerd, and when at last we descend toward Rookery, I close my eyes, for our airport is closely surrounded by hillocks of tall trees and I once overheard the captain tell his copilot at this point, "I hate landing in a teacup."

It's a lovely surprise to find Mary Sue waiting for me at the terminal. She drives me home. Mother too seems pleased to see her. In the twenty years since the breakup of my marriage, Mother and I haven't discussed other potential women in my life; she makes her opinions known entirely by nuance and gesture. She has, until now, withheld her opinion about Mary Sue, and so I suddenly feel lighthearted, hopeful, expansive. Having finally crossed the no-man's-land of Mother's withheld judgment, I'm now in friendly territory.

While eating Chinese, which Mary Sue has kindly brought with her in little paper buckets, I inquire about Richard Falcon. Did they realize he was about to return to Rookery?

"Oh, I wanted that to be a surprise, Leland," says Mother.

"Lucy and Ron and Claudette are driving him up here tomorrow, and they'll all be here for dinner."

We drive the block and a half to campus and park in front of the auditorium, arriving early in order not only to set up Mother's oxygen system, but also to greet Neil Novotny, who has not been back here since leaving his job in the spring of 1969.

There are half a dozen people waiting in the auditorium. Angelo, who's directing the Workshop, says that Neil has decided he's Mary Magdalene Peterson tonight, but he's nowhere to be found. He's checked his dormitory room, the cafeteria, the library. Over the next twenty minutes several people come in, two by two, and scatter themselves around the main floor and balcony. At the appointed time our celebrity is still not here, and Mary Sue begins to fume.

"It's okay if he's late," I tell her, "he's a novelist."

She thinks this terribly ridiculous. She gives out with a loud hiss, unfortunately, just as Neil steps forth from the curtains, followed by Angelo, and they approach the lectern.

Oh my. Neil looks worn out and spiritless, like a vagrant or convalescent. His gray hair is long and snarled. His T-shirt says *DIE YUPPIE SCUM*. He keeps a fearsome scowl trained on Mary Sue while Angelo introduces Mary Magdalene Peterson and I count the house—sixty or so, which means that we have attracted to campus, beyond the twenty-eight enrollees, about thirty additional fans of the "gospel-romance" genre, including L. P. Connor slouched in a seat at the rear.

There are a few gasps from the more innocent and unsuspecting of Mary Magdalene's fans when Neil then steps up to the microphone to read. With his eyes still locked on Mary Sue, he opens a fresh paperback which I recognize as one of those he has sent us lately; portrayed on its cover is a seductress wearing a halo. Someone behind us sputters something unintelligible that ends with, "Sheeeeesh!" I assume it's L. P. Connor. Mother, beside me, is shaking with silent laughter.

Neil shifts his scowl from Mary Sue to a group of latecomers who tiptoe in and quietly seat themselves. They include Edna and Emeric Kahlstrom making a rare evening appearance because they remember Neil from their younger and probably happier years. He responds to Edna's timid wave with a blank stare and then announces that instead of his most recent novel, *Under the Upper Room,* he will read tonight from *Candlelight at Cana,* because it's tamer and less demanding. Here he pauses to look us over as though challenging us to claim to be intelligent beings. *We are able to understand prose of this depth, Mary Magdalene, we can take the rough stuff.* But of course no one speaks up; we're all much too polite, or embarrassed for him.

He reads without one iota of feeling for what seems an eternity before we begin to shift in our chairs and clear our throats. Somebody coughs a deep wet cough. Somebody sneezes. The very sight of him makes me sad. He has obviously failed, if not at writing, then at some other pursuit important to his happiness. Or have his parents recently died?—Neil, like me, is an only child. Or maybe it's a washed-up love affair. Did I look this miserable after my divorce?

" 'So the young woman in the scanty white outfit went over to the young man in the blue toga and whispered in his ear, then slipped out into the night,' " he reads. " 'The young man in the toga's face lit up. The scantily clad young woman's father, seeing this, got suspicious. So did the young woman's mother. So did everybody else at the wedding feast.' " On and on he goes, apparently unaware that Philosopher Kahlstrom has fallen asleep; unaware that the little squeaks and moans that sound at first like a ventilator fan but which grow louder now, are coming from Mother who can no longer contain her amusement; unaware that Angelo, thank God, is edging toward the lectern to wind things up. Neil jumps a little when he feels Angelo's shoulder nudging his. He says thanks, bows his head to the sound of a brief bit of applause, and steps back as Angelo announces that coffee and cookies await us in the cafeteria, but first we have time for a few questions.

"Do you go out like this often and speak?" asks Mother.

"Not often," Neil replies curtly, his eyes returning to Mary Sue.

I ask, "And how do people usually react when they find out that Ms. Peterson is actually a man?"

"Reaction is mixed."

These answers are delivered with such obvious distaste that no one else speaks up. I suppose I ought to let his performance end here, but I can't help asking what part Rookery State played in his career, how he remembers his time here after twenty-five years away. I'm ready to point out that even if he learned nothing more than his dislike of being a faculty member—he was an utter failure in the classroom—it was a valuable discovery.

"Rookery State? I wasted three years of my life here."

"But surely you must have learned something from a career standpoint."

"Leland, the only thing I learned here was what a wasteland this is."

Okay, I get the point. I don't press him. I'm standing up, reaching for Mother's coat, when he launches off on a surprising topic: our old friend, the late, great, hard-drinking painter of mother-daughter portraits who colored his bass-playing with the deepest, darkest tones.

"Now I think of it, however, there was one person I never would have met if I hadn't come to Rookery. I'm talking about

Connor, the first truly dedicated artist I ever met." Neil speaks while fidgeting with his book and running a hand through his long and unruly gray hair. "He inspired me to give my writing everything I had. . . ."

I sit down and listen, gratified to hear Connor remembered for a change with the respect he deserved, and fascinated by the reaction this stirs in Connor's daughter, who has left her seat at the back and is drifting up the side aisle toward the speaker's platform as though in a trance.

Catching sight of her, Neil looks wary, turns the microphone over to Angelo, and steps down to join us, his hand extended to me.

I try to sound hearty. "It's great to see you, Neil. You remember Mother, of course."

He gives her a brief nod, distracted as he is by Mary Sue. It's her beauty that attracts him—I see that now, up close. His eyes, in fact, reveal such a deep fund of lust that I, too, am distracted: "And this is Sally," I tell him. "Or rather, Mary Sue."

I take Mary Sue's hand—a gesture of apology, protection, love. He seems not to have heard me misspeak. He keeps staring at her while Mother tries to fill the silence with small talk, and while Mary Sue, smiling benignly, bends my little finger painfully backward.

Outside, following the others along the lighted pathway to the cafeteria, I'm aware of L. P. Connor skulking along at the rear of our procession. Why, in January, did it seem such a brilliant idea to bring her together with Neil? I was out of my mind with anger. I felt so triumphant at the prospect of humiliating my nemesis, while at the same time disproving her gender-based theories of writing, that I forgot to be prudent, cautious, fearful— all the qualities she's been demanding of me, lo, these many years. I expect fireworks in the cafeteria.

But there is no outburst, no explosion. As we engage Neil in further conversation, Ms. Connor sidles up to Mother and stands beside her, smiling shrewdly at Neil between sips from a bottle of mineral water. He steals glances at her, presumably trying to place her in his memory. When she finally speaks, it is to ask, "Whatever became of *Losing Lydia*?"

He looks far off, as though searching the far corners of the room for the manuscript he struggled to complete during his time on our faculty. "I don't know," he says. "I may have used part of the plot in another book, the one about the riverboat gambler."

"Then how about the money my dad gave you to publish it?" This is an apt question. Neil solicited funds from several of us to help save his publisher, T. Woodman Press, from bankruptcy. We never saw the book in print. I myself responded to three of his appeals, to the tune of $750.

Unruffled, he sets forth some drawn-out and meaningless excuse involving stubborn editors, public taste, and the international monetary fund.

"Well, I read it," says L. P. Connor. "It was a good story till Lydia decided to go out to Oregon with that jackass she met on the boat. I'd like to help you get it back on track."

"You read it?"

"The day you left town, remember? I read it in the backseat of my dad's car on the way to Minneapolis. He drove you down there to the airport."

A spark of recognition comes into his eye. "You're not Laura Connor."

She nods. "Her brother finds her too soon. It's a great plot until she's found—then the story goes all screwy."

"Isn't that sweet," says Mary Sue a few minutes later, watching my nemesis leave the student center with Neil. "Your celebrity seems to have taken the sting out of Ms. Connor."

"I wouldn't be too sure," I tell her.

"She's leading him on," says Mother. "He'll be crucified before he knows it, he's such a fool."

The profane and exuberant Victor Dash arrives next morning with his wife Annie. I hear Annie's deep laugh in the corridor and Victor cursing, "We travel a thousand miles across this goddamn nation camping in our pup tent and sleeping like babies in the wilds—then we cross over into Minnesota and get eaten alive by mosquitos. Why don't they give this godforsaken state back to the Indians?"

They bound into my outer office like a couple of frisky pups, and Viola Trisco, her mouth agape, watches Victor greet me with a twisting and painful sort of handshake and Annie Dash leap into my arms—yes, leap; she's the sort of spirited little woman who will cling to your neck for a few seconds before backing away and gushing praise. "God, Leland, what a success story you are. Dean today, president tomorrow—what's next, the White House?"

"Where's Zastrow, that dink?" asks her husband. "I want to remind him what a dink he was during our strike."

"Oh, shush, Victor. How's Lolly, Leland? Is she still on the radio? Is she still full of beans?"

"Zastrow's gone. He gave our commencement speech, mostly on the many improvements he's seen since he took office, then he and his wife moved to their retirement home in Fargo."

"Goddamn," roars Victor, "weren't we the babes in the woods in those days, Edwards? We had no business going up against the College Board—we didn't have a goddamn thing to bargain with, remember?" His laugh is a high-pitched squeal. "But one thing we did have was guts."

I will always think of Victor Dash, a small, square, impulsive man with a voice like a boombox, as the person who introduced Rookery to the modern age. It was a quarter century ago that he hit town like a meteor, organizing a local chapter of the Faculty Alliance of America and leading us out on a strike for higher wages. Because such behavior was unprecedented on college campuses in those days, there appeared in the *New York Times* a photo of several of us—though not of me, thank the Lord—picketing in front of McCall Hall.

"Guts, Edwards, back then we had guts. And we were dirt poor. I couldn't afford to buy my kids a bicycle. Not like today's prima donnas, making seventy, eighty thou. You're probably making that yourself, Edwards, how much do you make?"

"Seventy."

"Think of it!—for sitting on your ass all day, not teaching a goddamn thing, just standing up now and then to greet your old friends." Another high-pitched laugh, another elbow-injuring handshake.

Victor, sixty-six and a retired union organizer, is devoting himself these days to finding fault on every level of the labor force. I've learned this from the news clippings he insists that Annie enclose with her letters to Mother, articles listing the incomes of CEO's, plumbers, street-sweepers and physicians, each article heavily impressed and sometimes ripped by some muckraking comment scrawled across it with a sharp ballpoint pen. Even his beloved pipeline workers, from whose ranks he rose (or fell, in his opinion) into teaching, are making too much money these days. *Look at this no-good asshole,* he wrote under a magazine photo of a man directing pipeliners across the Iranian desert. *Used to know him in S. Dakota. He's making a hundred grand per annum.*

The two of them go out for a stroll around campus. I call Mother. "The Dashes are here. Shall I send them over?"

"More the merrier, Leland. They can meet Richard Falcon."

"He's there, at the house?"

"He's not only here"—she lowers her voice—"he seems happy."

Happy, but unwell. I find the poet smoking on the front step, flicking his ashes into our bed of blue iris and looking pinched. He smiles and hails me as I come up the walk and says he is glad to see me—music to my ears, of course—and yet his handshake is weak and something is missing from his voice, something of his old tone of authority. I make bold to point this out to him before we go inside, ask if he's been sick in Omaha. He is in fine fettle, he insists, never better. The pressure is off. His poem is done and Peggy Benoit has turned her attention to another man, has married him in fact—so his daughter has reported—and he can now afford to relax.

"Relaxed, Leland, is all I am, not sick . . . You never saw me relaxed before . . . I used to shake your hand like a drowning man grabbing at a lifeguard." Speaking causes him to pant or gasp for air. "Because that's what you were, of course . . . You saved my life more or less, or rather . . . you saved my poem which *is* my life."

"Have you been in touch with your daughter?"

"I have. You're surprised?"

"And Peggy was actually the woman from Italy, chasing you?"

"I didn't feel I could tell you the truth, Peggy being an old friend of yours. . . . And then seeing her in Rookery that Sunday, I panicked . . . Ran away from the house you put me into with that woman wearing that funny dress."

"Kimberly Kraft. Eccentric, but a very old friend. Tell me, why did you risk contacting your daughter? You said she's unreliable. She might have led the authorities to Omaha."

He squints his right eye at me. His gray, wrinkled complexion reminds me of Nettie Firehammer's before she died of smoking. "What authorities?"

Has the man gone senile on me? "Your unpaid taxes, for God's sake! The publisher who's holding you to that old contract you signed!"

"Oh, I made all that up."

The door opens and Cousin Lucy comes out. Her embrace is followed by Claudette's. Above us Cousin Ron stands beaming in the doorway with Baby Detroit squirming and spitting in his arms.

On the way in to dinner I ask, "You mean I can stop being afraid of going to prison?"

"What?" He's perplexed.

My explanation about the IRS causes him to chuckle. "Well, I had to make a good case for myself, didn't I? . . . Had to be sure you'd find a place to squirrel me away."

A bitter mixture stirs in my chest—anxiety, sadness, a pinch of anger. "Mr. Falcon, your poem was the best case you could make for yourself. Wasn't it clear, after a month of working together, that I'd do anything you asked of me?"

This he dismisses with another little chuckle. He's on his best behavior during dinner, and yet my anxiety grows. Afterward I follow him outside again, badly in need of his assurance that my devotion is clear to him, that he won't forget me the minute he's back in New Hampshire. But how do I broach a topic so delicate, so close to my heart? I move upwind from his smoke so I can inhale the earthy aroma of neighborhood gardens drying out after the spring rains, and I stand there mute, rehearsing and rejecting various openings. Finally I revert to a more practical question that's been on my mind:

"Did you also make up the part about Jonathan?"

"No, Jonathan will always be troublesome. That's why I'd rather not go home right away—or at least one of the reasons." He gives me a sly smile. "What do you think, will that eccentric friend of yours take me back in her house?"

INAUGURATION DAY

Eighty degrees makes for a very hot day in Rookery, and on that rare afternoon when the temperature hits ninety—say once every second or third summer—a dozen cases of heatstroke are rushed to the hospital and a dog or two will drop dead in the street. At two o'clock on Inauguration afternoon the campus thermometer hits ninety-three. No leaf stirs. No songbird utters a syllable of song. Even on the shady lawn in front of McCall Hall, the still air presses heavily down on the padded shoulders of our academic gowns. Before Father Tisdale finishes his brief Invocation, his face is running with sweat, and so is mine. We northerners aren't used to such heat.

Attendance is no greater than I expected. In the front fifteen rows of folding chairs the faculty sits in the sweltering shade of their mortarboards. Mary Sue looks positively parboiled, what with her sunburned cheeks and nose and chin; this morning we went canoeing down the river, oblivious to the sun. This was the first time in the fifty years since my father's death that I'd taken the canoe down from the rafters in the garage and set it afloat. Canoeing requires a partner. Mary Sue loves to canoe.

A sunbeam, falling through an opening in the canopy of leaves, spotlights Faith Crowninshield and the guitar case she marched in with. She likes to keep her instrument close at hand at all public functions, in case she's asked to play. Next to Faith is the empty chair Emeric Kahlstrom sat in for two minutes before deciding to go home and cool off. Viola Trisco and April Ackerman are about the only support staff I see.

Behind the faculty sit invited dignitaries from State government, a scattering of students, as well as local citizens who like to keep an eye on the college. There are a dozen or so friends of Mother's and mine. Edna Kahlstrom is visiting in whispers with Annie and Victor Dash. Among the students I spot some of my recent freshmen: Carol Thelen, no doubt on extended coffee break from Petey's Price-Fighter Foods; Mrs. St. George, who has gone back to matronly-looking dresses now that school is out for the summer; and Edgar Curtis, the bus driver. It takes me a moment to recognize Kelly Evans because she's bald. On the grass beside Ms. Evans's chair there is a box containing copies of *The Rookery Chapbook*. I've put Ms. Evans in charge of mail orders and we're already into the third printing.

Sally, I see, is surrounded by a knot of old folks—Dot, Johnny, Hildegard, and—yes, that *is* Twyla Todd, brought down from her surveillance post on the fifth floor of the Hi-Rise. Does the tote bag on her lap contain her shortwave radio? Sally, as usual, looks quite cool, and so does Twyla, whose painful joints loosen in the heat. About the only other person not visibly suffering is the inscrutable Dr. Bhandi, our linguist from Bombay, clad in a sari.

The last seven or eight rows of chairs are mostly empty. Cousin Lucy is back there dandling Detroit between her knees, and next to her sits Mother, scribbling away in her notebook and imagining, I'm sure, the narration that will go with the video Cousin Claudette is filming with her camcorder. Cousin Ron is back there yawning. The rest of the O'Kellys (wisely, thought I; selfishly, thought Mother) stayed in Nebraska rather than cross the Midwest in the baking heat. Cousin Wesley and Bernadine responded to our invitation through Richard Falcon, sending their regrets and wishing me well and wanting to know if Rookery State would be sending down another geographer to take this one's place, or if they should go ahead and sell the house despite the falling real estate market.

Following the Invocation, Richard Falcon, my platform guest, steps up to the microphone and recites "Haying in the Heat," a poem about

> ... A hayfield in a torrid hollow in July
>   Where chaff and sweat and sunlight sear the eye ...

a poem so redolent of the kind of day it is that many of his listeners hang their heads in lethargy or despair. I see Sandor Hemm shaking his at the completion of each rhymed couplet. The poem is acknowledged with light applause, which quickly evaporates in the overhanging boughs.

The poet's voice has taken me so far into myself that I miss hearing Dr. Gail Ann Suderman's introduction of the chairman of the College Board (the CEO of the HMO), as well as most of the chairman's address. I'm going back in memory to the day I first ran across this poem while sitting under a tree. I was twelve or thirteen, and the tree, a giant oak, stood on the riverbank about ten miles downstream from Rookery. My father and I, who had been fishing since dawn, had beached the canoe in order to get out of the blistering sun and eat our midmorning lunch in the shade. When, having finished our sandwiches and Kool-Aid, my father lay on his back, pulled his hat down over his eyes, and began his customary twenty-minute nap, I brought out from the lunchbag the leather-covered edition of *Hopson's Modern Poets*, which the college librarian kept under lock and key and lent out only to her most trustworthy borrowers. I opened it at random, and my eye fell upon "Haying in the Heat." I remember how reading it seemed to intensify the muggy atmosphere of the river valley. The very page felt hot to the touch.

Isn't it odd that despite my love of poetry even at that age, I can't remember ever having a conversation about poetry with my father? In fact, I can't recall talking with him about much of anything. We were silent companions, seldom confiding in one another.

It isn't clear to me why the CEO's words should be met with such dour looks from so many of our female professors and such wild applause from Coach Hokanson and athletic director Burr until I open my program and am reminded of his subject: *Scholarship and Hockey since 1929: Educating the Whole Man.*

A few minutes later I find myself standing at the microphone, installed as the sixth president of Rookery State College and about to launch into my inauguration speech entitled "A Dean Speaks His Mind, a President Responds," in which I intend to enumerate the many shortcomings of our institution and suggest ways to rectify them, when it occurs to me that this gathering has already endured enough in my behalf. Therefore, waving my fifteen typewritten pages in the air, I tell the faculty that they will find copies in their mailboxes, and I will ask the editor to print it in an upcoming issue of the *Morning Call* for anyone else interested in reading it. By asking Father Tisdale to come forward for the concluding prayer, I gain for myself a standing ovation. After this, surely nothing I do as president will earn me such unanimous respect.

For the reception, we move to the only air-conditioned building on campus, the student center, where the first two people to approach me with smiles and congratulations are—believe it or not—L. P. Connor and her mother. The daughter's smile, though not to be trusted, is actually quite attractive, her straight white teeth having by some miracle survived her neglectful hippie period of the early 'seventies and her extended period of depression after her father's death and seem to be carrying her through her current punkhood in fine shape. Her mother's smile, of course, is fixed, having been applied with her garish makeup before she left home.

"I have permission from Neil Novotny to finish *Losing Lydia*," my nemesis proudly announces. "He's sending me the manuscript as soon as he gets home. I'm going to be a novelist."

"Be careful what you commit yourself to," I warn her. "How can you write a book and still be the full-time gadfly you've been all these years?"

She opens her mouth and lets out a funny, quiet sound from deep in her throat, a cross between a moan and a sigh that strikes me as somehow familiar. Nudged ahead in the receiving line, she and her mother are shaking hands with the chancellor and the CEO before I realize I've just heard Connor's rare and understated laugh as handed down to the next generation.

It's Johnny Hancock doing the nudging, and bringing the New Woman along by the hand. Both of them wear new clothes, he an off-brand bib overall stiff with sizing, and she a dark brown pantsuit resembling a UPS driver's.

"The rev-runt's dead, I s'pose you heard."

"I'm sorry, Johnny. It's going to be lonely at the men's end of the dining table, isn't it."

"Naw, I never had no time for sky pilots anyhow."

"Besides," says the New Woman, fluffing her oxblood hair, "we're getting married."

Johnny, dribbling spit into his pocket, pulls her past Mother to Dr. Suderman, to whom he exclaims, "I sold two and a half dollhouses. They wasn't sellin' as bat houses, and they wasn't selling as purple martin houses, so I sawed 'em in half and called 'em dollhouses and five of them dopes in the lobby bought 'em for their granddaughters."

"It was my idea," the New Woman calls back to us as Johnny pulls her over to the refreshment table where Dorcas Muldoon is sitting with her jaundiced finger on the coffee spigot and looking no closer to death than she did before she outlived Nettie Firehammer and Father Pyle; and yet when she catches my eye, drops her bony jaw, opens her toothless mouth, and sends me a finger-wiggle of congratulations, it seems like a message from beyond the grave. "We're getting hitched," I hear the New Woman tell her.

Next in line is Portis Bridges. "Let me know when you're ready to talk celebs again, Dr. Edwards, I've got somebody lined up you wouldn't believe."

"Wait'll you hear!" exclaims Reggie VanderHagen, his sidekick.

"Madonna, I suppose."

Portis is momentarily speechless. "How did you know?"

"Bullet bra herself," says Reggie with his mouth stretched in a smile of incredible width and beads of perspiration trickling down his bronzed and shaven dome. The smile is the servile one he perfected for President Zastrow, and I can't help trying to wipe it off his face by declaring:

"We'll be starting a summer theater program, Reggie."

"We?" Though his smile remains undiminished, his disappointment is apparent in his eyes. Reggie, instructor of drama as well as speech, has spent every summer since coming to Rookery in absolute idleness, sunning his skull in a deck chair on the riverbank.

Southern California has taught Portis one thing at least—how to look cool when the temperature's up. He stands there in his sky blue shirt, cream necktie, and tan pants with his stupidly happy eyes fixed on mine despite my telling him, "I probably won't require your agenting, Portis."

Both of them bend down to kiss Mother's cheek and say obsequious things to her before moving on to Dr. Gail Ann Suderman and revealing at last what they've had up their sleeves these past six months:

"Dr. Suderman," says Portis, pressing Reggie upon her, "I'd like you to meet somebody with all the skills of a dean."

Actually I'm relieved to hear it. If Reggie VanderHagen turns out to be his only competition, Angelo will be a shoo-in as my successor.

Next come the rest of the Bridges clan, followed by the extended family of Mayor Steadman. Then come the Coopers, our neighbors across the steet, asking me if Father Pyle's death was hastened by his slamming into their parlor with his car. I tell them I doubt it, he died of chronic bitterness. Next I accept the congratulations of the staff of KRKU and their families, who inquire of Mother about their weekend of tenting on Owl Lake. Then there's another of Victor Dash's twisty handshakes and another leap at my neck by Annie as well as a kiss on the mouth. Hugs and kisses, too, from Cousin Claudette and Cousin Lucy, who then make a beeline for the corner where Richard Falcon appears to be visiting civilly with Angelo and Gloria. A kiss as well from Sally, who breaks into the line to say she will have to get her seniors back in their air-conditioned niches at the Hi-Rise before the heat gets them down.

For the temperature in the student center, in deference to Dorcas Muldoon's cancerous and cooling bones, is locked in at 78 degrees, and those who found it such a relief to enter are beginning to find it oppressive and are heading for the comfort of their air-conditioned cars. Among them are a number of people I want to step out of the reception line and visit with, so I hold a quick consultation with Mary Sue, Sally, and Mother about an alternative space. "We need somewhere cool enough for people to sit still for a sonata," I tell them. "I want to go public again with the piano." Our sleeping porch, though it might easily hold three dozen guests and is equipped with a spinet, isn't air-conditioned; the Van Buren meeting rooms, though air-conditioned, are all booked. Mother suggests we follow her friends Hildegard, Dot, and Twyla home, so Sally rounds up her charges (including Richard Falcon, who awaits a decision from his prospective land-lady) and hightails it across town to get the place ready.

And that's how we end up throwing a cocktail party in the dining room of the Sylvan Senior Hi-Rise, surrounded by jigsaw puzzles hanging on the mustard walls. We're peered at by a number of bleary-eyed residents whose naps have been shortened by our invasion. Gail Ann Suderman has a fine old time discussing libraries with Dot Kropp, investments with Hildegard and Angelo, and cattle and pigs with a couple of farm widows. Mother pursues the CEO of the HMO up and down the room pulling her oxygen tank behind her, until she pins him down to an on-the-air phone interview. I've overindulged in brandy before I know it, judging by how tall I suddenly seem to be, and I keep listing to the left. To Father Tisdale, who asks me to deliver the eulogy at Father Pyle's funeral tomorrow, I reply giddily in words I will doubtless regret in the morning, "Of course, I'll be happy to eulogize that gloomy man."

Lucy and Claudette are in the kitchen making Sally laugh, Richard Falcon has just confided to me that his troublesome grandson isn't the main reason he wants to remain in Rookery indefinitely—I am the other reason—and the New Woman is blushing at a wrinkled newspaper clipping Johnny Hancock is pressing upon her when I determine that I'm tall enough and con-fident enough and free enough of inhibitions to accompany Mary Sue to the piano.

It takes a good bit of clinking a spoon against an empty bottle to bring Claudette and Lucy in from the kitchen and to get Dr. Suderman's attention away from the farm widows. With everyone quiet and Twyla's radio reduced to a staticky hum, I announce, "Here's your reward for suffering through today's ceremony, my friends. Mary Sue Bloom and I will now play for you Mozart's Sonata Number Two."

This is clearly one of Mary Sue's brittle days. She's way out ahead of me, beginning the second phrase as I come to the end of the first. Unless I skip a measure I'll never catch up. I skip several and even then, coming to the end of the first movement, I find her dawdling there, her eyes on her fingers, her mouth crimped in a severe little smile as she waits for me to sound the final chord with her; and then, having begun at this frantic rate, I continue at top speed, momentarily forgetting that this is the *andante* movement, which today Mary Sue has chosen to play with an exaggerated, dirgelike slowness; and it's on and on like this: the entire sonata presented in this unharmonious, leapfrog manner. Why is she eluding me? This isn't music, this is a comedy of missed communication. Because she's not feeling confident, that's why. Whenever Mary Sue's self-esteem diminishes, she invariably turns evasive. But why on this day of all days? Ah, well, there's a puzzle for the ages—the moods of womankind, their frequency, their intensity.

But the intensity of this one isn't so great that we're prevented from coming together at the end, thank God. Moving through the final three measures, I strike the keys with all my might—ta BOOM boom BOOM, ta ta Boom BOOM BOOM— coming down so hard on the final note that I hear a string snap inside this ancient, neglected instrument. Remaining on the bench, my arm lying across Mary Sue's shoulders, we acknowledge with a grateful sort of nodding and smiling the half-hearted applause emanating from those few guests and residents who listened through to the end; then I turn and ask, close to her ear, "Will you marry me?"

Her answer is an immediate "Maybe," damn it, accompanied by the same crimped smile directed not at the keyboard this time, but at me—a smile that says, primly, *You can't know what you're asking, it could be very difficult being married to me—better wait till your euphoria wears off.*

I hug her to my breast, my throat, my heart. " 'Maybe' isn't good enough," I murmur desperately. " 'Maybe' simply won't do."

"How about 'probably'?" She eases herself out of my embrace. Her smile has softened. "Would 'probably' be better?"

"Yes, oh definitely, if 'probably' means we're engaged."

"Oh dear." She looks suddenly apprehensive. "You mean *publicly*?"

"Of course. What other kind of engagement is there?" Seeing worry-wrinkles move across her forehead, I plead, "I'll make the announcement if you wish. Right here and now. Over and done with."

"I hate to tell you this, Leland—she's your own dear mother, after all—but I couldn't stand being the main topic day after day on 'Lolly Speaking.' "

I see her point. Being a daily feature on the radio isn't something to look forward to.

"But when will we tell her? The world has to know sometime."

"After the wedding, if there is one."

"Please, Mary Sue, will you stop being so negative?"

"Hey, Leland, how 'bout a little 'Twelfth Street Rag' for old times' sake?" This is Victor Dash, carrying two dishpans in from the kitchen, one of them enameled, the other plastic, while at the same time shedding his suitcoat into the hands of his giggling, adoring wife. Placing the pans, inverted, on the trestle table, he takes two long-handled wooden spoons from his back pocket and begins testing for percussive effects, filling the room with an insistent and irritating beat on the metal pan, punctuated by the echoless thud of Tupperware.

"Be with you in a minute, Victor." I lead Mary Sue out into the half-deserted lobby. "We need to talk, Mary Sue." I try edging her into the entryway, out of earshot of the four lobbyists planted at various depths in their adjustable Naugahyde rockers. These four aged women are all but strangers to me; I scarcely know them by name, so I can't tell if it's meekness or disapproval or a lack of interest that's kept them from joining the cocktail party. I'm guessing it's the last, judging by the boredom in the eight incurious eyes they turn in our direction.

Mary Sue, standing her ground, lowers her voice. "Look, so we're engaged. All I'm saying is let's keep it to ourselves."

"But I won't feel engaged unless we tell people. Making it public makes it official, don't you see?"

"You want to go public, do it like this."

So far gone in hopeless ennui are the four lobbyists that not even our lengthy kiss seems to interest them. For when we come up for air I see their gaze again directed outside the window at the endless string of cars going by.

I stand there panting as Mary Sue explains, "We do that a few times around town and people will get the idea, and yet Lolly won't have anything official to gush over."

It dawns on me then that being engaged to Mary Sue without telling Mother will prove to be stupendously satisfying. I have to swallow quite a bit of guilt of course, but it's guilt that has a delicious tang to it, a flavor I recognize from somewhere deep in the past, like the taste of a very dry wine drunk outside on a dark October night, lying on the beach where, only min-utes earlier, there had stood a mammoth pile of sticks and dead leaves.

And it dawns on me further—don't ask me how I know it— that this feeling is something my father, God love him, would have understood.

I scan the room for the poet. "Mary Sue, there's one person we absolutely have to tell."

"No, Leland, not Sally. I realize you tell her everything but at least spare her this."

"Richard Falcon."

"Oh. Well, then . . ." A moment's hesitation, followed by a decisive nod. "Sure."

He's left the party. Rising to his room—402, Worthington Pyle's room—I draw her to my side. "I love you, Mary Sue."

She says "Likewise," and turns and rises to my kiss as the door opens on two.

"Hee, hee," says Johnny Hancock, stepping in. "Goin' down are yeh?"

"Going up," I tell him.

"Then you're goin' down, hee, hee, ha!"

Johnny, regarding Mary Sue, clears his throat to speak, and I cringe—needlessly as it happens. "Wanna buy a bat house?"

"No, thanks."

"Birdhouse?"

"Nope."

"How 'bout a dollhouse?"

We get out on four.

The sight of Mary Sue at his door, as I expected, delights Richard Falcon. What I didn't expect was the degree of warmth he puts into welcoming us. He leads Mary Sue by the hand into his west-facing sitting room, where the late-afternoon sun is filtered through a haze of cigarette smoke. Before joining them, I switch on the ventilator hood over the stove and crush out a cigarette smouldering in an ashtray on the drainboard.

Then we tell him.

"Engaged to be married! Ah, Leland my boy, that's wonderful news, and right on the heels of becoming president, my, my, my." Standing before us in his shirtsleeves and loose necktie, he smiles at Mary Sue sitting next to me on the couch and adds, chuckling, "And to a woman as lovely as this." His chuckle becomes a coughing fit, from which he emerges bleary-eyed and needing a smoke.

"Has Kimberly called you?" I ask.

"Called to say she hasn't decided yet."

"She'll relent. She just wants you to stew for a few days."

He chuckles. "Says if I move in I got to promise to stay longer than last time." He puts his lighter to a fresh cigarette, then lowers his voice to its poetry-reading pitch. "Nobody deserves good fortune more than you, Leland."

It takes a moment or two for these words to sink in, and when they do, I close my eyes and bask in their meaning. What they mean is that I have the poet's blessing. How gratifying. How affecting. The words work on me like brandy. I'm much, much taller than ever before, and I'm imbued at last with the very sort of benevolent presidential power I'd expected to—but didn't—pick up at my installation ceremony. In short, I feel smug.

"And I envy you," he adds in a voice broken by what sounds like another cough coming on. "When I think of how I've worked in obscurity for the past twenty years, hoarding peanut butter off the commodities truck that comes in once a month from the welfare office . . ."

Mary Sue nudges me, and I open my eyes to discover his voice broken not by phlegm but by tears. The dear man is sitting on the arm of the couch, weeping.

"You aren't sixty yet, Leland."

"Fifty-nine."

"That's how old I was when I last published a book." At this, he's rendered speechless, and he holds out his trembling, empty hands in a beseeching gesture. His face is expressionless but tears continue to fall. He seems to be pleading for understanding, so I tell him I understand, and he nods as though satisfied, letting his hands fall into his lap. Actually, I understand nothing. I don't know if he overimbibed downstairs or if we're seeing the creator of a masterpiece in the throes of postpartum depression. Whatever the cause, his altered mood sweeps my smugness away.

Feeling embarrassed for him, I get up to go, half expecting him to object, but no, far from detaining us, he moves with surprising agility through the kitchen, wiping his shirtsleeve across his eyes, and opens the door into the corridor.

"You'll have to forgive me, the smallest things set me off lately."

"Never mind," Mary Sue tells him, and she kisses him on the cheek. I summon the elevator while she lingers in the doorway saying tender things. It strikes me that they might be father and daughter, standing there holding hands. And this, in turn, leads me to the realization that Richard Falcon, whether he knows it or not, is in Rookery for good. In his weakened condition, and as my surrogate father, he'll never be able to pull himself away from the care and support he's going to get from my two wives. I have two parents now as well, a full set, in decline. Arduous days ahead for all of us. Despite his living alone all these years this old man is in many ways less self-sufficient than Mother, and more demanding. And certainly more volatile. But that's okay. That's fine. I have the blessing of a father at last.

396 • THE DEAN'S LIST

He shuffles over to the elevator with Mary Sue, asking, "When's the big day?"

"We haven't set a date," I tell him.

"Don't hold your breath," says Mary Sue.

"Ah," he says, eagerly rubbing his hands together, "I have time then to write you a poem."

APPENDIX

The Rookery Chapbook

TEN POEMS
BY

Richard

Falcon

Rookery State College
Rookery, Minnesota

Squatters' Rights

Over needles
Under norways
I know a path
To the doorless doorways
And warping walls
Of a weathered house
Surrendered to
A covey of grouse.

Under ceilings
Under eaves
Under boughs
Of needles and leaves
Under a sun
As dim as the moon
They flutter and swoop
In the shadowy noon.

They roost on the porch
Drum on the chairs
Carry home berries
To eat on the stairs
Peck at pebbles
Evening and dawn
In the wiry growth
Of what was lawn.

And looking the part
Of a rightful heir
Disregarding
The disrepair
Grandfather Grouse
Disdaining to mingle
Watches his brood
From his favorite shingle,
Equally proud
Of his manmade house
And siring a strain
Of housekeeping grouse.

Haiku

Beaks and wingtips down
Geese like inverted saucers
Spiral to the pond.

Heavy with blackbirds
Before a houndstooth sunset
The leafless trees pose.

Reflection on the Water

The fish that takes the fatal bite
Is victimized by appetite,
Both his and mine.

Because I'm better at deceit
I satisfy his urge to eat
So I can dine.

Contrast

I wade and explore
In hazy noon light
The countryside smothered
In snow overnight
And find I'm unable
To comprehend white
With everything dark
Having vanished from sight.
I'm startled by color
No matter how slight:
An oak leaf in flutter,
A bluejay in flight.

To My Neighbor, Ann Docking, Who Wishes
Someone Would Write Her a Sonnet

The girl who longs for sonneteers has found
Herself four hundred years too young. Their moans
Of love in silence lie, compiled and bound
In heavy books as dusty as their bones.

Yet so urgent seem their pleas when scanned
Upon the page, she prays the distant age
Return when ladies could at whim demand
A knightly verse delivered by a page.

Instead her mail contains a card in prose
Demanding she present without delay
The book of sonnets with the fee she owes
For dreaming silly dreams an extra day.

I hope these fourteen lines may see her through
Until the age of Petrarch dawns anew.

A Brace of Dreams

Two golden pheasants
In a climate too cold
For corn to grow
Couldn't die old.

One I shot.
It ran though stricken
And jerked about
Like a chopping-block chicken

The other I fed
A diet so rich
It stiffened away
With hardly a twitch.

Cooled Acquaintance

Bound in snow
At the peak of a hill
Our crystals of ego
Are frozen and still
Recalling the spring
And summer we saw
Before we were ice
Awaiting the thaw
When disengaging
We'll freely run
Down opposite sides
Of the hill in the sun.
A trace of each other
We may retain
But silt will sink
In the April rain.

Postal

Creased carelessly, absorbing as lust,
Letters at first come enclosed with souls,
Odd as rusty buckets of spice.

Later letters are purely precise,
Empty as polished pitchers of dust,
Full of the news that everyone knows.

The Red Oak

Among the four seasons' perpetual jokes
Is the winter appearance of overdressed oaks.
Refusing to fall with the sleet and snow
Oak leaves cling, lifelike, through fifty-below
Until they are nudged by the force of the sap
Rising to fashion the oak a spring wrap.

I hope when it's autumn and winter for me
I can look as alive as the overdressed tree
And during the lengthening nights I can cling
To my wits and my heart—the tokens of spring—
Only releasing them into the sod
The moment I'm dressed in the glory of God.